PENGUIN BOOKS

The Shadow of War

1914: The Great War Series

Stewart Binns began his professional life as an academic. He then pursued several adventures, including that of a schoolteacher, specializing in history, and a stint as a soldier, before becoming an award-winning documentary-maker and latterly an author. His television credits include the 'In-Colour' genre of historical documentaries, notably the BAFTA and Grierson winner *Britain at War in Colour* and the Peabody winner *The Second World War in Colour*.

He also launched Trans World Sport in 1987, Futbol Mundial in 1993, the International Olympic Committee Camera of Record in 1994 and the Olympic Television Archive Bureau in 1996.

Currently chief executive and co-founder, with his wife, Lucy, of the independent production and distribution company Big Ape Media International, Stewart has in recent years continued to specialize in historical documentaries, including a series on the Korean War, the history of Indo-China and major studies of modern Japan and India.

His previous novels *Conquest, Crusade, Anarchy* and *Lionheart* – the 'Making of England' quartet – were published to great acclaim.

His home is in Somerset, where he lives with his wife and twin boys, Charlie and Jack.

www.stewartbinns.com

D0107843

The Shadow of War

1914: The Great War Series

STEWART BINNS

PENGUIN BOOKS

PENGUIN BOOKS

Published by the Penguin Group
Penguin Books Ltd, 80 Strand, London WC2R ORL, England
Penguin Group (USA) Inc., 375 Hudson Street, New York, New York 10014, USA
Penguin Group (Canada), 90 Eglinton Avenue East, Suite 700, Toronto, Ontario,
Canada M4P 2Y3 (a division of Pearson Penguin Canada Inc.)
Penguin Ireland, 25 St Stephen's Green, Dublin 2, Ireland (a division of Penguin Books Ltd)
Penguin Group (Australia), 707 Collins Street, Melbourne, Victoria 3008, Australia
(a division of Pearson Australia Group Pty Ltd)
Penguin Books India Pvt Ltd, 11 Community Centre,
Panchsheel Park, New Delhi – 110 017, India
Penguin Group (NZ), 67 Apollo Drive, Rosedale, Auckland 0632, New Zealand
(a division of Pearson New Zealand Ltd)
Penguin Books (South Africa) (Pty) Ltd, Block D, Rosebank Office Park,
181 Jan Smuts Avenue, Parktown North, Gauteng 2193, South Africa

Penguin Books Ltd, Registered Offices: 80 Strand, London WC2R ORL, England

www.penguin.com

First published by Michael Joseph 2014
Published in Penguin Books 2014
002

Copyright © Stewart Binns, 2014

The moral right of the author has been asserted

Set in Garamond MT Std
Typeset by Jouve (UK), Milton Keynes
Printed in Great Britain by Clays Ltd, St Ives plc

A CIP catalogue record for this book is available from the British Library

ISBN: 978–1–405–91517–5

www.greenpenguin.co.uk

To all those who endured the Great War

Author's Note

The Shadow of War is a work of fiction. Although largely based on real events (and with many of the characters borrowed from history), all names, characters, places and incidents either are the product of the author's imagination or are used entirely fictitiously.

Many of the characters speak in their local vernacular, especially the old Pennine dialect of North-East Lancashire. Largely gone now, it was still spoken into the 1960s and I remember well its unique colour and warmth. It was an unusual combination of Old English and the nineteenth-century 'Mee-Maw' – the exaggerated, mouthed reinforcements of speech used to overcome the noise of the looms in the cotton mills – made famous by comic actors such as Hylda Baker and Les Dawson.

The meanings of various East Lancashire dialect expressions, as well as examples of Cockney rhyming slang and background facts about military terms, Victorian and Edwardian mores and various historical references are explained in the Glossary at the back of the book.

Contents

PART TWO: JULY
Death in a Distant Land

PART THREE: AUGUST
Into the Boiling Cauldron

PART FOUR: SEPTEMBER

Your King and Country Need You

PART FIVE: OCTOBER

Race to the Sea

PART SIX: NOVEMBER
Graveyard of the Old Contemptibles

PART SEVEN: DECEMBER
Christmas Truce

Introduction: 1914

It is the early summer. Britain has an aura of timelessness; it appears to be a land of serene invincibility, populated by people blessed by prosperity and contentment. Britannia's mighty empire stretches around the world; her navy is pre-eminent; her army is a distinguished and proud elite of marksmanship and discipline.

But the patina of imperial greatness is fading; all is not as the country's privileged elite would like to think it is. The clear skies of June 1914 are misleading. The chill wind of social discontent is beginning to swirl around this sceptred isle.

Her poor and dispossessed are restless, no longer prepared to accept the oppression born of a centuries-old class system. The world is changing rapidly; the Empire is a drain on Britain's dwindling resources and ageing industries. Only a few decades after it reached its zenith, Britain's Victorian heyday is already a thing of the past.

Yet more ominously, there is also a terrible storm beginning to foment in Europe, the elements of which are the vainglorious posturings of Europe's ancient powers. It will soon become a freak and ferocious tempest that will be calamitous for all engulfed by it. When it strikes, its savagery will be beyond anyone's comprehension and will consume the whole world.

This is the story of five communities of Britain's people, their circumstances very different, but who will all share in the tragedy that is to come. They and their homeland will be changed for ever by the catastrophic events of the Great War.

PART ONE: JUNE

Champagne and Plovers' Eggs

Monday 1 June

Assembly Rooms, Presteigne, Radnorshire

The Reverend Henry Kewley, Rector of St Andrew's, Presteigne, is in full flow. Tall, silver-haired and supremely self-confident, he has been holding bi-monthly meetings for the town's business community for the past year. There has been a lengthy and tedious debate about the calibre of the town's police force and the condition of its jail, but Kewley is now addressing the issue of Presteigne's future livelihood.

'. . . So, as I said, because of the sterling efforts of all concerned, we have fought off attempts to remove the assizes from our town. Let us give thanks for that great victory. But let me also address our deeper, longer term problems.

'Gentlemen, I now come to a matter of great importance. The appallingly low prices our farmers are receiving are continuing to have a dreadful effect on us all. Let me give you some harsh facts. Although the town is now on mains water, almost all our houses are still waiting to be connected to a fresh, running supply. We have at least twenty cases of diphtheria every year, and the numbers of other serious illnesses – polio, in particular – remain stubbornly high. Our school population is still down, and the issue of recruiting quality teachers is as urgent as it was ten years ago.'

Henry Kewley has his audience of more than a hundred of the good men of the area, all neatly turned out with clean, well-ironed shirts and polished boots, in the palm of his hand. A hugely popular preacher, founder of the local football team and doyen of the boys' club, he is the unofficial leader of the community. He not only has the skills to hold an audience, his subject is of grave concern to everyone in the room. Presteigne has been in the doldrums for almost thirty years; its once prosperous High Street and pretentiously grand Broad Street are now full of boarded-up shops, closed pubs and empty commercial premises. The town looks grey; its people are disheartened, and many are pitiably poor.

'We are now a town of barely one thousand souls, far fewer than when we were all boys. Rather than bringing trade to the town, the railway has taken business away. The big houses now go to Hereford, or even London, for their fancy goods. The tannery, brickworks, nail factory and sawmill have all closed. Leominster and Ludlow's streets are full of motor cars and their grating horns. But, at the last count, we have only nine registered motor cars and three motorcycles in our entire area. Although I hardly relish the thought of their ungodly noise and dreadful fumes polluting our streets, motor vehicles are a good gauge of a town's affluence. Regrettably, our main modes of transportation remain the sturdy horse and the human locomotion of Shanks's pony!'

Kewley pauses to read his audience. Shopkeepers, small businessmen, artisans, farmers; he can see the anxiety on their faces, but also the expectation in their eyes, hoping that he is about to announce a new panacea to rid them of their woes.

'Coal has to be our future!' he cries.

There are audible moans from around the room as heads are thrown back in exasperation. Two years earlier, a wily prospector, Aaron Griffiths, formed a company and began to sink shafts in the local area in search of coal, the 'Black Gold of Wales'. The first shaft was sunk at Folly Wood, which many of the older and more cynical locals believe is a name which offers an all too apposite moniker.

Surface coal has been found in the area over the centuries, and it has often been said that there are rich seams underground. Griffiths has sold over 800 shares in his company but, so far, little of consequence has been found and the locals, not known for having a generally optimistic outlook on life, have become increasingly sceptical.

With Aaron Griffiths sitting directly in front of him on the front row, and undaunted by the groans, Kewley continues.

'I know we have not yet had a positive result, but we must support Mr Griffiths. He is offering more shares and is prepared to sell some in exchange for credit from his suppliers.'

Kewley is suddenly interrupted by an old farmer, who rises to his feet with a broad but contrived smile on his face.

'Reverend, you be a persuasive cove, there's no doubt o' that, but those drillings have brought up beggar all, bar a few ton o' stone and hundreds o' gallons o' water.'

There is laughter all around the room, but Kewley is unperturbed.

'Carwyn, dear old friend, we all know of your misgivings about the project. But we need something new to bring prosperity to the town. I appeal to you to be more patient and much less pessimistic.'

Carwyn's fabricated smile disappears, to be rapidly replaced by a sneer.

'Henry, you've called us 'ere again. We were a-thinkin' you had somethin' new to tell us, but yer just makin' another appeal for Aaron Griffiths, who's had enough outta us already.'

A large, handsome man just turned forty, resplendent in his frock coat and towering top hat, jumps to his feet. He is Philip Davies, the local auctioneer, Urban District Councillor and Reverend Kewley's most ardent supporter. Half a head taller than any man in the room and with a voice like a growl of thunder, he gives old Carwyn a withering look.

'Carwyn, you should temper your remarks. The good reverend is only offering his advice in the best interests of the town.'

The old farmer sits down, shaking his head. He is muttering a response as he does so, his comment just audible to those with a good ear.

'In the best interests of Griffiths and his bloody shareholders, more like.'

The meeting starts to break up as men leave from the back of the room. They have heard enough about Presteigne's coal escapade and are annoyed that Kewley and Davies have nothing new to offer to improve the town's prospects. Not only that, two hours of depressing town business and speeches – most of which have been dreary – have made the audience thirsty. The Duke's Arms, just down Broad Street, is the town's most popular rendezvous. It is a fine hostelry with a renowned bar and a revered home-brewed ale.

Already seated in a quiet corner of the low-ceilinged, timber-framed saloon bar are the three Thomas boys: Hywel, aged nineteen, the eldest, and his two younger brothers, Morgan and Geraint. All three work on their father's farm to the west of Presteigne. Once the source of a modest living, Pentry Farm is going through hard times, which have had a devastating effect on poor old Rhodri, their ageing and all but bedridden father.

Hywel's brow is etched by furrows of anxiety. His stare is vacant; his eyes do not register the simple furnishings and usual accoutrements of an archetypical British hostelry. His thoughts are elsewhere, seeing the lush green fields of Pentry populated by fewer and fewer sheep, its cottage farmhouse in urgent need of repairs to its roof and its barns increasingly dilapidated. Then his Da comes into his mind's eye. He used to worship the ground he walked on; now he has to carry him to his bed every night and change him when he soils his pants. He closes his eyes momentarily to stem the tears that are beginning to form.

With the Thomas boys is a friend from school, Tom Crisp, who, unlike them, is from English stock and proud of it.

Tom is the first to comment on the sudden influx of the well-to-do of Presteigne.

'Putting the world to rights again?'

Hywel smirks disdainfully.

'Aye, as usual. Trouble is, they couldn't hit their own arses with a shovel.'

Tom responds in defence of two of them, men he admires.

'I know most of them are busybodies who act like sheep, but old Kewley's a good man, and Davies is all right. They've been good to us young ones.'

'Aye, but the other buggers make me choke on me beer.'

The Duke's Arms used to be one of three pubs on Broad Street, a wide, elegant thoroughfare of medieval and Georgian structures that reflects Presteigne's better days. There were six more drinking haunts on the High Street, which has a similar mix of buildings. Now the Duke and two rivals are the only survivors.

It is Presteigne's hard times that have closed the pubs, not austere Welsh Presbyterianism. Although it sits in a small valley amid the picturesque rolling hills of Radnorshire, the least 'Welsh' of Wales's counties, it is also surrounded on three sides by the English border. Offa's Dyke is to the west, not the east, placing the town in England's domain since antiquity. Indeed, the Welsh name for the town, Llanandras – the holy place of St Andrew – has all but been forgotten.

England is within touching distance at several places around the town and begins at the small bridge on the River Lugg at the bottom of Broad Street, only a few yards from the ancient church of St Andrew. The Lugg is but six yards wide at the bridge. On its east bank is the cottage of the Lewis family, of Welsh descent, but who live in England. While on the other side is the Browns' cottage, who are English through and through, but reside in Wales.

Despite the porous border and the dominance of the English colossus next door, those locals who are Welsh, especially the hill farmers, are ferociously proud of their Celtic heritage. They speak their antique language at every opportunity, either privately within their families, or very publicly to affirm who they are. It is a badge of honour.

But, in the main, the language of Presteigne is English and its accent contains only a hint of a mid-Wales lilt, leavened by the rustic drawl of neighbouring Herefordshire. Even the Welsh-speaking farmers sound like rural English folk when they speak the language of their Anglo-Saxon neighbours.

The Thomas boys all speak Welsh, but only at home, or except when they want to annoy Tom Crisp, who invariably responds with the habitual litany of 'Taffy' jokes and insults about hill farmers' supposed carnal appetites for sheep.

Geraint, a lithe seventeen-year-old, a year younger than his brother Morgan, and two years Hywel's junior, is at the now crowded bar, having just ordered more beer.

Suddenly, the door of the Duke is flung open and a distressed young woman rushes up to the boys' table. It is their sister, Bronwyn, Morgan's twin. She has run the five miles from their farm and is flushed pink, her thick black hair clinging to a face soaked in tears and perspiration.

'It's Da . . . I canna wake 'im!'

The three Thomas boys are on the move in an instant. They tumble into their horse and cart moments later, leaving Tom to pay for the beer. But Bronwyn calls after him, pleading.

'Tom, come with us, please!'

Tom throws a shilling on to the bar, forgoes the change and chases after the Thomas clan.

The ride to Pentry Farm is a torture for the four Thomas siblings. They fear the worst. Da has been ill for years and, after his wife died suddenly two years ago, has become mentally as well as physically ill. He is morose and difficult to live with.

After only a hundred yards, Bronwyn grasps Tom's hand and begins to sob. They have been lovers since the winter, but have managed to keep it to themselves. Hywel has had his suspicions and, seeing the clasping of hands, realizes its significance. He smiles and rests his hand on theirs, a gesture which is a comforting acknowledgement for both of them. The younger boys do not even notice, they are too focused on the farm track ahead and getting home as quickly as possible.

When they reach the quaint but ramshackle cottage, Da is still slumped where Bronwyn left him, in his chair by the fireplace. His head is resting on his shoulder; trickles of saliva have run down from the corner of his gaping mouth and dripped on to his shirt. His face is cool to the touch, his pallor exaggerating the thick black stubble on his chin.

Hywel feels his father's forehead and checks for any hint of breath from his mouth, or the glimmer of a pulse at his neck.

'He's gone.'

His voice is clear, trying to control his emotions. Both the younger brothers walk out into the farmyard to hide their tears and Bronwyn collapses into Tom's arms.

Hywel goes over to comfort her.

'Bron, I know it's 'ard, like, but go and 'elp the boys. They need someone to mother them.'

He guides her gently to the door, hugging her as he does so.

'Tom, will you help me get Da on to the cart and take him to the undertaker? Bron will stay 'ere with the boys.'

Bronwyn watches as her father's body is taken away to Presteigne. It follows the same winding route the livestock take on their way to the slaughterhouse. But this is her Da. She tries to remember him before he became crippled in mind and body by age and anxiety. When he whistled while working in the yard, or when he told her wonderful stories about his own Da and Tad-cu, both of whom refused to speak English and could neither read nor write.

She wants to be strong for Geraint and Morgan but cannot stop the tears or the awful sense of foreboding about the future.

9

Tuesday 2 June

Royal Fusiliers' Albany Barracks, Parkhurst, Isle of Wight

Serjeants Maurice Tait and Harry Woodruff loathe the Royal Fusiliers' Albany Barracks. Both Cockneys and army veterans, they have served all over the Empire in some remote and dangerous outposts but, to them, the rural Isle of Wight might as well be India's North-West Frontier.

The nearest pub is a mile away and although their serjeants' mess is comfortable enough, and the barracks as good as any, a location in the green fields beyond a sleepy English market town is not their idea of home. To compound matters, the other battalions which make up the army's 9th Brigade at Albany – the 1st Battalion Northumberland Fusiliers and the 1st Battalion Royal Scots Fusiliers – both speak alien languages, 'Geordie' and 'Jock', which might as well be two dialects of Chinese as far as the two London boys are concerned.

Not only are the other soldiers provincials – 'peasants', as the Londoners call them – they like their beer full of hops, all pale and frothy, not like the rich malty ales of the south, which are much more to Maurice and Harry's liking. The Jocks and Geordies keep complaining about the beer in the south being 'flat' and 'sweet', leading Maurice and Harry to offer what they think is sound advice to remedy their dilemma: 'Fuck off back up north, then!'

'Let's walk into Newport, Mo.'

'Bollocks, mate; I'm knackered. Let's get some nosh 'ere and call it a night.'

'Come on, we'll just 'ave a couple, then stroll back; it's a nice evenin'. Maisy will do us some chips when we come back.'

'She bloody won't. Your "couple" will be six or seven, and the kitchen'll be closed when we stagger back.'

'So, we'll scoff some chips in Newport.'

'Bloody 'ell, 'Arry, you've got a cast-iron belly. I can't swill gallons o' beer like you, then load up on chips.'

'Is that right? What abaht two years ago in Dublin, then?'

'Ah, that was different. Mick beer is as weak as piss!'

As Harry knew he would, Maurice eventually gives in and they are soon striding down the road into Newport. It is a pleasant market town, not without a few little architectural gems, and typical of rustic England. But its charms are lost on two fusiliers who have travelled the world and much prefer the hubbub of London. Lifelong friends, they joined the Fusiliers in 1896 at the age of sixteen and are now about as experienced army veterans as it is possible to be. Now thirty-four years old, with eighteen years' service, they are approaching the twenty-one-year maximum permitted by British Army Regulations.

After serving for three uneventful and tedious years at the Curragh, the British Army's main camp in Ireland, twenty-five miles west of Dublin, they sailed for South Africa in 1899 to fight in the Second Boer War, an experience that was far from humdrum.

After some banter about the delights of a couple of Newport's voluptuous beauties, and some whistle-whetting endearments addressed to the ale soon to be consumed, their idle chatter turns to their greatest preoccupation: soldiers' tales of enemies fought and battles won and lost.

'D'ya remember that fuckin' big Boer what nearly did for yer at Colenso, Mo?'

'He 'ad no chance; I were ready fer 'im.'

'Bollocks! If I 'adn't plugged 'im, he'd 'ave skewered yer like a pig on a spit.'

'Yeah, yeah, but I tell yer what, I 'ope we never 'ave to face firepower like at Tulega Heights ever again.'

'Just stay close to me, mate; the bullet that'll do fer me ain't been made yet.'

'No, 'Arry, don't say things like that; it's tempting faith.'

'Tempting, *fate*, Mo; tempting *fate*.'

'Whatever it is, don't tempt it!'

Maurice and Harry took part in the relief of both Mafeking and Ladysmith, two events which saw the British Army at its heroic best, winning fierce encounters with courage and discipline. But they also participated in examples of British intolerance and brutality, where vanquished opponents were treated with contempt and worse. Such stories are never part of their reminiscences – in the hope that, if they are not mentioned, they will fade from their memories, but they never do. Even so, like most of their comrades, they have become inured to the horrors of battle and to the barbarity of war.

They returned from South Africa as non-commissioned officers, each with five battle clasps to their Queen's South Africa Medal and, much more importantly, the extra pay to go with them. They served in India for two years from the beginning of 1903, another sojourn that was hardly dull.

'D'ya think we'll ever get sent back to India?'

Maurice's face lights up.

'It would suit me. Don't mind a bit of warmth – and a hot black arse!'

'Delhi belly and a dose of the pox more like!'

'As long as we don't 'ave to trek up them fuckin' Himalayas again, chasin' after them mad Tibetees.'

The British Army's expedition to Tibet was typical of the kind of punitive action all colonial armies are required to undertake from time to time to deal with 'troublesome natives'. In atrocious conditions, the Royal Fusiliers trudged all the way to Lhasa to quell an uprising instigated by the Dalai Lama. It was a vicious action, where British forces with Maxim machine guns and Lee-Enfield rifles killed thousands of Tibetans armed only with matchlock muskets and sabres. Not particularly proud of what they had to do in Britain's name in another far-flung corner of the Empire, Maurice and Harry knew there was little point dwelling on it. They did what they were trained to do; they took a breath, stuck out their chins and got on with it.

They returned home with India General Service Medals and Tibet Campaign Medals, replete with Battle of Gyantse clasps, to add to the already strikingly colourful row of ribbons on their chests – and an extra sixpence in their pay.

Upon their return, they transferred to the newly formed 4th Battalion Royal Fusiliers to stiffen its ranks. They joined the same platoon, part of C Company, and were barracked at Parkhurst. With their service record, they have become senior soldiers of great renown and are well known as a couple of hard-nosed, seasoned veterans who you would definitely want on your side if 'push came to shove'.

They thought they had done well to avoid another stint in India, but soon regretted their transition to the 4th when, after a year or so, the bucolic delights of the Isle of Wight began to wear thin.

Now, as the two of them see Newport town centre in the distance and begin to sniff the malty aroma of Burts Bitter, which they regard as one of the island's few saving graces, they quicken their pace down Holyrood Street and are soon settled into the Railway Tavern, their favourite haunt. It is a quiet pub, full of friendly locals, and not popular with either the Geordie or Jock fusiliers. If it was, the two Londoners would go elsewhere.

Bitter is only tuppence ha'penny a pint in the Railway, whereas it is thruppence in London. As serjeants, they are earning 16 shillings a week. As single men, they are housed and fed by the army, so have plenty of silver in their pockets for beer and baccy.

Beer, baccy and the occasional liaison with the fair maidens of the island are the men's only distractions. If they get desperate, some of their female acquaintances are street girls from the town's back alleys, or tarts who set themselves up in 'nests' in the hedgerows near the barracks. Every now and then the top brass clear out the nests for a while, especially if there is an outbreak of venereal disease, but on the whole the girls are regarded as a necessary evil to keep the men content.

The life of a professional soldier in barracks is a long monotony of training, drills and exercises. Although discipline is enforced sternly, it is not as harsh as it used to be, when floggings were commonplace. Besides, experienced soldiers know how to deal with the 'bull' and to keep a low profile. The food and accommodation have improved dramatically since the service days of Maurice and Harry's fathers and grandfathers, when men were housed worse than cattle and fed like pigs. But boredom remains and leads to lethargy and often boils up into tension, bullying and sometimes violence.

The two veterans like and respect most of their officers. They often have to take orders from newly arrived young lieutenants who have hardly begun shaving, and some of the senior officers can be arrogant or unpleasant, but, on the whole, there is mutual respect and goodwill.

Harry's mood becomes more and more reflective as the Burts Bitter takes effect.

'Still fancy runnin' a boozer when you ged out?'

'I do, a nice little country job up in Eppin' Forest.'

'But you don't like the countryside!'

'Yeah, but it's nice up there and I'm talkin' about a boozer, not a bloody tea shop. It's on the railway, so it's easy to get into town and, of a Sunday, it brings all the Londoners up fer a day out.'

'Sounds like a nice little earner. If I went for a boozer, it would be up in Norfolk somewhere. I went there once as a boy with me old fella. It's as flat as fuck but pretty, like; you know, windmills and all that. Yeah, a nice quiet pub on the Broads, I fancy that.'

Maurice and Harry joined up together and hail from Leyton, East London. Not real 'Cockneys' by strict convention but, like most Londoners in the British Army, it is an appellation they are happy to accept – especially Harry, who cherishes his Jack the Lad persona.

'I don't s'pose life's too bad. We'll 'ave our pensions soon, and much better ones than our old fellas got.'

'Not 'alf! Twenty-five years in the Coldstream, both of 'em, right through the Crimea: Alma, Inkerman. Then they 'ad to sell their fuckin' medals when they retired to keep us warm and fed!'

When serving abroad or away in barracks, Woodruff and Tait senior were heavy drinkers, frequent brawlers and not averse to the charms of the opposite sex, which is why they never rose beyond the rank of corporal. On the other hand, they were, in the words of the vernacular, 'as good as gold' with their wives when at home on leave. Except, that is, if anyone challenged their good name, or insulted their loved ones. Then, retribution would be swiftly delivered and brutally effective.

No one messes with the Woodruff and Tait families. Their rented homes are just four doors apart in Bromley Road, Leyton, a modest mid-Victorian terraced row of neat houses with small bay windows to the front and tiny back gardens to the rear. The Drum, which Maurice and Harry still think is the finest ale house in the world, is just fifty yards away on Lea Bridge Road, where their fathers still drink every evening much to their mothers' chagrin.

As boys, Maurice and Harry were inseparable. They were good athletes. Maurice played for Essex boys at cricket and spent long hours every summer at the county ground on Leyton High Road. Harry was a classy footballer and went down to West Ham Park to play for Upton Park Football Club for a couple of seasons, the proud holders of the title '1900 Olympic Football Champions'.

However, both boys' sporting potential was thwarted when they joined the army. They now sometimes play for their battalion, but overseas postings have meant that opportunities have been few and far between.

Harry comes back from the bar with two more jugs of beer in his hands and a smile on his face.

'There are two Geordie corporals in 'ere. Bloody nerve! They're at the bar talkin' abaht the officers' mutiny at the Curragh – or at least that's what I think they was on abaht!'

Maurice has scant regard for officers at the best of times.

'Officers' mutiny! If the ranks had mutinied, they'd 'ave been shot! Ireland's a fuckin' mess; if the Micks want home rule, I say, let 'em 'ave it. As for those Unionist fuckers up north, running bloody guns from the Germans – they should be put up against a wall, startin' with that Carson bloke.'

Harry is less vitriolic about the senior ranks, but is not keen on the cavalry – neither its officers nor its men.

'The fuckin' Cherry Bums was at the heart of it – 6th and 15th Lancers – stuck-up bastards. I remember them from Ladysmith – tossers!'

'That reminds me, 'Arry, do you remember that Churchill fella from Ladysmith, riding in, wavin' 'is hat like the conquerin' 'ero? He's done all right fer 'imself, ain't he?'

'He has that. Lord o' the fuckin' navy, ain't he?'

'Yeah, he was all right, though; came up and spoke to us. Not many of 'em do that.'

'Funny little fella, baby-faced with a little ginger tash. Couldn't 'alf talk!'

'What about those Geordies in our boozer?'

'Oh, they're all right; one is a 'ell of a good left-hand bat an' a decent bowler.'

'That's all right, then . . . I didn't think Geordies played cricket.'

'Neither did I.'

Wednesday 3 June

Dieppe Harbour, Normandy, France

Winston Leonard Spencer-Churchill has been First Lord of the Admiralty for two and half years. Only thirty-nine years old, but a seasoned veteran of politics, war and controversy, he has always been a 'young man in a hurry'. Since his schooldays, he has been convinced that, like his prestigious ancestor John Churchill, the 1st Duke of Marlborough, it is his destiny to lead his nation to glory.

Winston has crossed the Channel on the Admiralty's yacht, HMS *Enchantress*, to spend a couple of days with his wife, Clementine. Heavily pregnant with their third child and having left her young children behind with their nanny in London, she has been staying with her mother, Lady Blanche Hozier, in Dieppe. Lady Hozier's home is a commonplace, bourgeois house in a narrow street close to the centre of Dieppe. Divorced from her husband, Sir Henry, she has sought refuge in Normandy, well away from the opprobrium caused by her reputation as a notorious gambler and a woman of dubious virtue.

As Clementine gets ready for dinner, in between sips of champagne, Winston is pacing up and down the First Lord's quarters rehearsing his latest speech.

'"I say this to you all, to the good people of this ancient land and to the people of our glorious Empire, we must take the measures I have outlined in order to protect our noble heritage. If we do not consider these threats to our future security, we will face grave consequences.

'"I say this to you now . . ."'

Clementine would have preferred a quiet dinner alone with her husband but, as usual, he has made sure that the *Enchantress*'s wardroom table will be full.

'Pig, why have you invited so many to dinner? I see F. E. Smith is here. He might be a brilliant lawyer and a good friend, but he encourages you to drink too much.'

'Darling Cat, don't fuss. FE has the sharpest mind in that dreary profession, and he amuses me with his very droll stories. He told me one this morning. Apparently, a friend of his, a very senior judge, was recently presiding over a case involving some very inappropriate behaviour by a senior civil servant and asked FE, "Could you tell me, what do you think one ought to give a man who allows himself to be buggered?" FE replied, without any hesitation, "Oh, thirty shillings or two pounds; whatever you happen to have on you."'

'Really, Pig, that's disgusting! I hope he doesn't repeat it at dinner.'

'I'm sure he won't, darling, not with the Mayor of Dieppe there. Mind you, as you have the best French among us, if he does, you will have to translate.'

Clementine's face breaks into a smile for the first time as she gives her husband a playful slap on the back of the hand. 'Clemmie', as she is known, is ten years younger than Winston. Sharp featured with warm, gentle eyes and wavy russet hair, she captivated Winston as soon as they met. They dote on one another.

Clemmie places her hand on Winston's cheek.

'Winston . . .'

'Oh dear, if it's "Winston", I fear a reproach is imminent.' He adopts a thespian pose. 'The dark clouds of doom hover above me; an awesome bolt of lightning is about to strike a poor defenceless soul.'

'Stop playing the fool! You're right; here's the bolt you fear. Despite your promise, I hear you have been flying again.'

Winston deliberately adopts a boyish docility.

'Only once.'

'Twice! I have my sources, you know.'

Winston abandons the theatricality.

'So you do. Well, twice then. But you've heard me say it many times: in the future, wars will be fought in the air as much as they're fought on land and at sea.'

'That's as maybe, Winston, but you won't be fighting in them. You will soon be forty; your days as a soldier are over.'

Winston suddenly looks forlorn. He knows Clemmie is right, but does not want to admit it.

Sensing that she has touched a nerve, she continues her onslaught.

'We will soon have a third child. I cannot support myself on my own, let alone with four mouths to feed. Dearest mother is practically living in penury, and my father has disowned me.'

Clemmie's eyes begin to fill with tears. Winston melts at the sight; he cannot bear to see his beloved cry.

'Darling, I'm so sorry. I know how difficult it has been for you.'

'Winston, I must insist, you are *not* to fly. You are First Lord of the Admiralty, not a serving officer!'

Winston looks at her closely. He sees that her ultimatum is absolute.

'Very well, no more flying.'

'As of today? And you will keep your promise this time?'

'Yes and yes, darling Cat, for you and the kittens.'

Clemmie dabs the tears from her eyes and kisses Winston on the cheek.

'How is the fiancée of that poor man who was teaching you, the man who was killed flying across the Channel?'

'Airlie Hynes, dear old Gilbert Lushington's girl?'

'Yes, that's the one. Poor girl!'

'I believe she is as well as can be expected. Lushington wrote to me on the morning of the day he died. I sent the letter on to her with a note from me. She wrote me a very sweet letter by return.'

'That was thoughtful of you. But her sad loss makes my point. It could so easily have been you, Pig.'

'I know, Cat, I know.' Winston gently places his hand on his wife's swollen belly. 'How's kitten number three?'

'Being a little beast; it's never still.'

'Then let's feed you and the brute, and see if another glass of Pol Roger will put it to sleep.'

The First Lord of the Admiralty adjusts his favourite black polka-dot bow tie, gives Clemmie his arm and strides the three of them off to dinner with his usual purposeful gait.

HMS *Enchantress* is a nautical oddity. It is a naval sloop, but powered by steam, resembling a cross between a sleek tea clipper and a stout cross-Channel steamer. The elegant lines of its gleaming black hull and lofty masts and rigging are ruined by a huge grey funnel amidships. Nevertheless, it serves as the Admiralty's showcase yacht and, at 320 feet, with a complement of 10 officers, 186 men and armed with four 3lb guns, it makes a splendid sight at sea and a stylish abode in harbour.

Winston has made *Enchantress* his personal domain and has spent a total of eight months on board during the previous year and a half. In fact, the frequency of his occupation and the large numbers of family and friends he invites on board for dinner, weekends and longer visits, including cruises around the Mediterranean, has caused questions to be asked in Parliament. But Winston is undaunted, pointing out that all the on-board hospitality is paid for out of his own pocket.

Not that his pockets are very deep. He is constantly in debt, his lavish lifestyle significantly outstripping his income.

It is only his copious writing, as a renowned author and journalist, which keeps him afloat, quite apart from the fact that he is notoriously lax in paying his bills.

A formal dinner in the *Enchantress*'s wardroom is a spectacular sight. The decor is a blend of polished mahogany and gleaming brass, the table glows with burnished silver and sparkling porcelain, and the officers look immaculate in their navy-blue uniforms and gold braid.

Tonight's gathering is highly convivial, even by Winston's standards. F. E. Smith tells stories, mainly of the bizarre happenings in Britain's courtrooms and the eccentric lawyers who inhabit them, while Winston holds forth about the most pressing issues of the day. Although on opposite sides of the House of Commons, F. E. Smith (the Conservative) and Winston (the Liberal) are very close.

A self-made lawyer from humble middle-class origins on Merseyside, FE failed the examination to get into Harrow and had to climb the academic and social ladder slowly and diligently. Winston, on the other hand, is aristocratic and able to move with nonchalance in the highest circles. Their origins have little in common. However, they both have an astonishing gift for words, boast a rapacious appetite for the good things in life and possess unquenchable ambition. They recognize the qualities each has, and they revel in one another's company.

Wardroom etiquette usually demands that three subjects are taboo: politics, religion and women (which means sex). But with Winston and F. E. Smith present, such taboos are futile.

Two officers at the far end of the wardroom table have spent most of the evening talking about Winston.

'You know, one of the most remarkable things about him is his rapport with the men. They all know he's a toff and can be very abrupt, but he has a way with him that they take to. Have you noticed, his voice does not have the cut-glass edge of the aristocracy? His accent is more middle-England.'

'You're right; that never occurred to me. Do you think he has cultivated it deliberately?'

'I suspect not. He's just different from the rest of us; a complete original, infuriatingly irresistible. He appears to sees no barriers between people and is just as comfortable talking to a stoker as he is to a member of the Cabinet. People sense that, and respond in kind.'

'You mean he talks down to both? And tells them what to think!'

'Yes, something like that.'

'How far can he go, do you think?'

'Good question; he'd probably make a great general or admiral.

'I recently read his thoughts about Nelson. He called him our "greatest commander". I could see him as a Nelson or a Wellington – or, of course, in the guise of his ancestor, Marlborough – but in politics, not much further than he is now. I don't think he's yet forty; he must drive the old boys to distraction, especially the Tories. He's too hot-headed for higher office, we'd be at war the entire time!'

Starved of the affection of both his mother and father, Winston had an unhappy childhood and did not enjoy school, where he was generally regarded as 'troublesome'. However, despite his turbulent demeanour, physical frailties, bright red hair, baby-faced features and a marked speech impediment, he has an astonishing effect on all who meet him. His wit, energy and fortitude are overwhelming and, despite his noticeable lisp, he can command an audience with oratory that is universally admired. He has seen action in Cuba. He fought, was captured and escaped during the Boer War. He served on India's North-West Frontier and was at the heart of the fighting at the Battle of Omdurman, the last cavalry charge of the British Army. All his adventures reflect a single-minded and relentless pursuit of his determination to be a leader of men.

All is good humoured at dinner until, in a momentary lull in the conversation – and to the horror of his commanding officer – a brazen young cadet speaks directly to the head of the nation's navy. He raises the most topical and divisive subject of the day: the continuing threats made by Sir Edward Carson, leader of the Ulster Unionists. The Unionists of the Protestant northern counties of Ireland are saying loudly and unequivocally that they will do all in their power to resist Irish home rule. They are adamant that they will take up arms to stay in the United Kingdom.

'Sir, may I ask, why do you not agree with Mr Bonar Law and the Conservatives that, if the Ulster Protestants do not want to be part of an Irish Republic that pays homage to the Roman Papacy, they should be allowed to remain with us in Britain?'

Winston bristles, but he knows that the young man is fresh out of Dartmouth Naval College and so tempers his reply.

'Well, sir, I never agree with Mr Bonar Law and the Conservatives as a matter of principle.'

Winston waits for the laughter to subside and hopes that the young man will be content with his flippant reply. But the boy is not satisfied.

'Sir, my question is a serious one. Is not loyalty to Britain and the Empire to be admired?'

Winston takes a breath.

'I was jesting, of course. Yours is a question of some merit, so let me attempt to answer frankly. With my good friend here, Mr F. E. Smith, I have spent many hours talking to the Unionists. They are a tenacious lot, but immensely loyal to Britain and the Empire and, if I may be so bold, to their own self-interests. I cannot fault loyalty and I understand self-interest, but where is the loyalty in forming a militia, armed with German rifles, to force the hand of the government at Westminster? Is that not taking self-interest into a corrosive dimension, young man?'

The junior officer begins to respond, eager to grapple with Winston, but F. E. Smith interrupts him.

'Sub Lieutenant, what do you think of the Montepulciano? Don't you think it's awfully good? I'm told the Pope is very fond of it.' He turns to Winston. 'Perhaps we should send a case to Carson, marked "With the compliments of Pius X"?'

Most at the table are unable to stop themselves enjoying F. E. Smith's barbed remark and there are a few chortles of laughter. Chastened, the young officer realizes he is being asked to desist and lowers his head to hide his blushes.

Winston smiles at him.

'Young sir, come and see me during our voyage back to Portsmouth and we will talk further about your laudable passion for Britain and the Empire.'

Clemmie places her hand on Winston's arm and whispers to him.

'That was kind, Pig.'

Winston looks down at his empty glass. He seems suddenly pensive and leans towards Clemmie and FE, seated next to her, making sure that only they can hear.

'Ireland has vexed us for years, but now it's the least of our problems.'

FE looks at Clemmie sympathetically. He recognizes the sudden look of melancholy on Winston's face just as readily as she does. He also knows what troubles his friend.

'There is a diabolical mechanism being primed in Europe which fills me with dread. The Kaiser and his generals are fuelling it with men and weapons. And their enemies, especially the French and the Russians, are reciprocating.'

Clemmie casts a knowing glance at FE and leans across to her husband.

'Winston, please don't become morose about the Germans again.'

'Clemmie, my darling, I'm not morose, I'm anxious. We

25

are certain to be dragged into it if comes to a fight, and our army's not numerous enough to fight a major war in Europe. I've tried my damnedest with the navy, which is all-powerful, but I worry about our army. We have so few experienced men.'

'Please, Winston, you'll give me and the kitten indigestion. You can talk war with the men later, when I've gone to bed.'

Winston has not really heard his wife's plea; he is staring out of the wardroom porthole, beyond Dieppe's harbour, into the English Channel.

'At home, working people are on strike everywhere, mostly with just cause. Will those men fight if they are called to arms? In God's name, I hope so.'

FE tries to reassure his friend.

'They will fight, Winston. We are a nation of fighters.'

'You are a Birkenhead man, FE. Tell me, in truth, what is the mood on Merseyside?'

'Well, there's no doubt there's belligerence. We've had more than our share of strikes and some appalling violence. But the unrest is about pay and standards of living. If they are called to fight for the King and the Empire, they won't hesitate.'

'That is comforting to hear; I suppose the same is true in my constituency, in Dundee.' His expression takes on an even more pained look. 'Not that I'm there very often, poor buggers. I don't think I do a very good job for them.'

He turns towards a painting of Horatio Nelson, the hero of Trafalgar, which hangs on the wardroom wall.

'My biggest unease is that we haven't fought in Europe for almost a hundred years – not since the days of that man and the redoubtable Wellington – and the German Army is formidable. I pray that French military elan is still what it was, that it can hold a German attack. Our army is pitifully small. It is used to confronting colonial mutineers brandishing swords and spears; it is too old-fashioned to support the

French in a significant way against a German attack. We need more heavy artillery and armoured vehicles, not cavalry horses and sabres.'

'Why don't you ask Asquith for oversight of all our defences?'

'I have, FE, believe me, I have.'

Clemmie clutches her stomach, wincing at another assault by her unborn child.

'Winston, please don't be so melodramatic; this is a dinner party, not a meeting of the Cabinet.'

Churchill does not look up, even when his glass is filled with more Tuscan wine, but FE responds to Clemmie's plea for bonhomie. He raises his voice above the chatter of the dinner table.

'The other day, a high court judge asked me what I would give a man who would let himself be buggered . . .'

Friday 5 June

'Grim news in *The Times* this morning, Father.'

'There's always bad news in the papers; that's what sells the damn things.'

Despite his father's indifference, John George Stewart-Murray, Marquess of Tullibardine, known to the family as 'Bardie', the eldest son of the 7th Duke of Atholl, begins to recite the headlines.

'"Suffragettes burn Wargrave Church, Henley".'

'I'd horsewhip the buggers!'

'Quite so, Father, if a little harsh.'

Despite his father's initial disinterest, which is now turning to irritation, Bardie continues his musings.

'"The Balkans in turmoil. Durazzo" – which I think you told me you visited once – "under siege".'

'Durazzo, bloody awful shitty place, full of Albanian cut-throats.'

'Well, everyone seems to be fighting over it.'

'Bardie, please; you are ruining my bloody breakfast. Where are your brothers? You can keep them amused with the headlines.' The old duke's bile has been well and truly stirred. 'Bloody Balkans. We need to stay well clear of all that. The world is in bloody chaos. That little bastard Welshman, Lloyd George, has put up supertax to a shilling and fourpence in the pound. The man's a damned communist. Everyone's on strike; even the buggers who make cricket balls walked out the other day. Bloody nerve! Some communist union will be at the back of that.'

As his father's tirade against the world gains momentum, Bardie finally realizes his mistake and pushes his head deeper into the protection of his newspaper. Fortunately, just as the old man launches into the vexing question of the Irish and their 'appalling' demands for independence, Bardie's two brothers arrive.

'Morning, Father.'

The two speak almost in unison to their father, John James Hugh Henry Stewart-Murray, Chief of the Clan Murray and Commander-in-Chief of the Atholl Highlanders, Europe's only surviving private army. As he does every morning, he inspects the attire of his two sons for its propriety and scrutinizes their shoes for the obligatory lustrous shine. Not that the boys have to polish their shoes, or prepare their clothes; that is all done for them by the valets belonging to Blair Atholl's regiment of servants.

'Why the hell are you two always bloody late?'

'We're not, Father; you and Bardie are early.'

The duke glances at the clock. It is two minutes to seven. The boys are right, but the old boy growls all the same.

'Oh, very well, sit down. Bardie wants to tell you about how the world is going mad!'

Perhaps wisely, Bardie chooses not to reveal any more news and, with Blair Atholl's exemplary staff hovering around them, the four men consume their more than ample breakfasts. A few minutes later, the duke breaks the silence.

'I'm off to see Inglis about the gardeners. They've cut that bloody hedge by the greenhouses too low again, trying to save themselves work – lazy buggers!'

The three boys smile at one another as their father leaves. Forsyth, the butler, bows as the duke passes and the first footman, Dougie, rushes to open the dining-room door for him.

The old duke's gruff manner disguises a much kinder disposition than appears on the surface. He loves his family, is loyal to his friends and is generous to those who work for his house and estate. Even so, his views about the health of the nation and the affairs of the world are somewhat blunt and his solutions to the ills he perceives in both are rather draconian, even by the highly conservative standards of the day.

As they are required to by their father – every morning, without exception – the three Stewart-Murray boys look immaculate in their Prince Charlie jackets and ties and the blue and green tartan kilts of the Murray Clan. Each learned Gaelic before English; they went to Eton in turn and then followed one another into the army. They are all decorated soldiers and veterans of the Boer War.

Bardie, the tallest and fairest of the three, is forty-three years old and Member of Parliament for West Perthshire. He served in the Royal Horse Guards and commands the Scottish Horse, which General Kitchener asked him to raise for the Boer War. Lord George, known as 'Geordie', is shorter, darker and more solid than Bardie, and his younger brother by two years. He is in the Black Watch, was a defender at Ladysmith and served in India as aide-de-camp to its Viceroy, Lord Elgin. The youngest brother, Lord James, who goes by the name 'Hamish' (the Gaelic form), is more in the mould of Geordie than Bardie and is the youngest of the family, at the age of thirty-four. He is a major in the Cameron Highlanders and was mentioned in dispatches in South Africa.

All three Stewart-Murray boys have perfected that air of aloof charm so typical of the social graces of the well-mannered aristocracy, who can make an art form out of affable superiority. Their neatly trimmed 'eleven a side' moustaches suggest order and discipline, but with a hint of rakishness.

Bardie, having finished with his newspaper, passes it to Hamish, who is keen to read the news – not so much to discern the details of the world's woes as to enjoy its latest scandals.

'I see that Frenchwoman, Henriette Caillaux, is going to stand trial.'

Neither Bardie nor Geordie appears particularly interested, but the brothers politely inquire about the identity of the lady in question.

'You two really need to take more interest in the world at large.'

Bardie sneers.

'You mean its tittle-tattle!'

'Call it tittle-tattle if you like, but listen to this; it is so French. Madame Caillaux is quite a girl. She is married to Joseph Caillaux, the French Finance Minister. Three months ago, *Le Figaro* printed a private letter, written by her husband, which was politically very damaging; something about a dodgy tax deal, with him in it up to his neck.'

Bardie and Geordie are listening now; there is nothing like a political scandal over breakfast.

'So Madame Caillaux is incensed and thinks her husband should challenge the editor of *Le Figaro*, a Monsieur Gaston Calmette, to a duel. Hubby thinks not; perhaps he's not a very good shot, or just a bloody coward. So Madame marches into the newspaper offices and asks to see Calmette, but he's out. So she calmly sits down in reception and waits for him for over an hour. There she is, sitting decorously, smiling sweetly at all who pass, but with a Browning pistol hidden in her fur muff! When poor old Calmette returns, she is shown to his office, where she tells him he's a scoundrel and bloody well empties the Browning's magazine into him. She puts six bullets in the bugger!'

Both Bardie and Geordie are open-mouthed.

'Dead?'

'Of course he is, dead as a proverbial door nail.'

'Bloody hell!'

'Hang on, chaps, wait for the best bit. With pandemonium breaking out all around her, she doesn't try to make an escape, but puts the pistol back in her muff, walks back to reception and sits back down again. When the police arrive, she confesses all, stressing that she used all six bullets to be sure that *le bâtard* was dead! She then refuses to be taken to the police station in a Black Maria but, with the police acting as escort, has her chauffeur drive her in her Daimler, which is still parked outside.'

Bardie is impressed.

'Hell's bells, she makes our suffragettes seem like pussy cats!'

Geordie is not so sure.

'Perhaps, but it's enough to put you off the fairer sex for life. Imagine going home to her and having to confess to a little dalliance on the side and she opens her knicker drawer and pops you with a bally pistol!'

Bardie changes the subject.

'I'm going up to Glen Tilt this morning. Would you two slouches care to join me?'

Hamish declines, but young Geordie's eyes light up.

Bardie has been involved in a scheme for over six years that both his father and Hamish think is hare-brained, but which Geordie thinks is fascinating. It involves a somewhat eccentric character called John William Dunne, the son of wild Irish aristocrat General Sir John Dunne.

As a boy, Dunne became obsessed with the novels of Jules Verne, especially the imaginary machines he described. He started making paper aeroplanes by the score and flying them from the roof of his family home in County Kildare. By the time he was a teenager, Dunne, as bright as he was odd, was designing elaborate flying machines in the manner of Leonardo da Vinci. He was encouraged to continue by the author H. G. Wells, a family friend, whose vivid imagination was also a lifelong inspiration.

Bardie met Dunne during the Boer War, when Dunne was a lieutenant in the Imperial Yeomanry, but afterwards lost touch with him for a while. In the interim, Dunne had got himself attached to a peculiar new military establishment, the British Army's School of Ballooning, on Farnborough Common. An American, William Samuel Cody, a man even more outlandish than Dunne, had a rather unique role at Farnborough: he was the army's Chief Instructor in Kiting.

Cody was extraordinary. Born William Cowdery in Iowa, he changed his name to 'Cody' after his hero, 'Buffalo Bill' Cody, and came to Europe in the 1890s with the 'Klondike Nugget' a Wild West act in which he displayed his horse-riding, shooting and lassoing skills. His long goatee beard, cowboy hat and leather chaps were laughably ostentatious, but huge crowds flocked to see him all the same.

Cody became fascinated by balloon flight while performing in Paris. He duly discarded the cowboy outfit and transformed himself into a leading expert in and exponent of balloon and kite flying. However, he retained his flamboyant whiskers, showman's persona and, significantly, a personal collection of rare photographs he had bought at an auction in New York.

The photographs illustrated the use of surveillance balloons by the Union Army during the American Civil War, images so striking that they convinced a few of the more enlightened souls in Britain's War Office that there might be something worth pursuing in this peculiar phenomenon called flying.

Cody proceeded to design several two-man 'war kites', one of which towed a small lifeboat across the English Channel. He also flew a manned observation kite from the deck of HMS *Revenge*, a feat witnessed by several gawping senior figures at the Admiralty.

When William Dunne heard that the grandiose American's latest fad was gliders and powered aeroplanes, he rushed to Farnborough to meet him. Dunne begged to be involved, then demanded to be. Fortunately, after each weighed the other up, one madcap inventor recognized a fellow eccentric and Dunne was accepted.

Cody later left Farnborough to pursue flying as a private enterprise. After setting many records and twice winning the Michelin Cup and several *Daily Mail* Round Britain Races, he was killed in an accident in 1913. His funeral at Aldershot Military Cemetery was attended by 100,000 people who witnessed an interment that took place with full military honours and generated national headlines.

Dunne had remained at Farnborough, but when it was realized that his experiments were readily visible in the local vicinity and were thus easily observable by Britain's enemies – especially the spies of Germany's new Imperial Air Service, the *Fliegertruppe* – he approached Bardie.

The Atholl Estate has many remote valleys and Dunne asked Bardie if one could be used for a secret development programme. Bardie discussed it with his father, who was very sceptical, especially when his son described Dunne's latest scheme. He hoped to develop a prototype aeroplane based on the aerodynamic characteristics of the winged seeds of the zamonia plant. At first, the old duke, a cavalry man first and last, was speechless, but he finally conceded when he was reminded that he had also thought electric lighting, motor cars and telephones were ludicrous ideas.

Glen Tilt, a few miles to the north of Blair Castle, was chosen for the clandestine work. Hangars and workshops were built and good progress made, with better and better versions of Dunne's designs being produced. However, in 1909 the sceptics prevailed at the War Office and Dunne's funding was withdrawn. So Bardie, undaunted, enlisted the support of his friends, Hugh 'Bendor' Grosvenor, the 2nd Duke of Westminster, one of the country's richest men, Baron Nathan 'Natty' Rothschild, the renowned Jewish philanthropist, and William 'Billy' Wentworth-Fitzwilliam, 7th Earl Fitzwilliam, the owner of Wentworth Woodhouse, the largest private house in Europe. After a little arm-twisting, each agreed to join with Bardie and take over the financing of the project.

Dunne's prototype development in Scotland began with 'Dunne (D) 4', which was dismantled at Farnborough, transported in secret to Scotland and reassembled at Glen Tilt. The project is now up to 'D8', which has already been flown successfully, persuading the War Office to place an order for two of them to be built for use in military manoeuvres.

While Bardie asks Forsyth the butler to prepare some lunch and organize wet-weather clothing, Geordie asks Bardie about future plans.

'It's costing us a fortune, but Churchill has written to me privately, encouraging me to press on, so we're very heartened by that.'

Hamish, about to go off shooting, is eavesdropping. He is not a Churchill fan.

'If the First Lord is so keen, why doesn't he write in an official capacity?'

'He's a politician, Hamish, so he has to be circumspect with his opinions, especially about a secret scheme, financed privately.'

'Isn't that so typical of Churchill? He wants it both ways.'

'Of course he does; he's a politician. And, if I may remind you, so am I.'

'I rest my case, m'lud!'

'Off with you, Hamish. Go and shoot something; preferably something edible. My partners are coming up for the weekend, they'll be on the four o'clock from London. You need to be at dinner tonight; it's a three-line whip from Father.'

'I know, I'll be there. Is it black tie?'

'Yes, the girls are coming up too; best behaviour all round.'

That evening, there are so many at Blair for dinner, that the duke has instructed it be served in the Castle Ballroom, a cavernous hall with a magnificent hammer-beam roof and a minstrels' gallery large enough to accommodate a small orchestra.

The 7th Duke, 'Iain' to his friends, is at the head of the table. But the old boy is a widower, so Bardie's wife, Kitty, Lady Katharine Stewart-Murray, four years younger than him, is the hostess. She is intelligent, feisty and is constantly at odds with her father-in-law.

Kitty is from the 'lesser gentry', a social stratum she regards as embodying Britain's strong moral backbone; a view firmly reinforced in her mind since her marriage to Bardie. She is contemptuous of the loose behaviour of those whose titles once defined them as her social superiors. Now, she will be a duchess herself one day. She loves Bardie, despite his own 'weaknesses', and is determined that she will redeem him from the sins of his peers. Nor will she allow herself to succumb to the temptations of the weekend 'bed-hopping' so relished by the Stewart-Murrays and those of their ilk.

As she looks at the dinner guests, a thin smile crosses her face. She notices the knowing glances being exchanged; she sees the false charm and the overt sycophancy. She catches Bardie's eye, who smiles at her warmly in his turn. Then she admonishes herself a little: she played her own little games with Bardie when they first met, so perhaps she should not be so judgemental.

Hamish and Geordie are there, as are two of the three daughters of the family. All three Stewart-Murray girls are older than the boys: Dorothea is almost fifty, Helen is a couple of years younger and Evelyn, something of a family 'black sheep' who lives abroad, is yet another year younger.

Bardie's partners in the aeroplane scheme are there, but without their wives, who have been left behind in England. William Dunne is also there, with two of his designers, as are several of Bardie and his brothers' local friends. However, there is no dearth of ladies. Bardie has been careful to invite several presentable young women from the well-to-do families of Perthshire and even a couple of socialites from Edinburgh, who have been driven up in Bardie's brand-new motor car, a midnight-blue Rolls-Royce Silver Ghost. Several of the ladies will, no doubt, be very keen to make the acquaintance of the immensely rich and titled guests.

It promises to be an entertaining evening and weekend when, concealed behind the imposing walls and turrets of Blair's white-stucco, Scottish-baronial splendour, the Anglo-Scottish nobility will indulge themselves in their notorious 'rakishness'.

As the dinner comes to an end, Kitty notices some of the more obvious pairings as they make their clandestine plans for the night. She allows herself a few lingering thoughts about the couplings to come and enjoys, briefly, the erotic thoughts she conjures in her mind's eye. Then she extinguishes them, reminding herself that they are not 'proper' and are to be resisted if one's moral fibre is to be kept intact.

Saturday 6 June

'Nice service, Hywel.'

'We'll miss old Rhodri.'

As people offer their condolences at the family reception after the patriarch of the Thomas family has been laid to rest in Presteigne's St Andrew's churchyard, there are many similar hollow platitudes. Disappointingly few people went to the service and even fewer have turned up to the wake, even though the Duke's Arms always does a nice shoulder of ham with fresh bread, and the family has provided half a dozen flagons of beer.

Hywel and the others smile appreciatively at the gestures of kindness. But, if truth be told, their father was always a curmudgeonly sort, who got worse as he got older and became so insufferable after his wife died that he ended up with few friends. Cathy Griffiths was the glue that held the family together, and when she contracted pneumonia during the cold January of 1912 and died within the week, life became an increasing strain at Pentry Farm. Rhodri's pride was shattered. For generations, Pentry had been able to keep a large family and the old man blamed himself that it could do so no longer.

Money became tighter as the value of lamb plummeted. And with every fall in price, Rhodri's mood darkened. All three boys had to earn extra money by working on neighbouring farms and, despite being a good scholar at school, Bronwyn was forced to take up cleaning work in Presteigne.

As the wake empties and Morgan and Geraint pour more

and more beer into themselves from the still half-full flagons, Hywel, Tom and Bronwyn are left huddled together in a dingy corner of the Duke's back parlour. It is not one of the pub's better rooms, dark and chilly with a flagstone floor and cream distemper walls. It is four in the afternoon and the pub is quiet. The shopworkers, factorymen and artisans will not be in for another half an hour and, as it is early June, the farmers are busy in their fields.

Bronwyn has put on her mother's black dress and coat and is as pretty as a picture, her long black tresses tied into a fashionable pompadour. It is the first time she has worn her hair up but, at eighteen, she is old enough. Indeed, it is not thought 'proper' that a grown woman should wear her hair down unless in the privacy of her bedroom.

The room is suddenly made much darker as the huge frame of Philip Davies blocks the light. He greets them all warmly and thanks them for the food and ale, then turns to Bronwyn.

'Bronwyn, I hear you're doing some cleaning. Clara is not too well at the moment, could you do two or three half days for us?'

'Yes, I could, Mr Davies . . .'

She pauses, delighted by the offer of more work, but also a little overawed. Philip Davies is the most prominent man in the village, a towering presence, both physically and in local esteem.

'Thank you, sir. When should I come?'

'When are you next available?'

'Wednesday afternoon?'

'That's perfect.'

Davies shakes everybody by the hand before leaving. Even without his top hat, he has to lower his head to pass under the door to the back room.

Hywel is looking tired and pensive. Tom, who has taken a day off from his work as a carpenter, tries to distract him.

'Another mug, Hywel?'

'No, ta, Tom. I should get those two boys home afore they empty those flagons.'

'Come on, have another! Tell him, Bron.'

Bron grasps her brother's arm.

'Come on, big brother, I'm goin' to 'ave one. Will you buy me a milk stout, Tom?'

'Of course.'

'No, you won't.' Hywel turns to his sister. 'I don't want you drinkin' at Da's funeral, it's not proper.'

Bronwyn is feeling raw.

'Hywel, don't you dare! I'm eighteen, a grown woman. You men are drinkin'; if I want a drink, I'll 'ave one. Tom, a milk stout, *and* a glass o' port wine, please.'

Tom, sensitive as always, knows that emotions are brittle and that a row is looming.

'Bron, perhaps Hywel's right. Why don't we take some beer home?'

Bronwyn sees a chance to be yet more provocative.

'Good idea, I can stay with you tonight.'

Bronwyn knows that there is no possibility of staying with Tom; he lives with his parents, plus his two younger brothers and two sisters, in a small terraced house in Presteigne. Her remark is simply intended to antagonize her brother. Quite apart from the impracticality, even if Tom lived in a palace, his parents would be horrified – except for a formal family gathering – at the thought of a girl of marriageable age crossing their threshold, especially to spend the night.

'No, Bronwyn, don't be silly. I meant home to Pentry. I can stay in the barn.'

'Tom, I'm not bein' "silly"; you sound like Hywel, or my father. Well, neither of you is my father. He's dead!'

She bursts into tears and rushes from the parlour. Tom gets up to follow her, but Hywel puts his hand on his friend's arm.

'Leave her be for a minute or two.'

Hywel looks severe, trying to sound like a man of forty, rather than a youth of nineteen.

'Sit down, we need to talk.'

Tom knows what is coming. It is a conversation he has been dreading since Monday, when Hywel realized how close he and Bronwyn have become.

'So how long 'as it been goin' on?'

'Hywel, Bron's of age –'

'That's as maybe, but I'm entitled to ask. I'm head o' the family now.'

Tom knows he has a point.

'Since Christmas.'

'Are you bein' careful?'

'Course we are; we're not daft.'

'How do yer find somewhere to do yer courtin'?'

'Hywel, come on, man. Be fair.'

'All right, sorry . . . but she is my little sister.'

'I know! I have sisters too.'

'I assume you'll be makin' an 'onest woman of 'er?'

'I will, Hywel, but I've nothin' to offer her at the moment.'

'Well, we're all in that boat. But remember, you'll answer to me if you hurt her.'

Tom takes the warning without rancour, knowing full well that it is no affront to the friendship he shares with Hywel, merely a genuine expression of the affection of an elder brother for his little sister.

'What will you do now that Rhodri's gone?'

'I don't know; it's a right bugger. Pentry can't keep four of us. Geraint and Morgan need to find more work, or I do.'

'What about that girl from Knighton you've been seeing? She was very keen on you last time I saw her.'

'Cari? She's keen, all right; fair makes me get a stalk on. But she's not a future Mrs Thomas.'

'Hywel, if things are tight, would you consider me moving

into Pentry with Bron? I pay my ma and pa rent, but they can get by without it, so I could put that into the Thomas family's pot.'

'There's no room, Tom. Bron only gets some privacy by sleepin' in the parlour.'

'I'll do up your wood store. It's got good thick walls, and the roof is sound.'

'You've been checking it out, then.'

'I have . . . Bron and I have done a bit of courting in there.'

'I bet you 'ave! But what will I do for a wood store?'

'Put the logs in the barn; there's room.'

'Suppose you've been doin' a bit of courting in there as well?'

Tom just smiles.

'Well?' Hywel grins back. 'Very well, let's shake on it.'

Tom is elated and jumps to his feet.

'I'll go and get Bron, and give her the news. Then you can take her home.'

'No, bring 'er back 'ere. The boys can carry on drinkin' a while, and I'll buy 'er that stout and glass o' port. You can come and stay with us tonight. As it seems it's not the first time you've spent the night in there, you and Bron can 'ave the barn!'

Keighley Green Working Men's Club,
Burnley, Lancashire

Keighley Green Working Men's Club is one of dozens of spit-and-sawdust drinking dens that help Burnley's weavers and colliers rinse from their throats the dust and dirt of the town's cotton and coal industries. Burnley is not called 'King Cotton' for nothing. The mountains of bales that roll out from its 100,000 looms mean that, by some distance, it is the world's leading producer of cotton.

Like every Saturday night, Keighley Green Club is packed. The steward, retired cricketer and local hero John-Tommy Crabtree, has his sleeves rolled up to reveal the powerful forearms of one of the town's most prodigious fast bowlers. He is pulling pints while keeping a wary eye on the rowdier tables. His starched white apron has seen better days and his stiff Gladstone collar and black bow tie are the same ones he has worn for twenty years. Prominent above the back of the bar is the heavy, lead-filled shillelagh he wields most weekend nights when the lads get a bellyful of ale inside them and lose all reason. Massey's prize-winning King's Ale is not called 'fighting ale' for nothing.

The air is a pungent fug of honest sweat and tobacco smoke. Dozens of cheap clay pipes are being enjoyed by the older men, while 'coffin nails' (rolled tobacco cigarettes) are the more popular choice among the younger ones.

The spittoons that sit by the bar and in the corners of the club will be full by the end of the night as the men rid themselves of the residue of the working week. Accurate and fulsome spitting is a matter of pride. Working men have to spit wads of it: grey-green in hue for weavers, black for colliers.

The tables are full of heavy glazed earthenware beer mugs, which are replenished at regular intervals by 'pot lads' carrying huge pitchers of frothy ale. They wear brown aprons with a large pocket at the front for copper change, keeping silver coins in their pockets, well away from wandering hands.

Sporting big moustaches and dressed in their creased and threadbare black jackets, collarless union shirts and cotton mufflers, the men look like siblings of one another. There are no single women to be seen; only a few mature wives of the older men are permitted to cross the threshold of the club. And those wives need to have strong bladders, robust bowels, or few inhibitions, as the only sanitation is a long tin lant-trough in the yard, which serves as a urinal, and a single long-drop privy with no door.

A painted white line, across which not even the older women may step, runs past the fringe of the bar and marks out a large open area where two billiard tables sit. They are surrounded by knots of animated men watching the challenge matches that are taking place. Adding significantly to the tension, considerable sums of money are being bet on the outcome of the contests.

At the dozen or so Britannia tables that circle the room, three-card brag – that uniquely brutal game for ardent bluffers with nerves of steel – is being played for piles of shillings and sixpences that none of the players can afford.

Close to the bar, beyond the 'lasses' scratch' – the members' name for the strict frontier between the sexes – there is a particularly raucous table of half a dozen young men. Tommy Broxup, a burly weaver a few years older than the others, is holding court.

'So t'new foreman, a cocky little bugger fra' Rochdale, comes up to me and says I were slackin'.'

The young lad next to Tommy is Vincent Sagar, only seventeen, his face full of freckles and mischief. A novice at nights of heavy drinking, he is all ears, obviously in awe of Tommy's bravado.

'What did tha say to 'im?'

'Nowt. But after a bit, t'lad went for a piss, so I followed 'im. Waited until he were in full flow, then I put me 'and on his shoulder. He looked round, freetened to death, and pissed down his pants. I told 'im if he ever spoke to me like that again I'd knock his fuckin' block off.'

Vinny nearly falls off his chair laughing at Tommy's story.

'Tha's a rum bugger, our Tommy!'

Weavers are in the vast majority and rule the roost in Burnley. But there are always clashes with their redoubtable rivals in the working-class pecking order, men without peers in working-class mythology, the local colliers.

Colliers are easily identified at the end of a shift as they trudge home to wash away the grime of the pit in the tin bath that hangs on a nail outside the back door of every terraced house. Black-faced and red-eyed, they are men coarsened by their back-breaking toil, who think weaving is 'work for women and girls'.

The antipathies between pit men and mill men invariably escalate into fisticuffs at closing time on Saturday nights, and again during the many cricket and football matches that are played on the town's asphalt recreation grounds every Sunday.

Tommy Broxup is a frequent participant in tussles with the town's colliers, many of whom drink at the Princess Royal on Yorkshire Street, not far from Keighley Green, on the other side of the canal culvert.

The Leeds and Liverpool Canal cuts through the middle of Burnley like a Victorian Offa's Dyke. Its 'Straight Mile', which runs along a huge embankment sixty feet above the town centre, is said to be one of the 'Seven Wonders of Britain's Waterways'. However, the older locals have a different view; they can remember their grandparents telling them how it ruined the town: 'Five years o' mess, £25,000 o' brass – fer what? Nowt but a long bath o' water!'

In the middle of the mile, a circular tunnelled culvert connects the two sides of the town. Once a fine piece of late-eighteenth-century engineering, it is now dripping with seepage from the canal above and offers dark shadows for those whose business is less than wholesome. It is home to several 'loose lasses' who hide in its murk and is one of the most popular venues for the town's 'cock' fights, in which its young lads use their fists and clogs to earn the title 'cock' of their district, or even of the whole borough.

There are seven pubs and three clubs within fifty yards of the culvert, which provide a baying audience for the frequent brawls that take place in the dank confines beneath the canal. Wisely, the police usually arrive when the mayhem is over and encourage the throng to go home to their beds.

Tommy's most famous encounter 'under t'culvert' happened a few months earlier. It was a pre-arranged fight with Joe Smalley, a big lad with a lot less brain than brawn. Joe had heard tales of the speed of Tommy's fists and the strength of his blows and had tucked a 3lb blacksmith's hammer into the back of his belt. Before blows were exchanged, following the usual courtesies, Tommy went to shake Joe's hand.

'No gougin', reet?'

Joe did not accept Tommy's handshake and seemed very tense; his answer was only a mumble, hardly audible.

'Aye.'

'Cloggin' or not?'

Joe did not answer but, to the dismay of everyone there, pulled out his concealed hammer and started swinging it. He was suddenly like a man possessed.

'Come on, Broxup, let's see 'ow fuckin' 'ard y'are.'

Tommy ducked several times, but Joe caught him with a heavy blow to the edge of his right shoulder, making his renowned right fist all but useless. Tommy had to think quickly and attacked in any way he could. He threw himself at the big collier, knocking him to the floor, taking the wind out of him. He used his right knee to pin Joe's left arm to the ground and his own left hand to hold his opponent's right wrist.

Without a good right hand, Tommy had nothing to attack with. He thought of head-butting the collier, but with Joe's head supported by the ground, it would probably do Tommy more damage than his opponent.

Joe was a strong lad and began to wriggle free, so Tommy had to act fast and decided to sink his teeth into his adversary's side, just below his ribs. Like a bull terrier, he did not let go and blood began to flow copiously. Joe tried to free his hammer but a fellow collier, outraged that a colleague had brought a weapon to a fist fight, stood on its shaft and pinned it to the ground.

Joe bellowed in pain; Tommy bit harder until the agony was too much to bear, forcing a cry of '*Enough!*' from his stricken foe. Tommy relaxed the grip of his teeth and spat out the blood that had filled his mouth. Joe, his shirt and jacket crimson with blood, was helped up by his fellow colliers.

Although Joe had surrendered, he felt humiliated. For him the fight was not over. He pushed his helpers away and wrested free his hammer. By then, Tommy had turned his back and Joe lunged at him, his weapon held high. There were gasps and cries and looks of horror, alerting Tommy to the danger. He turned in an instant and used his good left arm to parry the blow that might well have killed him. A swift but powerful kick to the groin made Joe double up in pain, which gave Tommy the chance to deliver a rabbit punch to the back of his opponent's neck, rendering him immobile until he collapsed to the ground.

Once more, Joe's colleagues took him away, this time more roughly, indignant about their fellow collier's behaviour. As they did so, a craggy old veteran of the pit approached Tommy and shook his hand.

'Yon Joe's a wrong 'un. But tha's fettled 'im reet enough; mind you, it's a reet good job tha's got thy own teeth!'

For weeks afterwards, the story of 'Tommy Broxup's 'ammer and teeth feight' was repeated across the town to the great amusement of all who heard it. Unfortunately, Tommy's collarbone had been broken by the hammer blow and he was unable to work for five weeks. His employers, knowing full well that he had injured himself in a fight, held no sympathy for him. They kept his job open, but he got no sick pay and his union could only offer him a third of his weekly earnings, a paltry 4 shillings a week.

However, every Friday evening, there was a knock on

Tommy's door, 54 Hart Street, the last terraced house on the long row of identical homes all owned by Daneshouse Mill, his employers. It sat directly beneath the looming bank of the canal in one of the town's poorest districts.

For each of the five weeks that Tommy could not work, the source of the knock was a little lad, no more than twelve, who would hand Tommy a crumpled manila envelope, saying, 'From t'lads at pit.' It contained between 8 and 10 shillings in both copper and silver. It was the proceeds of a regular collection taken at the pithead of Joe Smalley's Bee Hole Colliery, a small pit just behind Burnley's football ground at Turf Moor and only a few hundred yards from the famous ''ammer and teeth feight'.

After the final delivery, Tommy went to the pit to thank the colliers. As is their way, they were forthright with their responses.

'No need to thank us, lad. We made Big Joe put in a bob a week. He won't be feightin' again fer a bit.'

Despite its prominence, Burnley's canal is not the defining feature of the town. That honour goes to the forest of mill chimneys that stretches as far as the eye can see. When they can see them through the heavy smoke that belches out, the local children count the stacks. They say there are 'six dozen when it's reet murky' and 'eight dozen if tha can sken Pendle Hill'.

The acrid smoke that the chimneys vomit into the air sits over the town like a heavy shroud and masks the sun on all but the freshest days. In winter, when every household is burning 'best slack' in their grates to add to the puke of the mills, the air is so thick with soot it stings the eyes and makes it impossible to keep clothes clean, or even breathe without wheezing.

Paradoxically, Burnley, for all its ills and sins, sits in a hollow in the high undulating moors of the Pennines, a vast landscape of austere beauty. Tarnished only by the black infernos of the local cotton towns, Colne, Nelson, Burnley and Accrington, the moors offer welcome relief to the gloom and drudgery of daily life.

Almost everything in the area is built from Pennines' mill-stone grit, an attractive, soft yellow sandstone akin to the renowned limestones of the Cotswolds and Somerset in southern England. However, in the rural south, stone retains its golden hue for generations. In Burnley, gleaming new stone is black with grime within ten years.

The old adage, 'Where there's muck there's brass,' is of little comfort to the ordinary folk of Burnley, to whom 'brass' is never plentiful. They live huddled together in their endless rows of terraced houses that make linear patterns on the steep slopes descending towards the town centre. Most of the town's housing and many of its public buildings have been built within the last fifty years of rapid growth. They sit cheek by jowl with older, haphazard housing stock close to the town centre, the squalid homes of the old and the poor.

Burnley has all the seedy characteristics of a frontier town, its population exploding from 4,000 in 1800 to over 110,000 in 1910, often mixing the sons and daughters of impoverished Pennine hill farmers with even more destitute Irish migrants. Diphtheria, scarlet fever, polio, bronchitis and pneumonia are commonplace, as is the extreme bow-legged gait of childhood rickets, what the locals call 'bandy-legs'.

There are a few large and splendid Victorian homes for the mill owners on the fringes of the borough and a scatter-ing of not quite so grand Edwardian houses for the middle classes who serve them. But the vast majority of people live in identical two-up-two-down boxes, many of them back-to-back hovels, while a few have to endure the ravages of cellar dwellings, where large families live in almost medieval filth beneath street level.

'Long drop' and 'tipple' lavatories, emptied every week by the soil men with their horse-drawn carts, are the only sanitation, and the stench is usually overpowering in the poorest districts, especially in the summer. Flat caps, old Lancashire shawls and weavers' clogs are standard dress, and most people only possess the clothes they stand up in.

However, even though poverty is endemic for many, hard graft, long shifts and overtime bring in enough money to keep the market stalls busy and the pubs full.

Keighley Green was once an open, low-lying meadow between the old market town of antiquity and the new nineteenth-century boom town. But it is now one of those rough-house areas where the police walk their beats in squads of four with a horse-drawn Black Maria nearby to sweep up any miscreants. It is also home to the new police station and town lock-up, deliberately situated in the rowdiest part of the borough.

As a typical Saturday night in Burnley unfolds – this one warmer and more humid than most – Tommy Broxup continues to keep his friends amused. But his focus suddenly shifts to a face at the club bar he has not seen before.

'Who's yon big bugger?'

Vinny has no idea, but his best pal from schooldays, Nathaniel 'Twaites' Haythornthwaite, has. A short sturdy lad with a mop of white-blond hair, who hails from the Pendle village of Sabden five miles north of Burnley, he recognizes the newcomer immediately.

'By 'eck, that's "Mad Mick" Kenny. He's called "Cock o' Colne", not just because he's an 'ard case, but because o' t'number of women he's shagged. He's a collier; 'is dad were a Paddy.'

'A Paddy collier from Colne. What's he doin' in 'ere?'

Vincent sniffs the prospect of a rumpus.

'I'll go an' ask 'im.'

As he passes the steward, John-Tommy leans across the bar.

'Did tha laik at cricket today, lad?'

'I did, John-Tommy, we laiked at Ramsbottom.'

'And?'

'Forty-eight not out, and three fer twenty-one.'

'Good lad.' John-Tommy nods appreciatively and smiles broadly. 'But tha needs to be suppin' less ale if tha' wants to be a top laiker.'

Vinny walks on, only half listening to the advice. John-Tommy's look turns rueful, remembering that it was too many pints of Massey's that brought an early end to his own cricketing career.

Despite the crowd of bodies around the bar, Vinny is soon back with the other lads, looking chastened.

Twaites grins at him.

'What did t'big bugger say?'

'He told me to fuck off and mind me own business.'

'So what did tha say?'

'Well, he's an even bigger bugger up close than 'e looks at a distance, so I did as I was told, an' fucked off!'

They all laugh out loud, except Tommy, who is already pushing through the throng to confront the visitor. He has had a few pints and feels like warming his knuckles and burnishing his clog irons. Almost as tall as Mad Mick, he puts his face far closer to him than is necessary.

'This is a members' club, lad.'

The big lad smiles rather than take the offence that is intended.

'Course it is, wouldn't be a club if it didn't 'ave members.'

'But tha's not one of 'em.'

Again, no offence is taken; the smile broadens.

'Neither are 'alf t'lads in 'ere.' He rests a gentle hand on Tommy's shoulder. 'Can a non-member buy a member an' his pals a pint?'

Tommy is perplexed. He intended to provoke a fight, but gets a grin and a pint instead. The unexpected response draws Tommy's venom.

'Aye, we'll 'ave a pint wi' thee. But only one, then it's out-side fer a set-to.'

Three pints later, the two men are sharing stories, all talk of fighting forgotten. Then Tommy remembers that his new pal is a stranger to the club.

'So, Mick lad, why 'as tha come down to Burnley toneet?'

'To see thee.'

'Me, what fer?'

'Two reasons. First, I 'eard about thy set-to wi' Joe Smalley and I wanted to meet t'lad wi' teeth like a bulldog. Second, my missus, Cath, is a bit of a firebrand. She supports them suffragettes and 'as just joined t'socialists.'

'Bloody 'ell; votes fer women! My Mary's t'same. I can't vote mesen; I don't know any lad who can. Mary says we should all 'ave t'vote.'

'I know, Cath's 'eard that your Mary speaks 'er mind at t'mill. That's why I'm 'ere; Cath wants Mary to join t'socialists. But I wanted to speak wi' thee first.'

'That's reet gentlemanly of thee. I'll talk to Mary. But she knows 'er own mind and will suit 'erself.'

'Another ale, Tommy?'

'Aye, ta. 'Ow yer gettin' 'ome to Colne?'

'A've missed last tram; I'll 'ave to walk.'

'No, yer won't; it's seven mile to Colne. Tha can sleep in our front room and meet Mary in t'morn.'

'Good o' thee to let a collier through thy front door.'

'That's alreet. No pissin' in t'fire back, though. I know what you lads do fer a piss down t'pit.'

Monday 8 June

Before Blair Atholl's weekend guests catch the lunchtime train back to London, Bardie Stewart-Murray is anxious to show them and his fellow investors the fruits of three years' hard work trying to perfect William Dunne's flying machine. Despite a long weekend of daytime shooting and highly raucous night-time revelry, transport to Glen Tilt Aerodrome has been organized for 7 a.m. Breakfast has been sent up and served in one of the large hangars.

Bardie has been holding back from showing his guests Glen Tilt in order to spring a surprise. He has been in correspondence with Winston Churchill, Britain's First Lord of the Admiralty, for some time about their mutual interest in aeroplanes. On Saturday morning, he received a telegram from the Admiralty stating: 'WSC, First Lord, accompanied by CSC, will anchor in Firth of Tay, Sun 7th. Will be at Glen Tilt Mon 8th, 7.30 a.m. sharp.'

Bardie immediately cancelled the planned visit to Glen Tilt he had arranged for Saturday, citing 'technical difficulties', and rescheduled for Monday morning. Despite the fact that heavy drinking and other forms of wickedness were still going on at 3 a.m., all the guests have appeared and, apart from some pastiness around the gills, look fresh and are turned out immaculately. After all, debauchery is no excuse for slovenliness.

Bardie has only confided in his father and William Dunne about Churchill's visit. The former, not fond of Liberals, is unimpressed, the latter is rushing around like a man possessed.

Kitty, Bardie's wife, is curious about the breakfast.

'Champagne in the Glens on a Monday morning, Bardie. What's the occasion?'

'It's a surprise.'

'You mean the damn thing flies!'

'Of course it does. Don't tease; you've seen it fly many times.'

'So why the champagne?'

'We're expecting a guest.'

'Really, and who would that be? The Kaiser, perhaps?'

'Kitty, don't be beastly. Actually, it's Churchill.'

Kitty suddenly sheds her sarcasm.

'Goodness! Well done, Bardie; I rather like him.'

'Hmm, I'm afraid Father doesn't.'

'Your father doesn't like anybody very much – particularly me.'

'That's because he thinks you're a suffragette.'

'I've told him countless times that I have no truck with the Pankhursts. But because I have a tongue in my head, I must be both a suffragette and a socialist in his eyes.'

'Darling Kitty, he thinks I'm a socialist because I don't agree that men should work for a pittance and not be able to feed their families.'

Kitty and Bardie's banter is interrupted by the loud horn of a jet-black Admiralty car sent from Rosyth to transport the First Lord to Blair Atholl and its secret aerodrome. It pulls into the open space in front of the assembled breakfast gathering and, to the amazement of all, out steps Winston Churchill with his wife, Clementine, in his wake. He heads smartly for the duke, full of effusive geniality.

'Your Grace, good to see you again.'

He then turns to Bardie and Kitty, and does the rounds of the guests. Kisses and handshakes are exchanged.

'Ah, champagne! From the slightly pale complexion of your guests, I gather you still know how to throw a party. Must have been quite a weekend.' He takes a generous gulp from his goblet and turns to the duke's butler. 'Good morning to you . . .' He pauses.

'Forsyth, sir.'

'Good morning, Forsyth. Splendid morning! Do you happen to have any oysters?'

'I'm afraid we don't, sir; not very fresh in Edinburgh yesterday. But his lordship asked cook to prepare some plovers' eggs for you. She has sent some fresh bread, which we can toast for you if you like.'

'My goodness, this is heaven on earth! Thank you so much, and tell the cook she will assuredly go to heaven.'

Winston ushers Clementine to join the elderly duke at his table and begins to demolish his eggs. As he does so, he takes charge of proceedings.

'Bardie, your hospitality is beyond reproach. Now let's see how this contraption of yours performs.'

William Dunne takes his cue and signals to his mechanics at the adjacent hangar to wheel out his latest prototype. Dunne is not the showman that his mentor William Samuel Cody was, but he tries his best to introduce his marvel.

'Your graces, my lords, ladies, Mr Churchill, this is the D8, developed here at Glen Tilt by the Blair Atholl Syndicate Limited. It is the next major step in man's triumph over gravity.'

So far, so good, thinks Bardie. Dunne continues, trying, without too much success, to add gravitas to his delivery.

'The D8 is powered by a water-cooled, four-cylinder, sixty-horse-power engine. It directly drives a four-blade pusher-propeller, which saves considerable weight compared to the chain drives of previous prototypes.'

Bardie looks around at the gathering. Although Churchill and his investors are still engrossed, his father is already staring up at the high sides of the glen looking for roe deer, while the fixed smiles of his sisters and those of Kitty and Mrs Churchill are beginning to strain.

Dunne carries on regardless.

'The D8 is a tailless four-bay unstaggered biplane, my speciality, with its wings swept at 32 degrees. The outer struts are enclosed with fabric, forming fixed side curtains that provide directional yaw.'

Dunne suddenly catches Bardie's eyes, which are imploring him to stop talking and to fly his contraption. All but Winston have glazed over and are shuffling their feet impatiently. So D8's designer cuts short his technical outline, dons his flying helmet and clambers aboard a craft which looks for all the world like an oversized children's kite.

With its inventor at the controls, its propeller kicks into life with an ear-splitting roar and, despite its bizarre appearance, D8 makes bumpy progress down the glen. It shakes and rattles like an old boiler, but when it eventually becomes airborne, the propeller's sound suddenly becomes melodious and its struts, props and canvas take on the elegance of a bird in flight. It flies over Glen Tilt for nearly twenty minutes. Dunne, now in his element and feeling confident, is even able to fly low over the aerodrome and take his hands off the controls. Only a few feet from the ground, he waves to his audience as he passes. There are gasps from those watching, even the old duke smiles.

Winston is full of admiration.

'Very good show, Bardie.' He goes over to Bardie's investors and shakes their hands. 'Three lords a-laughing! I'm not surprised; very well done, gentlemen. This is a big step forward.'

When Dunne lands his plane, Winston is there to greet him.

'Mr Dunne, you have made dramatic progress. You have the future in your hands. Literally. Please, keep going.'

'Thank you, sir.'

Still beaming, Winston turns to Bardie.

'Clemmie and I are staying in my Dundee constituency tonight, so we have time for an early lunch. Shall we adjourn to Blair? I'd like to have a word with you and your backers.'

A casual buffet lunch is prepared at Blair Castle, during which Winston guides Bardie and his investors into the garden.

'Gentlemen, I know you have a train to catch, but I wanted to have a quiet word about your project here. It is very exciting; you must continue, full bore.'

Natty Rothschild bristles slightly.

'We shall, Winston, rest assured. But as you know, we're only financing it because the army withdrew its funding.'

Bendor Grosvenor then makes his feelings clear.

'There is only so far we can go as private investors. The War Office has to do more.'

Winston takes a deep draw on his cigar, sticks out his chin and exhales flamboyantly.

'I know, they turn the word "conservative" into a blasphemy. I'm sorry. But I am trying to bring flight under the wing of the navy, if you will forgive the pun. I'll get my way, but you must give me time.'

Billy Wentworth-Fitzwilliam asks the obvious question.

'How much time?'

'Give me nine months. I have approval for my naval budget for the rest of the year, but I'll work on the PM for the autumn review. He realizes the Germans are ahead of us, and the gap is widening. Asquith knows that only too well, but there are many doubters in the Cabinet. I'm working on them. Please keep going until March.'

Bardie walks towards the window and looks across the glens towards the east.

'Winston, this situation with the Kaiser, is it serious?'

'Yes, I'm afraid it is. It is a growing threat. I fear he will not stop until he has his way with the French –' Realizing that he may be sounding too alarmist, he breaks off and lightens his tone. 'So, gentlemen, look to the east and give me time.'

The four men look at one another for a moment before giving hesitant nods of agreement.

Winston, now in the mode of the jovial politician, shakes their hands and bids them farewell.

'Safe journeys to London. And don't worry, I'll have flying under the navy's wing very soon. Fear not, gentlemen, we will all be flying around in those things before you know it. You'll make a fortune.'

Monday 29 June

Mechanics' Institute, Burnley, Lancashire

Burnley Mechanics' Institute is the town's finest building. A neoclassical Victorian masterpiece, its Palladian façade, complete with Corinthian columns and elegant pediments, would readily serve as a gentleman's club in St James's, in London. Although it is beginning to acquire the grime that is the hallmark of Burnley's other buildings, its soft honey-coloured sandstone still stands out against the darker shades of the local millstone grit.

While it would sit well in London's club land, the clientele in the Mechanics' Reading Room on this warm sunny evening could not offer a greater contrast to the aristocrats of White's or Boodle's. The gathering is an odd assortment; they number fewer than thirty and have a wide range of views, but all are committed socialists of one kind or another. All, that is, except Tommy Broxup and Mick Kenny, who are there to see the kind of people their wives admire so much and seem to spend more and more time talking about.

The audience is devoted to improving the lot of Burnley's downtrodden masses, but few of them are from the town's impoverished communities. In the main, they are schoolteachers, civil servants and office workers; most have clean suits and are well turned out. There are only half a dozen men who look like mill workers or colliers, and two of them are Tommy and Mick. Only five of the gathering are women.

Mick's wife, Cath, and Tommy's wife, Mary, are seated at the front. The two men are at the back, trying not to be noticed. The two girls are at the front because they want to be close to the night's guest speaker, Mr Harry Hyndman, the mercurial leader of the newly formed British Socialist Party.

Cath has been committed to the cause since 1905, when her father took her to the annual conference of the Social-Democratic Federation, which was held in Burnley. Only just thirteen at the time and not able to understand much of the political jargon, she was, nevertheless, entranced, especially when Hyndman spoke. He talked of the 'regeneration and emancipation of humanity' and said that the mission of socialists was to 'remove from the great mass of the people all the hideous conditions of environment which make their lives a living hell'.

He finished with rousing lines that brought tears to Cath's eyes; words she would remember for the rest of her life.

'Those of us who would free others must themselves be free; those who would purify others must themselves be pure; those who would strengthen others must themselves be strong. If we are all those things, we will have in our hearts the first faint gleam of the dawn of a new social era. Comrades, let us march forward together.'

After Mick and Tommy's meeting in the Keighley Green Club, Cath and Mary have become firm friends and Mary is devouring the reams of socialist literature that Cath is giving her. Both excelled at school but, as girls, have no future other than a life in the mill. Mary left school at thirteen to become an 'under-fettler', a role for which a small child is ideal, as it involves cleaning the cotton waste from under the working looms.

She is now a fully fledged four-loom weaver and works at the Daneshouse Mill in Stoneyholme, where Tommy is a tackler, responsible for the maintenance of the looms. Cath works at the Trafalgar Mill in the Weavers Triangle in the centre of the town. Both mills are large and successful, employing hundreds of weavers. Cath and Mary are already notorious as 'troublemakers'. As the vast majority of weavers are men, and most of them resent women moving in and taking their jobs, the unions are almost as hostile to them as the owners. All the union officials are men and, as Cath puts it, 'left wing when it comes to men's wages and conditions, but right wing when it comes to women'.

Mr Hyndman is introduced by the chairman, a member of the local Fabian Society, who describes the guest speaker's illustrious record at Trinity College Cambridge, where he read mathematics, before becoming a lawyer and journalist. He was a first-class cricketer, playing for the MCC and Sussex, and travelled the world, becoming friends with, among others, Mr Karl Marx and Mr Friedrich Engels. Tommy and Mick are impressed by the visitor's cricketing pedigree but are clueless about the identities of Marx and Engels, except that they know they are not cricketers.

Hyndman gives an inspirational speech, which is received with rapturous applause. After the speech, there are numerous questions, few of which make much sense to Tommy and Mick, who are becoming restless. They have been in the pub and had a few jugs of beer, which is not conducive to intellectual insight. Suddenly, Tommy jumps to his feet to ask a question. When the chairman asks him to name himself and his affiliation, Mary and Cath turn round. A look of horror immediately flashes across their faces.

'I'm Tommy Broxup. I'm affiliated to nowt, but I'm still askin' me question. Mr Hyndman, tha can talk like a good 'un, I'll grant thee that. But when that lad introduced thee, he told us abaht Cambridge an' all that. So, I'm wonderin', when tha spouts abaht t'poverty o' workin' people, 'ow dost tha know what tha's talkin' abaht?'

There are a few ripples of laughter in the room, but most are embarrassed that a local man, speaking with an accent they are all trying hard to lose, should be so rude to their guest. Mick pulls Tommy's jacket to get him to sit down.

Mr Hyndman is unperturbed, smiling broadly.

'Mr Broxup, those of us who are fortunate by accident of birth to have been afforded many of life's privileges carry a great responsibility to help, where we can, to right the world's wrongs. I cannot hide my past, or pretend it didn't happen, nor would I want to. I'm proud of what I have achieved. All I would ask of you, as a fellow human being, is to judge me by what I do now and what I do in the future, not by my past.'

The speaker's thoughtful reply brings another round of enthusiastic applause, particularly from Cath and Mary. It also impresses Mick. He looks at his new pal, Tommy, who, despite his somewhat inebriated state, is thinking deeply. A few more questions are asked before the meeting is brought to a close. As it does so, Tommy gets to his feet and walks to the front of the room. The audience, knowing Tommy's predilection for violence, is anxious, but Hyndman seems untroubled and strides forward to meet Tommy halfway. He is as tall as the Burnley man, but much larger, with his long auburn beard making him look quite formidable.

Tommy grasps Hyndman's hand and shakes it vigorously.

'I were out of order, Mr Hyndman. Tha's reet, tha' musn't judge a man by 'is background.'

'My name is Henry. May I call you Tommy?'

'Aye, yer may. I hear tha laiks at cricket. Me an' a couple o' lads are laikin' agin Lowerhouse tomorrow. Come an' 'ave a knock.'

'But I'm an old man. And not registered, Tommy.'

'It doesn't matter, we're only Burnley Thirds. Just a few o' t'lads; casual, like.'

'Well, I'm speaking in Nelson at seven thirty, and I haven't wielded a bat in many a year . . .'

'Tha'll be alreet, we start at five thirty. We'll get the Lowerhouse lads to concede t'toss and tha can open fer us. Rose

Grove Station is just up t'road. Nelson is only fifteen minutes.'

'Well, Tommy, on that basis, how can I refuse?'

The following evening, at five thirty on the dot, to the bewilderment of the twenty or so spectators and to the chagrin of the Lowerhouse Third Eleven, Henry Hyndman, founder of the British Socialist Party, opens the batting for Burnley Cricket Club's Thirds. Over seventy years old, and several stones heavier than when in his prime, he bats with the trousers of his heavy woollen suit pushed into his socks and tucks the bottom of his beard into his waistcoat. There are many in the crowd who remark on the uncanny resemblance to the great cricketing legend, 'The Champion', Dr William Gilbert Grace.

Tommy also opens, but is out for two in the second over, bringing in Vinny Sagar, Tommy's pal and the club's most promising youngster. When Hyndman has to retire an hour later to catch the train to Nelson, he has scored 78 off just 51 balls, including 3 sixes and 13 fours, with Vinny contributing a commendable 16. The great socialist leader leaves the field to a standing ovation and a handshake from the members of both teams.

Tommy is the last to grasp his hand.

'Thanks to thee, Henry.'

'Thank you, Tommy; I hope you go on to win.'

'We will. Vinny'll get fifty, he ollus does, and we'll make a hundred and sixty, thanks to thy seventy-eight. They'll be lucky to get a hundred and twenty.'

'It was my pleasure, Tommy. I thoroughly enjoyed myself.'

Tommy walks over to the boundary with Hyndman and beckons to one of the spectators to escort his guest to the station.

'Tell me, Henry, this socialism malarkey, every bugger bein' equal an' all that, will it ever 'appen?'

'Undoubtedly, Tommy. In fact, it already has – for example, during the Paris Commune, and a few other places – albeit briefly. If we can persuade men like you to believe in it, instead of old fuddy-duddies like me, it will happen for certain. And soon.'

Tommy is lost in thought as he watches his guest leave. Then the opposing captain bellows at him. It is his turn to umpire.

'Art laikin' Tommy, or what?'

Burnley Thirds win the game easily.

That evening, Mick and Cath Kenny and Tommy and Mary Broxup are sitting with the team to enjoy a few post-match drinks in the Lowerhouse's small wooden pavilion. Cath is a teetotaller and is only drinking ginger beer, but Mary is fond of Mackeson, the new milk stout that is growing in popularity.

The men, who have played in their working clothes, have stripped off to their vests and trousers and taken off their clogs and socks. Mary and Cath are still wrapped in their long voluminous skirts and petticoats, their head and shoulders covered by heavy Lancashire shawls, the standard dress for mill workers. Only well-to-do ladies wear the latest Edwardian styles with pleated skirts, tailored jackets and feathered hats.

Cath is concerned that young Vinny is quaffing ale as quickly as Tommy and Mick.

'Our Vinny, tha doesn't 'ave to drink them pints as quick as these two daft buggers.'

Mary agrees.

'Our Tommy were a grand cricketer an' could laik a fair game o' football until he started suppin' ale by t'gallon.'

Tommy springs to Vinny's defence.

'Stop moitherin', woman, t'lad'll be alreet. Let 'im enjoy his ale.'

64

Mick thinks it's a good idea to change the subject.

'So, Tommy, tha were impressed wi' Hyndman's battin', but what abaht 'is politics?'

'Aye, he can bat; he's a proper cricketer. He's what, seventy? Not bad fer an old 'un.'

Mary notices that Tommy has not answered the other part of Mick's question.

'An' his politics?'

'Well, I've been thinkin'. He meks some good points, I'll give 'im that. Mary's told me abaht that Paris Commune thing. But it's all them long words – prola . . . terrion . . . or summat.'

Cath comes to his rescue.

'"Proletarian", Tommy; that's us, t'workin' class.'

'You mean them as got nowt!'

'Reet. T'socialists want to end all that an' create a fair an' equal world.'

'It'll ne'er 'appen, lass.'

'Oh it will, Tommy. Won't it, Mary?'

'I 'ope so, Cath. But it means daft buggers like this lot comin' to their senses.'

Mary begins to raise her voice.

'Dost tha' know, you men, two million o' thy comrades are on strike down south reet now? London's buildin' workers, dockers, an' all sorts; they've bin out fer weeks.'

Tommy tries to calm his wife down.

'Mary, keep thy voice down. We're in a cricket pavilion, not a public meetin'.'

'I won't keep me voice down! You lot need to listen, an' all t'other men in 'ere. That Mrs Pankhurst were arrested last week fer t'eighth time. An' they've been force-feedin' t'suffragettes fer years; it's not reet.'

Tommy rises to the bait, but with a mischievous grin on his face.

'There's some what reckon they should be flogged. Or their husbands need to give 'em a good seein' to!'

Mary is livid and clips Tommy around the ear. It makes little impact, and he starts to laugh loudly. So Mary picks up his half-empty mug of beer and throws its contents in his face. There is a sudden silence in the pavilion, and Tommy's expression changes dramatically. Mick sees what's happening, rests his hand on Tommy's arm and nods at Cath to get Mary home.

'Tha'll be needin' another pint, our Tommy. Vinny, ged 'em in.'

Mary bursts into tears as Cath leads her to the door, where they bump straight into Nat 'Twaites' Haythornthwaite, who has arrived to join the evening's drinking.

'Eh, what's up 'ere, then?'

Mick pulls him into a chair.

'Shurrup, Twaites, an' sit down.'

PART TWO: JULY
Death in a Distant Land

Saturday 11 July

Winston and Clemmie Churchill have taken a small Norfolk cottage for the summer. Clemmie, the children and their nanny have been there for almost a month, while Winston comes up from London by train most weekends. On this occasion, he came ashore from HMS *Enchantress* on Friday, leaving the Admiralty yacht anchored at sea, much to the fascination of locals and holidaymakers alike.

Unlike many grander holiday retreats in the area, Pear Tree Cottage is a modest abode. It has three bedrooms and a bunk room and is hidden down a narrow lane a few yards from the small cliffs that fall down to the North Sea. Overstrand and nearby Cromer have become very fashionable holiday destinations since the old Prince of Wales stayed here in the 1890s. As a consequence, several of London's well-to-do have built large seaside villas along the coastal road.

Winston's younger brother, Jack, and his family have taken Beehive, a similar cottage nearby. The cottages bring back fond memories for the Churchill brothers as the area was a favourite resort of their mother's when they were small. Despite the six years between them, Jack and Winston have been close since childhood. They served together in South Africa, where Jack was badly wounded and was mentioned in dispatches. They have also shared the many stigmas attached to their family, especially the rumours that their father, Lord Randolph, died of syphilis and that their mother, the New York-born beauty Jennie Jerome, later Lady Randolph

Churchill, has had many lovers, including the old king, Edward VII, when he was Prince of Wales.

Lady Randolph is only recently divorced from her second husband, George Cornwallis-West, an officer in the Scots Guards who is the same age as Winston and who is renowned for his charm and virility. She remains one of London's most glamorous women and is still notorious, even at the age of sixty.

With both Winston and Jack at Overstrand for the week-end, sandcastles on the beach are the order of the day. Like Winston, Jack holds a commission in the Queen's Own Oxfordshire Hussars as a reservist and has the same passion for all things military. As Winston did before him, Jack spent many happy hours playing with the family's unique collection of tin soldiers at their ancestral home, Blenheim Palace. With the image of their ancestor the Duke of Marlborough at the moment of his great victory in the Battle of Blenheim in 1704 staring down at them from the huge tapestries above, the boys would dream of victories past and glories to come.

A wide stretch of Overstrand's golden sands has taken on the appearance of a battlefield. As usual, Winston is playing the role of Marlborough, in command of the armies of Britain and the Holy Roman Empire, while Jack is Marshal Tallard, commander of the Franco-Bavarians.

'Puppy, try to manoeuvre Chumbolly so that he refrains from sitting on our artillery!'

'Puppy' is the family name for Winston's daughter, Diana, who will soon celebrate her fifth birthday. She has been told of the crucial importance of Marlborough's artillery at the Battle of Blenheim by her father since before she could walk. So she tries earnestly to persuade 'Chumbolly' – her younger brother, Randolph – not to sit on the square of sand that represents Captain Blood's artillery battery. Unfortunately, Chumbolly is only just three and not yet familiar with

Churchill family lore, so is oblivious to all attempts to clear his rump from a crucial sector of the battlefield.

Jack, nobly playing the role of the soon-to-be-vanquished Tallard, only has his son, Peregrine, 'Pebbin', on his side. But Pebbin is only a year old, so Jack's wife, Lady Gwendoline, 'Goonie', has been enlisted to carve out the lines of the French and Bavarian infantry. Winston, who has a pet name for everybody, calls Jack and Goonie's family the 'Jagoons'.

Clemmie smiles to herself as Winston barks out his orders. '*Now*, Puppy! Push on with the infantry!'

Winston has borrowed one of Chumbolly's clockwork trains for a squadron of British infantry. But as Puppy pushes it through the sand towards the French line, the little Chumbolly bursts into tears and crawls after it, destroying the entire British left flank and bringing an entirely novel ending to the legendary Battle of Blenheim. Goonie summons the nannies to gather up the children, all of whom are now crying, while Jack goes off for a quick swim.

Winston and Clemmie are left sitting on the sand. Winston is suddenly quiet.

'What's the matter, Pug?'

'Oh, nothing, darling.'

'Come on, I know when something is troubling you.'

'It's just a shiver from the past. Watching dearest Jack in the sea; it reminds me of an unfortunate experience we had years ago.'

'In South Africa?'

'No, in the lake at Ouchy, in Lausanne, when we were boys. I nearly killed us both, and it was my own stupid fault.'

Clemmie recognizes the sudden change of mood she has seen many times before. Winston looks at her like a little boy lost.

'We were sailing on the lake. It was a beautiful day, not a breath of wind. We decided to go for a swim, so I lowered the sail and in we went. We'd been in the water for about ten minutes, diving down to see how far we could go, when the wind suddenly got up and opened enough of the sail to get the little boat moving. I told Jack to stay where he was and started to swim towards to it, but every time I got close, the wind pushed the confounded thing away. I don't think Jack knows to this day how perilous our position was; we were a long way from the shore and I was getting very tired. Suddenly, I saw Death as near as I think I have ever seen him.'

'Oh, Pig, how terrible! Why did you never tell me?'

'I've never told anyone. I made one last attempt and just managed to grab the side. It was my last ounce of strength; after that "Two Little English Boys Drowned in Lac Léman" would have been the next day's headlines in the Swiss newspapers.'

'Darling, don't get yourself upset. It was a long time ago.'

'I know, and we've both cheated Death several times before and since. But I fear for Jack if this thing in the Balkans flares up.'

Clemmie knows that the political situation in Europe has been worrying her husband for days and causing his increasingly sombre mood. She knows enough of the background through listening to Winston and is aware that the murder in the Balkans of the Archduke Franz Ferdinand, heir to the Austro-Hungarian throne, has created a dangerous crisis.

'The assassination?'

'Yes, there have already been riots in Vienna. It seems that the royal carriage had almost no protection and that the Serbian military was behind the plot. I fear this is only the beginning. Like the high tide, which will come later today, forces are in play that we may not be able to stop.'

'Come on, Pig, enough of depressing subjects! Goonie and the nannies are doing all the work with the kittens; we must help with tea.'

'Puss, do you mind if I go for a stroll along the beach? I need some air. Jack will help with tea.'

'Mr Black Dog again?'

'I think so, darling; he's been sniffing around lately. The Unionists are getting me down, and now those lunatics have murdered the Archduke. I need to clear my head.'

'Don't let Mr Black Dog come too close; fight him off, be a brave soldier.'

'I will, Puss, I always do. But be patient with me.'

Winston's bouts of depression are often intense and can be prolonged. Clemmie has suggested all kinds of remedies – from pills and potions to German psychiatrists – but her husband is proud and stubborn. He bumbles along in his own way until he eventually shakes off his dark moods.

That night, the two Churchill families leave the children in the care of a local nanny and are guests of Sir Edgar and Lady Leonora Speyer at their nearby home, Sea Marge. Speyer is a wealthy Jewish banker and a very good host. He normally enjoys Winston's wit and stories, but on this occasion very little of either is forthcoming.

The evening drags until, unwittingly, Speyer hits a raw nerve by asking Winston's brother, Jack, a simple question.

'So will you go back to the Hussars if the balloon goes up?'

Winston's face reddens.

'No, Jack bloody won't! I want him behind a desk if, as you put it, the "balloon goes up". There will be carnage on an unimaginable scale. It won't be cavalry and sabres; it will be machine guns and six-inch howitzers!'

Clemmie manages to change the subject and, thoughtfully, Speyer pours Winston another drink.

'I'm sorry, Winston, you're down here for a weekend's rest, not to talk about war.'

Winston smiles thinly at his host, but says very little throughout the rest of the dinner.

Nor does he say much at breakfast the next morning or,

indeed, for the rest of the weekend before he is rowed out to *Enchantress* to resume his duties on Monday morning.

A few days later, Clemmie receives a letter from her huband.

Darling Cat,

I felt so forlorn as you and the kittens slowly faded from view when I left on Monday. I know I behaved atrociously at dinner on Saturday, please convey to the Speyers my heartfelt apologies – good people, they don't deserve an ogre like me at their dinner table. Hope the Jagoons didn't take anything to heart, I was only thinking of Jack.

I'm feeling much better – now immersed in all the shenanigans before the Ireland Conference, which begins next week. It will be a brawl, but at least it's made Mr Black Dog slink back into his corner.

Missing you, darling one; kisses for the kittens. Hope to get to Pear Tree on the 24th or 25th.

Your ever loving,
Pug

Sunday 12 July

The Kettledrum Inn sits on the edge of the wild moorland above Burnley. Behind the rustic little pub, the vivid summer colours of the moors create a scene as pleasing on the eye as any you can imagine. On the other side, the view is less appealing, where the dry-stone walls of Red Lees Road snake through the fields towards the distant gloom of the town.

However, for once, the vista looks relatively clear and people can breathe fresh air for a change. It is the end of Burnley Fair, the traditional two-week annual wakes holiday for the entire borough. The mills, pits and most of the shops are closed. Two-thirds of the population are either at the seaside at Blackpool or taking day trips into the Dales. The foul chimneys are at rest, with not a hint of smoke from any of them. The steam engines are still; their boilers and flues are being cleaned and painted. The weaving sheds are being swept and the tunnels and shafts of the pits are undergoing annual maintenance and inspection.

Everyone is streaming back home to be ready for tomorrow morning and another year of toil. Today is the last chance for the families and friends of Tommy and Mick to enjoy their well-deserved holiday. They have had a couple of days in Blackpool, climbed the local beauty spot, Pendle Hill, been to the fair in the marketplace several times and made the annual pilgrimage to see Jack Moore's monkey down Barden Lane.

As Sunday promised to be warm and sunny, they decided to walk up on to Widdop Moor and take a picnic with them.

It is now seven o'clock on Sunday evening, opening time at the Kettledrum, and they have timed their descent from Widdop perfectly – although their timing didn't need to be so precise. Despite the licensing laws, the Kettledrum has been open all day. It is a long way from Burnley's police station, and the pub has been the venue for an illicit gathering to join in the ancient Pennine trap and ball game of Knur and Spell.

Vast amounts of money have been gambled on how far the local professionals can hit a small pottery ball across the moorland with a long flexible mallet. All over the pub's garden, and the nearby moor, there are groups of men sleeping off the effects of the afternoon while, wisely, the winner of the contest – who pocketed over £30 – has long since gone home with his considerable victor's purse. The local winner is often the great Jerry Dawson, born within the range of a long hit from the Kettledrum, the goalkeeper at Burnley Football Club and one of Knur and Spell's longest hitters.

Tired and scorched by the sun, the wanderers from Widdop need a few drinks before walking back into town. Thankfully, it is downhill all the way to their homes. When Mick sees the human residue from the afternoon's activities, he grins.

'Bugger me, there's bin a reet good do 'ere. There's lads all over t'place; they look like they've been shot!'

Vinny Sagar and Twaites Haythornthwaite, who are both unattached, have joined Mick and Cath and Tommy and Mary for the day. They are at the bar ordering the first round of drinks, with plates of stew and 'hard'– the local delicacy of cow's foot and marrow stew – served cold on tin plates with crispy havercakes.

The four senior members of the group are sitting outside enjoying the cool evening air.

Cath is grinning from ear to ear.

'Afore t'lads come back, me an' Mick 'ave got summat to tell thee.'

Mary's eyes start to widen in anticipation, before her friend continues.

'I don't want them two young 'uns to know just yet, cos it's early days, but I'm expectin'.'

Mary shrieks, but is quickly hushed by the others. Even so, she cannot stop herself hugging her friend. Tommy grabs Mick's hand and shakes it vigorously, until the return of Vincent and Twaites puts an end to the celebrations.

Vinny, always a live wire, makes a flamboyant show of placing the pots of ale on the trestle table in front of his friends.

'There, first o' many.'

Twaites digs him in the ribs with his elbow.

'Go on, get 'em told.'

Vinny also has some news that he is desperate to impart.

'Football lads are back in trainin' tomorrow.'

Tommy has noticed the self-satisfied smirk on Vinny's face.

'Which "football lads"?'

'Burnley.'

'You mean at Turf Moor?'

'Aye.'

'So?'

'Well, I'm seein' Mr Haworth tomorrow neet. He's gonna 'ave a sken at me.'

The open mouths around the table are soon replaced by handshakes and kisses of congratulations. Vinny is already a very promising cricketer but, before the Burnley Fair began, one of the Burnley Football Club's scouts saw him playing football for Burnley Boys Club. He immediately recommended him to John Haworth, Burnley's manager and the man who, in just four years, has transformed the team from English Football League mediocrity to being the best team in Europe.

Burnley won the FA Cup in April, beating Liverpool 1-0 at Crystal Palace in front of the King and 70,000 fans, over

30,000 of them from Burnley. The town has been gripped by football fever ever since. The team is full of England and Scotland internationals and has just returned from a tour of Europe, where they beat the best teams in Germany, Hungary and Austria.

'Does that mean tha'll meet Tommy Boyle?'

'Aye, I reckon so.'

Tommy Boyle is Burnley's captain and part of the impregnable half-back triumvirate of Halley, Boyle and Watson. Tommy cannot contain himself.

'Bloody 'ell! Freeman, Mosscrop? Jerry Dawson?'

'Aye, all of 'em.'

Tommy jumps to his feet.

'Mick, come on, lad, we need more ale. This is gonna be a grand neet, except fer Vinny, he's goin' on t'ginger ale from now on!'

It does become a grand night, after which the friends make their way home via a succession of pubs until they get to Burnley town centre, where each of them go their separate ways.

As they walk the short distance to their home in Hart Street, Tommy asks Mary about Cath's pregnancy.

'Dost tha think she meant to get in t'family way?'

'I'll ask Cath when I see 'er, but I wouldn't 'ave thought so. At least they're now in Burnley, it would've been a reet bugger if they'd still been in Colne, wi' Mick 'avin to travel all that way to t'pit.'

Mick and Cath have just moved to Stoneyholme, which is within easy walking distance of Mick's pit at Bank Hall, Burnley's biggest colliery, and not far from Cath's mill in the Weavers Triangle.

'Dost think they're wed, or livin' o'er t'brush? I've ne'er talked to Cath abaht it.'

'Dunno, I've ne'er asked Mick. Either way, it's gonna be 'ard fer 'em. As me mam used to be agate, "Weddin's nowt, 'ousekeepin's all."'

Mary stiffens with indignation.

'Aye and tha's not t'first and won't be t'last. Not until summat's done abaht how families feed th'sels when t'wife 'as childer.'

'We can 'elp 'em, lass, can't we?'

'Aye, we can.'

Mary stops and looks up at Tommy.

'Know what, our Tommy? When tha's got thy temper fettled, tha's a good lad.'

Tommy cranes his neck to kiss his wife.

'When are we gonna 'ave a little Broxup?'

Mary pushes him away coyly.

'Not yet, tha daft bugger! We need a few more bob in t'Co-op before we start thinkin' o' childer. Besides, there's talk o' war brewin' in Europe.'

'Where?'

'In t'Balkans.'

'Where's that?'

'Don't know, but they say it could spread.'

'Well, it won't be coming 'ere, will it?'

'Don't suppose it will.'

Tommy squeezes Mary suggestively.

'So abaht this babby.'

'Bugger off, yer big lummox, wait til we get 'ome!'

When the two of them get home, Tommy and Mary enjoy with relish one of the few things that Burnley's impoverished circumstances and limited horizons cannot deny them. Tommy, local hard case, and Mary, vociferous renegade, have a volatile relationship. He is old-fashioned and is frequently disconcerted when he finds it hard to follow Mary's thoughts and ideas. She finds Tommy's temper and penchant for violence abhorrent, but admires his courage and strength.

They are an odd mix, but very much in love.

Wednesday 22 July

Serjeants Maurice Tait and Harry Woodruff have just arrived at Wellington Barracks, the London headquarters of the Royal Fusiliers. The barracks, a fine Victorian Gothic building in the heart of the Tower of London, is grand enough to house 1,000 men and was built in the 1840s by the Duke of Wellington while he was Constable of the Tower.

With revolution in the air in Europe and the Chartists rampaging for political reform in Britain, the Conservative government of Sir Robert Peel had feared a working-class uprising and a significant strengthening of London's military barracks was seen as a wise precaution.

In the midst of a similarly febrile atmosphere, Maurice and Harry's C Company of Fusiliers, 180 men under Major George Ashburner, has been sent to London to provide an experienced military presence and to be on standby should trouble break out.

Particular shivers of alarm have been felt in the corridors of power in recent weeks after it was discovered that hundreds of police officers have been joining a fledgling union in secret; a chastening fact for the government. Strikes have been endemic for three or four years and working-class discontent is growing. Strong hints of similar dissatisfaction among police officers are seen as potentially disastrous. In the week of the King's Buckingham Palace Conference on Home Rule for Ireland, security resources are stretched to breaking point and nerves are taut.

Maurice and Harry are enjoying a breath of air and a mug

of tea with their immediate superior, Company Serjeant Major Billy Carstairs. Maurice treads carefully when asking Billy, another veteran and a notorious disciplinarian, about the reason for the long journey from the Isle of Wight.

'So, Sarje, what's the story?'

'The usual; backin' up the bobbies, in case of a barney. There's talk of lots of junior policemen not being very happy with pay and conditions.'

Harry, always more forthright than Maurice, is less inhibited with their CSM.

'They should be so bloody lucky. I'm not very 'appy with my lot an' I 'ave to get shot at by Fuzzies, Wogs and Boers!'

'I should keep those thoughts to yourself if I was you, Harry. The brass is all nerves at the moment.'

'What, about a few strikers? They'll always be up in arms.'

'It's not just that; they're worried about the Micks. And then there's all the talk of war in Europe.'

'You mean over that archduke what got shot?'

'Apparently. If the Austrians kick it off, then they'll all be at it: the Frenchies, the Ruskies, the Fritzes. Threats are flying around between 'em all.'

Maurice starts to smile.

'So who'll we be fightin' this time? The Russians, like me old fella?'

'No, Major Ashburner says they'll be on our side.'

'So it must be the French.'

'No, they'll be on our side as well.'

Harry looks perplexed.

'So, who then, Sarje?

'The Germans and Austrians, Harry.'

'Bugger me, I'd rather fight the French; the bloody Germans are tough sons of bitches.'

For the next two days, C Company waits in reserve in Green Park, close to Buckingham Palace. The assignment is tedious, not the sort of job professional soldiers enjoy at the best of times, let alone on the streets of their own capital city. The soldiers are asked to keep a low profile and stay close to their lorries.

By Friday evening, the Buckingham Palace Conference has ended without an agreement between the Irish Nationalists and the Ulster Unionists. But in the press, and within political circles, Ireland suddenly seems to be a minor annoyance; all the talk is of war.

But not on London's streets. The weather is warm, the pubs and restaurants are full, and everyone is looking forward to the weekend.

Maurice and Harry have settled themselves down under a tree close to Piccadilly and are watching people make their way home. Maurice smells the air and soaks in the bustling atmosphere of the city. The streets are full of colour and life. Everyone is on the move. The noise of car horns fills the air, horses' hooves clatter on cobbles, the street vendors holler; the noise is almost deafening. But it is a comforting din, because it is normal and reassuring. The familiar mingling aromas of exhaust fumes, horse dung, restaurant fried food and stale beer are being carried on the breeze.

'This beats the bloody Isle of Wight, mate. Good old London town!'

'Too right, Mo. Don't you just love it?'

Harry, always on the lookout for a pretty girl, can see plenty to tickle his fancy.

'Better class of girl up west, that's for sure.'

'You're not wrong, 'Arry. Look at that little filly over there!'

'Bloody hell, she'd fair make you hot under the collar.'

'She would that, lovely curly hair; I reckon I could make it curl a bit more given 'alf a chance.'

'Just watching 'em is making me 'orny. If we get some leave at the end of this little jaunt, I think I'll be tapping on Big Marge's door.'

'Good luck; you'll need a big 'ammer and a big nail!'

'You been there?'

'Might 'ave.'

'You dirty little feather-plucker.'

Maurice carries on gawping but changes the subject.

'You know what the CSM was talking about the other day, a coppers' union and all that? Well, I had a chat with a couple of 'em the other day, down by the Palace. It's true, the peelers are not 'appy.'

'Join the club! Who is, these days? The toffs are larfin', but the rest of us just 'ave to grin and bear it.'

'I know, 'Arry, but it's a bugger when the Old Bill is starting a union and talkin' about goin' on strike.'

Friday 24 July

Weighed down by ominous events at home and abroad, Winston Churchill has caught the lunchtime train from London to enjoy a weekend with his family. He spends the afternoon with his brother, Jack, discussing the worsening situation in Europe. Later he declines a Churchill family dinner, preferring instead to spend the evening with his wife, Clemmie.

'Are the kittens asleep, my darling?'

'They are, Pug. Nanny has turned in; all is quiet.'

'I should be taking you out to dinner, but I wanted this weekend to be just the two of us.'

'How sweet of you. I can't think of anything better. Supper is in the oven, ready in fifteen minutes.'

Winston pours wine for both of them and sits by the fireplace staring at the empty grate.

'May I talk shop for a while? I'm greatly troubled, my darling, and you are always such a comfort to me.'

Despite her heavily pregnant midriff, Clemmie pulls up a pouffe, wraps herself around her husband's legs and rests her head on his lap.

'As you will have read, the King's conference on Ireland at the Palace, although well intentioned, has achieved nothing. It stumbled and fell on what I consider to be no more than an inconsequence: the bloody boundaries of Tyrone and Fermanagh! They are prepared to take Ireland to a civil war over a few miles of bog and moor, and drag the rest of us into it. The King does not know which way to turn, and the

Cabinet is split down the middle. Jack says, "Bugger the lot of them, and impose a solution from Westminster!"'

'I tend to agree with him, Pug. There is only so far one can go with blind obstinacy.'

'Well, after several hours of debate on it during Cabinet, with the PM his usual urbane self, Eddie Grey was passed a note. When he read it to us, the already sombre mood darkened like a gathering storm. It was the Austrians' note to the Serbs, following the assassination, quite the most shocking set of demands I have ever heard – so draconian that no country could possibly agree to them. It was a declaration of war, not an ultimatum.'

Clemmie squeezes her husband tightly.

'What will happen now?'

'War, my darling, a most terrible war, which it will be impossible for us to avoid. The trials and tribulations of the humble parishes of Tyrone and Fermanagh are but nothing compared to the behemoths glowering at one another in Europe.'

'Surely it can't be as bad as all that.'

'I'm afraid it can, Cat. War is like the coitus of the beast; it is relentless and all-consuming, and only abates when its lust is sated.'

'What a terrible picture you paint! Do you really think it will come to all-out war?'

'Indeed I do. I fear for Jack and for you and the kittens; nothing will be the same again. Eddie Grey, who is an erudite and perceptive soul, is sure we are at the precipice and said so to a Cabinet that sat and listened to him in stunned silence. They looked like frightened rabbits – except Asquith, of course, who looked like a benign headmaster – while Lloyd George just kept shaking his head. Grey is very depressed.'

'And you? Is Mr Black Dog lurking?'

'Strangely, he isn't. Despite the impending horror of it all,

I feel exhilarated by these events. I don't know why, but I am; awful, isn't it? The thought of impending battle invigorates me. Perhaps it's in my inheritance, but if there's a fight in the offing, I want to be in its vanguard. It was true in South Africa and at Omdurman, and it's still true now.'

'My darling Pug, many men are the same. Don't fret about it, it's the nature of the male of the species.'

'Are we really so simple?'

'Yes, you are; but you are no ordinary warrior. You are a general, a leader of men.'

'You know me so well, sweetest thing, but you are in danger of making my notorious ego even more inflated. Perhaps a little unwise, given my weary reputation in certain quarters?'

'Let me be the judge of that. I can live with your ego, and so can those who are devoted to you. As for the rest, bugger them!'

Tears form in Winston's eyes. Clemmie is everything to him; she is both his emotional anchor and his political confidante. He kisses her warmly and caresses her swollen belly.

'Come, Cat, let's eat and get you and kitten number three to bed. I suspect tomorrow will be a long day. There is a car coming in the morning from the Admiralty. We will have four handsome Royal Marines for company. They are here to protect you and the kittens for the time being.'

There is a look of horror on Clemmie's face.

'Good God, has it come to that already?'

'Just a precaution, darling, no need to be alarmed. Come, let's eat. I have to go to Cromer post office at eight tomorrow morning to telephone Lord Louis and agree the disposition of the 1st and 2nd fleets.'

Winston's gaze is fixed on the back of the empty grate of Pear Tree Cottage; the furrows in his brow become ever deeper. Clemmie gets up, but not without some difficulty, to retrieve supper from the oven. Although it is the end of July and the day has been warm, she feels the sudden chill of the evening. It strikes her like the icy gauntlet of winter. She thinks of her children upstairs and the one coming to fruition in her womb. She looks back at Winston, hunched in his chair, a cigar in one hand and an almost empty glass of claret in the other.

'Darling, your glass needs refreshing, and so does mine.'

The next morning, Winston has his conversation with Prince Louis of Battenberg, the First Sea Lord. A special operator has arrived with the marines to take charge of Cromer's telegraphy, much to the annoyance of the incumbent, who has served the community loyally for several years.

When Winston returns to Pear Tree Cottage, Clemmie, Jack and his wife, Goonie, are waiting to hear his news.

'Well, the navy has never been more ready. I have ordered that, as a precaution, they do not disperse to their home ports, but remain on standby at their stations. However, the encouraging news is that Serbia has accepted the outrageous demands of the Austrians!'

There is look of astonishment on Jack's face.

'But that's extraordinary!'

'I know, I find it hard to believe. I didn't think any nation would accept their draconian terms. Let's hope Vienna calms down now. But come, let's gather our forces on the beach; it's time to relive past glories!'

'Not Blenheim again, Winston?'

'No, Jack, let's do the final hours of Waterloo. I'll form the British squares and you can attack with Ney's cavalry, the bravest of the brave!'

Jack smiles. He knows that no matter how courageous Ney and his cavalry will be at the impending re-enactment of Waterloo, Winston's resolute squares of red-coated British infantry will break them.

The chief of Britain's navy, the greatest the world has ever seen, is, for the moment, content. The weather is glorious, England's shores glisten, and its hinterland glows, verdant in the warm haze of a summer morning. His mighty navy is at anchor, protecting his beloved homeland. From Cromarty to Dover, in their various sally-ports, his flotillas lie in wait to snare any aggressor. In the Channel, the great super-dreadnoughts brood, their awesome 13.5-inch guns ready to bombard any threat that dares come within range.

The Battle of Waterloo is won once more and Winston, victorious yet again, collects the spoils of the battlefield – two buckets, their spades and a watering can – before suspending hostilities for lunch. When they reach Pear Tree Cottage, a walk of only a few yards, an earnest marine colour serjeant is waiting for them.

'Sir, the Foreign Secretary, Sir Edward Grey, has sent a telegram asking that you return to London this afternoon. He will be at home at Eccleston Square. Supper will be prepared.'

'Very well, Colour Serjeant. Does Sir Edward say any more?'

The man hands Winston the telegram. His eyes are immediately drawn to a clipped sentence, 'Austrians still not content,' before folding the paper neatly.

'Destroy the telegram immediately. Please ask the telegrapher to reply that I will be with Sir Edward by nine.'

Clemmie and the children are distraught.

'Pug, it's been less than a day –'

'I know, darling, but Eddie has asked me to return because the situation is deteriorating. The colour serjeant here will stay with you.'

The marine casts a concerned glance at Winston.

'But, sir, I have strict orders to stay with you.'

'I understand, Colour Serjeant, but the safety of my family is paramount. I'll take your lance corporal with me on the train. You stay here and report to my brother, Lieutenant Churchill.'

Although clearly reluctant, the colour serjeant, realizing that he is speaking to the First Lord of the Admiralty, a man more senior than all the ranks in the entire Corps of Marines, agrees.

Winston makes a rapid exit from Pear Tree Cottage and catches the afternoon train to London. There are tears all round, not only because his stay has been so brief and his departure so sudden, but also because of the ominous news.

Everyone knows that the unfolding events are about to affect them profoundly.

Saturday 25 July

84 Eaton Place, London

Eaton Place is the London home of the Stewart-Murray family. One of London's finest town houses, Bardie and Kitty pass most of their time there and regard it as home. After spending Friday night at his club, the Carlton, where all the talk was about the situation in Europe, Bardie's father has had lunch with the King at Buckingham Palace. The King was still fuming about the failure of his conference to resolve the Irish Home Rule crisis and was not particularly good company.

The old duke then spent the afternoon with one of his mistresses, a lady unknown to the family but who Bardie suspects may well be Winston Churchill's mother, Lady Randolph, only recently divorced from her second husband, George Cornwallis-West.

Although well over seventy, the duke still has an eye for the ladies, young or old and from any echelon of society. His indiscretions are well known to the family, who refer to them as 'Father's latest'. Sometimes they are high-born society ladies, but often they are local Perthshire girls, happy to romp with the ageing stag and especially grateful for the small gratuity that will follow in the wake of the dalliance.

Thanks to his afternoon's cavorting, the duke arrives at Eaton Place in excellent humour. He is a man who, perhaps more than any other man in Britain, is a law into himself; he can, more or less, do as he pleases. Unlike the King, a close personal friend, he does not have the eyes of the nation turned towards him every time he appears in public. Isolated on his vast estate in Scotland, hidden behind the walls of his ancient, fairy-tale castle, he is ennobled with more titles than any other peer: a dukedom, two marquisates, five earldoms, three viscounties and seven baronies. He is the grandee of grandees, monarch of his own principality and commander of his own private army.

'So, Bardie, what's for supper? I could eat a horse.'

'Well, Father, I'll check with Jarvis, but I think he said leg of lamb. I don't imagine Allens of Mayfair would think of themselves as a *boucherie chevaline*, but I can get cook to ask when she next places an order with them.'

'Very amusing, Bardie. Jarvis, where's my Glenmorangie!'

Unnoticed by him, Jarvis, the family's London butler, has been hovering next to the duke for some moments. He immediately proffers him a silver tray with a crystal tumbler awash with a generous quota of his favourite malt. Jarvis bows and waits while, from a matching crystal jug, the old boy pours a thumbnail of water into a tumbler etched with the elaborate Atholl coat of arms.

'Where's Kitty?'

'She will be down directly, Father.'

Kitty and her father-in-law do not see eye to eye on many things. The 7th Duke likes his women to be decorous and supine. Any other kind is either a communist or a suffragette, or both. When Kitty went to Blair Castle for the first time, the duke was initially charming and even danced with her after dinner, delighted that her Scottish dancing was commendably proficient. But matters deteriorated the next morning when he led a walk down the glen. He, Bardie, his brothers and the other male guests formed the vanguard, leaving the ladies to bring up the rear. Kitty took great exception to this and immediately turned on her heels and headed back to the house. Relations between the two of them have been no better than tepid ever since, with occasional blasts of iciness, usually caused by squabbles over trivialities.

'So the King is fuming?'

'He is. He has a soft spot for the Unionists and doesn't want to relinquish his title as King of Ireland. He says it took us long enough to bring them to heel and can't understand why the politicians want to give it up so easily. I agree with him.'

'I take a different view.'

'I thought you might. Are you absolutely sure you're a Tory. Half the time, you sound like a bloody communist!'

'Hardly, Father; I just like to see both sides of an argument.'

'Well, in this argument there are two sides, but only one is right. Where's your bloody wife? I'm starving!'

At that moment, Kitty appears in the doorway.

'Bardie's "bloody wife" is here.'

She gives the duke a stare that would turn most men to stone, kisses Bardie on the cheek and sits down at the dining table. The duke, not discomfited in the slightest, joins her and stands at the head of the table. He then waits for the first footman to push in his chair so that he can lower his ample rump on to it. He notices that there are five places set for dinner.

'Are we expecting guests?'

Bardie takes a deep breath. His father's good humour has not lasted long.

'Yes, Father, we are.'

'Well, they're bloody late.'

'They're not late. I said eight, and it's only just turned the hour.'

'Bloody nuisance! I hope they're amusing.'

Kitty smiles, but thinly, through clenched teeth.

'I invited them because he's very well read and very bright. She runs a charity for homeless children and is absolutely charming. He's finishing his doctorate at Birkbeck College and acts as our personal secretary on a part-time basis.'

The duke flushes puce and his grey beard quivers as he convulses and coughs.

'Do you mean to say that you expect me to dine with your bloody servant!'

Bardie intervenes.

'He's not a servant, Father, he's a very learned academic chap who happens to be helping us out with some admin. He's more a friend than anything else.'

'So you're befriending your servants now. Bloody nonsense! You're a bloody fool, Bardie. Kitty is filling your head with all sorts of damn silly notions.'

The duke stands and throws his napkin on to the table. The butler hovers discreetly to one side.

'Jarvis, whistle for a cab; two minutes.' He turns to Bardie. 'I'll be at the Guards Club, where the servants serve and do as they're bloody well told.'

The duke pushes back his chair, which tumbles into the desperate grasp of the footman, and storms from the room. As he does so, he pushes past the evening's guests who, totally bewildered, stare at an image of utter disdain on the enflamed face that passes them in the hallway.

Dinner begins awkwardly without the duke. But Bardie and Kitty excuse his behaviour, using the King's conference on Irish Home Rule and his subsequent anger as a disguise. They pretend that the duke has been summoned by Queen Alexandra to help placate the King's mood by joining them for supper.

After dinner, during which both Kitty and Bardie drink too much wine, and as soon as their guests have departed, the evening's frustrations boil over.

'Your father is unbearable; I've had enough, Bardie. I don't want him here again, and I will not go to Blair while he's there.'

'Kitty, darling, I miscalculated. He's never lived in London and can't imagine a friendship with someone outside his social milieu. I should have known better.'

'Are you defending his boorish behaviour?'

'No, just trying to explain it.'

'Well, he doesn't mind cavorting outside his "social milieu" when it comes to the floozies he meets in the Burlington Arcade!'

'Kitty, please; he's no worse than most.'

'That's no bloody excuse! He talks about manners, discipline and values; he's a hypocrite, plain and simple.'

'He's also my father; I've got to live with him.'

'Well, I don't!'

Kitty rushes from the dining room in tears and slams the door behind her.

Several minutes later, after he has consumed a couple of large cognacs, Bardie joins her in bed. Somewhat drunk, he is feeling amorous. Kitty, still crying, is furious that sex should be on his mind in the aftermath of the heated exchange about his father's behaviour. She pushes him away firmly.

'Kitty, come on . . . I'm feeling romantic.'

'Romantic! Don't take me for a fool, Bardie. You're feeling like an engorged stag; it's just lust. I'm not in the mood for romance, and I'm certainly not prepared to accommodate your drunken passion.'

Bardie begins to succumb to the alcohol.

'For Christ's sake, woman, that's why I have no heir. You rarely let me near you. And when you do, there's no pleasure in it. I have my rights, you know!'

'Rights! Don't you dare. If you want to rut like an animal, go back to your tart in Mayfair; she's already produced one bastard for you. I'm told she'll open her legs for any Tom, Dick or Harry!'

Bardie loses control and slaps Kitty across the face with some venom. She screams out loud before kicking him and punching him with all her might. Fortunately, Bardie does not retaliate but backs away until he is left cowering in the corner of the bedroom, his own tears now flooding down his face.

Like his father, Bardie has produced at least one illegitimate child that Kitty and the family know about. She suspects that there are others. She and Bardie have just celebrated their fifteenth wedding anniversary and she is now almost forty. They both know she is unlikely ever to produce children.

Kitty was first introduced to little Eileen Macallum last year, when the girl was invited to Blair for a summer holiday. Nothing explicit was said, but Bardie's brother, Hamish, talked of the 'Macallum mystery'. The girl is thought to be the granddaughter of a 'Mrs Macallum, 6 Curzon Street, London' (a fact Kitty gleaned from a letter glimpsed over Bardie's shoulder) but the identity of the mother remains a mystery.

Eileen is a pretty and vivacious child. Kitty has grown to tolerate her and is even beginning to show a fondness towards her. However, her inability to have a child of her own is a constant source of sadness and the cause of frequent rows with Bardie.

After several minutes, despite still feeling the sting of his slap on her face, Kitty begins to feel sorry for Bardie, who is still cowering in the corner, sobbing like a child. Taking pity on him, she goes over to comfort him. He is full of remorse for having struck her and begs for forgiveness.

They do have sex, on the floor where they lie. It is more passionate than usual and is satisfying for both of them. They repeat the exercise the next morning – again, it is more fulfilling than usual – helping them forget the extraordinary behaviour of the duke and their own row from the night before.

Kitty reflects on how strange are the responses of people in the grip of extreme emotions.

Sunday 26 July

The four Thomas siblings have just arrived at Willey Lodge, a spacious country house a few miles north of Presteigne across the English border. They have been invited for afternoon tea by its owner, Mr Aaron Griffiths. Local auctioneer and town worthy Philip Davies is there, as is the Reverend Henry Kewley, the unofficial leader of the local community.

The three men, each steadfast pillars of local society, are staunch liberals; Kewley and Davies are Anglicans, but Griffiths is a Primitive Welsh Methodist and extremely proud of his Celtic roots. Other than religion, the three of them agree on most things, especially the need to revive the local economy, and have been striving for several years to find new sources of revenue for Presteigne.

Hywel, his two brothers, Morgan and Geraint, and his sister, Bronwyn, have no idea why they have been asked to tea, but they know it will be more than a convivial social gathering. Bronwyn is accompanied by Tom Crisp, who has recently become her fiancé. As agreed with Hywel, Tom and Bronwyn have been living together at Pentry Farm for the past two months, where Tom has converted the farm's old wood store into a one-room home for the two of them.

After a few minutes of polite conversation, during which Mrs Griffiths places huge piles of sandwiches and cakes on the dining-room table, Henry Kewley adopts his most charming manner and beckons the guests to sit.

'So, Hywel, how are things at Pentry after the very sad loss of your father?'

'Not thrivin', Reverend Kewley, but we mustn't crib, we're luckier than some.'

'Well said, Hywel; times are hard for everyone.'

Tom looks around at the expensive finery of Willey Lodge and the needless mountains of food, then casts a glance at Bronwyn. He wants to say, 'Present company excepted,' but knows he cannot.

'Hywel, let me come to the point. As you know, Mr Griffiths here has been digging for coal in Folly Wood for a while now. Mr Davies has also sunk a shaft near Caen Wood; he and I are shareholders in Mr Griffiths's company, the Radnor Coal Syndicate. But, on another matter, Mr Griffiths has a proposition for you.'

Aaron Griffiths steps forward, a beaming smile on his face, and greets them in Welsh.

'*Cyfarchion, ffrindiau.* Forgive me, but I must continue in English for the sake of our English friends.' His smile broadens and he raises his arms, as if preaching. 'I would like to buy Pentry Farm –'

Hywel, visibly shocked, interrupts Griffiths.

'There's no coal on Pentry's land, if that's what yer after, Mr Griffiths.'

'I'm not after coal, Hywel. There are several springs on the land, are there not?'

'Aye, there are; good strong 'uns. And the water's as sweet as apples, as pure as anywhere.'

'That's right, lad, and that's what I'm after. You've heard of Llandrindod Wells?'

'Aye, of course.'

'Well, we think Presteigne could become a flourishing spa, like Llandrindod.'

The Thomas family look at one another with expressions of bewilderment mixed with anxiety. Bronwyn, the most perturbed, grasps Tom's hand. As she does so, she casts an awkward glance at Philip Davies, whose house she has been cleaning since June. He smiles at her with an expression that surprises Tom and makes her feel uncomfortable.

She speaks out, hesitantly at first.

'Mr Griffiths, sir, Pentry has been in our family fer generations. Where'll we live?'

'Well, young lady, listen to my proposal. First, I will give you seven hundred and seventy-five pounds for the freehold of the land and the cottage. Second, I will draw up a five-year tenancy agreement for your family to rent the cottage and the land at a rate of forty pounds a year. My plan is to divert one of the springs to a new building I will construct at the bottom of your lower pasture, where I'm going to bottle the water. The water from the other springs is yours to use as tenants.'

Hywel does the mental arithmetic quickly. The price for the land is fair; it is a good offer, and he knows he can cover the annual rent from the farm's income.

'And after five years?'

'There's no reason why we can't continue the tenancy thereafter. I'm not interested in the farm, just its springs.'

'When do yer need an answer by?'

'Shall we say tomorrow evening? I can come to you at Pentry, if you like.'

Hywel looks around at his brothers and sister. They look bemused. Morgan nods his head slightly, suggesting interest.

'Very well, Mr Griffiths. We'll give you a bit o' tea. It won't be like Mrs Griffiths's spread, but we'll do our best.'

Before the Thomas family leave, Philip Davies offers them his advice.

'Hywel, I know that you face a difficult decision, but I also know how hard it is for you to make ends meet at Pentry. I've sold more land and properties than I care to remember, and Mr Griffiths is making you a very generous offer.'

'Thank you, Mr Davies. We'll go and ponder on it.'

*

The family goes home to Pentry to discuss the offer. Hywel opens some of their own scrumpy and the debate begins.

Bronwyn's position is immediately unequivocal.

'I don't want to sell. We have to make Pentry work. Ma and Da struggled for years to keep it goin', as did Mam-gu and Tad-cu before 'em.'

Looking crestfallen, Hywel, who is slumped in his father's favourite chair by the fire, asks everyone for their views.

Geraint is also clear.

'I agree with Bron, let's keep it. Morgan and I 'ave found good work this summer, we can find more if we 'ave to.'

Morgan is less sure and is tempted by the windfall.

'We could make a new start with nearly eight hundred quid; it's a lot o' money.'

Bronwyn reacts sharply.

'What do yer suggest? Knowing you, a pub, no doubt!'

'Good idea, Sis. But I was thinking o' two or three charabancs.'

'What for!'

'Just think, Presteigne's miles from anywhere. The railway only goes to Leominster. Motor cars are fer the well-to-do. How will everybody else get round? In charas o' course. They're the future for sure.'

Bronwyn laughs out loud. She loves her brother but thinks his fanciful ideas are ridiculous – and this is just one of many hare-brained schemes he has thought of.

Hywel turns to Tom.

'What do you think, Tom?'

'I should keep my thoughts to myself; it's not my farm, or my family inheritance.'

'No, but it soon will be. You're entitled to a say in this.'

Tom looks a Bronwyn for reassurance. She nods her approval.

'Well, Morgan has a point. If there's to be no recovery in farming in the near future, it might make sense to try something else. Perhaps open a business in Hereford or Ludlow.'

Hywel is intrigued.

'Like what?

'Charabancs are not a bad idea. But what about a building firm? We'd have the capital, and I'm a trained craftsman. You're all very good with your hands. We'd have a labour force of four, and Bron could run the office. She's better at figures than all of us, and very well organized.'

Bronwyn bristles once more, wishing she had not agreed that Tom should have a say.

'Tom, don't you dare include me in yer plans. I want to stay 'ere.'

'Bron, Hywel asked me what I thought. It's only a suggestion. Don't you think "Thomas Brothers' Building Company" has a nice ring to it?'

'No, I don't! We're farmers, not builders. Besides, I don't want to live in a town; I'm a country girl.'

Tom turns the question back to Hywel and asks him for his view.

Hywel is weighed down by the dilemma and takes a while to answer.

'Tom, bach, I don't know. It's tempting to think of havin' a lump o' money in the bank and the chance of a new beginning. But I 'ate the thought that I might be the one to sign away the Thomas home after so many generations.'

A good deal of scrumpy is consumed before Hywel decides that everyone should sleep on the offer and that a decision should be taken after breakfast the next morning.

When the family gathers again, Geraint and Bronwyn remain adamant that they should reject Aaron Griffiths's offer. Tom and Morgan are still in favour of accepting and making a fresh start. Geraint makes the point that Bronwyn and Tom are being given two votes when, strictly speaking, they should only have one, but Hywel dismisses his objection out of hand.

After listening to everyone air their views once more, he gets to his feet and goes to the kitchen window, where he can see Pentry's fields stretching into the distance towards Presteigne. It is a fine summer morning and the ground is warming rapidly. It is scene he has woken to every day of his life; to him, Pentry is heaven on earth.

Hywel has his back to his family; they cannot see the tears in his eyes. He takes a deep breath.

'We'll sell.'

'No, Hywel!'

Bronwyn screams in anguish. Hywel does not turn round, but walks to the kitchen door. As he leaves, he repeats himself.

'I'm sorry, Bron, we're selling.'

Bronwyn pushes Tom aside as he tries to comfort her. She rushes into the farmyard and runs into the fields in a state of great distress.

No one sees her for the rest of the day. When she reappears in the late afternoon, she hardly utters a word and refuses to say where she has been, even though it is obvious she has not been doing her cleaning work.

When Aaron Griffiths appears that evening, Bronwyn refuses to be party to the decision. Hywel goes ahead without her and shakes hands on the deal. Griffiths says the paperwork will be ready by the following week.

Tom, Hywel and his brothers spend the rest of the evening talking about how 'Thomas Brothers' Building Company' might work, an idea that becomes increasingly attractive the more they think about it.

Bronwyn appears just before bedtime, but refuses to talk to any of them, especially Tom, and stalks off to their little bolt-hole.

Hywel tries to reassure Tom.

'She'll be fine tomorrow, Tom.'

'No, she won't; you know her as well as I do.'

'Do you really think we could make a success of your idea? The boys are beginning to be excited about it.'

'I think we could. We would need to get out of Presteigne, where work is scarce. Some of the bigger towns are doing well at the moment. There's good money there, but we'd have to be quality builders – the bigger houses, that's where there's money.'

'And Bron?'

'I don't know, Hywel. She's been strange lately.'

'Get wed and give 'er a few little Crisps to worry about. That'll sort her.'

Friday 31 July

Admiralty House, Whitehall, London

As the situation in Europe worsens by the day, Winston has been sleeping at the Admiralty all week. The Royal Navy remains at station and, although largely secret, plans for a full military mobilization in the event of war are moving ahead at a pace. Guarded by their Royal Marines, Clemmie and the children and Jack and his family are still at their holiday cottages in Overstrand.

Courtesy of Sir Edgar and Lady Speyer, the Churchills are able to speak to one another by telephone almost every day. When they do so, because Winston fears that German spies may be monitoring their calls, they speak in a childish code they have invented for themselves. They use 'Old Block' for Asquith, the Germans become 'Cabbages', the Irish are 'Spuds' and the British 'Bowlers'. Ships become 'Rum Buckets' and the army 'Blenheim Tinnies' and so on.

They also write to one another daily, their letters being sent by military courier to ensure security.

Darling Cat,

As I write, I am looking over the Admiralty's splendid curtain wall into Whitehall, where London is at peace. How strange it is. It is Friday evening, approaching midnight, the usual revellers have made their way home at least an hour ago. The mood is increasingly sombre here, all I can see beneath the gas lights are shadows. It is an eerie scene.

Eddie Grey and I had dinner with the PM in Downing Street tonight. The company was excellent, as was the claret, but the food was dire. The Old Block is a fine PM, very generous with his fine wines – which, I swear, he can consume more of at a sitting than I can – but he has the palate of a street urchin! Probably a result of his humble Yorkshire origins, bless him.

The OB was serene as always and Eddie G said again how grateful he was that I rushed back to see him last weekend. He made a point of asking me again to pass on his gratitude to you for your forbearance in disrupting our family weekend.

We talked quite a bit about my conversation last week with the Hamburg shipping magnate, Herr Ballan, who I don't think you've met. It was no coincidence that I was placed next to him at dinner. We all agreed that he was clearly on a fishing mission instigated by the Kaiser. Ballan is a charming chap in a Teutonic sort of way, but I made it clear to him that we were ready to fight if cornered, or if our friends were compromised. He will certainly have taken my words directly back to the Kaiser. Perhaps it will deter the bugger.

That the Austrians have rejected the Serbs' acceptance of almost all their draconian terms is extraordinary. What do they want – blood? Of course they do! I see war as inevitable. The house of cards is stacked high and the slightest quiver will bring it crashing down. Make sure those marines are close to hand and have their eyes peeled and ears pinned back.

The world's markets are stuttering to a halt, credit can't be had anywhere. There's panic in Threadneedle Street. The Bank Rate is at 8 per cent and Lloyd George says it will go higher. By the way, LG is playing a canny game, clever as buggery; his status in the party is rising all the time. The Stock Exchange closed its doors this morning. Thank God we have very little invested.

The Cabinet is split, more than two-thirds for peace; only Eddie and I want to take a belligerent line. But the mood of pacification won't last. As soon as the first shots are fired, the complacency will evaporate. I'm hell-bent on us defending ourselves at the first act of aggression. How strange I am: the preparations for war and this mood of impending mayhem hold an awful fascination for me. How dreadful that I am made this way. But I am, and that's that.

The Germans are playing a spiteful and cunning game. They are asking what our reaction would be if they promise not to take French territory – just a few of France's colonies for indemnity – what a nerve! They say they will not invade Holland but make no mention of Belgium, which is their obvious route to Paris. Eddie Grey has written to inform them, in no uncertain terms, to bugger off. They say they just want to bloody some French noses, but believe me, my darling, their real aim is to recreate the Holy Roman Empire with the Austrians and then strike east against the Czar.

The problem is this: will our position make the situation better or worse? My view is simple. If we let them go ahead with impunity, they may well succeed and we will be faced with a continental monster as formidable as Napoleon and his Grande Armée. We must support the French at the outset and kill the creature before it can grow to the height of its power.

My darling, I'm so sorry for the diatribe. But the situation is grave, and I know you understand.

To matters more mundane. I have sent you a cheque for Pear Tree. Please have Jack scrutinize the account. I'm concerned that our bills for this month alone are over £150. The bank will be on my back again. Hodges – the weasel! – wrote to me the other day, telling me that he had received two cheques which pushed us beyond our overdraft limit. He asked what I expected him to do with them. So I wrote a little note on the bottom of his letter and posted it back to him. It just said, 'Pay them, man!'

If it goes quiet from me for a while, it will be because the balloon has gone up. But know that I will be thinking of you and the kittens every hour of every day.

Burn this letter, dearest one.

With all my love, my darling Cat, from your ever loving, lonely husband,

Pug

After Winston finishes his letter to Clemmie, he retires to his bed on the top floor of the Admiralty, but is unable to sleep, even after he has poured himself a hefty cognac. Eventually, he decides to get some air and take a stroll across Horse Guards and into St James's Park. He is accompanied by John Gough, a Special Branch serjeant, who is assigned to him whenever he is in London.

The night is warm, the sky clear and the moon is waxing well beyond its first quarter, casting long shadows across Horse Guards. Lights are burning brightly in Downing Street and the Foreign Office, but Winston is certain that the Prime Minister's will not be one of them. Herbert Asquith, the sturdy Old Block, will be sleeping the sleep of the just as he always does, despite the presence of his mistress beside him.

When they reach the lake in St James's Park, Winston sits down on a bench. He sighs.

'Serjeant, do you have one of those new battery torches with you?'

'I do, sir.'

'Good, then shine it over there, in the bushes, below Duck Island Cottage.'

There is a sudden flurry among the reeds, just where the serjeant is directing his beam.

'Look, just there; see how beautiful they are.'

With two tiny balls of grey fluff frantically trying to keep pace with them, a pair of black swans, their twin cygnets in tow, come scuttling out from the foliage.

'I've been watching them for a few days. Is there a more beautiful creature in the whole world?'

'No, sir, very fine they are.'

Winston asks his minder to switch off his torch and beckons to him to sit beside him. They watch the family of swans circle for a while, as the adults look for a new refuge for the night.

'Where is home, Serjeant?'

'Deptford, sir.'

'Ah, Deptford docks, the site of the knighting of Sir Francis Drake. And where Raleigh laid down his cape for Elizabeth I.'

'My goodness, sir, you know your history! I was born right by the docks.'

'What days those were, Serjeant, when the Royal Navy stood bulwark against the mighty Armada. I fear we face exactly the same predicament today.'

'Will there be war, sir?'

'Yes, Serjeant, I think we will be at war by the end of the week.'

The serjeant takes a breath and turns to his charge.

'Well, sir, in that case, shouldn't we get you back to the Admiralty?'

Winston smiles at the apposite remark and springs to his feet.

'Quite so, Serjeant. Let's make haste to our battle stations.'

PART THREE: AUGUST
Into the Boiling Cauldron

Sunday 2 August

Harry Woodruff and Maurice Tait are again on emergency duty with the Royal Fusiliers in London. As fears about the likelihood of war heighten, they have been sent back to Green Park to be close to Buckingham Palace and Whitehall. Within the government and the military hierarchy, there are concerns about how the nation, beset as it is by internal problems, will react as the threat of war increases and the tension rises. There is particular concern about the impact war might have on the economic turmoil that is blighting the country, increasing the calls for strike action and civil unrest.

Harry and Maurice had hoped to enjoy a long Bank Holiday weekend's leave at home in Leyton, but a telegram delivered late on Saturday afternoon to their parents' homes had summoned them back to barracks for no later than 9 p.m. that evening.

At least they had enjoyed Friday evening with their fathers in their favourite pub, the Drum, where all the talk was of war. After views were aired and old soldiers' stories told, it was unanimously agreed that, if it came to it, they would prefer to fight anybody except the Germans. They all knew the reputation of the Prussians of old, recounting tales of their resolve and discipline. In contrast, it was decided that the legendary Napoleonic traditions from the days of their great-grandfathers had long since disappeared and that the descendants of France's *Grande Armée* had 'gawn soft'. So, if they could pick their adversary, it would be the French; Wellington and the boys broke them at Waterloo and would do so again. On the other hand, they know that 'Kaiser Bill' has built a huge army, the like of which Britain has not faced since the war against Napoleon.

The talk left Harry and Maurice apprehensive. Boer farmers, tough as they might be, or a few crazy tribal warriors are one thing, but these German boys sound like they mean business and would be something else altogether.

As he promised himself he would, Harry also managed to see 'Big Marge' and has had a spring in his step ever since, despite the early recall to barracks and this morning's 6 a.m. reveille.

Rumours about war – where, when, against whom – dominate all the conversations in their serjeants' mess. But as the two men stare out across a deserted Piccadilly on a quiet Sunday lunchtime, they find it hard to see what all the fuss is about.

'What time is it, Mo?'

'Nearly two o'clock.'

'What a pain in the arse this is. I could be at 'ome givin' Big Marge another seein' to.'

'You ought to be careful, you could get a dose from 'er.'

'Nah, she's all right, told me she hadn't seen another fella all week.'

'You pullin' my chain, 'Arry? For a two-bob bit, she'd give anythin' a Barney Moke.'

A few minutes later, Harry and Maurice take a break and stroll down to St James's Park and into Horse Guards. They are hoping to bump into some Household Cavalry men for a bit of banter and a few well-directed insults.

As their boots crunch the gravel of the huge parade ground, they see the distinctive and dapper figure of the First Lord of the Admiralty, cigar in hand, walking towards them.

'Eh, Mo! That's that little Churchill fella.'

'Bloody 'ell, so it is. Mind yer Ps and Qs, 'Arry.'

Winston salutes them, as does his Special Branch minder, John Gough.

'Good afternoon, Serjeants; Fusiliers, I think. What are you up to?'

'Guard duty, sir, up at Green Park.'

Harry follows up Maurice's answer.

'Sir, we seen you at Ladysmith . . . a long time ago.'

'Indeed, gentlemen. But it was a good day.'

'Yes, sir. S'pose, yer gettin' ready fer another rumble.'

'Well, not at the moment. I'm going to see my swans.'

'Your swans, sir?'

'Yes, on the lake. Come with us; you can help me feed them.'

Despite Maurice and Harry's incredulity, they spend the next twenty minutes idly enjoying the tranquillity of St James's Lake and Duck Island, with its resident black swans. Winston describes their origins and monogamous breeding habits and enthrals the men with his easy manner and broad knowledge. When he finally bids them farewell and strides off towards Downing Street, he departs with a warm handshake for both of them. As he does so, his mood suddenly darkens and he rests a hand on Harry's arm.

'Within hours, we will be involved in a terrible struggle, above and beyond anything we encountered in South Africa. Are you up for it?'

Harry is the first to answer as they both nod enthusiastically.

'We are, sir, good an' ready.'

'Very good; that's the spirit. It will be a long and bitter road, but we will prevail.'

Maurice and Harry watch him go.

'So, 'Arry, sounds like that's that. We're orf to war.'

'Right, we'd better get back on duty. Nice fella that Churchill, ain't he?'

'Yeah, not a bad bloke fer a toff. Don't look like a soldier wiv his little baby face an' wispy ginger tash, but he don't 'alf sound like one.'

When they get back to Green Park, CSM Billy Carstairs suddenly appears.

'We've just had a message from the Old Bill at Piccadilly Circus. There's a right crowd gatherin' there, an' at Trafalgar Square; they're makin' one 'ell of a commotion. Take your squad down there an' 'ave a butcher's.'

Harry and Maurice decide it is probably wise to walk down Piccadilly in a relaxed manner, rather than in marching order, but as they approach the gates of Green Park, they see a sudden change of mood transforming the scene before them. What was a quiet Sunday afternoon is now a blur of activity. People begin talking animatedly as groups form around individuals holding opened newspapers. Harry's attention is drawn to a young newspaper vendor on the corner of the Ritz Hotel. He is surrounded by a growing crowd and has a pile of *Evening Standard*s on his arm, which he is selling as quickly as he can hand them out.

'Mo, it's Sunday, ain't it?'

'Yes, mate. It looks like they've printed special editions.'

'*War in Europe! War in Europe!*' is the incessant cry of the paper boy. Behind him, his news-stand's banner headline is just one word: 'WAR!'

'Bloody 'ell, the balloon really 'as gawn up!'

The newspaper lad changes his tune.

'*Kaiser declares war on the Czar . . . first shots fired!*'

The paper-seller repeats his cries over and over again as the crowds grow and grow.

'We'd better form up if we're gonna go to the Circus.'

The squadron of fusiliers manages to march no further than fifty yards before the crowd begins to applaud them. By the time they reach Piccadilly Circus, they are all but mobbed by a throng several hundred in number. In between wild cheering, choruses of 'God Save the King' break out. Union flags appear and cloth caps and boaters are thrown into the air. Several groups of men form up like soldiers and, with newspapers and umbrellas over their shoulders as improvised rifles, start marching up and down next to Eros.

Bottles of beer and wine and even champagne materialize, as if by magic, and the mood becomes more and more jubilant.

'Mo, it's time to beat a retreat. I've already 'ad one girl ask me if she can 'ave a cuddle wiv an 'ero!'

'Too right, our shift will be over in a couple of hours, let's get back to barracks, get into our civvies and get back up 'ere. A big night is in the offin' – we're 'eroes, good an' proper!'

'Or ear'oles! Either way, I'm up fer it. If we don't get a goose and duck tonight, I'm a Chinaman.'

The night of Sunday 2 August 1914 becomes a never-to-be-forgotten London occasion. Pubs and restaurants that have been closed for the second half of the week, because of anxieties about the banks and the drying up of credit, suddenly open their doors. The West End becomes the setting for a celebration of a kind not seen since the end of the Boer War.

Thousands mill around in a state of euphoria, but there is none of the brawling that usually results from long nights of drinking, and the mood remains joyous. Harry and Maurice get lucky; they meet two girls from Balham and do not get back to the Wellington Barracks until an hour before reveille the next morning.

Fortunately for them, CSM Carstairs, despite being a strong disciplinarian in military matters, is an understanding sort when it comes to the temptations of the opposite sex and usually turns a blind eye to such indiscretions, as long as they do not happen too often and are committed by men he trusts. If his two serjeants are on parade on time and look presentable, all they will receive by way of reprimand is a knowing look, followed by a frown and his favourite rejoinder, 'Dirty bastards!'

Bank Holiday Monday becomes an extraordinary extension of the night before. Britain has not yet declared war, but everyone feels that it is inevitable. The mood all over the country is the same. Old animosities begin to disappear and, overnight, what was a nation divided becomes a people united in common cause. Union leaders call for an end to strikes, the suffragettes discuss a truce and, in Ireland, both the Nationalists and Unionists throw their weight behind Britain's cause.

Despite the temptations, Harry and Maurice decide not to return to the girls in Balham on Monday evening, but choose an early night in barracks. They have heard that a full mobilization of the army is imminent and they may well be on a train to the Isle of Wight by midday on Tuesday. After a couple of beers in their mess at Wellington Barracks, they go for a stroll along the Tower battlements overlooking the Thames.

'These last few days 'ave been a right two an' eight, 'Arry.'

'Not 'alf! You'd 'ave thought we'd won a war, not just started one.'

'It was a good larf. But all that celebration about a war that 'asn't 'appened yet –'

'I know! But it's because none of the silly buggers out there 'ave ever fought in one.'

Thursday 6 August

Blair Atholl Castle, Perthshire

After German troops marched into Belgium on Tuesday 4 August, invading a country whose neutrality Britain had vowed to protect, King George V signed a momentous Declaration of War. The Foreign Office issued the following statement.

> Owing to the summary rejection by the German Government of the request made by his Majesty's Government for assurances that the neutrality of Belgium will be respected, his Majesty's Ambassador to Berlin has received his passports, and his Majesty's Government declared to the German Government that a state of war exists between Great Britain and Germany as from 11 p.m. on 4 August 1914.

By midnight, five empires were at war: Austria-Hungary, Germany, France, Russia and Great Britain. All thought victory would be swift and decisive.

The Kaiser, shocked that his British cousins – allies since they had fought together against Napoleon at Waterloo – should take such a step, relinquished his honorary titles as Field Marshal of the British Army and Admiral of her Fleet. The German servants at the British Embassy in Berlin removed their uniforms, spat and trampled on them and refused to help the British diplomats pack up and leave.

The dramatic news that Britain was at war reached every corner of the nation like a shock wave. The normally peaceful Blair Atholl Estate soon became a scene of confusion and upheaval.

Two days later, the old duke's notorious irritability has been provoked not only by the hectic activity but also by the realization that his Golden Jubilee celebration as duke of his demesne, scheduled for today – his birthday – must be cancelled.

A magnificent gathering of 2,500 guests had been expected, including the entire Scottish nobility and almost every man, woman and child for miles around. His own Atholl Highlanders were due to march past the castle in all their finery, accompanied by men from the Scottish Horse, the Cameron Highlanders, the Black Watch and a full fife and pipe band. A chamber orchestra from Edinburgh had been booked for the evening, enough catering companies were standing by to feed a small army, and Brocks Fireworks had sent its pyrotechnics experts all the way from Hemel Hempstead to organize the largest display Scotland had ever witnessed. All this has been cancelled at vast expense, lending a yet deeper shade to the duke's mood.

Of his six children, only Lady Helen is at Blair, newly arrived from Belgium, where she has been to see her sister, Evelyn, and now has to contend with her father's ire.

'What a bloody miserable day! The boys are all off playing soldiers. Your sister Dertha is too busy thinking about how she's going to cope with her husband's new commitments. But what about me? I'm a bloody commitment; my own jubilee and not a bugger in sight to celebrate with!'

'Don't swear so, Papa! I'm here, we can have an agreeable dinner together; I'll ask Forsyth to have a bottle of the '05 Margaux brought up.'

The old boy calms down a little.

'I'm sorry, Helen, but I'm not keen on the idea of a celebratory dinner on such a miserable day, even with your engaging company. The place is in chaos. Half the staff have gone!'

The duke has lost his valet John Seaton, his factor Robert

Irvine, his second chauffeur David Scott, his head stalker Peter Stewart, five gamekeepers and six junior men from his household; all reservists who have been called to the Colours.

'They've all gone off to fight for the King, thinking it's going to be a jolly, like a weekend's manoeuvres in the glens. Little do they know! I spoke to Shimi Lovat yesterday, who saw Churchill in London on Tuesday. He said it's going to be bloody. The German is a resolute cove and will take some beating.'

'Oh, Papa, our poor boys! I'm worried for them.'

'So am I. Hamish is somewhere in the Firth of Forth with the Camerons, George will be in Aldershot tomorrow with the Black Watch, and Bardie is running around like a blue-arsed fly, back and forth to Dunkeld, trying to get the Scottish Horse into shape. The bugger has taken all my good horses and left me just a few fat-bellied old nags.'

'Papa, please stop swearing.'

'Sorry, I'm just at sixes and sevens with it all.'

The old boy's face begins to mellow from fury to bewilderment. He looks at Helen wistfully.

'How's Evelyn?'

The duke rarely mentions his third daughter, a year younger than Helen, a forsaken child, now-middle-aged; he has not seen her for many years.

'The same; her letters are lucid, as always. But when one sees her, she's as timid as a mouse. It's still difficult to have any kind of conversation with her.'

'Her companion?'

'Yes, she's a good sort; they seem to get on well together.'

Lady Evelyn is something of a family embarrassment. She has been withdrawn and difficult since childhood, a malady the duke is certain was caused by a notorious incident that has not been talked about since. When not much more than a baby, she was lost in deep snow for over an hour by a careless nanny. She became ill and eventually developed diphtheria – although the duke did not accept the doctor's diagnosis, preferring to think it was 'all in her troubled mind'.

When Evelyn finally recovered, she began to resent her mother, exhibiting an antagonism that became so entrenched it persuaded the duke, with the full agreement of his wife, to send her away into the care of a governess. She was sent first to Switzerland and later to Belgium. When she became an adult, a series of companions were found and an apartment bought for her in the old district of Malines, near Antwerp.

'Strange child, perhaps we should never have sent her away. At least Dertha is normal.'

'Dertha' is the family name for Dorothea, Helen's elder sister, who lives in England with her husband, Colonel Harold 'Harry' Ruggles-Brise. Harry, in his youth a fine athlete, excelling at cricket and tennis, is a superb shot and a decorated Boer War veteran. He is now a Grenadier Guards career soldier and Commandant of the British Army School of Musketry at Hythe.

Helen bristles slightly at what she thinks may be her father's hint that she too might not be 'normal'. Unmarried at the age of forty-seven, she has assumed the role of nominal Duchess of Atholl, a task she has undertaken since the death of her mother over ten years before, and has since devoted herself to her father and the estate.

The duke notices his daughter's discomfiture.

'Helen, dearest, I didn't mean that *only* Dertha is normal. You're the most sane of all of us. I don't know what I'd do without you.'

Helen, much reassured by her father's words, moves to place her hand on his arm, but he turns away. She can see that there are tears in his eyes and knows that he would not want her to see him in a moment of weakness. He has ruled his realm for just over fifty years and fears that his private fiefdom is about to change in ways that he will find hard to cope with.

Helen leaves him alone, knowing that he will soon be taken by carriage to one of the cottages on the estate to spend the night with his latest mistress, a humble widow from Perth who he met only a month ago. She will be his only companion for his seventy-fourth birthday dinner, an occasion that was supposed to be a glittering celebration befitting a duke of the realm. Helen feels desperately sad for him but knows that, despite his bluster, many titles and elevated status, he is a very weak and docile man, who will find contentment in the simple comforts his lover will provide for him.

Later that evening, Bardie makes a surprise return from Dunkeld, hoping to join his father for dinner. Helen, now alone, is sipping sherry in Blair's huge and ornate withdrawing room, a habit of which she has become increasingly fond.

'Hello, Helen, where's Father?'

'Fulfilling a social engagement.'

'Don't be ridiculous, it's his birthday!'

Helen does not answer, but looks uncomfortable.

'Don't tell me he's up the glen with that Grant woman?'

'Yes, of course; he's feeling sorry for himself, and old habits die hard. He became quite melancholy this afternoon. It's a shame he didn't know you were coming, it would have made all the difference.'

'Bugger! I was only just able to get away at the last minute.'

'Well, he's gone; we won't see him until after lunch tomorrow. At least he might be in a better mood by then. What news from Dunkeld?'

'Sis, it's extraordinary what's happening. The recruiting office is overwhelmed by queues of men, young and old;

there are farm boys, solicitors' clerks, teachers, factory workers. It's the same all over the country. All the old antagonisms seem to be evaporating. The strikers, the suffragettes, all are suddenly amenable, the papers are full of it. Quite remarkable! The mood is ever so jolly.'

'Let's hope it lasts, Bardie – especially when the fighting starts.'

'Don't be so gloomy, Helen, it will be a real adventure. The Germans can't hold the French on one side and the Russians on the other, especially without our help.'

'That's not what I've heard; you're forgetting the central Europeans. What about all those Austrians and Hungarians?'

'Have you been talking to your Edinburgh friend again?'

Helen has become acquainted with an Edinburgh businessman and accomplished sculptor, David Tod, a man several years her senior.

'Bardie, don't be inane. You know my friendship with David is entirely platonic.'

'Darling H, I wasn't suggesting otherwise, don't be so touchy.'

'Well, David says the war will be a calamity and that we should stay out of it.'

'Does he now! You should be careful about him. Father will be furious if your liaison becomes more than platonic.'

'Don't be beastly! It is not a "liaison", as you so inelegantly put it. I won't be jumping into bed with him, not at my age. But even if I did, why would it matter?'

'By all means have a roll in the hay with him, but don't let it get serious.'

'Why not?'

'Come on, old girl, Father would have a fit; the man's a wholesaler.'

'Bardie, you are an arse! David runs a number of very successful businesses and is a very fine sculptor.'

'That's as maybe, but you know how stuffy Father is.'

'Fiddlesticks!'

'By the way, your man knows bugger all about military matters. Calamity, indeed; the Germans will be sent packing within six months!'

'Is that so? David is very well read and has been to Germany several times. Besides, he's entitled to his opinion.'

'Of course he is, but his opinion happens to be misguided on this occasion.'

Helen feels the beginning of tears of frustration.

'Bardie, let's not argue about war. Get yourself a drink and I'll have Forsyth serve some supper. I had promised Papa a bottle of his '05 Margaux. Shall we have it?'

'What a divine idea! Let's start with a glass of fizz, and I'll tell you about how splendid the Scottish Horse are looking.'

Friday 7 August

Pentry Farm, Presteigne, Radnorshire

It has been a long week at Pentry Farm. Tom Crisp has been working on a new shop front for Newells' ironmongers in Broad Street, while the three Thomas boys have been harvesting in their fields from dawn until dusk. Bronwyn's days have been equally long. She has now found more houses to clean in the town, which keeps her occupied for six days a week. She and Tom walk to and from Presteigne every day, a round trip of ten miles.

A truce has been called over the issue of selling the farm. The terms of the domestic armistice involve Bronwyn going off to bed after supper every night so that Tom and her brothers can discuss the details of their new building business. There is also an agreement that the subject is never mentioned within her hearing – not even by Tom, and especially not when they are alone.

Everyone accepts that the truce will only last as long as it takes for Aaron Griffiths's solicitors to draw up the legal papers for the sale. They were due to appear this week, but have not yet been delivered. As usual, Bronwyn has gone off with a tilley lamp and retired to the little love nest that Tom has converted from Pentry's wood store, leaving the boys to continue with the planning of their future.

They have made good progress. Ludlow is the choice of location for their enterprise. They know what kind of premises they need, how much investment in tools, equipment and transport is required and, without Bronwyn's superior skills with numbers, have done some financial calculations that seem to suggest that the venture will be viable.

However, the news about Britain's declaration of war has led Hywel to have doubts about the whole venture.

'Tom, bach, if this fist fight with the Germans kicks off properly, there'll be no money about.'

'Possibly, but it could represent a big opportunity for us. There may not be as much domestic work if money gets tight, but there'll be lots of government work – army barracks, naval dockyards and the like.'

'But that will mean moving away, won't it?'

'Aye, it will. But think about how big the contracts will be. And there'll be a shortage of labour if lots of skilled men go off to fight.'

As Tom continues to describe the kind of work that war might create, Geraint and Morgan look at one another, impressed by his insight, and smile.

Morgan puts his arm on Tom's shoulder and fills his mug of scrumpy.

'You're a clever sod, Tom, that's what I say.'

Geraint's face suddenly takes on a thoughtful look.

'I've been thinkin'. Shouldn't we be decidin' about joinin' up? Lots o' boys are talkin' about it?'

Hywel adopts his head-of-family pose.

'None of us is joinin' anythin'. We've got a business to run.'

Hywel's firm response stops any further discussion, but both Geraint and Morgan are tempted by the prospect.

After another long day on Saturday, the family decides to go to St Andrew's Church on Sunday morning for Reverend Henry Kewley's service. They are not entirely driven by religious devotion; after the service they hope to see Aaron Griffiths in the Duke's Arms to ask about the paperwork for the sale of Pentry. Although Griffiths, a fervent Primitive

Methodist, would not be seen dead in St Andrew's, his evangelical piety does not prevent him from being one of the Duke's most committed consumers of its landlord's Best Bitter, a potent elixir which is brewed lovingly on the premises every Thursday morning.

When they arrive for the service, Henry Kewley rushes forward to greet the family on the path to the church porch and ushers them to one side.

'I'm glad you're here today. I was going to come out and see you this afternoon. I'll have to be brief; I've only got a few minutes before I must begin the service.' The Reverend is breathless and looks anxious. 'I have some very bad news. Aaron Griffiths died yesterday afternoon. It's a terrible blow all round; his family are inconsolable.'

The news strikes the Thomases like a thunderbolt. Hywel is the only one able to mutter a few words.

'We're really sorry, Reverend Kewley. Please send our condolences to Mrs Griffiths. How did he die?'

'A heart attack, we think. He was at home, just walking upstairs; he was dead before he hit the floor . . .' He pauses, knowing what it will mean to the family. 'I'm afraid that, for obvious reasons, the purchase of Pentry won't be going ahead now. I'm so sorry for all of you. Come and see me this afternoon, if you want to talk about it.'

Kewley shakes all their hands before rushing back into the church, his surplice wafting in his wake, to greet the rest of his congregation.

He also leaves a stunned silence behind. Again, Hywel is the first to speak.

'That's an end to that, then.'

Bronwyn has mixed feelings. She is relieved that they will not be losing Pentry, but knows that there will now be no relief from their dire financial circumstances.

Geraint, impetuous as ever, asks the obvious question, but one that is better not asked.

'What are we going to do now?'

'Well, Geraint, if you mean right now, much as I admire Henry Kewley, I'm in no mood for one of his sermons. Let's go to the Duke and raise a toast to old Griffiths, the man who very nearly saved our bacon.'

After two somewhat sombre hours of 'what might have beens' and 'if onlys', thanks to the curative effects of the Duke's Best Bitter, the gloom enveloping Tom Crisp and the Thomas family begins to lift.

The Duke, with its hotel licence, is the only pub in Presteigne open on a Sunday. As the Presbyterian and Anglican services are now over, it is full to its ancient rafters. All the talk is of war, much of it very animated and jingoistic. For over an hour, Geraint and Morgan have been part of a large group of young men at the bar, many of whom were at school with them. When they return to the corner table where Tom, Hywel and Bronwyn are sitting, they are somewhat inebriated and grinning from ear to ear. Geraint puts his arm around Hywel's shoulders rather clumsily and makes his brother spill some of his beer.

'Morgan and me will be off your hands soon. Pentry won't need to feed us.'

'How's that?'

'Bron's just told us – Philip Davies let on to her this week – that he's a reserve officer in the Welch Fusiliers. He's been mobilized an' 'as already left to join the regiment.'

Geraint gulps, trying to draw breath, so Morgan takes up the story.

'Davies 'as sent word. He's organized for a group of local lads to go to Llandrindod to volunteer.'

Morgan's words have a dramatically sobering impact on Hywel.

'Listen, the pair of you. Neither of you've got much more than bumfluff on your chins and you're talkin' of goin' to war! Not a chance, boys.'

Bronwyn is also horrified.

'Bloody 'ell! Are you mad? When I told you about Philip's offer, I didn't expect it to include you two. Over my dead body – do you 'ear me? – over my dead body!'

'Come on, Bron, for King and country . . . an' to save Pentry.'

'I'm not bothered about savin' Pentry if it means you two gettin' skewered on the end of a German bayonet!'

Morgan begins to laugh loudly and act out bayonet thrusts on Geraint.

'There ain't a German ugly enough to spear two fine Welsh warriors like me an' Geraint.'

Geraint joins in the theatrics.

'That's right, little brother! The Welch Fusiliers are the finest regiment in Wales. We'll have those Germans on the run, back to wherever they come from.'

Bronwyn cuffs Geraint across the back of his head as hard as she can.

'They come from Germany, you 'alf-wit! It's not your brawn that bothers me, it's that lump of lard that passes for your brain!'

Hywel brings the exchange to a close.

'Look, you two, you're not signing up for anything, not even the Boys' Brigade!'

Back at Pentry later, the night is warm and humid. Bronwyn and Tom find it hard to sleep.

'Bron, since when have you been on first-name terms with Philip Davies?'

'What do yer mean?'

'Tonight, in the Duke, when you were talking about his offer to help men join up, you called him Philip.'

'Did I? I don't remember. If I did, it was a slip of the tongue.' Bronwyn, a little flustered, changes the subject.

'Tom, you 'ave to help us with Geraint and Morgan. They admire you.'

'Help you do what?'

'Persuade 'em not to be so daft and join up.'

'I'm not sure it is daft.'

'How do you mean?'

'I think it's very worthy of them to want to fight.'

'Tom, how can you! Are you mad?'

'I don't think so; I've been thinking I should join up myself. I like Philip Davies, and I admire him if he's prepared to give up his good job to go off and fight for his country. He must be in his late thirties.'

Bronwyn sits up and lights the candle by the bed. She looks dumbfounded.

'Let me see yer face. Look me in the eye and say that again.'

Tom stares at her with a steely resolve.

'I think I should join as well. I'm not Welsh, but I was born in Radnorshire, so if they'll have me in the Welch Fusiliers, then I think I should join up with your brothers.'

'I don't believe what I'm hearin'.'

'There are all sorts of good reasons. Without Aaron Griffiths's money, God rest his soul, Pentry is in a lot of trouble. Hywel will need to mortgage the farm to raise cash, which is a road to ruin. So it makes sense for the boys to think of other options.'

'But what about you?'

'Bron, this is hard for me to say. I don't want you to think that I'm not happy here. I love you very much and want to make my life with you, but all the talk about starting a business has got me thinking. I don't want our life together to be in a small town in a forgotten corner of Wales. Now we're at war, and that changes everything.'

Bronwyn begins to cry.

'Tom, what are you sayin'?'

'I'm not sure, but I think if Britain calls for its young men to fight, we should answer. The Germans are challenging us and we have to stand up to them. But it's also more than that for me; enlisting gives me the opportunity to see what the world has to offer beyond our little valley.'

'And what about us? You're talkin' about "you" all the time.'

'I mean "us", of course.'

'But I don't want to leave this "little valley". It's my home, and I love it 'ere.'

'I know you do, but there are many valleys in many places. There are towns and cities as well, full of challenges and opportunities. I want to experience some of them, but with you.'

Bronwyn does not respond; she just turns away and puts her head on her pillow. Tom stares at her still form, not seeing the tears trickling down her cheeks.

The last few weeks have been an awful concoction of emotions for Bronwyn Thomas. Driven by powerful yearnings since early adolescence, when images of the farm animals copulating filled her idle thoughts by day and her dreams by night, she finally found sexual fulfilment with Tom. When they began to live together at Pentry, she could give full rein to her desires and sex consumed her to the point of exhaustion.

She began to plan for the life that she had always dreamed of on her beloved farm: love, marriage, children and happiness ever after. But those dreams are now in ruins.

When she ran from Pentry two weeks ago, after the row about the sale of the farm, she did not hide herself away or wander aimlessly across the fields. Nor did she think to return to find solace with Tom, her fiancé. She rushed instead into the arms of her lover, a man old enough to be her father. Now she is lying in her fiancé's bed, the bed of the man she thought she loved but now doubts whether she does.

Her job as a cleaner for Philip and Clara Davies started well enough. Their home, just to the north of the town centre, on St David's Street, is an elegant Georgian mansion, one of the grandest in the area.

But the work is taxing, with many pieces of fine furniture to dust and polish and with paintings, porcelain and ornaments everywhere. The Davieses have a maid and a cook, but the cleaning is more than enough for one person, so Bronwyn does the upstairs and the bathrooms, leaving the maid to do the ground floor and help in the kitchen.

She hardly sees Clara, who seems to spend all day locked away in her darkened bedroom, a room she does not share with Philip, who has a room of his own. When it is time for Bronwyn to clean Clara's room, she will sit in the morning room, staring into the garden with a vacant look on her face.

Bronwyn soon began to feel sorry for Philip. His wife, still a handsome woman, tall, with long black tresses and clear, pale skin, seems to have had all the vitality drained from her. Bronwyn imagined that, for Philip, life with Clara must be like living with a ghost.

Then, early in July, two incidents turned Bronwyn's life upside down. The first came when she was cleaning Philip's study. It is full of collectibles and memorabilia, mainly books, but also ceramics, militaria and prints. It resembles an antiques shop and is a nightmare to clean.

She had finished cleaning one morning and, in need of a moment to catch her breath, sat in Philip's captain's chair at his desk. She began to pick up some prints that were lying in a pile. Always a good reader, the titles were easy for her to follow. One of them was 'Lysistrata'. Although the words were easy to read, the images were much more challenging. Bronwyn had never seen erotica before, and the sight of women taunting men who sported grotesque, erect phalluses shocked her to the core. But the bizarre images also aroused her, making her feel very confused.

'They are Aubrey Beardsley's illustrations for *Lysistrata* by Aristophanes, a Greek comic playwright from antiquity, written early in the fifth century BC. I hope they don't shock you?'

Bronwyn had not heard Philip come into the room. His study is next to his bedroom, and the door had been left slightly ajar. She jumped to her feet but, as she did so, knocked several of the prints on to the floor, compounding her embarrassment.

'No . . . well, yes . . . I'm sorry, sir. I was just tryin' to clean your room.'

As she scampered to pick up the prints, all of which portrayed highly suggestive imagery, Philip bent down to help her.

'I hope to sell them next week in Ludlow. They are very collectible.'

'I can't imagine who'd buy them; perhaps only lonely old men.'

He smiles at her.

'You'd be surprised, Bronwyn. I sell quite a few to female collectors as well. Aristophanes' comedy is based around a woman called Lysistrata, who wishes to bring an end to the Peloponnesian War between Athens and Sparta by convincing the women of Athens to withhold sexual privileges from the men until they agree to declare a peace, effectively holding the men's libido hostage. Don't you think it an interesting coincidence with war looming in Europe?'

'War, sir?'

'The heir to the throne of the Austrian Empire was assassinated three days ago. They say it may lead to war. Perhaps you women will prevent it happening.'

Bronwyn did not really hear what Philip was saying. She just wanted to crawl into a hole and disappear.

'I don't know about war, sir. But if I may say so, those things are just filth in my eyes.'

'Well, that's interesting. Beardsley's dead now. He was only twenty-six when he died, but before he died he converted to Roman Catholicism and begged his publisher to destroy his erotic drawings because he thought them an abomination. Luckily for his devotees, and for me, he didn't.'

'Well, I think you should burn 'em. He was right, they are an abon . . . im . . .'

'Abomination.'

'Yes, one of those.'

Bronwyn, scarlet in the face and sweating profusely, hurried from the room, closing the door behind her with a boom before bursting into tears.

She was left with her mind in turmoil. Philip had talked about the prints in a matter-of-fact way, as if was talking about the art of the great masters of painting. He had also spoken to her with kindness, without embarrassment, and had treated her as an adult. The more she thought about the incident, the more she forgot about how embarrassing the circumstances had been. Over the next few days, the images began to fill her head with lurid thoughts that led her to fantasize about recreating the scenes with Tom.

On the next two occasions when she cleaned Philip's study, he was away working in Ludlow – selling his 'dirty prints', she imagined. But the Beardsley prints were not the only ones she found. There were others, by illustrators with exotic foreign names like Count de Waldeck and Paul Avril, which were far less grotesque, but equally explicit. Bronwyn's initial shock and revulsion soon turned to fascination, and the images became central to her love-making with Tom. Gradually, and to the sweet torment of her vivid imagination, the large and powerful lover who dominated her secret fantasies came to resemble Philip, not Tom.

The second incident took place a week later and has filled her with remorse ever since.

Clara Davis had been taken for a carriage ride by her brother, who lived nearby. The house cook and maid were in

Presteigne at the shops and Bronwyn knew she was alone with Philip. Despite knowing full well that it was inappropriate – and potentially perilous – her mind raced and she felt her heart thumping in her chest.

She found herself cleaning his study, even though it was not the day for her to do so, when she heard him splashing in his bath. The door to his bedroom was partly open and she noticed that, by looking at the mirror over the mantelpiece in his study, she could see the door to his bathroom.

When she heard him step out of his bath and let out the water, she positioned herself so that she could catch sight of him. Philip is a big man, built like a warrior or an athlete, his body covered with thick hair. Compelled by a heady brew of mixed emotions – intense guilt, fear, but also a much more exhilarating sense of anticipation – she looked between his legs and there she saw that his manhood matched his powerful frame. It seemed partially erect, a sight that sent a wave of adrenalin through her body.

What happened next was an inevitability, entirely instigated by Bronwyn, who merely pushed the study door fully open and stepped into Philip's bedroom.

In the days that followed, in between sessions of intense love-making, Philip began to tutor Bronwyn, not only in the nuances of erotic art, but also in many other subjects. After a few days, he hired another cleaner, so that he could spend more time with her. He also paid the charges for two of her other cleaning jobs so that she could cancel them and come to him almost every day. Bronwyn's mind is alert and perceptive, and their conversations became more and more erudite as she charmed him with her questions and insight.

Their couplings were sometimes wild, but often tender. Bronwyn felt satisfied in ways she had not experienced before, as sex became an intellectual experience as well as a physical one. She became besotted with him, leaving her with the anguish of loving two men at the same time: her gentle fiancé, sweet, considerate Tom, and Philip, her masterful older lover.

She continued to make love to Tom, partly because she had to, but also because her passions of the day often carried over to the night, a sin that only worsened her feelings of guilt. Philip asked her about Tom and she told him the truth. He became jealous and asked her to keep herself for him alone, only adding to the shame she felt.

She was wrestling with her dilemma and was on the point of deciding to break off her engagement to Tom, when war intervened. When Philip told her he was leaving, it was as if the world had ended. She had no idea he was a reserve soldier. He made arrangements for Bronwyn to have access to a post office box in Presteigne and for her to withdraw her cleaning fees, much augmented by Philip, from his account at the town's Bridgnorth Bank.

Then he was gone, summoned to his regiment and the impending war.

Bronwyn's tears still flow on to her pillow. She is traumatized: exhausted by the intensity of her relationship with Philip and ashamed by her lustful behaviour and the web of deceit she has had to spin. Her mind spins in a whirlwind of intoxicating memories and dreadful remorse.

Philip has gone. She knows that many reservists are preparing to go to France; she may never see him again. Next to her is her fiancé, now deeply asleep, a man for whom she no longer has the same feelings she had just a few weeks ago.

Her tears soak into her pillow. Her dreams are shattered; she thinks her life is over.

Saturday 8 August

Despite the traditional conventions that apply to their gender, Cath Kenny and Mary Broxup have insisted on joining their menfolk for their Saturday drinking session at Keighley Green Working Men's Club. Although they are much younger than the 'older married ladies' tolerated in the club, they are with 'Tommy Brox' and 'Mad Mick' – two of Burnley's most notorious hard men – so their presence goes unchallenged.

Tommy and Mick have agreed that their wives can join them on the strict understanding that it is not taken as a precedent. Cath and Mary have also had to agree to behave themselves by not raising three taboo subjects: their support for the suffragette cause, their socialist beliefs and their commitment to pacifism, which has been nurtured by the growing opposition among some left-wing groups to the war with Germany.

Cath and Mary have been espousing anti-war sentiments all day. For the past week, the mee-maw in their mills has been all about the outbreak of war and its consequences.

At that morning's tea break at Cath's mill, the Trafalgar, a union official produced a copy of *Labour Leader*, the journal of the radical Independent Labour Party, and read out its exhortation: 'Workers of Great Britain, down with war! You have no quarrel with the workers of Europe. They have no quarrel with you. The quarrel is between the ruling classes of Europe. Don't make the quarrel yours.'

A very heated debate followed, which left Cath in a tiny minority who agreed with the ILP's stance. As many fellow socialists pointed out, the left-wing *Manchester Guardian* has come out in favour of supporting the war, as has the ILP's rivals, the Labour Party, and, indeed, Cath and Mary's hero, Mr Harry Hyndman, leader of the British Socialist Party. Much the same debate happened at Daneshouse Mill, where Mary works, leaving her in a small but vociferous minority. Mary's Irish roots had not helped her cause; accusations of disloyalty and even treason were levelled at her, including by some of her union colleagues.

Although Keighley Green's typically carefree and raucous Saturday night atmosphere still holds sway, there are nevertheless several grave and animated discussions to be heard. Through the usual din there is much argument about the morality and efficacy of Britain's declaration of war. One of the most contentious issues among the club's members, almost all of whom are weavers, is the thought that the town's colliers are certain to be excused military duty on the basis of the importance of coal to the war effort.

Phrases like 'fuckin' colliers' and 'lucky bastards' drift by Mick's ear – he is probably the only miner in the room – but they have no effect on him. As usual, his demeanour is remarkably placid.

In contrast, all the conversation at the Broxup/Kenny table is focused on young Vinny Sagar who, that very afternoon, has had the honour of playing in a trial match at Turf Moor for Burnley Football Club's youth team against Blackburn Rovers' youths.

The new season is less than a month away and Vinny is hoping he might get a part-time apprenticeship at the club, the first step to becoming a professional footballer. Burnley, currently the FA Cup holders and riding high in public esteem both locally and throughout the land, are the bookies' favourites for the 1914–15 league title. Joining the illustrious club would be a dream come true for Vinny. His ambition is to play cricket in the summer for Lowerhouse, a famous old team based on the outskirts of the town and one of the stalwarts of the renowned Lancashire League, and football in the winter for Burnley, the leading team in the land.

That morning, he had rushed to the ground after his shift at the mill. He had no time to eat the sandwich in his snap box, threw his working clothes at his ever-present companion, Twaites Haythornthwaite, and made it on to the pitch with only minutes to spare. Nonetheless, he made an excellent impression on John Haworth, Burnley's manager. Burnley beat Blackburn 3-1 and Vinny scored the third goal, late in the second half.

He and Twaites have been celebrating in the club since arriving at five o'clock and have lost count of how many pints of Massey's King's Ale they have consumed. They can just about see the bar, but most of their other faculties are fading rapidly.

'Tha should 'ave sken me goal, it were a belter! Must 'ave been thirty yard; went in like a bullet.'

Twaites takes issue, if a little incoherently, with Vinny's claim about the distance of his 'wonder' goal.

'More like eighteen yard, our kid, tha were only just outside t'penalty box!'

John-Tommy Crabtree, the club steward, himself a fine footballer in his day and one of the town's greatest fast bowlers, suddenly appears behind them.

'I 'ear tha laiked fer Burnley Youths today, lad.'

'I did, Mr Crabtree – scored an' all.'

'Well, tha won't be scorin' many more if tha keeps suppin' ale like tha does.'

'I've only 'ad three.'

'More like six or seven. You and Twaites can 'ave one more, then it's 'ome for t'pair o' thee.'

Vinny tries to argue, but Tommy Brox puts his hand on his shoulder.

'John-Tommy's reet. One more and you're on thy way down t'road.'

After Vinny and Twaites are sent packing to their beds, the conversation between Mary, Cath, Mick and Tommy, well lubricated by alcohol, turns to the impending war. The discussion quickly becomes strident. Mary is doubly disappointed. Not only are most left-wing groups on the British mainland supporting the war, most of her Nationalist kin in Ireland are suspending their demands for independence in order to lend support to Britain and the Empire.

'I can't believe it. After 'undreds o' years, an' just as independence were agreed, our Irish brothers and sisters 'ave bowed to their oppressors in Westminster. They must 'ave gone soft in th'eed!'

Cath nods in agreement with Mary, but neither Tommy nor Mick respond. They are eavesdropping on a loud conversation taking place at the bar, where several men in a group of weavers are arguing about the merits of Britain's declaration of war. One of them, Jimmy Dowd, an old adversary of Tommy's from schooldays, is as drunk as a skunk and eager for a confrontation. He has three equally belligerent friends with him as he staggers over to where Tommy and his group are sitting. Jimmy Dowd is six inches shorter than Mick and Tommy, but as wide as a barn door, and one of Burnley's most notorious scrappers.

He gets drunk most Fridays and Saturdays when, with sufficient Massey's inside him, he usually leads his little group of fellow nutters in a mass brawl with whichever similarly inclined pugilists they can find. The bobbies know to come gang-handed, crack a few skulls and then lock them up for the night.

'So, our Tommy, what does tha reckon to this feight wi' t'Germans?'

'I 'aven't thought abaht it much, Jimmy.'

'I 'ear thy missus is not only a peacemonger, but also a

fuckin' suffragette. What abaht thee? Is tha freightened o' feightin'?'

'Tha knows me better than that, Jimmy.'

Jimmy turns to Mick with a sneer on his face.

'What abaht thee, lad? I hear you're a collier an' a Paddy. We don't normally let colliers in 'ere, especially Mick colliers.'

Mick doesn't rise to the bait, but Cath does.

'Why don't you bugger off back to t'bar an' 'ave another ale?'

Jimmy looks at Cath with contempt.

'We don't normally let young lasses in 'ere either. Unless they're up for tuggin' a few cocks!'

Cath manages to reach Jimmy before Tommy does and lands a clenched fist on the side of his jaw. All hell breaks loose as chairs, tables, pots and bodies go flying. Cath and Mary retreat behind the bar, where they pass John-Tommy Crabtree, shillelagh in hand, on his way to sort out the brawl.

By the time the doughty steward reaches the combatants, only Tommy and Mick are standing. Jimmy Dowd and his friends are prostrate, bloodied and bowed. Jimmy looks the most damaged. Where his nose was prominent only moments ago, there is now a mess of blood and cartilage.

Tommy looks at Mick.

'Alreet, lad?'

'Aye, I'm fine. I'd 'eard tha's quick wi' them fists. But, by 'eck, tha can 'andle tha'sen.'

'Tha's reet 'andy tha'sen, Mick, lad.'

Tommy turns to John-Tommy, who is still holding his shillelagh with intent.

'Sorry, gaffer –'

'Not thy fault. I should 'ave chucked 'em out an hour ago. Will you lads 'elp me get 'em outside? Then you can 'ave one on th'ouse.'

Later that night, as Tommy and Mick stroll home a few yards behind their wives, Mick asks Tommy about the war.

'What dost reckon to this set-to wi' t'Germans? Will tha feight if it comes to it?'

'Aye, I think so. In't it our duty to defend our country an' our families?'

'What abaht Cath? She won't like it.'

'I know, but I'm me own man. What abaht thee?'

'I s'pose so, but Mary 'as been lecturin' me abaht it. She never lets up. It's our Irish roots more than owt else. She reckons that if Ireland doesn't get independence, we shouldn't fight. Mind you, that's apart from not believin' in wars in t'first place!'

'Vexin', in't it?'

'Aye, then there's our babby on t'way. That's thrown cat among t'pigeons; it's a reet bugger.'

'Well, t'feightin' 'asn't come to owt yet. It might all blow over.'

'Aye, let's hope so.'

Monday 10 August

The British Cabinet has been in its fourth successive emergency session since 8 a.m. It is now nearly lunchtime. The Prime Minister, Herbert Asquith, is chairing the meeting with his usual calm aplomb, but he's tired. He is almost sixty-four years old and beginning to feel the strain of the enormous task ahead of him.

'Mr Churchill, you wanted to make a point.'

'Indeed, Prime Minister. If I may, would Lord Kitchener confirm that he does not feel the need for mass conscription, even though our army stands at little more than one hundred thousand men? France has four million soldiers, the Russians six million. And the combined force of Germany and Austria-Hungary stands at seven and a half million men.'

Kitchener does not look irritated that he should be asked to explain himself again after making his position clear several times. He has gone public over the weekend, openly stating that he would prefer to create a new volunteer army, rather than introduce compulsory conscription.

'Mr Churchill, I am grateful to you for giving me the opportunity to reiterate my views. May I also congratulate you once more on the preparedness of the fleet; its status is a credit to all concerned, but to you in particular. Before I state my position, Prime Minister, I should stress that it is in no sense a criticism of my predecessors. Nevertheless, it is a fact that, while our Senior Service is the mightiest fleet the world has ever seen, the British Army is a relatively small, albeit highly trained and professional, army when compared to the hordes assembled by our neighbours on the Continent.

'The latest figures I have suggest we are eleven thousand short of our designated strength of two hundred and sixty thousand men. Approximately half of those are on the British mainland as of today; the rest are in garrisons throughout the Empire. Obviously, our army is much more focused on the particular needs of our colonies, rather than on the strategic problems of Europe, where massed land forces are strategically vital. However, suddenly to conscript millions of men would be folly. We have none of the facilities to cope with them: we lack men to train them, barracks to accommodate them, even weapons with which to arm them.

'Our reservists are substantial and are flocking to their muster points as I speak. But I am uneasy about putting them into combat too soon. Sadly, several battalions will be made up of at least fifty per cent reservists when they get to their Channel embarkation points.'

There is obvious consternation around the cabinet table at Kitchener's remarks. Asquith feels compelled to interrupt.

'Are you suggesting that the reservists are not up to scratch?'

'Well, Prime Minister, they are all experienced soldiers and many have fought in very challenging places, including, of course, South Africa. However, by definition, they are older men and not in full-time training. Secondly, this is a war in Europe against formidable modern soldiers, whose marksmanship and training are excellent and who have heavy artillery and machine guns. I am confident that our musketry is superior to any in the world, but I would prefer it if our reservists were between ten and fifteen per cent of enlisted men, not up at around forty to fifty per cent, as in many battalions.'

'Very well, Lord Kitchener, I think we understand. Let us

pray that resolving this squabble in Europe is a brief encounter.'

As Asquith makes his comment, Eddie Grey and Winston Churchill exchange disbelieving glances. Kitchener notices the doubt on their faces and decides to speak out.

'I fear this war may well be a protracted and bloody affair, Prime Minister. Vast numbers of men and huge volumes of materiel are about to be unleashed on a scale not seen before. If France falls, which we must pray it does not, the first phase will be over quickly. Then, God help us, we will be staring at the Kaiser's enormous army across a meagre twenty-two miles of English Channel.

'If France holds her ground, then a stalemate will ensue, which could be very costly indeed. Whatever happens, we need to train a new army, either to stiffen French resolve in the long term, or to confront the German Army if it dares threaten our shores. Such an army will not be created in weeks; it will take months. But the process has begun, and the reaction from every corner of Britain and the Empire has been extraordinary.'

The mood in the room darkens. A few members shift uneasily in their chairs; one or two cough nervously.

'So, my immediate plan is in two parts. First, to get an expeditionary force of the best of our men across to France as quickly as possible, where they will hold the left flank of the French border, which, as you know, is highly vulnerable to a German attack through neutral Belgium. Secondly, beginning this very day, a long-term recruitment, mobilization and training strategy will start to build the foundations of a new citizen army for the eventual defence of Britain and for victory in Europe.'

There is a peculiar stillness in the room after Kitchener finishes his eloquent summary. It is as if the enormity of what Britain is facing has suddenly become real. The Cabinet table is surrounded by men not averse to airing their views.

Meetings are usually typified by strident debate, where men vie with one another to speak, and silence is a rare occurrence.

The Prime Minister, Herbert Asquith, looks out across Horse Guards, lost in thought. The Foreign Secretary, Sir Edward Grey, stares at Kitchener, as if stunned by what he has heard. Then, suddenly, he speaks.

'Prime Minister, I think I should like to put on record that we have many things to be thankful for, but one of them surely is that, in Mr Churchill and Lord Kitchener, we have two men at the heart of the defence of our country in whom we can have the utmost confidence.'

As cries of 'Hear, hear!' ring around the room, the Prime Minister adjourns the meeting for lunch.

'We will reconvene at two o'clock sharp, gentlemen, please. This afternoon, Lord Lucas will introduce to us the new, long-term provisions being made for emergency food production by the Board of Agriculture and Fisheries.'

While the majority of the Cabinet eats in Downing Street's small dining room, Winston Churchill persuades Kitchener to join him alone for an al fresco lunch in the garden.

'I hope you weren't too dismayed by my question. I know that you've already said what you intend to do, but I wanted the full Cabinet to hear your very persuasive thoughts in detail, especially those who go straight to Fleet Street with their tittle-tattle.'

'Quite so, Winston. The sooner everyone understands what we're facing, the better. We've relied on the navy for far too long. Our land forces are minuscule, and most of our reservists have only signed up for domestic duties.'

'I wholeheartedly agree with you, K. We also need air power and armoured vehicles.'

'I'm not as convinced as you about the immediate efficacy of these new devices, but they will, I'm sure, be of importance in the long run. I have more immediate issues. I'm having all sorts of rows with John French. Pressured by the French High Command, he wants to commit to an immediate landing of the entire army, with as many reservists as can be got ready. But I'm only going to commit four infantry divisions and one of cavalry. I intend to hold back the other two here on the south coast.'

Winston nods knowingly.

'You fear the worst in France?'

'I do; we could be cut off from the sea or, worse still, suffer drastic casualties. I know your dreadnoughts are our greatest bulwark but, should doomsday come to pass, I want sufficient men to remain here to defend the south coast.'

'I understand. But "doomsday"? Surely not!'

'I know you're a warrior at heart, Winston – it's in your blood – and that the possibility of defeat never enters your head, but it's an ever-present thought in mine. The French will fight bravely, their officers will conduct themselves with their usual elan and their tough little poilus, full of national pride, will fight for the honour of the Republic. But their generals are thirty years behind the times, as are their weapons and tactics. The Germans, on the other hand, are cunning, well-equipped and hungry for conquest.'

'You paint a depressing picture, my Lord K.'

'Don't misunderstand me, Winston, we can win. We have the navy and we have the Channel. But if we are to have an army to win this war, we're going to need time to build it. What the Romans took two hundred years to create, we're going to have to do in eighteen months.'

'How many men?'

'One million, perhaps closer to two.'

'Bugger me! Can it be done?'

'Of course, but I'm going to have to break a few eggs and crack a few skulls to do it.'

'You can count on my full support, both within government and in the country.'

'I am grateful to you, Winston.'

'Not at all! Quite apart from the kindnesses you showed to me in the Sudan, all those years ago, for which I will always be grateful, all of us need to support you in your noble efforts.'

'You're very kind. You and I go back a long way, do we not? Now this great responsibility has fallen to us. May God give us the wisdom and the strength to carry it through.'

Later that day, Winston telephones Clemmie, who is waiting for the call at the post office in Overstrand, where she is staying with their children at Pear Tree Cottage.

'What a day it has been, Clemmie. Lord Kitchener gave an admirable account of his intentions; very impressive it was too. We had a private lunch together, and I think we are going to cooperate very agreeably. Mind you, I made something of a faux pas when I exclaimed at one point, "Bugger me!"'

'What do you mean, Pug?'

'Well, let's put it this way, he's not married and surrounds himself with a coterie of handsome young officers.'

'I had no idea . . . such a handsome, strapping chap as well.'

'I know, but, as it's often said, anyone who has served in Egypt comes back with a penchant for sodomy –'

'Oh, Pug, really! Not over the telephone, darling.'

'Don't worry, dearest one, this is a secure line.'

'I'm not concerned about security, I just don't want to hear about men buggering one another over the telephone.'

'Oh, dearest Cat, buggery doesn't happen over the telephone . . .' He pauses, but there is no response to his crass humour. 'Sorry, Cat. Let's change the subject. How are the kittens?'

'Well, but Chumbolly is being difficult, as usual. I know you are trying to change the subject, Winston, but I've been hearing the most dreadful stories about how the Germans are behaving towards the Belgians.'

'I don't want to distress you any more than is necessary, but the reports suggest they are being absolutely bestial. There have been mass executions, dreadful reprisals against soldiers and civilians alike, it seems they've gone mad; it's bloodlust.'

'Oh, my darling, how awful! Those poor people –'

'Lord K's organizing our Expeditionary Force; the first battalions have already left. The rest will be on their way soon.'

'Oh, I do hope so.'

'I must go, darling Cat. Lord Louis is coming to dinner. The *Goeben*, one of Germany's biggest battlecruisers, has evaded our entire Mediterranean Fleet and got through to Constantinople. The poor chap is coming to explain how it happened.'

'All right, Big Pig, many kisses from me and the kittens.'

'And from me to all of you. Make sure those marines keep their eyes peeled. Love you, Cat.'

Rouen, Normandy, France

Philip Davies, professional auctioneer and reservist captain in the Royal Welch Fusiliers, has had a frantic time. Within three days, he has had to make provision for his mentally ill wife to be cared for in his absence, arrange for his household and businesses in Presteigne to be run while he is away and rush to join the fusiliers who are already billeted in Dorchester Town Hall. And he has done all of this while in the throes of an intense affair with an eighteen-year-old cleaning girl who has become obsessed with him, and he with her.

He has vowed to write to Bronwyn every day, using the post office box he has arranged in Presteigne. But he has been too busy, so far, to send anything more than one short, scribbled note. He knows how smitten she has become by him, but his first few days away from her have allowed him to think more deeply about his feelings for her. Does he love her? He has repeatedly asked himself this question. He knows how totally infatuated he has become, but is it love? He is not sure.

At Dorchester, he was given a precautionary medical and granted command of two platoons in A Company, most of whose men are seasoned veterans – not the easiest baptism for a reserve officer with only a modicum of real military experience. Philip's top hat and tailcoat have been put away, to be replaced by British khaki. His auctioneer's gavel has been exchanged for a Webley Mk IV revolver.

The Royal Welch Fusiliers sailed from Southampton at 2 a.m. this morning and arrived in Rouen in the middle of the afternoon. They are the first British troops to arrive in Normandy and are given a rapturous welcome. As they march through the streets, they are cheered, kissed and embraced by men, women and children alike. They are given flowers, wine, food and cigarettes and hailed as saviours of a land about to be overrun by a horde of barbarian Huns.

The fusiliers are given a temporary billet in a local convent, only just vacated by nuns who have gone south to their sister house in Bordeaux. When his men are settled in, Philip calls them together.

'Stand at ease, men. Welcome to France, land of wine, women and song, at least two of which delights are only to be enjoyed in very small doses and one of which is likely to give you a dose!'

Their new officer's towering presence and blunt humour make an immediate impression on the forty-eight men in the room. They had expected a 'chinless wonder', probably an English one – or at the very least one with a cut-glass English accent – but Philip speaks like they do, or like the school-teachers they remember from childhood. He fills his address with humour and detailed information not usually given to private soldiers. He finishes with a final flourish.

'Serjeant Powell is handing out a pamphlet. It is from Lord Kitchener, the Minister for War. It is warning you against temptation, especially those emanating from bottles and brothels. Read it! If any of you have any difficulty with reading, just ask Serjeant Powell, Lieutenants Jones or Morgan, or myself.'

Philip likes soldiering; he is ideally suited to it. If it had paid more, he might well have become a career soldier rather than an auctioneer.

'Rouen is off-limits tonight. You need to get some sleep as few of us had any last night. We have no orders at present; I expect they will come down to us over the next day or two. Now, Serjeant Powell, get the men off to bed.'

Rules Restaurant, Covent Garden, London

Also en route on 10 August are two of the Stewart-Murray boys from Blair Atholl. While Bardie remains in Dunkeld with the Scottish Horse, Geordie is at Aldershot with the Black Watch, preparing to leave for Southampton, from where they will sail in three days' time. Hamish is with the Cameron Highlanders, who will also leave from Southampton on 13 August. They are billeted at the Duke of York's Barracks in Chelsea. As both men are close to one another, they arrange to have dinner together at Rules Restaurant in Covent Garden. When they arrive, they are part of a majority of diners who are in uniform.

As usual, Hamish does most of the talking.

'Have you heard from Father?'

'Not a dicky bird. I expect he'll be as grumpy as hell. Half the staff have gone to the Colours.'

'I hope Nellie-Hellie is holding the fort.'

'She will, don't you doubt it.'

'Do you know which boat you're on?'

'Yes, the SS *Gando*.'

'What the hell is that?'

'A cattle ship probably!'

Despite the economic gloom that has descended on the country after the outbreak of war, the mood inside Rules is buoyant. The patriotism, a sentiment some would say borders on jingoism, is palpable. The restaurant's famous cellar is being plundered with abandon and its traditional English fare being consumed as if its nourishment will make the difference when a British bayonet clashes with a German one. After all, how can a weapon wielded by a man fed on sauerkraut possibly be a match against one brandished by a doughty Brit sustained by Rules's steak and kidney pie?

The waiters are run off their feet, the laughter becomes louder and the women swoon ever more at the sight of their handsome, khaki-clad heroes. Some diners break into song, even though there are few tuneful voices to be heard. For Hamish and Geordie the atmosphere is irresistible.

'Shall we go down to Dalton's Nightclub after dinner?'

'Hamish, you're incorrigible!'

'Of course I am. Good heavens, we may not see one another, or Blair, or Blighty, ever again! I intend to get drunk and fornicate right royally with at least one little darling tonight.'

Geordie can see that Hamish means business.

'I'm not going back to the Duke of York's; I'm staying at the Langham. You should do the same, Geordie. Why go all the way back to Aldershot. But you can't sleep on my sofa! I intend to have company, so you'll have to get your own room. Perhaps you'll strike it lucky yourself?'

It proves to be a debauched night for both of them. They eschew Dalton's and go to the Gaslight Club in St James's instead, where they meet a pair of willing ladies. A couple of shop assistants who have digs together in Maida Vale, they are more than happy to spend the night with two uniformed lords of the realm. They have never met aristocrats before and are impressed by their officer's garb, especially under the influence of fine champagne, the opulence of the Langham Hotel and the cornucopia of a breakfast served to them at three in the morning.

To cap a raucous night, at eight thirty in the morning, Hamish gives them a five-pound note – enough to pay the fare to Edinburgh and back – for a cab back to Selfridges, where they are due at work in the Perfumery Department. They were all smiles and giggles as they left, but perhaps were not looking quite as spruce as they had done the day before.

For their part, Hamish and Geordie have sore heads for the rest of the day, are sullen with their superiors, bad-tempered with their fellow officers and vindictive with their men. But it was a jolly good night!

Royal Fusiliers' Albany Barracks, Parkhurst, Isle of Wight

Maurice Tait and Harry Woodruff have much more spartan accommodation for the night of 10 August than Regent Street's Langham Hotel.

The 4th Battalion Royal Fusiliers reported to the Ministry of War the previous day that it is fully mobilized and ready to leave for France, but Parkhurst Barracks is far from a picture of precise military organization. In fact, it is chaotic. The battalion's ranks have been swollen by over 700 reservists: middle-class Londoners, artisans, plus a few working-class lads from military families. Most are totally bewildered, frantically trying to get their kit and clothing together. The noise of serjeant majors bellowing orders and the timpani of army boots clattering on cobbles is deafening.

'Get a move on, lad!', 'Don't run, you're a soldier, not a

bloody whippet!' are just two of the confusing orders to be heard.

Every spare space at Parkhurst has been requisitioned and blankets issued so that men without beds can sleep in corridors. Eventually, after every inch of covered space has been deemed full, tents have had to be erected on the parade ground to accommodate the last groups of arrivals.

New rifles, kit bags and ammunition have arrived from as far away as Catterick and Colchester, yet still the armourers and storemen are struggling to get every man fully kitted out.

CSM Billy Carstairs has done his share of shouting; now he is almost hoarse and is relaxing over a bottle of pale ale in the serjeants' mess.

'Where's your lot, Mo?'

'In B Block, Sarje, all tucked up like bugs in a rug.'

Maurice and Harry have managed to get their platoon into proper beds in the attic space of B Block at Parkhurst.

'What sort o' bunch 'ave yer been landed with?'

'All right, the regular boys are corkers, but some of the reservists are a bit dodgy.'

Harry is much more forthright.

'Dodgy! Some of 'em are shittin' themselves. After a few years away from it, odd weekends on Salisbury Plain and exercises in the local drill hall don't make a soldier. Two lads, one of 'em a solicitor's clerk, the other a fuckin' undertaker, tried to report sick. I told 'em to fuck off to bed an' 'ave a wank.'

Billy Carstairs laughs out loud.

'That's your answer for everythin', ain't it, 'Arry?'

'Certainly is, Sarje. You know what they say? "A ham shank a day keeps the medics away"!'

'Well, the one who's an undertaker will come in useful on this little jaunt. We're being issued with a hundred and fifty rounds of ammo, and that's just for starters.'

'Bloody 'ell, that's a lot! Sounds like a proper war.'

'Too right, matey; Major Ashburner's just told me that we're sailin' from Southampton on Thursday, so we start movin' out tomorra afternoon.'

Harry has a mischievous grin on his face.

'How abaht that, Mo? We'll be in France for the weekend. All them little mademoiselles just waitin' to be kissed by an 'ansome English boy. I'll be all right, but I don't know abaht you two ugly bastards!'

'Mademoiselles! You'll 'ave no sap left fer them after you've carried your pack a few miles.'

'I've carried packs across deserts and into the Himalayas, Sarje.'

'Not these, you 'aven't. I reckon they'll weigh nearly seventy pounds when we've finished fillin' 'em; that's not countin' yer rifle and ammo.'

'How far is it to Germany, then?'

'Far enough, 'Arry, far enough. That's if we ever get there.'

'We'll get there if we 'ave to. If we can fettle the Boers, we can fettle the Kaiser.'

'Not sure that's our brief. Ashburner reckons the Germans will roll over the Frogs in weeks. We're just going to hold the Channel ports til Kitchener can build a new army to fight the Germans when they invade.'

'Invade Blighty! They wouldn't 'ave the nerve. But if they did, we'd give 'em a bloody nose, wouldn't we, Mo?'

'If you say so, 'Arry.'

'I just want one of those silly spiked 'elmets they wear.'

'The pickelhaube?'

'Whatever you say, Sarje. I want one to go wiv the leather fedora I nicked off a Boer major at Colenso.'

'Dead, was he, at the time?'

'I should cocoa; shot 'im through the gullet at thirty yards.'

Monday 24 August

As is his wont, Winston is working in bed in his room at the Admiralty. His breakfast tray has been put to one side and he is working through his ministerial box, creating a mess of documents around him, some of which have cascaded on to the floor. He is dressed in his monogrammed pyjamas and red velvet dressing gown and is halfway through his first cigar of the day. It is just turned 7 a.m.

The bedroom door opens with a flurry. There is no knock, just the sudden looming presence of Britain's Minister for War, Herbert Horatio Kitchener.

Both he and Winston have spent a restless night. They knew yesterday evening, following some skirmishes involving British cavalry patrols, during which the first British shots of the war were fired, that the British Expeditionary Force had encountered the German Army. But, at 11 p.m., there had been no news.

The general situation in Belgium had become grave. Liège had fallen on 16 August and General Alexander von Kluck, Commander of Germany's 1st Army, arrogant and fiercely determined, had continued to sweep through Belgium in pursuit of the German grand plan to march through their neutral neighbour, encircle Paris from the north and defeat the French in just forty-two days.

With the British Expeditionary Force safely across the Channel, and with at least a majority of men as prepared as they could be, Sir John French, Commander of the BEF, chose his ground. With reports coming in from Royal Flying

Corps reconnaissance flights that huge numbers of German troops were on the move, John French chose a defensive position around Mons, the centre of the Belgian coal-mining region.

The Mons–Condé Canal offered a modest defensive line, but it was little more than six feet deep and twenty-five feet wide – hardly a major obstacle.

'Bad news, Winston.'

Kitchener hands over a telegram from French, which Winston reads with a perceptible tremor in his hand.

> My troops have been engaged all day with the enemy on a line roughly east and west through Mons. The attack was renewed after dark, but we held our ground tenaciously. I have just received a message from GOC 5th French Army that his troops have been driven back, that Namur has fallen and that he is taking up a line from Maubeuge to Rocroi. I have therefore ordered our retirement to the line Valenciennes–Longueville–Maubeuge, which is being carried out now. It will prove a difficult operation if the enemy remains in contact. I think that immediate attention should be directed to the defence of Le Havre.

Winston hands the telegram back to Kitchener. All the colour has drained from his pink cheeks.

'Bloody hell! Namur, that's the pivot; they've got us on the run.'

Kitchener is not only bereft, he is furious.

'I fear French has got the wind up; you know how excitable he is.'

'What are you going to do?'

'Well, I'm off to see the PM and give him the grim news. Then I'm off to Dover. I'm sailing this afternoon; I've got to keep French squared up.'

'Could you replace him?'

'I'd love to, but he's a bloody field marshal; I can't fire him on the first day of the war.'

'Go easy on the Old Block, he'll be mortified.'

'I will. But do you think Asquith is strong enough for what's hurtling towards us?'

'There's no doubting his acumen; it's his staying power that could be an issue. He's tired.'

As Kitchener goes to Downing Street to see the Prime Minister, Winston gets dressed and walks across Horse Guards to the Treasury. He is unnerved. His knowledge of Britain's military history is second to none and, as he crosses the great parade ground of the King's Household Division, he thinks back. This is a moment unparalleled since Elizabethan times, when his beloved land faced the Armada of Philip II of Spain, and reminiscent of the Napoleonic Wars when the formidable army of Republican France threatened to subject 800 years of British history to the whim of a military demi-god.

When Winston finds his quarry, he is surrounded by Treasury and Bank of England officials, junior ministers, industrialists and men from the city and leading banks. It is still early, just turned nine thirty, but the group of worthy men are unshaven and a little bedraggled. Remnants of breakfast are strewn on tables and chairs. They have been working all night. At the centre of the group is a diminutive Welshman, Winston's friend and political ally, David Lloyd George, Chancellor of the Exchequer.

Winston catches his eye and beckons him into a small room the size of a broom cupboard.

'What's the matter, Winston?' Lloyd George, speaking with the lilting vowels of his Welsh homeland, grabs Winston's arm and remarks, 'Winny, this is where we keep the tea and biscuits.'

Like a conspiratorial schoolboy, Winston whispers earnestly.

'It's grave news from France. The Germans have broken through and we are, as French's telegram puts it, "retiring". Namur has fallen, which is the worst news of all.'

'Fuck! And the French?'

'Fighting bravely, as always, singing the "Marseillaise" as they go. But they're outnumbered, out-gunned and dying in droves.'

'And our French?'

'Lord K thinks he's wobbling.'

'Well, he'd better get out there and straighten the bugger out.'

'He's on his way.'

'Does the PM know?'

'He will by now.'

'I'd better go and see him; he'll need a bit of a lift. And before those buggers in the Cabinet try to convince him to bring our boys home.'

'Listen, David, French is warning Kitchener about a possible evacuation from Le Havre.'

'Already! We've only been fighting for a couple of days.'

'I know, it sounds grim indeed. I will send a note to the fleet this morning telling them to be aware of an impending operation in the Channel. But, if there has to be a withdrawal, I would feel better about it being from the Cotentin – probably Cherbourg, or even St Nazaire.'

'That's a bloody long way to walk.'

'Better a long walk than be stuck on the end of a Prussian bayonet.'

'Well, thank God we've still got you and the navy, Winston.'

'Thank you. You know, this is going to be a rough ride.'

'Well, let's make sure we come through it.'

'How are things here?'

'It's been a buggers' muddle. The City boys are running around like blue-arsed flies, bankruptcies everywhere, money flying across the Atlantic. Everyone wants gold; there are runs on the banks everywhere. But we're on top of it; we'll be fine. The country is coming together behind our soldiers and sailors. They must be our priority. They built our Empire, now we must help them defend it.'

'David, you are an inspiration! Thank you.'

'You go off and make sure your dreadnoughts are facing the right way, and I'll go to see Asquith. He's a good old boy, but he'll need a couple of malts before lunch.'

Winston feels invigorated by Lloyd George's resolute manner and is reassured that, should Asquith falter, the Welsh Wizard would be an ideal replacement. He returns to Admiralty House to dictate a telegram to the fleet. It reads:

Personal. News from France is disappointing and serious results of battle cannot be measured, as fighting still continues over an enormous front.

We have not entered the business without the resolve to see it through and you may be assured that our action will be proportional to the gravity of the need.

I have absolute confidence in the final result.

No special action is required from you at present, but you should address your mind to a naval situation which may arise where Germans control Calais and French coasts and what ought to be the position of the Grand Fleet in that event.

Winston then goes to his room to write to Clemmie, something he has failed to do for almost a fortnight.

My Dear One,

Humblest apologies to you and the kittens for the silence, but you have never been far from my thoughts despite the traumas of recent days. It is a tonic just to write to you, and it is my second fillip of the day. I've just left DLG. He picked me up by the lapels. He was so full of vigour and strength, just like his Mansion House speech when he took on the Tories over Agadir. I sang as I walked through the Downing Street Tunnel and skipped across Horse Guards like a schoolboy.

The news is not the best from France. The BEF has had a bloody nose at Mons and are in retreat. No hard facts yet, but French is pulling them back. We may face some difficult days ahead.

I want you to come home soon. Summer is nearly over and kitten number 3 an impending joy. Close up the cottage and come home to your ever loving husband. The marines will help, and I will make arrangements for transport. Tell Jack the news so that the Jagoons can come home with you.

Tender love, dearest.
Your ever loving,
W

Bougnie, West Flanders, Belgium

Sunday 23 August 1914 had become one of those days, like so many that summer, when history moves forward, not with a measured step, but with an abrupt lurch.

On the morning of that day, at Obourg, north-east of Mons, men of A Company, 4th Battalion, Middlesex Regiment saw the massed ranks of German field-grey uniforms for the first time. The West London boys, the 'Die Hards' of the Peninsular War, opened fire. Their commanding officer, forty-year-old Major William Abell from Worcestershire, died instantly from a bullet through the head, the first named British casualty of the Great War.

So unexpected was the coming together of the two armies – 36,000 men of the BEF and many more on the German side – that in the villages around Mons the local

Belgian civilians were on their way to church, in their Sunday suits and feathered hats, when the firing started.

Church bells suddenly stopped ringing. The gentle sound of worshippers' footsteps on dirt and gravel became the grating noise of people running in panic. Women and children screamed in anguish; men shouted instructions, trying to keep control. A quiet Sunday in an inconspicuous corner of rural Belgium had become the first great battleground of the war.

It was said that an angel appeared that day, forbidding the Germans to go any further, the 'Angel of Mons'. If only it were true. The reality was a long August day of brutal killing. At the end of it, the BEF had suffered 1,600 casualties, while German losses may have been as high as 5,000. The 4th Middlesex lost 15 officers and 353 men.

The Belgians to the north of the BEF fell back, as did the French to the south. The Germans were there in too great a number; the position was untenable and Sir John French ordered a retreat. Chaos ensued. The British Army was not used to retreating.

Hamish Stewart-Murray has, so far, missed the anguish of the Battle of Mons. He arrived from Le Havre on 14 August and, after being fêted by the French population at every turn along their route south, his company, C Company, the Queen's Own Cameron Highlanders, was immediately attached to Headquarters, 1st Army. He was designated as escort to General Douglas Haig, Commander of the 1st Corps, and billeted at Haig's HQ at Bougnie, six miles south of Mons. As a result, he has only heard the thunder of distant artillery and seen the glow in the sky from burning buildings.

However, since dawn this morning, a constant stream of wounded, exhausted and disorientated men have been traipsing into Bougnie from the direction of Mons. General Haig has been hurried away, out of danger, to the west. Hamish has been ordered to take a platoon in the direction of the walking wounded, to Bavay, a reasonably sized town across the French border, fifteen miles to the south-west, to see what he can do to help inject some discipline into the retreat. It takes him most of the day to get there. The roads are full of bedraggled groups of men moving in the same direction, all devastated by fatigue, many in need of medical care.

The local Belgian and French citizens are doing what they can to help, but many of them are also in the process of fleeing from what they fear is a host of bloodthirsty Huns about to descend on them.

When Hamish gets to Bavay, he is confronted by a scene of utter chaos. The exception is the contingent of 200 or so men from the 4th Battalion, Middlesex Regiment, who are in excellent order despite having lost all their officers. They are commanded by the impressive presence of their company serjeant major, who has marched them into the centre of the town as if they are on the parade ground and ordered them to clean their rifles and kit. As for the rest, the elite of the British Army, they look like they have been campaigning for a year. Most can walk no further and are lying around in various states of distress.

Hamish asks the Middlesex's CSM to get his men to organize a muster point outside Bavay's *hôtel de ville* and to begin a roll call.

'Your name, Serjeant?'

'CSM Brown, sir.'

'Major Stewart-Murray, Mr Brown, very well done.'

'Thank you, sir.'

'Your officers?'

'Gone, sir. They were together, lookin' at a map. Direct hit by a big 'un. Thankfully, they didn't know what hit 'em.'

'I don't suppose there are any ambulances around or any Medical Corps chaps?'

'No medics, sir. There's a group of vets a mile or so back, but they've got 'undreds of 'orses to deal with. One of my corporals said that there are some Queen Alex's nurses in a school over there.'

'Very good, Mr Brown, carry on. But don't take your men off without liaising with me. I'm sure I'll need you during the day.'

'Very good, sir.'

CSM Brown snaps a salute before marching off. Hamish watches him go, hugely relieved that men like him are at the heart of the BEF. He has heard a story that the Kaiser said that he is going to crush Britain's 'contemptible little army'. It seems that, although the British Army is relatively small, it is full of men of outstanding calibre like CSM Brown and that the Kaiser will underestimate them at his peril.

Hamish takes his platoon over to the school, where he finds several dozen men lying on stretchers in the playground. In the middle of them, trying to cope, are two nurses and a sister from Queen Alexandra's Imperial Military Nursing Service. There are also several local French people offering help, bringing soup and water and even wine and brandy.

The nurses' once immaculately starched white aprons and pale grey dresses are covered in blood and more closely resemble the uniforms of slaughtermen than the garb of nurses.

'Sister, can we help?'

A woman of no more than twenty-five turns sharply. Her hair has begun to fall from its tight bun and strands of it are matted to her face by perspiration.

'Yes please, sir.'

'My men will start taking the wounded into the school, so that you can start doing dressings.'

'That's helpful, sir, but I'm afraid we don't have any bandages left.'

Hamish immediately calls over his NCO.

'Serjeant, take six men, see if you can find some transport

and go around Bavay. Requisition all the sheets from any hotel or boarding house you can find. Don't brook any argument' – he pulls out a handful of pound notes and gives them to the serjeant – 'and give them one of these for their trouble. Now, do you need anything else, Sister?'

'A case of morphine, an operating table and a surgeon . . . sir.'

Hamish just smiles at the sister's sarcasm.

'Don't you have anything for pain?'

'I have a little morphine, but very little else. Perhaps some blankets would help – and any food your serjeant can find.'

'What happened to your medical officer?'

'He's gone up to see where the men are coming from, taking his ambulance, his orderlies and half my nurses –'

'Well, we'll help you as much as we can.'

'Thank you, sir. By the way, your general, Haig, came through earlier. He's got terrible diarrhoea.'

'Has he, by Jove. That will teach him to eat oysters in the middle of a war!'

The sister smiles for the first time.

'May I know your name, Sister?'

'Of course, sir. Margaret Killingbeck.'

As always when Hamish sees a woman worth pursuing, he does not think twice, even amidst the carnage around him.

'Interesting name.'

'Yorkshire Dales, sir.'

'Well, I'm Hamish Stewart-Murray. My batman has a couple of bottles of claret in his knapsack. Would you like to have a glass or two this evening?'

Not surprisingly, the sister looks disconcerted at the suggestion and glances at the sea of stretchers around her.

'That's very kind, Major, but don't you think I might be a little busy this evening? Perhaps some other time.'

Hamish, suitably chastened that he has had to be reminded of the dire circumstances which surround them, smiles meekly, then rolls up his sleeves and begins to help get the wounded inside the school. He talks to each one with genuine concern, especially a young Gordon Highlander whose dark green kilt is dripping with blood from an abdominal wound.

'Where are the rest of your platoon?'

'I dunno, sir. Our officer got shot by the canal, then we lost both our serjeants when we had to pull back. A lot of men went down around me. When I got hit, I fell into a ditch an' lay still until the Germans passed.'

'How did you get here?'

'Walked, sir.'

'With a bullet in you?'

'Aye, but it's gone right through, sir – just on me side, beneath me ribs – I dinna think it hit anythin' important.'

Hamish can't help smiling.

'You've done well, soldier. What's your name?'

'Hamish, sir, frae Aberdeen.'

'That's a good name to have. Let's see if we can get you patched up.'

The lad's mood suddenly changes. He has lost a lot of blood and is exhausted. He starts to talk animatedly.

'It went well at first, sir. It was like shootin' practice on the range. They came in massed ranks, like toy soldiers, shoulder to shoulder; we couldna miss. A squadron of their cavalry tried to come over the bridge, but they went down like ninepins; horses and men fell into the canal. It was a terrible sight, sir.' The young man grabs Hamish's hand and starts to shake it violently. 'But they kept comin', sir, thousands of 'em. We couldna hold 'em any longer.'

One of the nurses takes the young Highlander away; he is still talking excitedly.

All the men have similar stories. Thousands of German soldiers, their field-grey uniforms making clear targets in the green fields of summer, came through the trees in close order, only a few hundred yards from the British line. Then they fell like fairground ducks, easy targets for the extremely accurate fire of the British infantryman. But the defenders were outnumbered by at least three or four to one in many areas, and the German superiority in numbers eventually made the difference.

Hamish is keen to find out what has become of the Black Watch and, specifically, his brother Geordie. To his relief, he hears that his brother's regiment is still in reserve and was not involved in the fighting at Mons.

Inchy, Nord-Pas-de-Calais, France

By the evening of Monday 24 August, the 4th Battalion Royal Fusiliers have reached Inchy, a French village over fifty miles from Mons. They are exhausted and have suffered heavy casualties. Mons has cost them five officers and over 150 men. Six more officers and over 100 men are wounded.

Maurice and Harry are unscathed. They saw many Germans in their rifle sights and shot too many to count but, other than some artillery shells that landed close to them, they were never under threat. They are now waiting to be addressed by Major George Ashburner. When Ashburner appears among the fusiliers, they are resting on the platform of Inchy railway station and, despite their desperate weariness, they immediately spring to attention.

On Ashburner's nod, CSM Billy Carstairs orders the company to stand at ease. Both Ashburner and Carstairs are well turned out, their uniforms tidy, their faces shaved; but it is obvious they have been in the thick of it. Ashburner manages a broad smile.

'Gentlemen, I am a proud man this evening. You have acquitted yourselves with great distinction today. Even though we are withdrawing, it is against overwhelming odds and there is no shame in that. Our information is that C and D Companies faced two whole battalions of Germans on Sunday and we gave them a lesson in British marksmanship. So, a proud day for the Royal Fusiliers.'

Ashburner bows his head and looks at the list in his hand of known C Company casualties.

'But it is not without significant cost, and we mourn the loss of many brave colleagues today. I will give Mr Carstairs the list, which he will post whenever he can find somewhere appropriate. Men, you are tired and need rest, but I have one particular story to tell you. It is a sad tale, but one of extraordinary heroism that illustrates who we are and what we do. It occurred at the Nimy railway bridge, where our young Irish Lieutenant Maurice Dease commanded our machine-gun section. The section came under extremely heavy fire and several men were killed or injured and had to be replaced. Their position was very cramped and Lieutenant Dease was wounded twice, but he continued to help his section keep firing.'

Ashburner looks down; the men close to him can see that their commanding officer has tears in his eyes.

'Both our machine guns had, by now, jammed, but Private Sid Godley rushed forward, cleared one of the guns and resumed firing. While his comrades made their escape, Private Godley continued firing for almost two hours until he ran out of ammunition. Witnesses think that he was hit during this time.'

By now, there are many fusiliers, even the most battle-hardened, with lumps in their throats.

'Even so, he began to dismantle his gun and throw its parts into the canal. As far as we know, Lieutenant Dease died during this action and we saw his body being removed by the Germans. As for Private Godley, he was also taken away, but all who witnessed it say he was alive at the time. Let us hope that they are merciful to him.'

Ashburner nods at CSM Carstairs once more, who bellows at the men, '*Attention!*'

Ashburner takes a deep breath.

'Let us bow our heads and remember our brother soldiers who have fallen at Mons.'

After a full minute of silence, a voice from the back of the company begins to sing the famous soldiers' song from the Boer War, which is soon taken up by the entire company, including all the officers.

I have come to say goodbye, Dolly Gray,
It's no use to ask me why, Dolly Gray,
There's a murmur in the air, you can hear it everywhere,
It's the time to do and dare, Dolly Gray.

So if you hear the sound of feet, Dolly Gray,
Sounding through the village street, Dolly Gray,
It's the tramp of soldiers true in their uniforms so blue,
I must say goodbye to you, Dolly Gray.

Goodbye, Dolly, I must leave you, though it breaks
   my heart to go,
Something tells me I am needed at the front to fight the foe,
See, the boys in blue are marching and I can no longer stay,
Hark, I hear the bugle calling, goodbye Dolly Gray . . .

Maurice and Harry sing as loudly as the rest. Boer War veterans themselves, it brings back fond memories, but also puts the events of the last few days into perspective.

'This ain't South Africa, is it, Mo?'

'No, it ain't. Bloody 'undreds of 'em and they kept comin', no matter how much of a pastin' we was givin' 'em.'

'This war could get nasty.'

'Not 'alf; it's already 'airy enough!'

'I'm knackered and I reckon we'll be on the move agin soon. Ashburner will want more distance between us and the Hun than this.'

Harry is right; after only four hours' sleep, they are on the move again. The weather is not kind. After days of stiflingly hot August weather, the heavens open and the temperature drops dramatically.

'Bloody 'ell! I'm fuckin' freezin', 'Arry.'

'Too right, mate, it's brass monkeys. Where do yer reckon we're off to?'

'I 'aven't a clue! But we'll know when we get there.'

They march until three thirty, and the first hint of dawn, on Tuesday 25 August. Maurice can see the French road sign in the early light. It reads 'Le Cateau'.

'Let's 'ope it's got a boozer.'

'A bath would do me. I'm beginning to feel lousey.'

'You're not kiddin', you whiff like a fuckin' badger.'

Bavay, Nord-Pas-de-Calais, France

By the late evening of Monday 24 August Hamish Stewart-Murray has managed to get all the fit and able British troops out of Bavay. Of the wounded, most have been evacuated, leaving only those too badly injured to be moved. There are just three requisitioned transport buses waiting to make the final withdrawal. But the lead troops of the German advance are thought to be making camp only two miles down the road.

Sister Killingbeck and her two Queen Alexandra's nurses are still treating the casualties. She wants to stay with them until the Germans arrive; Hamish is insisting that she leave on one of the final transports.

'You must come with us, Margaret; we need you on our side of the line. There will be lots more men to treat before this is over.'

'But what about these men? They are my responsibility.'

'The Germans have got excellent medical facilities, they

will be well taken care of. I want you on the final transport. If you want me to make it an order, I will.'

'Very well, Hamish, if you insist. But first I need your help with something. I've been looking after a badly injured Welch Fusilier captain; he is still conscious, but not very coherent. When he's cogent, he asks for a senior officer.'

'How's he doing?'

'It's astonishing he's still alive; he's a very strong man, but he won't survive the night. He's got two bullets in his chest and one in the right leg. He's bleeding internally.'

'Is there nothing you can do?'

'He needs surgery, but we can't move him.'

'Should I see him?'

'It would be kind.'

'What's his name?'

'Captain Philip Davies. He was taking a message from his battalion, took a wrong turn and rode straight into a German patrol. He survived for five hours in a ditch, then dragged himself two hundred yards to a crossroads, where he was found by the Middlesex boys.'

'Is he in pain?'

'Yes, rather a lot. I've no more morphine to give him.'

Hamish does not relish his task. There has been no sign of a chaplain since he arrived in Bavay and he fears the dying man wants to make a confession, or at least be comforted in his death throes.

The captain has been put in a small office in the school, where he can die in peace. The room is dark, but as Hamish enters he can hear the death rattle in the man's breathing very distinctly.

'Captain Davies, Hamish Stewart-Murray.'

The stricken man stirs slightly and blinks rapidly, as if trying to clear his head.

'Good evening . . . I can't see your pips?'

'Major.'

'Good evening, sir. Do you mind coming closer? I can't really turn my head to see you.'

'Of course.'

'Where are you from, sir?'

'Please call me Hamish. I'm from Blair Atholl, Perthshire.'

'Stewart-Murray, Blair Atholl . . . then your father must be the Duke of Atholl?'

'He is, indeed. Do you know him?'

'Yes, slightly, I sold him a few things last year; I'm an auctioneer and dealer in Civvy Street —'

Philip suddenly winces with pain and begins to cough blood. Hamish desperately summons help.

'*Sister!*'

Sister Killingbeck rushes into the room. She knows what to do instantly.

'Let's lift him.'

The two of them lift the dying man's shoulders, and his throat clears. But the sister knows from experience that it won't be long.

'I'll have to stay, Captain. I need to keep your throat clear.'

Philip stares at Margaret plaintively and grabs her hand.

'This is a terrible question to ask, but are you a woman of the world, Sister?'

'I think I probably am, Captain.'

'Then I must ask you to forgive me. If you are going to stay, you will have to be privy to what I want to ask of Major Stewart-Murray. I don't have much time.'

'We have to keep you upright, but I doubt I'll be shocked by anything I hear. And nothing you say in this room will go any further.'

'That's reassuring, Sister, but my request actually involves something that must leave this room.'

He turns to Hamish.

'Hamish, will you do a huge favour for a complete stranger?'

'Of course, old boy.'

'HQ will have my details, but I'm from Presteigne in Radnorshire. When you're next on leave, would you deal with a matter of some delicacy? It is an awful imposition, but my circumstances leave me little choice, and I don't want an entirely innocent party to suffer.'

Hamish looks at Margaret; both can guess the gist of Philip's dilemma.

'There is a girl, Bronwyn Thomas, she is very young, engaged to a fine young man in the town. My wife is not very well and couldn't cope with the house. Bronwyn, a farmer's daughter, a lovely girl, came in to do some cleaning for me' – he squeezes Sister Margaret's hand – 'oh dear, this is so embarrassing . . .'

Both Margaret and Hamish smile at Philip, wanting to reassure him.

'Listen, old chap, don't worry, I have the morals of an alley cat. And although I'm sure Sister Killingbeck's are impeccable, listening to men's infidelities comes with her job.'

Margaret smiles warmly and nods her head.

After a brief moment, Philip appears to lose consciousness and Margaret shakes her head; she fears he has gone. But Philip suddenly opens his eyes, his face twisted in pain.

'There's a key . . . in my knapsack . . . It is to a safety-deposit box at the Midland Bank . . . in Ludlow . . . Whatever is in there should go to Bronwyn . . . some silver and jewellery, it should make a fair bit . . . There's also . . . a letter . . .'

His words falter and, at last, he goes limp in their arms.

Hamish helps lay Philip down before rummaging through his knapsack, where he quickly finds the key and the letter tucked into one of its side pockets. He turns to Margaret, who has tears in her eyes. She looks at Hamish for the first time without the ascetic look of a professional nurse who has seen it all before.

'What tangled webs we weave.'

'I'm afraid many of us are weak when it comes to life's temptations; I know I am.'

'Will you do as he asked?'

'Of course.'

Both Margaret and Hamish think that Philip has died, but he suddenly squeezes Margaret's hand. She leans towards him to hear what he is trying to say. His voice is barely audible and beyond Hamish's hearing.

'What did he say?'

Margaret's tears are now flowing down her cheeks. She pauses, trying to compose herself. Eventually, she takes a deep breath.

'He said to tell Bronwyn that she made him very happy. And that she should take wing and fly.'

Margaret feels for a pulse. There is nothing. She covers Philip with his bed sheet.

'I don't normally cry. I have lost eleven men here today, but this is so sad. To experience all that mental torment on top of his pain. And that poor girl, just a cleaning maid. When you go to see Bronwyn, may I come with you?'

'I would be greatly relieved if you would.'

Tuesday 25 August

Contrary to the wishes of Sir John French, Commander-in-Chief of the BEF, a momentous decision has been taken by General Horace Smith-Dorrien, Commander of the British II Corps. A courageous veteran of the Boer War and the Battle of Omdurman, he was one of only a handful of men to escape the slaughter of the Battle of Isandlwana against the Zulus in 1879.

Realizing that his exhausted men will soon be overrun by the rapidly advancing Germans, he has decided to make a fight of it. He has 40,000 British and French troops at his disposal and hopes that a courageous stand will derail the German momentum and grant Douglas Haig's I Corp, and the bulk of the French 5th Army, time to regroup.

Maurice and Harry are dug into a light trench on the western side of the Cambrai–Le Cateau road. They are not with the 4th Fusiliers, who are stationed behind the line in reserve, near Troisvilles. Maurice and Harry and eight of their platoon have been sent forward with a consignment of ammunition to replenish the supplies of the 1st Battalion Lincolnshire Regiment. Like the entire BEF, the Lincolnshire men are exhausted. They have marched all night and, after being given bread and tea in the village of Inchy, have taken up a position ready for an imminent German attack. As the onslaught is expected at any moment, the Lincolnshire's CO has told Maurice, Harry and their men to choose their ground and join the defensive line.

French civilians – men, women and children, the few locals who have not fled eastwards – are still to be seen. They have been helping dig trenches and readily sharing whatever food they have left.

Unlike Mons, where the British position looked across an urban canal to factories, pitheads and slag heaps – not unlike the coalfields of Wales or the North of England – Maurice and Harry are now looking out over rolling green fields reminiscent of the Home Counties. In the few minutes' lull before the inevitable storm, the mist of dawn is clearing and birdsong is in the air.

It is unlikely that many of the British defenders realize it – and the French certainly do not – but it is the anniversary of the Battle of Crécy, in 1346, a battlefield not a million miles away, when English archers shot twelve arrows per minute to destroy the army of the French King, Philip VI. If, today, the British infantry can fire their Lee-Enfield rifles at fifteen rounds per minute, as they did at Mons, it could have the same effect on Alexander von Kluck's 1st German Army.

On the stroke of 6 a.m., a huge German artillery barrage destroys the early morning serenity. The deafening noise scatters the French civilians far and wide and wakes all but the most stubborn of the Lincolnshires, asleep with their chins on their rifles. A few are so tired that, despite the roar, they have to be shaken like rag dolls to rouse them from their slumber. The Germans have learned an important lesson from Mons. Before their infantry attacks en masse, they are going to intimidate the British marksmen and decimate their ranks in preparation for a frontal attack. The bombardment is relentless.

'Fuck me, 'Arry! 'Ow many howitzers 'ave they got?'

'More than us, that's for sure.'

The British guns are brought closer to try to knock out some of the German artillery, but they are vastly outnumbered. After about two hours, during which Maurice and Harry can also hear heavy infantry battles to their right, a German shell explodes only yards from them.

'Stretcher-bearers! Stretcher-bearers!'

The same cry goes up from several men at once as clods of earth and human flesh land like heavy spots of rain at the beginning of a storm. Some men are crimson with the blood of obliterated colleagues.

'*Stretcher-bearers!*' One of the cries becomes increasingly hysterical. It issues from the throat of someone in the fusiliers' platoon, one of Harry's men.

'What the fuck is wrong with 'im?'

'I think 'e's gawn marbles and conkers, 'Arry.'

'Fuck! I'll 'ave to go and sort 'im; come wiv me, Mo.'

The two veterans make their way along the line towards their panic-stricken comrade, who is screaming uncontrollably and being held down by the two men on either side of him. Harry is livid.

'It's that tosser from 'Ackney. I'll lamp 'im when I get over there.'

As he makes his remark, the rat-a-tat-tat of German machine guns suddenly begins. Many voices shout that field-grey German uniforms can be seen in the meadows on the other side of the road. Harry and Maurice's focus is no longer on their distressed fusilier.

'Look to your fronts, lads; here they come! Let's give 'em an old "mad minute"!'

While German machine-gunners to the left and right keep up murderous fire, their infantry advances across open ground. They are in more open order than they were at Mons, making them more difficult targets. Nevertheless, they still suffer significant casualties, but they do not falter. They just keep coming on like a grey tide crested by spiked beige helmets. Almost one helmet in three falls to the ground as its wearer is hit by a British bullet. On the British side, the number of men hit by the German machine guns is fewer, but their loss is depleting a much smaller number of men.

Harry looks over to where the hysterical soldier was acting up. His minders, now too busy to give him any attention, have left him and he is sitting behind a tree, head in hands, rocking from side to side.

'Look at 'im, Mo! I'm gonna shoot that twat when this is over.'

Almost before he has finished speaking, fusilier John Savage, aged thirty-one, from Hackney, reserve soldier and tailor at Henry Poole on Savile Row, has jumped out on to the main road with his hands held high in surrender. One of his comrades tries to pull him back, to no avail. Savage starts to walk towards the advancing Germans.

The intensity of the machine-gun fire is so great, he only takes a few strides before he is shot, not once, but several times. He staggers backwards with the multiple impacts. Two bloody holes appear in the rear of his tunic, made by bullets that have travelled straight through him. His arms fall to his side, then he stumbles forward, appearing oblivious to the pain he must be feeling.

Another bullet penetrates his skull. A German Army standard-issue Gewehr 98 Mauser bullet is half an inch wide and makes a terrible mess of a man. The one that strikes the young fusilier creates a deceptively small, neat entry hole just above his left eye, but the back of his head explodes as the missile exits. He falls to the ground in a twisted heap. Now the pain has gone; he will never feel anything again.

Harry looks at his men and the Lincolnshire lads around them to assess the impact of the incident. To his relief, it has made them angry and, after a moment of reflection, they renew their accurate fire into the ranks of the German infantry. The fight goes on for most of the morning; the number of dead and wounded rises relentlessly. The stretcher-bearers are exhausted, unable to cope.

The advancing Germans take cover on the other side of the road, only making occasional forays forwards.

'How many rounds 'ave yer got off, Mo?'

'Lost count, but enough fuckin' lead to cover a church roof.'

'My barrel's as hot as a poker. I'd like to ram it up the arse'ole of that Hun machine-gunner over there. I've been tryin' to plug 'im for twenty minutes, but I can't getta bead on 'im.'

A minute or so later, Harry exclaims and throws his cap in the air.

'Got the cunt! What a fuckin' shot; took 'is fuckin' pickle helmet right orf. It must be six hundred yards.'

Maurice is impressed. He retrieves Harry's cap and throws it at him.

'Put it back on, yer daft bugger. I'll give you four hundred yards, no more. But not a bad shot, I'll grant yer that.'

Artillery shells are still falling all around them, sending huge tremors through the ground. Most men are covered in soil or the blood of their comrades. The German machine guns are relentless, as is the rifle fire from their infantry. The enemy is finding secure positions from which to fire, producing a stalemate. The continuous noise is overwhelming, making most men feel disorientated.

Bullets make many different noises when they hit home. Some 'ping' when they strike stone or metal, others 'thud' into soft ground, but when they hit men they produce more sickening sounds: the 'splash' of hot metal tearing into flesh, the 'spray' of blood that the impact produces and, finally, the tormented scream of the victim.

To live through the sights and sounds of war is to become what is called 'battle-hardened'. Some men survive the experience, some men are devastated by it, but no one is ever the same again.

The British and French line at Le Cateau is over ten miles long and is being breached in places, especially where it is receiving machine-gun fire from its flanks.

By two o'clock in the afternoon, Harry and Maurice can see that several sections of the British line are in retreat. Of the eight men they brought, in addition to the stricken John Savage, two more men have been killed and two have been wounded.

Word is passed along the line: 'A tactical withdrawal in fifteen minutes.'

'So we're orf, 'Arry.'

'Scarperin' again. I thought the British Army didn't do that kinda thing; certainly not twice in three days!'

'I think we might 'ave to get used to it. We could be doin' it all the way to the fuckin' Channel at this rate.'

Although the British position is crumbling, Smith-Dorrien's decision to stand and fight at Le Cateau proves to be a masterstroke. Having seen him hold his ground, and after witnessing the quality of British musketry, the German High Command hesitates, giving the BEF a vital few days of grace to regroup and allowing the French to organize courageous counter-attacks. For the 4th Battalion Royal Fusiliers, it means many more hours of marching, but they have bought themselves some valuable breathing space.

The initial casualty figures from France are a shock to the nation. Large numbers of war dead have not been a familiar phenomenon for the British people in modern times. During the two and a half years of the Boer War, some twelve years earlier, Britain suffered almost 21,000 men killed, missing or dead from disease. So far, in just three days of fighting in France and Belgium, more than 1,600 have been killed at Mons, 5,000 at Le Cateau and another 500 in peripheral fighting. Another 2,500 men have been taken prisoner.

The Times's report of the events is sobering: 'The battle is joined and has so far gone ill for the Allies. Yesterday was a day of bad news and we fear more must follow.' Although British numbers are significantly smaller than French and German figures, they create alarm at home, but also indignation, which strengthens the mood of patriotism, swelling yet more the numbers of those flocking to army recruiting stations.

PART FOUR: SEPTEMBER

Your King and Country Need You

Tuesday 1 September

Winston and Lord Kitchener are having a private dinner in the War Office. Kitchener has ordered food from the ministry's excellent kitchen and Winston has brought some claret from his stock at the Admiralty, plus an almost full bottle of Hine, his favourite cognac. The First Lord's contribution to the feast reminds Kitchener of one of Winston's increasingly well-known sayings, his four 'Essentials of Life': hot baths, cold champagne, new peas and old brandy.

Winston is keen to hear more about a message that has arrived from Sir John French, outlining his decision to pull the BEF back to the west of Paris and thus leaving it to the French to be solely responsible for the defence of their capital city.

'It seems foolhardy in the extreme. What are his reasons?'

Kitchener shakes his head in exasperation.

'He doesn't think he has enough men, armour and supplies – which he hasn't, of course. But he's known that all along. He was sent to make a fist of what he'd got, not to come crying as soon as we suffer a reverse. Thank God, Smith-Dorrien made a stand at Le Cateau, otherwise we would have been completely swamped.'

'What will you do now?'

'The French PM has been on to Asquith; he wants to know where we stand. The PM's adamant, we're holding our ground. So I'm off to Paris first thing for another encounter with our French, which I'm not looking forward to; he's such a cantankerous customer.'

Winston has every sympathy for Kitchener, a fine soldier, but who has been asked to sit in a politician's chair.

'I saw the note from our ambassador in Paris.'

Kitchener shakes his head.

'I know, hundreds of thousands streaming out of the city, and makeshift barricades being built. It doesn't sound too promising.'

'Have another cognac, K.'

'I think I will. I hear the French government is off to Bordeaux tomorrow – no shortage of cognac there, what?'

'Quite, but I like the sound of the new military governor of Paris, General Gallieni. He said yesterday that his orders were to defend Paris and that he would do so until the very end. That's the spirit! Our French comrades need to gird themselves with the spirit of Napoleon's Imperial Guard refusing to surrender at Waterloo.'

'You're such a romantic, Winston, but I agree, a bit of French elan would make all the difference. It's their bloody country, after all. You're fond of them; have they got the stomach for it?'

'I am very fond of them. The Napoleonic *esprit de corps* is still there, and I'm sure they have the bottom. They'll pull through.'

'Our boys don't have a lot of time for them.'

'Yes, but our men are professional soldiers, whereas most of theirs are conscripts – peasants and factory fodder. They're republicans and I'm avowedly a monarchist, but they revere their *liberté, égalité, fraternité*. Now that the very existence of their great republic is at stake, they'll fight.'

'By God, I hope you're right, because tomorrow evening I'll be telling John French to hold his ground. And put in peril the lives of a hundred thousand British troops.'

*

The next morning, as Kitchener makes his way to France, Winston, speaking for both the navy and the army, addresses the Cabinet concerning the latest situation in France and elsewhere.

It has been a difficult meeting. Lloyd George's summary of the current economic situation, although painting a much less gloomy picture than the previous week, has unnerved many members, especially those with domestic portfolios. Unlike most in the Cabinet, Winston gets to his feet, as usual, before speaking, confirming the impression his detractors have of him, that he is a 'dangerous young windbag'.

'Prime Minister, gentlemen, let me address, first of all, the latest news from France as of this morning. We have reached a moment of relative calm. In close liaison with General Lanrezac's 5th Army, the BEF is moving back to regroup and find a stronger defensive position. Significantly, following General Smith-Dorrien's inspired holding action at Le Cateau, Lanrezac struck a major blow three days ago with a ferocious counter-attack, forcing the German 2nd Army to deflect its advance towards Paris. The momentum the Germans have enjoyed for many days has been halted.'

Winston is suddenly interrupted by Reginald McKenna, British Home Secretary.

'Mr Churchill, I am sure you saw the distressing article in the special edition of *The Times* on Sunday, in which Arthur Moore reported on the wretched condition of our men after Mons. He wrote of "broken regiments", "men scattered across swathes of countryside", "battered by marching".

'Now, I am the last person to question a man like yourself, who has such a shrewd grasp of military matters, but if the situation is "calm", as you maintain, why has Sir John French said he wants to pull back the BEF to the west of Paris? And why is he talking about fortifying Le Havre, in order to be able to get our boys home safely . . . ?' McKenna pauses for effect, looking at several Cabinet colleagues as he does so, before continuing smugly, 'Which – dare I say it? – is where they belong.'

Winston tries to hide his annoyance.

'Mr McKenna, forgive me, but this is not the time for scoring debating points. Lord Kitchener is seeing John French tonight to reiterate his position, the Prime Minister's position and my position, which is that, having made a tactical withdrawal, we will now, with our French comrades, make a stand, east of Paris – not to the west – to halt the German onslaught.'

Winston catches the Prime Minister's eye. Asquith nods approvingly.

'I should add some more detail to put the current situation into sharp perspective. The position is extremely grave; it has been from the moment war was declared. Sir John is under great strain, as are we all. The elite of the French officer corps is being cut to ribbons. General Foch, Commander of the French XX Corps, has lost his only son and his son-in-law. French losses are in the tens of thousands. The Germans are within touching distance of Paris; vast columns of people are streaming west, and the government is about to transfer to Bordeaux. On the Eastern Front, news is coming in of a catastrophic defeat for the Russians in East Prussia. Initial reports suggest losses approaching one hundred thousand men, leaving Germany's generals, Ludendorff and Hindenburg, a free run through Poland.'

Winston is in his element. He appears to be making McKenna's case for him, but his voice rises. Asquith smiles to himself; he knows his First Lord of the Admiralty well, and can guess what is coming next.

'But only last Friday, ships of our Grand Fleet gave the Kaiser a black eye off the Heligoland Bight, sending three of his cruisers to the bottom: the *Mainz, Cöln* and *Ariadne*. We know that he has already issued orders for his High Seas Fleet to remain skulking in its harbours until further notice.

Not only that, General Smith-Dorrien's masterstroke has bought us vital time to regroup. Our army in France is but a welterweight, and we have stepped into the ring with a cruiser-weight who has knocked us on to our backside at Mons.'

Winston's voice rises another notch.

'But this is only round one. We have absolutely no intention of throwing in the towel so early in the fight, especially as Lord Kitchener is building a new army, the like of which we have never seen before. It will be a true heavyweight to match our magnificent navy. The last thing we need now is to be casting doubt on our military capabilities – especially not in this room, of all places.'

Undaunted by Winston's eloquence, Charles Hobhouse, Postmaster General, asks Asquith if he may make a comment. The Prime Minister, reluctantly, signals his approval.

'Mr Churchill, I have a little army experience myself, with the 60th Rifles. There are many in military circles who agree with Sir John French and my friend Reggie McKenna that the army should be on the Kent side of the Channel, ready to defend our island, rather than have them spill their blood in a lost cause trying to prop up the soft-bellied French.'

Winston is incensed.

'Prime Minister, forgive me for being blunt, but I must say this to my Cabinet colleague. There is only one "military circle" that makes any difference here and it is scribed by a small but resolute arc containing only the Prime Minister, his Minister for War, Lord Kitchener, and your humble servant, the First Lord of the Admiralty. There is no other "military circle" of any consequence to the war effort. Indeed, ours is a triumvirate, not a circle; it is a triangle of iron will which is unbending, unwavering and untiring.'

Asquith's smile becomes a visible one. Winston's supporters in the Cabinet also smile; some, like Lloyd George, have a hint of moisture in their eyes. The Prime Minister intervenes to sum up.

'Thank you, Mr Churchill. Let me call a halt to this, save to say that the First Lord has expressed very clearly the view of this government. Lord Kitchener is making that view plain to Sir John French today, and I will do the same to the French government later this morning. We must be unified on this. I will not tolerate any public dissent. Differences of opinion must not go beyond this room.

'Now, I have some sobering news to impart. We have received preliminary casualty figures from the first week of the war: over seven thousand dead or missing, and at least two thousand five hundred taken prisoner. These are appalling losses, and telegrams with the dreadful news are arriving in homes across the country as I speak.'

The Prime Minister's head is bowed, staring at the lists of British dead.

'I ask that we hold a few moments of silence in honour of those who have died and that we pray for those who will soon resume the bitter fight.'

After Cabinet, Winston and Lloyd George walk to Pall Mall for lunch at the Reform Club. They are hugely popular figures because of their work together on the National Insurance Act three years earlier, and now because of their support for the war, so they are cheered by everyone who recognizes them and many rush up to shake their hands. Although both men resigned from the Reform Club the year before over the blackballing of a friend, they have been given a wartime dispensation, as the club is so close to Whitehall, to attend for lunch. When they arrive, they receive many more warm handshakes and appreciative gestures before they sit down in the club's splendidly gilded Coffee Room.

'Dazzling this morning, Winston, very impressive, quite brought a tear to my eye!'

'Thank you, David. The "60th Rifles" bit got my goat. He's never picked one up in anger in his life!'

'Neither have I.'

'But you don't make inane comments in Cabinet.'

Lloyd George has a mischievous smile on his face.

'Do you know, Winston, I often wonder about you. Here we are at the home of the Liberal establishment, but are you sure you belong here? Aren't men of your ilk supposed to be at the Carlton with the Tories?'

'I rather think my "ilk" is entirely of my own making but, as you ask so bluntly, let me be candid in response. I think, at heart, I am a Tory. But, for the time being at least, my head is inclining me to Liberality – especially as most of the current Tories are buffoons.'

'Well, I'm delighted to hear it. Let me know if your heart begins to rule your head. I pray it doesn't just yet, because we need you.'

'Very kind of you to say so.'

'Now, about the situation with John French. How will he react to Kitchener laying down the law?'

'Not well – in fact, he'll be livid. They don't get on, as you know, but he regards me as a friend – which I am, of course. He will write to me, begging me to help stop this "political interference", arguing that K should stick to the politics and leave the soldiering to him. But he forgets that the Old Block picked K for the War Office precisely because he's our senior soldier. Believe me, David, if I'd been in the Old Block's shoes, I would have made myself Minister for War and made it absolutely clear to French that he was to do as he was bloody well told!'

'I don't doubt it for a second.'

Lloyd George gulps a mouthful of wine as the two men watch a loin of pork being carved at the table.

'Listen, Winnie, to change the subject to a bit of gossip. Is it true that Kitchener's queer?'

'Well, it's a widely held rumour. He is inseparable from his aide-de-camp, a fine young chap called Captain Fitzgerald, and is surrounded by a group of young officers – what John

French calls "Kitchener's Band of Boys" – but all these tales are only innuendoes. And you should remember that there is a lot of envy directed towards him.'

Lloyd George, his ample moustache now dripping with pork gravy, has a wicked look on his face.

'You spend a lot of time with the old buffer. Has he never asked you to walk round his rose garden, so to speak?'

'Certainly not!' Winston pauses . . . 'Why his rose garden?'

Lloyd George laughs loudly and deliberately exaggerates his Welsh accent.

'Well, you see, it's supposed to be decorated by several pairs of naked bronze boys on marble pedestals; all with lovely pert backsides!'

'Don't, David, we're having pork for lunch!'

Saturday 5 September

Wellington Hotel, Brunshaw Road, Burnley, Lancashire

The Ministry of War has made strong representations to the English and Scottish Football Associations and to the Football Leagues of both countries to request cancellation of the 1914–15 football season. But both associations and both leagues have decided to go ahead with their competitions, despite the outbreak of hostilities.

The Wellington Hotel, the nearest public house to Turf Moor, the home of Burnley Football Club, is packed with fans and there are many more on the pavements outside. It is a warm evening. Unusually, autumn has not yet come to North-East Lancashire.

'The Clarets', their new nickname following their decision to wear claret and blue just four years ago, have started their season today with a shock home defeat to Bradford City, losing by a single goal. Over 11,000 fans – an excellent gate – have turned up, full of expectation that, following victory in the FA Cup in the spring, this will be Burnley's year and will bring the club's first league title.

There is much head-shaking and muttering about the performance. The ominous events in France could not be further away, even though there are posters everywhere asking for volunteers for 'Field Marshal Kitchener's New Army'. Recruitment leaflets were issued before and after the game, but most men are too preoccupied with the loss of two points at the beginning of the season to pay much attention to events a very long way away.

The vast majority of Burnley's fans are poorly educated,

semi-literate weavers and miners. Although most will have had schooling up to the age of twelve or thirteen, many would have been truants or poor performers in the classroom, which typically housed up to forty children. Burnley's weavers and miners have little knowledge of the events of the day, beyond local concerns such as what is in their pay packet, or the price of beer and cigarettes. Nor do they have much sense of deference or respect for the British class system and the privileged elite who sit at its pinnacle. To many, the war in France is not their fight – at least, not yet.

A particularly despondent group sits at a corner table, readily made available by the Wellington's landlord, who knows they will help him sort out any trouble if it should occur later. Not only are they disappointed at the afternoon's result, they are also weighed down by significant personal issues.

Tommy and Mary Broxup have both lost their jobs, as have Mick and Cath Kenny. Vinny Sagar still has his job, but his ambition to become a professional sportsman has been dealt a severe body blow. His pal, Twaites Haythornthwaite, is heartbroken for Vinny but has also suffered a personal calamity of sorts: he is still smarting from yet another female rejection the night before.

Vinny trained with Burnley's trialists last weekend, played in a trial-team friendly against Preston North End on Monday evening and had two more evening training sessions during the week. However, on Friday evening he was called into the office of John Haworth, Burnley's manager, who was with one of the club's directors, Bob Wadge. The presence of Wadge led Vinny to think his moment had arrived, that he was about to be offered a contract as a junior apprentice. Sadly, nothing could have been further from the truth; he was about to hear the fateful words uttered to many an aspiring footballer.

'Listen, Vinny lad, you're a quick 'un and tha can thump a

ball alreet. But tha's not big enough, or strong enough, fer top level. Tha could play at a good amateur level, but not as a pro.'

Vinny almost bursts into tears; the news is devastating.

'Is tha sure, Mr Haworth?'

'Aye, lad; I'm reet sorry.'

Then the reason for Wadge's presence becomes clear as he passes Vinny a small envelope.

'There's a few bob in there, lad. Get tha'sen some beers.'

Vinny has had twenty-four hours to recover from the news, but is still feeling very raw. His state of mind is not helped by a severe hangover induced by the bellyful of ale consumed by Twaites and himself as they made good use of Bob Wadge's silver.

For Tommy and Mary, Mick and Cath, their dilemma is even more traumatic.

Accrington, Burnley's nearest neighbour, six miles to the west, is smaller than Burnley, but almost its Lancastrian twin. It is another cotton town but also famous for its 'Accrington Iron', the world's toughest building brick, used to build the base of Blackpool Tower and other monumental buildings, and for the lining of most of Britain's sewers.

Since the beginning of July, Accrington has been tormented by a bitter industrial dispute that has brought the town to its knees. Howard and Bullough, the borough's leading employer, is the world's largest producer of power looms. Its huge Globe Works sits in the middle of the town like a red-brick colossus; it, too, is built with Accrington Iron.

On 2 July, Howard and Bullough's 600 engineers went on strike. Its management had refused to meet the demands of the Amalgamated Society of Engineers for recognition as a trade union and to consent to its demand for a minimum wage for the company's employees. Six days later, the management locked out the whole workforce of nearly 5,000 men and boys. Although members of the ASE have since received

20 shillings a week lock-out pay, and 1,100 members of the Gasworkers and General Labourers Union have been given 10 shillings a week, some 2,000 non-union workers have been left without any income. Local charities and voluntary collections at mill gates and in pubs and clubs have provided their only means of survival.

After war was declared, Howard and Bullough's management decided to relent and, beginning on Monday 17 August, agreed to open the Globe's gates to those who wanted to go back to work. Many decided to return, but the ASE, which still had not seen its demands met, told its members to stay out.

After work on 17 August, local socialists and political activists flocked to the Globe Works' picket lines. Over 100 Burnley union members travelled in a fleet of buses to show solidarity with their Accrington colleagues. Cath Kenny and Mary Broxup were among them. They had organized their shifts so that they could be there and, as violence of some sort was almost inevitable, had insisted that Mick and Tommy went with them. When non-union engineers emerged from the factory, many drafted in from the Midlands, all hell broke out. Bottles and stones were thrown and, wielding their batons, mounted police charged the crowd.

There were also some in the throng looking for trouble. It was said they were hired thugs brought in by Howard and Bullough to discredit the picketing. Fist fights began everywhere, and Tommy and Mick were soon in the middle of them. After they had both been badly beaten by police truncheons, they were arrested by snatch squads and taken to Accrington Police Station in a Black Maria.

When Cath and Mary went to try to get them released, they were locked up as well. All four spent the night in the cells: Mick and Tommy with dozens of other strikers, most with cracked heads and other injuries; Cath and Mary with Accrington's female drunks, down-and-outs and prostitutes.

Although not charged with a criminal offence, they were not released until lunchtime the next day and thus missed a day's work.

The outcome of the incident was catastrophic for the four of them. North-East Lancashire's local employers closed ranks and all of them lost their jobs. Cath and Mary had become infamous as troublemakers, and their arrests had given their employers the perfect excuse to sack them. In Mick and Tommy's case, they had crossed swords too many times with their foremen and supervisors, who were terrified of them, and the altercation in Accrington had provided an ideal opportunity to settle old scores.

Neither Tommy nor Mick is a union man, so their income has disappeared overnight. Cath and Mary's union have given them three months at half their normal wage, but the union will not offer any other support, nor fight their dismissal. They have few friends in the union hierarchy, most of whom resent women taking what they think are 'men's jobs' and who dislike their avowed support for the suffragettes.

Cath Kenny is now four months pregnant and beginning to show. Her anguish is perhaps the greatest of those at the table, all of whom are in a melancholy mood. But she tries not to talk about the predicament they face and asks the men about the afternoon's game.

'So 'ow did they laik?'

'Like eleven Mary-Annes!'

Mick is blunt, but Tommy is even more vociferous.

'More like watchin' fuckin' blind school laik. That one Bert Freeman missed; I coulda blown it in wi' me cap! The big pillock!'

'I thought he were a good 'un.'

'Aye, he usually is, Cath, he's played centre for'ard fer England; but he laiked like a reet barm cake today.'

Mary is oblivious to the banter about Burnley. She is trying to read various pamphlets and papers on her lap, a task not made easy by the constant jostle of men passing with mugs of ale in their hands. The heavy haze of tobacco smoke and the rising volume of animated male voices does not help much either.

While the men were at Turf Moor, she and Cath were at the Burnley headquarters of the British Socialist Party. The party is in turmoil, both locally and nationally, split asunder by arguments about the ethics of the war effort. Its leader, Henry Hyndman, who Cath and Mary both revere, has spoken out in favour of supporting Britain's cause. The news has shocked the majority of grass-roots members. Most not only see the war as a fight between ruling aristocracies, in which working-class people are no better than cannon fodder, but are also instinctively pacifists and reject all forms of violence.

For Cath and Mary, it is another ethical dilemma to add to the quandary created by the suffragettes' decision to suspend their protests and to support the war. Mary can see the worry etched on Cath's face.

'How's t'bairn?'

'Alreet, I think. I can't feel anythin' yet, but I've got a grand bump showin'.'

Cath's eyes begin to fill. She looks at the men, still talking football.

'What are we goin' to do, Mary? These daft buggers don't know what day it is.'

'They're just men; can't 'elp th'sels. Most o' time, when I'm talkin' to Tommy, it's like talkin' to a wood stoop. I've been readin' all this stuff. I don't know what to think any more.'

'Neither do I, lass. Pankhursts are arguing. They reckon Sylvia wants to carry on protestin' and is very anti-war. Now Henry's come out in favour o' t'war. I don't know what to mek on it all.'

'I'm t'same. What chance 'ave we got to fathom it, if they can't agree wi' all their fancy education?'

Mary hands Cath a newspaper cutting.

'One o' t'lads gimme this today.'

Cath reads it intently. It is from the *Burnley Express*, a placed advertisement, a nationwide appeal to the men of England from Lady Louise Selina Maxwell, the wife of Sir John Maxwell, a senior army officer and veteran of Omdurman and the Boer War.

Must we be ashamed to be Englishmen when we see you skulking at home watching football or cricket matches, lying in the grass in the sun, safe and secure – as you fondly delude yourselves – while the manhood of Europe is shedding blood on the battlefield. Awake!

I am a woman, alas! I cannot go. But my man has gone. England needs you to save her liberty. Wives, give up your husbands. Mothers, send forth your sons. It is time the women rose and bid you go, or they must hang their heads in shame before the brave women of other countries, who have given their all for their country's sake. Awake! Awake! England needs her sons.

'Forgive my French, Mary, but who the fuck does she think she is!'

'I know, she sounds like a reet stuck-up cow. But read this one from t'*Accrington Observer*. It's from a lad called Clayton, addressed to the strikers at Howard an' Bullough.'

Mary presses a crumpled page of newsprint into Cath's hand.

What are you doing in this time of stress and trial? Shall I tell you the plain and unvarnished truth? You are sitting on your heels on the kerbstones. You are traipsing aimlessly through the already overcrowded streets. You are lounging, sitting and standing near the war office in Dutton Street discussing tactics and methods of a warfare in which you will not, either with hammer or gun, play your part for the honour of your country.

'Who's "Clayton"?'

'I don't reetly know. There are other letters, signed "Patriot" and "Loyalist". They all say t'same thing. Here's summat else; read this.'

It is a front-page story from the *Burnley Express*, with the headline: 'German Atrocities. Shocking Stories from Belgium.'

In the towns and villages they begin by requisitioning food and drink, which they consume until intoxicated. Then the scenes of fire, murder and especially pillage begin, accompanied by acts of deliberate cruelty, without respect to age or sex. After a preliminary attack and massacre, they shut up the men in the church and then order the women to return to their homes, but to leave their doors open all night.

Cath looks up sharply.

'What, so that t'Germans can use 'em like tarts?'

'O' course! Th'*Express* is too soft to say so, but that's what it means.'

'Bugger, that's terrible! Dost think it all true?'

'Well, somebody t'mornin' said t'stories were made up by t'government. I don't know; Jack Mosscrop says it's true, and 'e works on t'*Colne Times*. There's lots o' lads joinin' up after readin' stories like it.'

'I don't know, Mary. I'm reet confused.'

'Apparently, men can sign up an' serve together as a bunch o' lads. They're callin' 'em "Pals Battalions", wi' local officers, not southern toffs.'

'That's a good idea. At least they can put all t'coffins on t'same train 'ome.'

'I know, but better to feight wi' yer pals than total strangers. It said in t'*Guardian* that Liverpool 'as already produced three battalions and Manchester four. An' that in London, stockbrokers, sportsmen, Jews an' all sorts are joinin' up together.'

Cath looks at Mick and the others, merrily drinking ale and still discussing the game.

'Tha's not sayin' that this lot should join up? That's agin all our principles!'

'Is it? Not accordin' to Henry Hyndman and t'suffragettes. I don't believe in feightin' and killin' poor native people so that we tek their land from 'em. But even some o' t'pacifists think this do wi' t'Germans is different. An' there's summat else: tha's expectin', Cath. Think on; we'll soon not 'ave a penny comin' in to either of our 'ouses. 'Ow will we pay t'rent? Kitchener's sayin' he'll give recruits twenty-one shillings pay an' billetin' allowance. An' when t'men are away, twelve shillings an' sixpence for a wife, an' two shillings an' sixpence fer each o' t'childer.'

'That's more than we were getting' at t'mill, workin' four loom!'

'Reet. Temptin', in't it?'

''Tis that, but we'll be called traitors to t'workin'-class cause an' all that.'

'I know we will; not by all of 'em, mind. But it's our families that come first.'

'But these four lummoxes might get th'sels shot. 'Ave yer seen t'casualty figures?'

'Aye, but this lot are too daft to get shot.'

'I don't know, lass. I can't bear t'thought of it. I'll talk to Mick abaht it.'

'Well, if Mick goes, Tommy'll go wi' 'im. An' if those two go, Vinny'll go. An' where Vinny goes, Twaites goes.'

'Aye, he'll go to keep an eye on Vinny. He won't want t'silly bugger to get 'issen shot.'

'That's as good a reason as any, Cath. Let's hope none o' them gets shot.'

Winston Churchill's family have finally returned from an extended stay in their holiday cottage in Overstrand and are now back in London. As Clemmie is now heavily pregnant and Sir Edward Grey is still using their house in Eccleston Square, Winston has moved Clemmie and the children into a flat in the Admiralty.

It is Saturday night, but London is in a strange mood. Many people are still gripped by a martial fervour, a zeal that is part jingoism – indignation that someone should have the audacity to threaten Britain's pre-eminence – and part anger that, if the press stories are to be believed, the Germans have been committing dreadful atrocities in Belgium. The 'Hun' is being painted as a marauding beast, a monster threatening civilization itself. Lurid descriptions of brutality by German troops are everywhere, as are voyeuristic images of naked Belgian damsels being molested by savage Huns who resemble snarling hyenas or vicious bears.

But some people have become less warlike. Shocked crowds have gathered at ports all over the country to see the convoys of ambulances bringing the wounded from France. The casualty figures are far greater than anybody expected and the newspaper reports about the BEF in full retreat in a parlous state have added to the alarm.

Winston has been neglecting his family. The copious flow of letters between him and Clemmie has been reduced to a trickle. As his brother, Jack, is preparing to leave for France, Winston has organized a private supper at the Admiralty for Clemmie, Jack and Goonie. He has also invited his great friend F. E. Smith and his wife, Margaret. The six of them have dressed formally and Winston has ensured that the food, drink and service are commensurate with the fare offered at the finest of London's restaurants.

The first half of the dinner is devoted to family chatter, niceties and the usual banter between Winston and FE. It includes a couple of FE's legendary tales, which Winston encourages him to repeat. Both were comments he made to judges on the Northern Circuit while he was cutting his teeth as a barrister in Liverpool.

On one occasion, he was chastised by a judge who said, 'Mr Smith, having listened to your case, I am no wiser.'

To which FE replied, 'Possibly not, m'lud, but you are now much better informed.'

In another fabled moment, a very senior judge, whose wisdom was doubted by many, asked him, 'What do you suppose I am on the Bench for, Mr Smith?'

To which FE responded, in an instant, 'It is not for me, Your Honour, to attempt to fathom the inscrutable workings of Providence.'

Having given FE the floor for a while, Winston begins to hold court. He is in jubilant mood, which is a surprise to his guests. They felt sure he would need succour, given the worrying news about the BEF's anguished retreat from Mons.

'As you know, I am not inclined to crow unless, of course, it is an irresistible necessity driven by overwhelming achievements in which I may have played a minor role.'

All five smile. Winston is in one of his rampant veins. They know that what will follow will be an oratorical tour de force.

'At sea, our ships have muzzled the German Grand Fleet and it has run back to its ports, where I'm sure its sailors will spend the autumn idly polishing the brass and mahogany of their captains' wardrooms. The Heligoland Bight encounter was a stunning blow. Three of their cruisers and a destroyer are on the bottom, many more damaged. We had some impairment to one of our cruisers, but Commodore Roger Keyes's battle plan was outstanding. Old Jelly Bones is crowing about it, but it was all Keyes's doing.'

Goonie looks confused. 'Jelly Bones' is one of Winston's many pet names with which she is not familiar. Jack comes to her aid.

'John Jellicoe, my dear. Winston has just made him a full admiral and given him command of the Grand Fleet.'

Winston suddenly turns, with a fiery look in his eye.

'And he had better bring home the bacon for me, or I'll have it sliced off his rump!'

He then resumes the acclamation of his and Britain's prowess; he gets to his feet, goblet of claret in hand.

'I have more to tell: I wrote a memo three years ago, outlining what I thought would be the disposition of German forces if they were to launch an attack on France and how the subsequent conflict would unfold. Among many other things, I suggested that the German lines of communication would become too stretched and that their rapid advance would be curtailed within forty days.'

Then Winston gives an illustration of his extraordinary memory.

'I can quote from it now: "By the fortieth day, Germany should be extended at full strain and this strain will become more severe and ultimately overwhelming." Well, today is the thirty-sixth day of their assault, and it has come to pass. Of course, our army high command did not take my advice. I suggested that we should wait in reserve to strike at the right time but, pressured by the French, who panicked a little, we threw in our lot immediately and hence the unnecessary mauling at Mons. However, I do take some small comfort from being vindicated – especially as Kitchener and others have said as much.'

Despite Clemmie's hugely pregnant midriff, she jumps to her feet to kiss her husband.

'If they listened to you more often, my darling, the army might be in the same unassailable position as our navy.'

'Thank you, Clemmie, dearest heart. But actually, you have brought me to my next piece of news. Lord K has asked me to take control of all our air defences and add the Royal Flying Corps to my Royal Naval Air Service. He hasn't the time to devote himself to air power and is not really an advocate of its potential. But he knows I am very passionate about it. So, as well as our oceans, our skies are mine to command!'

All the listeners are enthralled; there are squeals of joy.

'I have already established a new squadron at Hendon and ordered a fleet of armour-plated Rolls-Royce cars to go to France to help establish forward air bases fifty miles inland. Twenty-four planes have already left, and we have launched our first aerial bombing sorties over German positions. The world's first air war has begun. I'm exhilarated by it all!'

Jack calls for a toast, which is made with great cheer. Clemmie remembers their visit to Glen Tilt to see Bardie Stewart-Murray's experimental machines.

'Does that mean you can commission some of those things we saw at Blair Atholl?'

'Ah, yes; that's going to be a little embarrassing, Clemmie. Those Dunne prototypes don't quite cut the mustard according to our engineers and experienced pilots. They're fine for civilian use, but they are not robust enough for a war zone.'

'Oh dear, such nice people.'

'Indeed, and Bardie's investors are all good friends of mine. But the two planes that were commissioned just couldn't stand up to the kind of sudden movements necessary under fire. Bardie is with the Scottish Horse in Dunkeld. When he comes south for embarkation to France, I'll break the news to him. I'd rather do it in person.'

Jack then intervenes.

'Why are you so sure he'll be going to France? The Scottish Horse is not on the latest list.'

'Oh, Jack, dear boy, I predict that by the time this is over, every able-bodied man in the realm will be involved in one way or another. And, if I may say so, ladies, every woman as well.'

Goonie grabs Winston's arm.

'So it won't be over by Christmas, as many are saying?'

'No, Goonie. Not this Christmas, not the next. And maybe not the one after that.'

'My God, Winston! With the casualty figures we've read so far, that means tens of thousands will die.'

'No, Goonie, hundreds of thousands, maybe millions.'

There is a sudden pall in the room.

Winston seeks to reinvigorate his guests.

'But let's face all that when the time comes. I have more to tell you – much more. And it's good news.'

Winston is now striding up and down the room. He has refilled his glass and the deep red claret is perilously close to the rim as he becomes more and more impassioned.

'Now, let me come to the best news since war was declared: the opportunity predicted by the scenario I outlined in my 1911 memorandum. All intelligence, especially from aerial reconnaissance, is indicating that von Kluck is swinging his army south-east of Paris.'

Clemmie looks perplexed.

'Why would he do that, darling?'

'Paris is too tough a nut to crack in a frontal assault. That was never part of the German plan. They wanted to encircle the city from the north, defeat the bulk of the French Army on the battlefield and then squeeze the life out of the city until it was forced to surrender. Now they are trying to do the same thing, but in a southerly arc, because the northern route is too much of a stretch, as I said all along.'

Clemmie is still baffled.

'So why is that good news?'

'Because he is exposing his left flank to a swift counter-attack from the French railheads in the city. Not only that, the French have been blessed by an astonishing stroke of luck. Three days ago, a German officer returning from von Kluck's headquarters to his own division took a wrong turn and drove straight into a French patrol. His car was sprayed with bullets and he was killed.'

Goonie lets out an impromptu gasp.

'Oh dear! That poor man –'

'Goonie, don't be ridiculous, he was our sworn enemy; this is a fight to the death.'

'I know, Winston, but he's probably a lovely village boy, only twenty-five years old, with a sweetheart and mother at home.'

'Quite so, but I'm more concerned about *our* lovely boys. Anyway, this sweet Prussian boy had a map of von Kluck's current disposition in his pocket and, more importantly, drawn on it in pencil were the lines of his intended movements. He is heading for the River Marne, and the plans show General Lanrezac exactly where to put his 5th Army. It shows the French the precise point from where to spring an ambush. The BEF will support Lanrezac and will share in what I'm sure will be a great victory.'

Jack is wide-eyed in astonishment.

'What an extraordinary piece of good fortune.'

'Quite right, dearest Jack, God always smiles on the righteous!'

FE then produces a copy of *The Times* newspaper.

'Talking of the righteous, I've got a copy of your Guildhall speech yesterday. I love this bit.'

FE gets to his feet, a great orator in the courtroom and parliament in his own right. He mimics Winston's voice, complete with his renowned lisp and flamboyant gesticulations.

'"You only have to endure to conquer. You have only to persevere to save yourself and all those who rely on you. You have to go on and at the end of the road, be it short or long, victory and honour will be found."'

Clemmie and Goonie applaud both men: FE for his perfect impersonation, and Winston for the stirring power of his words. Clemmie then tugs at Winston's jacket.

'Tell everybody what the Prime Minister said to you yesterday.'

'No, it was nothing.'

'On the contrary, it was very important. Four of us are Churchills, and FE and Margaret are honorary members of the clan; they would like to know what he said.'

Before Winston can respond, FE makes a little speech of his own.

'Really, Clemmie, honorary Churchills? What a rare privilege! But does it mean we have to agree with Winnie all the time?'

His wife, Margaret, answers immediately.

'Of course you do; I have to agree with you all the time, so why shouldn't you toe the Churchill line? You'll get used to it – I've had to!'

Everyone laughs; Margaret's wit is almost as sharp as FE's renowned jocularity.

Winston is being coy. In truth, he needs little encouragement to reveal what Asquith said.

'Very well, the Old Block had been talking to the lovely Venetia, his . . . erm . . . private secretary. She said she was worried about me, that I had the look of a ravenous wolf, desperate for the kill, and that she sensed the last thing I wanted was peace. I think OB meant it as a warning to mind my rhetoric in public. But I made it very clear to him that we Churchills are a family of fighters; it is in our blood, and I make no apologies for my demeanour as an uncompromising warrior.

'I explained that I cherish peace as much as the next man, but not above victory over an enemy who is so uncompromisingly ruthless in his ambitions. We must meet force with superior force. When the clarion call of war is sounded, we must answer until the account is settled. Nothing must be spared until victory is achieved; then we can enjoy the peace.'

There is silence for a moment.

Clemmie's eyes fill with tears as Jack and FE shake Winston's hand, and Goonie hugs him. All five at the table are thinking the same thing: he might be like a ferocious animal, but thank God we have him.

Rue du Marteroy, Jouarre, Seine-et-Marne, France

The 4th Battalion Royal Fusiliers has been acting as rearguard for the retreat from Mons for two weeks. They have marched over 140 miles with full packs, are footsore and totally fatigued. Dozens have dropped out from sheer exhaustion or from feet so blistered they can no longer walk. They have been living off the land, to preserve their rations, but have taken care to pay their way and not to alienate their French civilian hosts, who are, after all, their allies.

The Germans, however, have been less than courteous. The small town of Jouarre has been left resembling the kind of pitiful scene that follows an attack by a plague of locusts. The local people are nowhere to be seen. Every house has been ransacked, anything valuable taken and everything else destroyed.

Harry and Maurice have been ordered to take their platoon and check all the local houses for lurking Germans, or any sick or wounded soldiers and civilians.

'They're bloody animals, Mo. Look at that, some arse'ole's 'acked into that larder wiv an axe.'

Harry then goes upstairs.

'Mo, look at this lot. They've used the small bedroom as a shitter, dirty bastards. Jesus, what a pong!'

'Everything's gone, 'Arry; there's not a stitch in the 'ouse. They've nicked everythin'. Billy Carstairs says we're movin' up, not back, so we'll soon be able to 'ave a pop at the bastards.'

'I've lost track. I 'aven't a bloody clue where we are; we seem to 'ave been marchin' since last Christmas.'

When their platoon returns to the open fields behind the Abbey of Notre Dame, where the battalion is being billeted, they are just in time to hear an address from Major Ashburner. Already well liked by his men, his reputation among C Company has grown with every step from Mons. He gave up his officer's cavalry mount after Le Cateau and has since walked every yard with his men, carrying his own pack.

'Relax, men, and get yourselves comfortable on the ground – which, thank God, is still dry.'

He looks around at them. His face glows with pride.

'When my wife heard that we would be departing for France in August, she said, "Don't get sunburned!" But all we've had is thunderstorms and blisters!'

He gets the laugh he was hoping for.

'As you know, I let my charger go after Le Cateau. I thought I preferred blisters to saddle-sores.'

This time, the laughter is louder and much more heartfelt.

'Now, to the matter in hand, gentlemen. We stood our ground at Mons against overwhelming odds, bloodied their noses at Le Cateau and then withdrew in excellent order. Now we have a chance to teach our Teutonic friends a lesson.'

Maurice looks at Harry quizzically and whispers.

'What the fuck's a Tu-tonic?'

'Dunno, Mo . . . must be a German.'

Billy Carstairs sees Harry and Maurice whispering to one another and glares at them. Major Ashburner does not notice. He is in full flow.

'Now we have a chance to strike back. As you will have realized, we have swung round and, after falling back to the south-east for what seemed like an eternity, we are moving forwards, to the north-east. Paris is behind us and soon we will move up to the River Marne, where General Lanrezac's 5th French Army is attacking in vast numbers as I speak . . .' He pauses and smiles at his men. 'I want to read something to you. It is from the Commander of the French Army, General Joseph Joffre, a decorated veteran and highly respected soldier. It is his order of the day, issued this morning.

'I know the French troops look a little comical in their red pantaloons and blue tunics – and they certainly make for easy targets – but rest assured, they can and will fight. These are the general's words to his men: "Now as the battle is joined, upon which rests the future of our country, you must know that this is not a time for looking back. Every effort must be made to attack and throw back the enemy. A unit which finds it impossible to advance must, regardless of cost, hold its ground and be killed on the spot rather than fall back. In the present circumstances, no failure will be tolerated. *Vive la France!*"'

Ashburner scrutinizes the faces of his men. He can see that they are impressed.

'Rest well tonight. Bathe your blisters. As you relax, and again before we march out, just look around you and see what the Germans have done here in France and all through Belgium. Sister Anne-Marie, Abbess here at Jouarre, has told me that they even desecrated the abbey. They were rude and threatening to the monks and nuns, they got drunk and brought in women, some against their will. They even used the crypt, a holy place that is over a thousand years old, as a latrine. Tomorrow you will be able to repeat what you did at Mons and remind Fritz of his manners!'

A huge cheer goes up from the fusiliers, some of whom jump to their feet in anger, waving their rifle bayonets in the air like native warriors brandishing their spears.

*

The next morning, just before dawn, Maurice and Harry are breaking camp and prompting their platoon into life. They are as well rested as an eight-hour open-air bivouac will allow. They have eaten better than they have for the previous two weeks and have managed to bathe and dress their blistered feet. Most significantly, they are eager to get even with Fritz after the retreat from Mons and are indignant at the behaviour of fellow soldiers, albeit German ones, towards the local population.

'All set, Mo?'

'Yeah, as good as I'll ever be.'

The men of C Company spend the rest of Sunday 6 September in a long march in the heat of a warm, late summer day. They head north-east, from which direction they can hear distant artillery, rifle and machine-gun fire sufficient to indicate that a major battle is going on ahead of them.

They make camp at Château-Thierry. As their transport fails to appear yet again, they bivouac in the open air. Harry is rummaging around in his knapsack.

'Mo, what 'ave yer got for tucker?'

'A tin o' Moir Wilson's. What about you?'

'A Maconochie's.'

'That's a result, let's boil 'em up together and make a nice stew. Tell ya what else I've got, a bottle o' beer.'

'Where the fuck did yer get that from?'

'Been savin' it. Picked it up two days ago from an officer's table outside a café. He went fer a piss at just the wrong time for him; right time fer me. I'll share it with yer.'

'You're a good sort, 'Arry. 'Ere, 'ave one of my fags. Afraid it's one o' them filthy Frenchie ones – Sweet Caporal!'

'Fuck knows why they call 'em "Sweet", they're like smokin' dog shit!'

Harry and Maurice settle down for their feast of army rations and a bottle of beer. It is a long way from the comforts of home cooking, or the beer at the Drum in Leyton, but they feel better than they have for days. They are in a meadow just south of the Marne river, three miles east of Château-Thierry. Behind them is the main road from the town to the east. The road is congested in both directions with long columns of fleeing civilians going towards Paris and French troops moving the other way, both in vast numbers.

'Look at that lot, Mo! Black as the ace o' spades, some of 'em.'

'French native troops, 'Arry. North Africans, by the look of 'em.'

'But some are black.'

'I know, mate. They get about, them darkies.'

Led by French officers, thousands of French colonial troops join the battle for the Marne and for control of the approaches to Paris. Even more colourfully dressed than their French army comrades, they march past proudly to fight for the Republic.

There is suddenly a melee along the road as car horns sound and cheers ring out.

'Bugger me! The Frenchies are moving men up in cars.'

'They're bloody taxis, 'Arry. Hundreds of 'em. They must have come from Paris.'

'That's a good bit o' thinkin' by some Frenchie clever dick. None of our generals would 'ave thought o' that. Except for transportin' themselves, o' course.'

'What do yer reckon to the French boys?'

'Warmin' to 'em a bit, now that they're turnin' and makin' a fight of it. I still prefer the girls, though.'

Instead of moving up, Harry and Maurice spend the next two days watching the events on the Marne unfold. They take their platoon down to the main road on a regular basis to help the movement of soldiers and civilians. More and more French troops move up from Paris, while more and more wounded move the other way. Some French units have lost half their men and two-thirds of their officers. The Moroccans they saw the day before, proud and marching in good order, return bedraggled and with only about a third of their number. But from what they understand from the French soldiers, the battle is going well and the Germans are falling back.

'Looks like old Ashburner was right, the Frenchies are makin' a damn good fight of it.'

'Abaht time! Shame we're not in it. We were promised a scrap, but we're not gettin' it; a soldier's lot, I s'pose.'

'Shouldn't worry, 'Arry, I think there'll be plenty o' time fer that.'

'I'm gonna 'ave a word wiv Billy Carstairs, see if we can nip into the village tonight. The locals will be in a good mood, so we might get our legs over. And if nothin' else, we can 'ave a couple o' their bubbly beers.'

Tuesday 8 September

Major Hamish Stewart-Murray's Cameron Highlanders are advancing towards the Marne river. Close by, his brother Geordie's battalion of the Black Watch are part of the same deployment. Both battalions have reached Saint-Ouen-sur-Morin, where they camp for the night. Hamish and Geordie have not seen one another since they had dinner together in London and indulged in their night of debauchery at the Langham Hotel with the girls from Selfridges.

Sister Margaret Killingbeck and her Queen Alexandra's nurses have been travelling with the Camerons since they coincided in Bavay two weeks ago. Margaret and Hamish have become close since the trauma of the death of Captain Philip Davies of the Welch Fusiliers, but it has remained a platonic relationship. Margaret's personal circumstances are a mystery to Hamish. She has revealed little of her status or background, and Hamish has chosen not to probe.

All three have been billeted in the town's main hotel, the Auberge de la Source, and have agreed to have dinner together. The auberge is an old coaching inn and would be an idyllic location for a convivial stay, were it not for the fact that a calamitous battle is taking place only a few miles away. Nevertheless, the proprietor is hurrying from table to table, serving the best of his kitchen and cellar, just like he did only last week for German officers.

Margaret is anxious and feeling a little guilty. She is a farmer's daughter from Muker, a tiny village high in Swaledale, the most remote of all the Yorkshire Dales. Fine dining played no part in her upbringing and has only been an occasional part of her life in recent years when, as a senior nurse at Guy's Hospital in London, some of the wealthier doctors took her out to the West End. She left her childhood sweetheart in Swaledale and has since enjoyed only an occasional, inconsequential fling. She joined Queen Alexandra's nurses in 1912, but this is her first overseas posting.

'I must be back to relieve one of my girls at eleven. She's been on duty since this morning without a break.'

'Of course, Margaret, we understand. Geordie is off early tomorrow, so we should all have an early night.'

Margaret is a little overawed. Meeting one son of a duke was disconcerting; now she is having dinner with two of them. Their self-confident bearing and impeccable manners are disconcerting, but she likes the look of Geordie; he has a nice smile and is warmer than Hamish.

'So, Geordie, do you have titles like Hamish?'

'Well, yes, but it's very complicated. I'm the second son and will only inherit if Bardie, our elder brother, gets on the wrong end of a German bullet. As for Hamish here, he will have to wait for both of us to go. We've also got three sisters, all older than us, but they can't inherit the dukedom, only the boys.'

'Seems unfair.'

'You may well be right, but tradition is a difficult thing to change.'

'It's a big family.'

'It is; Father's a prodigious old stag.'

'And do you all get along?'

'More or less. Helen, our second-eldest sister, rules the roost and keeps us all in order. But what about your family?'

Geordie is not as reticent about delving into Margaret's past. Hamish is all ears; he is hoping, finally, to hear more about the intriguing Sister Margaret.

'I'm a simple farmer's daughter. We have sheep in one of

the prettiest places in England. I suspect it's not unlike your part of the world.'

'So what brought you to nursing?'

'I did well at school, the teacher took a shine to me, but Muker was too small for my ambitions. It's a tiny place, fifteen miles up the valley of the Swale, with no mains water and no electricity. The same families have lived there for generations. We even have our own language that only the locals understand!'

'That's interesting, we were all taught Gaelic as children. Perhaps your local language is similar?'

'I'm not sure; I think ours is just Old English. Most Pennine folk have their own words.'

'So you left your little village?'

'Yes, I went down the valley to the Friary, a small hospital in Richmond, and fell in love with nursing. Then I went to Guy's Hospital in London and joined Queen Alex's two years ago.'

Hamish wants to learn more and risks asking a rather impertinent question.

'So what's your ambition after nursing? To start a family perhaps?'

Margaret is maddened that Hamish's only thought about her future is that she might want to 'start a family'.

'What, and bring children into this? I don't think that would be a good idea.'

'That's a bit melancholy, isn't it, Margaret?'

'Is it? You should try dealing with what I deal with every day. Yesterday, I had to patch up a boy who had lost his right foot and taken a bullet in the abdomen. He'll live, but will never have children and will pee like a woman for the rest of his life.'

Hamish and Geordie gulp and look down at their menus.

'I'm sorry, but I have to cope with that kind of thing all the time.'

Geordie sees that the evening's conviviality is rapidly disappearing and changes the subject.

'I hear the French are doing rather well up ahead. I think we should have some champagne to celebrate. And I'm tempted by the chateaubriand. Who'll join me?'

They all choose the chateaubriand, a rare treat, and soon the champagne, prime beef and a bottle of Burgundy get the evening back on track. Smiles begin to soften Margaret's face as she relaxes into the evening. But exactly on cue, at ten thirty, duty calls and she says her goodbyes, leaving Hamish and Geordie to drink cognac alone.

'So, Hamish, how long have you been pursuing her?'

'Two weeks.'

'She's a corker! A bit frigid, but a few pokes with what you've got under your kilt will sort that.'

'I'm not wearing a kilt, Geordie –'

'I know that; I'm talking metaphorically, dearest brother.'

'Well, the problem is, I don't think she likes me very much. I think she's intrigued – Scottish lord, and all that – but that's about it.'

'Well, that'll do for a start. Try and get your leave to Blighty to coincide with hers. Give her a dinner in the West End, take her back to Eaton Square, show her our illustrious ancestors on the wall and she'll swoon – guaranteed!'

Hamish is not convinced and looks forlorn.

'Perhaps . . . but the trouble is, I want her now. God knows when we'll get leave.'

'Listen, she'll come round; she just needs a bit more warming up. She's a bit of a suffragette type. No more talk about starting a family; that went down like a lead balloon!'

'I know, but I'm not very good with the modern girl – too clever for me. Anyway, when are you off?'

'At six o'clock sharp. The CO has promised us a ding-dong with Fritz tomorrow.'

'Well, keep your head down if it comes to it. I don't want you getting a bullet through that thick skull of yours.'

'It would bounce off! Don't fuss so.'

Hamish then remembers to tell Geordie the conclusion to a story he began back in June.

'By the way, do you remember the story I told you about Henriette Caillaux, shooting that newspaper chap in Paris?'

'Indeed I do; extraordinary business.'

'Well, she got off scot-free!'

'Good God! On what basis?'

'Crime of passion. Her lawyer said that women's emotions mean they are incapable of premeditation. Therefore, the shooting was an act driven by feminine passion, which was the only feasible explanation. She walked from court a free woman surrounded by hundreds of well-wishers.'

'Hell's bells! Couldn't happen in England.'

'I know; we are going to give them the bloody vote, and the French think that they're not capable of thinking straight. Strange world, isn't it?'

The two brothers shake hands formally, but Hamish puts his hand on his elder brother's shoulder just as he turns to leave.

'Be careful, big brother.'

'I will. And you make sure to get some Scottish beef between the legs of that nurse before she becomes an old spinster. It'll do her the world of good.'

Thursday 10 September

Mary and Tommy Broxup are sitting in front of the cast-iron range in the back room of their tiny terraced house in Burnley. The gas board has cut off the gas, so they are sitting in candle-light. There is half a scuttle of coal left by the grate; it is the last fuel they can afford. They have sold their net curtains and all the furniture in the front room to make ends meet.

The house is bare, save for one double bed upstairs, a kitchen table and the two chairs they are sitting on. Their only food for the week has been mutton stew and dumplings, enlivened on odd days by the local delicacy 'stew an' 'ard' as a treat.

The tap above the old stone slop sink is dripping incessantly. Tommy is easily able to put in a new washer, but he cannot afford to buy one now that he no longer has a wage coming in. There is little prospect of work for Mary either, and they have had no money since her union pay ran out after they were both sacked following the trouble at Howard and Bullough's.

It is ten o'clock in the evening. They would usually be at the pub at this time, or at the Keighley Green Club, but they have no money in their pockets.

In recent weeks, Mary and Tommy have heard rumours that John Harwood, the Mayor of Accrington, has been in feverish correspondence with the War Office since the Declaration of War, asking for permission to raise a Pals Battalion from Accrington and the surrounding area.

Finally, on Monday 7 September, Harwood heard from

Harold Baker, MP for Accrington, hotfoot from London on the afternoon train, that the War Office has agreed to the raising of a new volunteer battalion for Kitchener's Army. It will be called the 11th Battalion East Lancashire Regiment (Accrington Pals) and 158th (Accrington and Burnley) Brigade, Royal Field Artillery (Howitzers). With the proviso that Harwood must raise an entire battalion of 1,100 men, recruitment will begin on Monday 14 September.

Still in two minds about the war, Mary has spent the day walking around Burnley's weaving sheds, listening to the arguments about Britain's involvement and how it is affecting ordinary people. There are strong views on both sides.

'What dost think o' these pals battalions, Tommy?'

'Not much. It's like bein' in t'Boy Scouts, like them Burnley Grammar lads, who look like reet little tossers!'

'That's what many o' t'lads I've talked to say. But there's many as reckon we should weigh in to keep t'peace in Europe.'

'What dost tha reckon, our kid? Tha's cleverer than all on 'em.'

'Can't decide, Tom. Fer folks like us, there's nowt much to feight fer. But it's all we've got. And I know one thing: if what some o' t'lads who've been in t'army say is true, then we can't beat Germans wi'out ordinary lads like thee. If that's reet, then maybe tha should feight.'

Tommy looks perplexed.

'What dost mean, Mary?'

'Well, if thee and thousands o' others feight for King and country, then they'll 'ave to gi' thee reet to vote for King and country at end on it!'

Tommy smiles warmly at Mary. Proud of his shrewd wife, he puts his arms around her.

'They should put thee in charge. You'd 'ave 'em told!'

'I would, but it'll never 'appen; we've to get t'vote first.'

'Reckon I should get that Boy Scout kit on, then?'

'Mebbe, Tommy. We'll 'ave to do summat, or we'll starve.'

Saturday 12 September

Vailly-sur-Aisne, Picardy, France

French resolve, with not a little German indecision, has won the day on the Marne. The French soldiers have been galvanized by the proclamation of General Ferdinand Foch, Commander of the French 9th Army, issued on 9 September: 'I ask each one of you to draw upon the last spark of energy, which in its moments of supreme trial has never been denied to our race. Everyone must be convinced that success belongs to him who holds out longest. The honour and security of France are in the balance. One more effort and you are sure to win.'

The Germans retreat in the face of renewed French attacks; they lose over sixty miles in just a week and are driven across the Marne and the Aisne rivers. More atrocities occur, adding to the bitterness of the conflict, especially between French and German troops. German units take hostages from villages in exchange for wounded men they have to leave behind. Many of the hostages are mistreated, and some are executed.

The French newspapers are full of gruesome accounts. In Varreddes, a town north of the Marne, the Germans left twenty wounded men in the *hôtel de ville* and took twenty elderly citizens with them as hostages. When two of them, men in their late seventies, could walk no further, they were shot in the head at point-blank range; a third was killed by a blow to the head from the butt of a rifle.

Encouraging reports of columns comprising hundreds of German prisoners being rounded up are passed through the ranks of the British Expeditionary Force. Many of the accounts talk of German infantry, abandoned by their officers, hiding in attics and cellars in a drunken stupor. Thousands of cavalry horses have been left by the sides of the roads, which are littered with vehicles for which there is no fuel, surrounded by a plethora of stolen booty that has become a hindrance to the retreat.

The respect most of the British soldiers had for their German opponents is replaced by contempt and loathing. Conversely, the doubts they had about the courage of their French allies are replaced by admiration.

Although Harry and Maurice's platoon were not involved, the 4th Battalion Royal Fusiliers has suffered severe casualties in the last two days. Seeing at first hand the wanton destruction of the German occupation, it had been advancing into the territory vacated by the enemy's rapid retreat, when an opportunity to engage again suddenly occurred.

After crossing the Marne unopposed on Wednesday the 9th, reports came in from a marauding troop of 6th Dragoon Guards. They came galloping down the road to report that the Germans ahead had not yet broken camp and were enjoying a leisurely breakfast.

The fusiliers attacked immediately, but walked straight into a hail of machine-gun fire. Thirty men were lost within minutes, cut to pieces before they could take cover. It was an ambush of sorts. Although the Germans were, indeed, taking a relaxed breakfast, they had taken care to cover their position with well-hidden machine-gun posts. Lieutenants Tower, Beazley, Jackson and Longman were wounded, the latter two severely. Despite the losses, the fusiliers pressed on and soon overran the German camp, taking over 700 prisoners, all of whom they had confronted in combat before. There was great satisfaction in the British ranks, knowing that opponents who had forced them out of Mons would not take any further part in the war.

Harry and Maurice's C Company have enjoyed two quiet days, on the 10th and the 11th, during which time they have heard almost no gunfire. Now, on the morning of Saturday the 12th, they reach the Aisne river, which they have to cross by means of wooden planks lashed together by army sappers. These are either hasty French or German constructions; whichever they are, it is a precarious crossing.

By the time they have crossed, it is pitch dark and rain is falling heavily. C Company takes up position in and around Maison Rouge Farm. Reports suggest that the enemy is only a few hundred yards away, so there is no opportunity to make camp or take cover. The men face a miserable night in the open, with the dark skies cascading their contents down upon them; it is the middle of September and the chill of autumn is an ominous reminder that winter beckons.

Harry and Maurice have got their men into a series of outbuildings at Maison Rouge and most have some cover, but the two friends have chosen an exposed position by the farm entrance so that they can see the track leading to the farm. They protect themselves with their standard-issue groundsheets, one underneath them and one above.

'It's gonna be a long night, Mo.'

'And a wet one. At least we 'ad a good night wiv those little ladies in Jew-ar-ray, or whatever it was called.'

'Yeah, but I 'ope we don't get a dose off 'em. I don't reckon they was innocent virgins!'

Maurice adjusts his cap, which is poking out from the top of their impromptu shelter. As he does so, the rain that has accumulated on its felt surface runs down his neck and face.

'I think nights like that are gonna become few an' far between, ol' friend. Let's take it in turns to snooze; two hours on, two off?'

'All right, mate. You go first. D'yer reckon Fritz is sleepin'?'

'I 'ope so, 'Arry. I don't fancy a set-to in this fuckin' rain.'

*

The morning of Sunday 13 September breaks with an autumnal chill in the ground, but the rain has stopped and the sky above begins to clear. However, a thick ground mist has descended over Picardy. France's long hot summer is over. The scene now more closely resembles the dank weather of Britain than the balmy climes of continental Europe. The hot sweats of conflict in the long August days are about to be exchanged for the cold sweats of battle in the cloying mud of autumn, only to be followed by the unyielding rime of winter.

Harry raises his hand to alert his friend, and whispers.

'Mo, can you hear that?'

'I can; it's fuckin' German voices. They can't be more than two hundred yards away.'

Harry calls over to a couple of corporals and, in a hushed voice, tells them to keep the noise down and to pass the word among the men. Then their new captain appears, a fresh-faced lad who looks like he should still be at Sandhurst. He is called James Orred. He is friendly and far less pompous than his predecessor, whom they have not seen since he was concussed by an artillery shell at Mons. He is called 'Orrid' by everyone, a nickname he has had to live with since his youngest schooldays.

Although he likes to use the expression 'Orred by name, 'orrid by nature', the men do not fall for it. Orred is a soldiers' officer: firm but fair, brave but not foolhardy, astute but not aloof. His accent suggests he went to one of the better public schools but he is happy to rough it with the lads and spends more time with them than with his fellow officers.

'Good morning, men, I trust you slept –'

'Quiet, sir, Fritz is just over there, through them trees.'

'Sorry, Serjeant.'

Maurice tugs at the officer's arm to pull him down behind the farm gate of Maison Rouge. Orred gets out his field glasses and trains them on the trees.

'Good heavens, the woods are swarming with the buggers. It looks as if they've gathered themselves and are going to mount a counter-attack. Serjeant Tait, get the men to choose good positions and stand to. Send Corporal Smith to Major Ashburner and tell him that half the German Army is about to come down this farm track!'

'Sir!'

'Serjeant Woodruff, we need as much ammunition as we have with us to be brought forward right away.'

When Maurice and Harry return, orders carried out, Orred looks at his watch.

'Sunrise was at five twenty yesterday, so a couple of minutes later today. It's now five twenty-five. Brace yourselves; I think the attack will either commence in five minutes' time, or at six sharp. Fritz is very precise with his timings.'

Maurice nods subtly at Harry; they are impressed. Orred seems calm and collected. Given his tender years, he cannot have been under fire before, but he is acting like a seasoned veteran. CSM Billy Carstairs appears.

'Where do you see them, sir?'

'Serjeants Tait and Woodruff spotted them first – or rather, heard them. They're in those woods over there, Mr Carstairs. I estimate at least a couple of companies.'

'Very good, sir. I'm sure the major will send another platoon forward as soon as he hears.'

'I hope so; we'll hold this ground for as long as we can.'

When Orred puts his field glasses back to his eyes to check on the Germans, Billy smiles at Maurice and Harry. It is a warm smile, signalling that he too is impressed by the young officer.

'Hold your ground, lads. And look out for the captain's back.'

The German attack does not come at five thirty, but on the stroke of six. All hell breaks loose with an earth-shattering artillery barrage. Thankfully for C Company, the Germans have assumed that the British are positioned next to or near the Canal Latéral, parallel to the River Aisne. However, C Company is several hundred yards ahead of that, so the artillery barrage passes harmlessly overhead. The 1st Battalion Lincolnshires, the fusiliers' relief battalion, are not so lucky; the open ground between the canal and the river is exactly where they made camp last night and precisely where the shells are landing.

Up at Maison Rouge, the fusiliers are looking anxiously at the trees two hundred yards in front of them. They know that as soon as the artillery barrage stops, which could be a ten- or fifteen-minute burst, German infantry battalions will come streaming through the trees en masse.

At six twenty precisely the attack begins. A huge wave of shadowy grey figures emerges from the trees. They run, semi-crouched in open formation, their officers urging them forward with their swords held high. Captain Orred looks round to check that his platoon is in place and that his two lieutenants are prominent in encouraging their men. Finally, he looks at his machine-gunners, to ensure that each gun is primed and its gunner has a bead on the rapidly encroaching Germans.

'On my order. Take steady aim . . . wait for it . . .'

He waits for what seems like an eternity. Fingers twitch impatiently on triggers.

'*Fire!*'

An intense volley of lethal fire is released. There is a moment's silence as the fusiliers reload; German bodies fall to the ground, some with obscenely distorted movements. Even at this distance, blood can be seen cascading through the air when a bullet strikes a head or neck. Some victims are propelled backwards by the impact, especially if they are hit more than once in the torso.

By the time the enemy has closed to within one hundred

yards, its front two or three ranks have been devastated. But there are hundreds more men behind them. Harry and Maurice look at one another. The arithmetic is easily done; there are far too many Germans bearing down on the fusiliers for them to be able to hold their ground for long. They can see Captain Orred looking around, hoping to see reinforcements moving their way.

Then a German machine gun begins to open up from a small copse of trees to their left. What has so far been a one-sided fairground shooting challenge is suddenly a more even contest. Fusiliers are now being hit, including Lieutenant Hobbs, who is hit in the chest and is dead within minutes. Next to him, Jimmy and Nobby Parsons, brothers just nine months apart, two chirpy little fellows from Pimlico, are both cut down in the same burst of machine-gun fire. The agonizing cries of stricken men rise above the rat-a-tat-tat of gunfire. Stretcher-bearers scurry backwards and forwards, leaving a gory trail of blood and human remains along their route.

'Fuck me, 'Arry, this is not lookin' too good. We need to leg it.'

'You're not kiddin'! Where's old Ashburner when we need 'im?'

'He needs to get a move on, or we'll be fucked!'

As the fighting continues, Harry becomes more and more incensed. He has killed men before and been close to his own demise more than once, but the intensity of this war disturbs him.

'This ain't like other wars, Mo. So many fuckers tryin' to kill one another, an' so much firepower.'

'Let's 'ope it won't last long; mebbe a few months.'

'I pray to God it don't drag on, or we won't be drawin' that pension!'

The Germans are within fifty yards when Billy Carstairs and Major Ashburner lead two more platoons of fusiliers and an extra machine-gun team into the farmyard and round its buildings. The new men make a dramatic difference. Their added firepower forces the Germans to take cover, and an impasse develops that extends well into the afternoon.

The fusiliers are almost surrounded, but the track to the main road behind them, under the cover of defensive positions, is still in their control and they have the advantage of the protection of the farm buildings. On the other hand, they are significantly outnumbered, and Major Ashburner has been extremely brave – or perhaps reckless – in bringing more men into the middle of what might be a total encirclement.

Ashburner comes over to Orred and asks him about his situation.

'John Hobbs has gone, sir. We've lost at least two dozen men, but we've held our ground, thanks to your arrival.'

'Well done, Jim. We now need to think how we get back to the safety of the battalion.'

'Right, sir. By the way, I thought Fritz was supposed to be retreating.'

'Indeed! Perhaps a fizzer has come down from German High Command, demanding a death and glory charge.'

Ashburner then turns to Billy Carstairs, Maurice and Harry. He has new orders for them.

'Mr Carstairs, you and CSMs Woodruff and Tait have seen it all before. I want you three to gather together a covering squad for Captain Orred. They must all be top boys, good with a bayonet. I'm going to lead us out of here. I'll deploy the machine guns to give you covering fire as we go, but you will be the rearguard. It will not be easy; the floodgates will open when they realize we're pulling back. Any questions?'

There are none, but Harry and Maurice exchange glances. They know that what they have been asked to do is fraught with danger and a likely death sentence for several of them.

Ashburner's withdrawal is done with classic military precision. Men retreat in squads, covering one another as they go. The major makes sure the farm track is protected by covering fire so intense that it is some considerable time before the Germans realize what is happening. The first group to reach the main road comprises the stretcher-bearers and medical orderlies, followed by the rest of the support troops.

Billy Carstairs and Captain Orred organize the rearguard action. It is done with speed and the utmost discipline, but even so, three men fall before they reach the track.

As one group, under the command of Carstairs and Harry, provides covering fire the other, under the command of Orred and Maurice, sprints for new ground. But there is just not enough firepower to keep all the Germans at bay, and Carstairs and Harry's squad is left exposed.

From his firing position on one knee, Carstairs shouts, '*Fix bayonets!*'

He and Harry and the eight men in their squad are soon surrounded by more than a dozen Saxon Guards who appear from a ditch behind them. There is a hail of bullets from them, felling at least three of the fusiliers. The lunge and parry of a bayonet skirmish begins immediately. The Saxon Guards are experienced soldiers, but British infantry bayonet techniques, like its musketry, are second to none and the Germans lose several of their number in a fierce close-quarters encounter. But more Germans are rising from the ditch all the time.

Orred's and Maurice's squad reach the security of the buildings by the main road, about 100 yards away, where they meet more reinforcements from the battalion. They are soon able to direct significant fire towards the Saxon Guards and force many of them to seek cover.

Captain Orred has stepped into the open and is bellowing at his men to make a dash for it.

'Mr Carstairs, get your men out of there!' He then implores

those around him, 'Come on, men; more volleys! Those boys need covering fire.'

Maurice shouts at his captain, beseeching him to get behind cover, but Orred ignores him. He raises his pistol to fire; then he stops. For a moment he is motionless, before his raised right arm flops to his side. His knees sag; he releases his grip on his pistol, which hits the ground with a clatter. Maurice realizes that he has been hit and rushes forward to help. He reaches the stricken captain just as he staggers sideways, and manages to stop him falling.

'Stretcher-bearers!'

Captain Orred's body goes limp in Maurice's arms and his head lolls backwards. His eyes are already closed as he is pulled towards the cover of the buildings. As Maurice struggles with Orred's lifeless form, several bullets strike the wall behind them. One hits the butt of Maurice's rifle, another takes his peaked cap clean off his head and a third punches into his stricken captain's midriff with a sickening splash.

By the time they reach the safety of the rear of the building, Captain James Orred is dead, a trail of blood marking the path of the last few moments of his life. The first bullet he took, entering the left side of his chest just above his heart, killed him within moments; the second one just added an unnecessary affront to a mortal wound. Maurice lays his body down carefully and asks the medical orderlies to check for his pulse.

There is not a flicker.

'Take 'im back carefully, fellas; he was a brave man.'

Maurice then rushes back to see what has become of Billy Carstairs and Harry.

What he witnesses makes him stop in his tracks and yell out loud, 'Fuckin' leg it, 'Arry!'

Harry has got Billy Carstairs on his back and is stumbling down the track carrying a weight that is, in normal circumstances, too much for him. And yet, somehow, he manages to carry him. Of his squad, only two fusiliers are with him, both running in a crouched position to make themselves as small a target as possible. Harry's face is a contortion of punishing exertion, but he clings to Carstairs's webbing to keep him steady with one hand and is still able to hold his own rifle in the other.

Just as they reach the corner of the building, one of the two men with them is hit in the back and careens against the corner with a dreadful thump. A bullet has gone straight through his lower back and exited through his stomach, splattering blood and guts on to the wall and the men standing next to it.

Maurice helps Harry get Billy Carstairs on to the ground. Harry gulps for air.

'He's taken two bayonet wounds in 'is ribs from a big Fritz.' Harry's face is dripping with sweat. 'I got the fucker, though. Only just managed to get Billy on me shoulder.'

Harry takes several more lungfuls of air, watched closely by his friend.

'He's a heavy bugger, Mo.'

Maurice has been looking at Billy's injuries. He glances up at Harry with a look of desolation on his face.

'He's also a dead bugger, 'Arry. He's got two 'oles in 'is back; must 'ave taken 'em while you was carryin' 'im.'

'Fuck! Poor old Billy; he was due 'is pension soon.'

Harry looks down at his dead comrade. There is no trace of sadness on his face, more an expression of bitterness.

'This war is bollocks, Mo. Look, there's only me and that fella over there that made it back. Almost the whole fuckin' squad is gone!'

Mo is not feeling any less angry. The captain's death has affected him deeply.

'We've lost Orred as well; shot right through, poor lad.'

'That's a proper shame; he was all right.'

Harry screws up his eyes and shakes his head, trying to rid the horror from his mind.

'It's bollocks. This ain't a war, it's a fuckin' slaughterhouse!'

'Steady, 'Arry; some of the lads are listenin' —'

'I don't give a fuck; it's all fuckin' bollocks, I tell you!'

Harry picks up his rifle and knapsack and strides off towards the centre of Vailly. Maurice shouts after him.

'Hey, 'Arry! Yer can't just go walkin' off.'

'Can't I? You just watch me. I'm gonna find a bottle o' brandy; then I'm gonna drink it. Then, if I get lucky, I'm gonna shag somethin', anythin'! When I'm sober, I might be back. Or I might not; I might walk all the way to Leyton.'

Maurice watches his friend go. He thinks about going after him, but knows it is better to leave him be. Billy Carstairs's blood has turned the back of Harry's khaki tunic a sickly brown colour. His knapsack has two holes in it. They must have been made by the bullets that killed his company serjeant major.

The 4th Battalion Royal Fusiliers will hold the farm and surrounding area at Maison Rouge for the next seven days, after which they will be relieved by the Lincolnshires. During the initial encounter, they have lost five officers and over 317 men. But their firm resolve is crucial in ensuring that the advances earned by the French Army to their right flank are not outmanoeuvred by a spirited German counter-attack.

Harry is as good as his word. Twenty-four hours after his 'disappearance', he emerges from Vailly looking calm, if a little bedraggled.

'You, all right?' Mo asks him.

'Yeah.'

'Did yer find yer bottle o' grog?'

'Yeah, but it weren't brandy, just some French bollocks; like fuckin' turps, but it didn't 'alf 'ave a kick to it. Was I missed?'

'Yeah, but I told 'em you'd gone to find a dressin' station. I should keep that blood-stained tunic on an' make sure everyone sees them 'oles in yer knap.'

Harry has not noticed the holes and looks at them in amazement. He rummages around in his knapsack and retrieves two G98 Mauser bullets.

'Jesus! If I'd seen them fuckers, I'd 'ave 'ad two bottles o' grog.'

The next day, Maurice and Harry are summoned to see Major Ashburner. They fear the worst. With the major is Battalion Serjeant Major Jack Coles, a veteran even more gnarled and fearsome than old Billy Carstairs.

'You two deserve much praise for what you did the other day. Captain Orred and Mr Carstairs were fine men, and what you did to try to save them was highly commendable – especially you, Serjeant Woodruff.'

'Thank you, sir.'

'But there's a fly in the ointment, I'm afraid.'

The two men look at one another and then at BSM Coles, who fixes them with an unremitting scowl.

'First of all, you, Serjeant Tait.'

'Sir.'

'Did you not inform my adjutant that Serjeant Woodruff had gone to a dressing station?'

'I did, sir.'

'Is that true?'

'Well, sir, he has two big 'oles in his knapsack an' 'is tunic is covered in blood.'

'Yes, I can see that. Very well, Serjeant Tait. Let me ask you, Serjeant Woodruff, is it true?'

'Well, yer see, sir, I was a bit confused after Fritz 'ad given us a bit of a seein' to –'

BSM Coles intervenes sharply.

'Listen, Woodruff, you was seen in Vailly. You could 'ardly 'ave been missed, covered in blood, wanderin' around wiv a bottle in yer 'and, shoutin' an' propositioning the young ladies of the town. I think you should make a clean breast of it. You was lucky the military bobbies couldn't find yer, or you'd be in detention now.'

'I expect one of them young ladies took pity on me, Mr Coles.'

'Don't you give me any lip, Woodruff.'

Major Ashburner gets to his feet and walks up to Harry.

'Woodruff, your record is exemplary. You and Tait have got more medals and clasps than the rest of the battalion put together. What on earth got into you?'

Harry rests his chin on his chest and takes a breath.

'Forgive my manners, sir, but I was well pissed off. Billy Carstairs was a good bloke, and so was Captain Orred. This war is not like anythin' I've ever seen before. It's mad; mass slaughter, on both sides.'

Maurice tries to catch Harry's eye to stop him talking, but to no avail.

'I just lost control for a while, sir. I'm hot-headed, always 'ave been.'

Major Ashburner circles Harry, staring at him. BSM Coles now puts his head on his chin as if to say, 'Silly bugger!' before Ashburner turns to him.

'Well, Mr Coles?'

'It's a court-martial offence, sir. Or, at the very least, a reduction to the ranks and three months' field punishment.'

Ashburner circles Harry once more. His expression becomes sombre.

'I want to tell you something. Two days ago, Thomas High-gate, a nineteen-year-old private in the Royal West Kents, was shot for desertion in Jouarre, just up the road. He was found hiding in a barn in civilian clothes. General Haig said that an example had to be made of him. If you had been picked up in Vailly, Serjeant Woodruff, you might well be in the same position now.

'However, what men like you have done since we came to France has made me very proud. I'm going to read you a short note addressed to the 4th Battalion Fusiliers from Sir John French, CO of the British forces here. We received it yesterday: "No troops in the world could have done better than you have. England is proud of you, and I am proud of you." Well, that's what you two embody – the best of the world's finest professional army.

'I also think this is a war like nothing we have seen before. And I suspect that what we have witnessed here is only the beginning. However, we are here to fight the war, not pass judgement on it. Do you understand that, Serjeant?'

'Yes, sir.'

'If you had not disappeared into Vailly to get drunk and cavort with the locals, I would have recommended that you receive the Distinguished Conduct Medal. As it is, I think your extraordinary stupidity is just about compensated for by your bravery in carrying a man such a considerable distance under fire.'

The major turns to BSM Coles, who is ready to record his senior officer's verdict.

'Let it be noted in the battalion diary that Serjeant Woodruff suffered a minor wound at Maison Rouge and, after treatment, was given twenty-four hours' leave in Vailly.'

'Very well, sir.'

Harry, a very relieved man, asks Ashburner for permission to speak. He waits for the major to nod his approval.

'Thank you, sir. It won't happen again.'

'Make sure it doesn't. You will not get away with it a second time.'

Monday 14 September

Troyon Sugar Factory, Vendresse, Champagne-Ardenne, France

Major Hamish Stewart-Murray is with the Cameron High-landers as they approach a bare, open plateau beyond a ridge above the village of Vendresse, forty miles north-east of Rheims. Across the ploughed fields in front of them is the red-brick edifice of the Troyon Sugar Factory. It is 6.30 a.m., and the day is going to be autumnally dank and murky.

So far, the Camerons have had few major encounters with the enemy; they are itching to prove themselves on the battle-field, especially now that the French seem to have forced the Germans on to the retreat.

Hamish is no longer attached to General Douglas Haig's headquarters, but is back with the Camerons' D Company and is leading platoons 13 and 16 in a wide-ranging British advance.

Hamish is used to being in the public eye – indeed, he has been a leader of territorial soldiers for many years – but has never led men into the teeth of a real battle. He is nervous. Somewhere ahead of him is a large force of German infantry, probably well set in defensive positions and supported by dis-guised machine-gun posts. There may be German Uhlans with their fearsome sabres and lances, hiding in the trees; there may be batteries of deadly artillery with their trajectories aimed towards the Camerons' advance. This morning is for real, far removed from a training exercise, and even more distant from the splendid nostalgia and ducal pomp of Blair Atholl's toy-soldieresque private army, the Atholl Highlanders.

The third son of a duke, he is supposed to have been bred to confront daunting situations like these. Courage is central to his family's heritage, part of his education from when he was a small boy; leadership defines his class and his nation. But, at this moment, in the chill of a misty morning in Champagne, he derives no strength from the breeding of his ancestors. He feels very lonely and grossly inadequate.

He looks around. He is surrounded by fellow Scots, the vast majority of whom are coarse and hard wee men from Scotland's poorest villages and towns. They are inured to adversity. He, on the other hand, has lived a life of almost unbounded privilege, where neither hardship nor suffering has played a part. Now, he is exposed. The comforts of Blair Atholl are a long way away. His gun will soon be pointed at a resourceful enemy who will return his fire with at least equal ferocity, not at a defenceless grouse or stag which cannot shoot back.

Hamish's pistol hand is shaking. His men are looking to him to lead, but he feels like a nervous schoolboy on his first day of boarding. He is thirty-five years old, but feels like he is thirteen. He is a son of the most titled aristocrat in Scotland, who is a close friend of the King, but he wishes he was a son of a humble forester.

Fortunately for him, Angus Farquhar, his redoubtable company serjeant major, hollers at him. His authoritative voice and familiar accent stop Hamish's mind wandering to places where it should not go.

'The factory is empty, sir; there are no Germans in sight. Will we move out?'

Hamish does not respond with the same confident authority, and barely gets out the appropriate response.

'Yes, Mr Farquhar, let's go.'

'Are you all right, sir?'

Hamish steels himself.

'Yes, just a bit of Bombay belly, bloody field rations, Mr Farquhar.'

'Aye, sir, well, stay close to me. The lads will be makin' a brew when we get into that factory. I've got a wee flask in me knap, a tot or two o' that'll sort yer out.'

'You're very kind, Mr Farquhar; I'll look forward to that.'

'Are we advancing to the pipes today, sir?'

'No skirl of the pipes today, Mr Farquhar. We don't want to let the Hun know we're coming.'

Hamish feels much better knowing that he is with men like Angus. He has a flask of his own in his pocket and decides that when they reach their destination, he will add a couple of shots from his supply to those from his CSM. It might be 'Dutch courage', but it will be very welcome.

Platoons 13 and 16 continue to advance over open ground towards the factory, which is now about 400 yards ahead. It looks deserted and an advanced reconnaissance patrol has confirmed that the Germans moved out some time ago. To his right are more platoons of Camerons stretching along the plateau. To their right are the Black Watch, where Hamish knows Geordie will be, and to the left are several platoons of Scots Guards and the Coldstream.

Just after the sudden, deafening squawks of a parliament of rooks fade into the distance, there is an ever more ear-piercing fusillade of gunfire. Rifle retorts and machine-gun chatter fill the air and echo down the valley. The mechanical din is soon supplemented by human clamour – the sounds of men in torment. Highlanders fall all around. Many are killed outright; others receive terrible wounds as bullets tear into their flesh.

CSM Farquhar hollers at his men.

'They're in the woods above and to the left! Find targets in the trees, and try to keep your heads down.'

He then turns to Hamish. He can see that his captain is bewildered.

'Platoon 13 to give covering fire, sir; platoon 16 to make a dash to the factory?'

Hamish is galvanized by the danger and answers firmly.

'Yes, Mr Farquhar, get them going. I'll organize covering fire.'

His hand has stopped shaking as his adrenalin begins to flow. He is aware of bullets cutting through the air close to him. Some whine as they pass, some whistle, a few make a sound like a bird in flight. Then there is a muted yelp behind him. He looks around just as Company Serjeant Major Angus Gordon Farquhar, a decorated veteran with twenty-two years' service, falls in a heap fifteen yards away. His khaki kilt apron is immediately covered in blood, which is running into the green, red and purple of his regimental plaid and down his bare legs to his hose and garters.

For some bizarre reason, despite the horror of what is in front of him and the threat from the bullets flying all around him, the sight of his CSM's exposed alabaster-white thigh and backside covered with trickles of crimson makes Hamish pause to reflect. He thinks how odd it is that Scottish soldiers still go to war in kilts, just like their ancient ancestors. As an officer, he is in cavalry britches and riding boots. They are suddenly a great comfort to him. If he is to fall into the cold, sickly soil of Troyon, he would prefer not to expose his lily-white flesh in the process.

Farquhar's beige tam-o'-shanter is lying on the ground a yard from his head, which has a gaping hole where his jaw should be. The man's eyes are still open, frozen in the moment of death. Hamish has to look away. The handsome highlander he has just spoken to, who had the presence of a man well-nigh indestructible, is now a hideous corpse.

Hamish goes over to the body. He feels compelled to straighten the man's kilt to cover his exposed buttocks. It seems the least he can do.

He feels very fragile again. If a man like Farquhar can be killed so easily, what hope is there for lesser mortals like him?

Then, before his burgeoning panic can manifest itself, he

is hit too. It feels like a red-hot poker has been thrust through his left thigh. He looks down and sees blood spewing down his leg and over his cavalry boots. He tries to stay on his feet, but cannot. He makes the mistake of trying to put weight on his stricken leg. Pain sears through him and he collapses to the ground. A young corporal rushes over, shouting for medical help, and tries to support his captain.

The pain has banished Hamish's fear.

'Corporal Tovey, we need to get the platoon to the cover of the sugar factory. Where's Serjeant Murray?'

'Dead, sir.'

'Macpherson?'

'Wounded, sir.'

'Then you must get the men moving.'

'They're already on their way to the factory. We've got to get you going as well, sir.'

Hamish hears another dull thud, just above his head, and his corporal's torso falls across his chest. John Tovey, a 25-year-old veteran from St Andrews with eight years' service, is still breathing. But his chest is rapidly filling with blood, which he is spluttering out of his mouth in involuntary spasms. The blood flows on to Hamish's tunic and seeps through to his shirt. He can feel its syrupy warmth. He can also feel the heaving of Tovey's chest. But then the rhythm stops.

Another mother's son is dead.

Hamish is about to push the body off him when another bullet plunges into it. Others hit the ground close by, some of which are so close that he can feel the quiver they make as they strike the earth. He realizes that the Germans are targeting him. He needs Tovey's body as a barricade and decides to lie still in the hope that the German marksmen will assume he is dead. He is afraid to move his head, to take a look, but hopes that the remnants of his platoon have made it to the safety of the sugar factory.

Minutes pass into hours and his body begins to lose

feeling. His leg is throbbing mercilessly, and occasionally the pain is all but unbearable. Bursts of fire are still happening at regular intervals, but the Germans seem to have stopped using him as target practice.

He tries to assess his predicament. He cannot be sure how bad his wound is, or how much blood he is losing. Help is unlikely to arrive until darkness, at the earliest, and there is a chance that the men of his platoon will be under too much pressure to venture out from their cover. They may even think that he is dead already and leave him, like so many others who have been left to die on the battlefield.

At what Hamish estimates to be late morning, the punishing rhythm of the firing diminishes. About half an hour later, it ceases completely. But by now he is in a bad way. The dampness of the ground is making him shiver uncontrollably. He has lost a lot of blood and is feeling faint. Worst of all, claustrophobia is taking over. He has been lying with a dead man across his chest for a long time, a weight that is now restricting his breathing. He begins to push at Corporal Tovey's body but, to his horror, he no longer has the strength to shift it.

A blind terror overwhelms him; he is finding it hard to breathe and, despite his strivings, he cannot release himself from the weight lying across him. All the while, he is staring into the face of the young corporal, a face that has now lost all its colour and whose lips have taken on the hideous powder blue of death.

Then comes blessed relief. The ashen face in front of him is replaced by an encroaching darkness – a liberation that he knows will mean his death.

The terror recedes into a void of unconsciousness.

'Major Stewart-Murray . . . Major . . .'
The voices Hamish hears later are distant and indistinct. They come in waves. There are only voices, no images.

Then they fade away; silence and emptiness resume.

When he eventually becomes conscious, Hamish is in a convent in Armentières. It has been turned into a forward field hospital and is full of badly injured British soldiers.

His vision is not completely clear, and his head thumps like the worst of hangovers. But he feels no pain from his leg, and the terror of his final moments on the battlefield at Troyon has gone. He is in a room on his own, in one of the nuns' cells. Standing by his bed is a young subaltern from the Camerons and next to him is Sister Margaret Killingbeck, looking immaculate in her starched white apron, grey uniform and red-trimmed nurse's bonnet.

'How are you feeling, Hamish?'

Margaret's gentle voice is such a comfort. Her tone sounds almost angelic to Hamish's ears.

'You have been very fortunate. You lost a lot of blood; another hour or so on the ground and you would not have made it.'

Hamish croaks a question.

'How did I get here?'

The Camerons' subaltern provides the answer.

'Sir, the Germans withdrew from the woods under pressure from the Coldstream boys on their flank, so we were able to retrieve you. Corporal Tovey's body saved your life. It was riddled with bullets when we found you both.'

'How many did we lose?'

'I'm afraid the numbers are grim, sir. Eighteen officers and four hundred and fifty-six men from the battalion killed, missing or wounded. In your company, D Company, the numbers are worse still. When we came to do the roll call, of its five officers and two hundred and twenty-two men, none of the officers and only eighty-six men reported in. You are the only officer to survive.'

'Good God! I need to get back on my feet.'

Margaret swiftly intervenes.

'You won't be back on your feet for quite a while, and certainly not in France. You're going home.'

'I can't, Margaret. We have no officers left.'

'That's as may be, but you've been unconscious for over a week. You nearly lost your leg, and you have a hole in it the size of a cricket ball. Fortunately, the bullet missed the bone and the artery, otherwise you wouldn't be here. But the wound is now infected –'

Hamish tries to interrupt, but Margaret will have none of it.

'You're going home. There's nothing more to be said. The doctors and I give the orders here, and you will do as you're told.'

Hamish remembers his fears before any shots were fired at Troyon. He then recalls the tormented faces of the men who died around him. Finally, the horror of his predicament on the battlefield invades his senses. He breathes a huge sigh; Margaret's words are suddenly a great comfort. Home seems like a good idea.

He remembers his brother, Geordie, and turns to the subaltern.

'What have you heard about the Black Watch, Lieutenant?'

'They got a mauling like us, sir; very heavy losses, I'm afraid.'

'Will you do something for me?'

'Of course.'

'Please find out what you can about Captain George Stewart-Murray, B Company.'

'Straight away, sir; I'll go over to the brigade myself. Their HQ is just down the road.'

'Thank you.'

The Camerons' lieutenant salutes and leaves. When he has gone, Margaret touches Hamish's hand.

'We nearly lost you, Hamish, and that leg is going to hurt. We can't give you much morphine – we haven't got much – so you're going to face a lot of pain. You need a long convalescence in that castle of yours.'

Hamish's latent feelings for Margaret rise to the surface.

'Come with me, Margaret.'

She smiles at him warmly.

'Sorry, Hamish; it's a nice thought, but a million Germans down the road are not going to let that happen.'

Hamish then remembers the promise he made to Captain Philip Davies.

'At least take some leave and come with me to deliver on my promise to that Welch Fusilier.'

'I'm afraid there's no leave for me just yet. And you must go straight home; your leg is already septic, you can't go wandering off to Wales.'

'But what about that poor girl?'

Margaret then has a thought.

'I've been asked to go back to Britain for a month. We are desperately short of nurses and, with Lord Kitchener recruiting a new army, we're going to need even more. A few of us are going to be touring all our general hospitals in a recruitment drive. I could see if I can be given Shropshire and Herefordshire, then I could deliver the letter and key.'

'That sounds ideal, Margaret. I think we will both feel better when we have relieved ourselves of that particular burden.'

Hamish Stewart-Murray is invalided home from Le Havre aboard the HMS *Asturias* on 21 September. While in the Channel, he writes to his father, the Duke of Atholl.

I'm afraid the reports about Geordie I have received are very scant. The lieutenant I sent off to the brigade to make inquiries came back only with hearsay. It was said that Geordie had received a wound to the head as a result of a shell exploding close to him. But he is not with his battalion and is not in any of the hospitals. Some men said that he was alive when they last saw him and that the Germans may have taken him to their medical facilities. Officially, he is listed as wounded, but that will soon be amended to missing. I am going to stay at Eaton Square for a while and hope to be at Blair soon, when I'm sure we will have good news about Geordie.

Hamish's letter to his father is not as blunt as it might be. Before he left for the coast, he heard reports that during the retreat from their encounter with the Black Watch, the Germans had shot all the wounded Scots they found on the battlefield.

He fears Geordie may have been one of them, if he was not dead already.

Tuesday 22 September

Duke's Arms, Presteigne, Radnorshire

Margaret Killingbeck has organized her nurse-recruiting tour of the hospitals of the West Midlands so that she can travel to Presteigne to fulfil Hamish Stewart-Murray's promise to a dying Welch Fusilier.

As her mission is somewhat delicate, she decides to make some discreet inquiries at the Duke's Arms, the town's main watering hole. She chooses her time carefully, just a few minutes after the pub's 11.00 a.m. opening time, when it has yet to welcome any customers and the landlord is tidying the bar for the day ahead.

'Good morning, landlord. Would you have a room available for tonight, and dinner perhaps?'

'Yes, indeed, miss. Our rooms all have fireplaces, and our bathroom has lots of hot water. As we're at the end of the season, I can let you have the room for three shillings and sixpence, including dinner.'

'Very good, I'll take it.'

'Your name, miss?'

'Margaret Killingbeck.'

'Would you like to go up now?'

'In a moment . . . Perhaps you can help me with an inquiry before I do? Is there a Thomas family in the town?'

'Well, Miss Killingbeck, this is Wales; we have a few of those.'

'Of course! This one would have a daughter called Bronwyn, a young girl about seventeen or eighteen.'

The landlord's jovial demeanour changes dramatically.

'Sorry, miss, can I ask why you want to know?'

'My mother is Welsh – also a Thomas – and she thinks Bronwyn and I are cousins.'

'Oh, I see.'

The landlord still looks at Margaret quizzically.

'And her brothers, of course?'

Margaret suspects the landlord may be asking the question to catch her out, but she has prepared herself well.

'I'm not sure about any brothers; we only have an old letter from many years ago, which talks about Bronwyn's birth.'

The landlord is a little more at ease following Margaret's answer.

'I didn't mean to pry, miss, but there's been a bit of an upset in the Thomas family. There're lots of rumours about, which I shouldn't talk of. But, as far as I know, only Hywel, the oldest boy, is up at the farm. The other brothers, Geraint and Morgan, Bronwyn's twin, have joined up with Kitchener.'

'And Bronwyn?'

'Gone as well, miss. She was engaged to young Tom Crisp, a nice boy from the town, a carpenter. He's gone as well, but nobody knows where.'

'Have they gone off together?'

'I don't know. But I don't think so . . . not if you listen to the stories.'

'Can you get someone to take me to the Thomas farm after lunch?'

'Of course. Old Carwyn will take you up to Pentry in his trap.'

There is a biting westerly wind to greet Margaret when she arrives at Pentry Farm. The chill of the autumnal air is an abrupt reminder that, when she gets back to France, she will not only have the wounded and dying to deal with, she will soon also be fighting every soldier's most bitter enemy: winter.

She asks Old Carwyn to wait for her, in the hope that a simple question to Hywel will produce a straightforward and brief answer. Despite the noisy arrival of Old Carwyn's trap and the incessant barking of the farm sheepdogs, Hywel is nowhere to be seen.

'He'll be around somewhere, miss. Young Hywel never comes down to Presteigne no more; he'll be around.'

Then Hywel appears from behind the wood store that Tom Crisp made into a modest home for Bronwyn and himself. He looks windswept and unkempt. He has about a week's worth of stubble on his face and his clothes are covered in the detritus of his agricultural occupation. To add to his shabby appearance, his manner is abrupt, almost to the point of snarling.

'If you're from Grundy's Solicitors, I told the last chap that I don't know where she is an' there's nothing of hers left here. So you can go back to where you came from.'

'I'm not from a solicitor's office; I'm a nurse.'

'So what do want here?'

'I'm looking for your sister, Bronwyn.'

Hywel's manner changes to a less threatening demeanour. 'Is she in hospital?'

'No, that's not the reason for my visit . . .' Margaret hesitates. 'May we go inside?'

Somewhat reluctantly, Hywel guides Margaret into Pentry's kitchen, where she is greeted with a scene of domestic chaos bordering on squalor.

'Sorry, miss, I don't have much time to look after the place. The farm is more than enough on its own; I've no time to look after the house.'

'That's as may be, Mr Thomas. But if I may say so, there's no excuse for a mess like this.'

'Well, it's a good thing it's none of yer business, then!'

'Look, I grew up on a sheep farm in Swaledale, in the North of England, so I know what it's like.'

'Swaledale! I know all about Swaledale, half o' my flock are "Swarddlers", as we call 'em . . .' He pauses and looks Margaret up and down. 'You're dressed up good and proper for a farmer's daughter, aren't yer?'

'I'm not a farmer's daughter any more; I'm a nursing sister with the army in France.'

'So what brings you to Presteigne an' asking after Bron?'

'I have a couple of things that belongs to her.'

'Well, you can leave them with me.'

'No, I can't, Mr Thomas; they belong to her.'

A sneer of a smile breaks across Hywel's face.

'Don't suppose this 'as something to do with a certain officer in the Welch Fusiliers, do it?'

Margaret is dismayed by Hywel's question and is not sure what to say.

'Would you like me to help you clean this place up a bit? I can tell Old Carwyn to come back later.'

'No, thanks, I'd rather know what it is yer 'ave for Bron.'

Margaret takes a deep breath and makes a decision. She walks outside and asks Old Carwyn to come back at six thirty. When she returns, she takes off her coat and rolls up her sleeves.

'Let's talk while we sort this mess out.'

'Suit yourself.'

Hywel watches as Margaret begins to bring her nurse's training and military discipline to Pentry Farm's kitchen.

'Mr Thomas, if you will tell me what's happened, I will tell you the circumstances that brought me here.'

Hywel spends some time thinking about how to respond. Eventually, he begins to help with the clearing up. His tone becomes less hostile.

'What 'ave you heard in town, miss?'

'Please call me Margaret. I've heard nothing, other than the Thomas family has had a bit of upset and there are lots of rumours around.'

'Well, we've certainly had an "upset" and there're lots o' rumours. Sorry to say, most of 'em are true.'

Hywel sighs, a prolonged sigh of despair, then turns to Margaret and tries to summon a smile.

'Would you like a cup of tea?'

'Only if I make it and wash up the mugs myself!'

Margaret's mockery does make Hywel smile. As she makes the tea, he carries on with the chores and begins his account of recent times at Pentry.

'I knew for a while that Bron wasn't very 'appy and things weren't right with Tom, her fiancé. He lived 'ere with her an' was a good friend to me an' the boys – one of the family, really. We'd all 'ad a big setback when an offer to buy the farm fell through because the buyer died suddenly. The whole thing caused a big rift between us, an' I thought that was what the problem was with Bron.'

'You'll have to drink your tea black, Hywel; I can't find any milk.'

'I know, I've had to sell our cow.'

The misery of his situation is borne out by the look of utter wretchedness on his face. Hywel then continues his story.

'So, that was back at the end o' July. Bron 'ad been doin' some cleanin' for Philip Davies for a few weeks, to make ends meet. He was a local bigwig an' a proper gent, or so we thought. When war broke out, that brought more problems. Davies went off with the Welch Fusiliers. Not many even knew he was a territorial. One day he was 'ere, next day he was gone.

'Bron became very moody; she and Tom rowed all the time. I don't know whether Tom twigged anythin' – I certainly didn't – but about four weeks ago, Clara Davies, Philip's wife, gets a telegram telling 'er that he's been killed in France. She's a funny woman to begin with, but she goes mad. She comes up 'ere shoutin' and screamin' at Bron, accusin' 'er of havin' an affair with Philip, and starts throwing all these drawings all over the farmyard. Filthy stuff that Davies apparently used to sell on the quiet. She kept shoutin' over an' over again, "I know what you've been up to with these drawings, you little whore. You're not the first, you know!"'

Hywel's eyes begin to redden as he fights back tears. Margaret watches as he struggles to control himself.

'Clara then shouts, "Now he's dead! So your disgusting little games will never happen again." Bron doesn't say anythin' at first – she's stunned, like – but then she bursts into a fit of screaming. Tom appears, wantin' to know what all the noise is about. He tries to comfort Bron but she pushes him away, shoutin', "No! No! Dear God, no!"'

'So he gets angry with her. She starts on at him, tellin' him to leave her alone. It's obvious to him that something has gone on with Davies, and he starts shakin' Bron. I 'ave to pull him off her. Then Clara says she knows all about a bank account that Davies has been puttin' money into for her. It was 'orrible' – Hywel throws his head back in anguish – 'like the whole world was fallin' apart.

'Even though she was still carryin' on, I made Clara's driver take her back home. By the time I'd finished, Tom was already runnin' down the road to Presteigne. Bron took about ten minutes to collect a few things before she was off 'erself. She went the other way, towards Llandrindod Wells.'

'Didn't you go after her?'

'No, I should 'ave done . . . but, to tell you the honest truth, I was disgusted. She was my little sister and he was a middle-aged man!'

'She's still your sister.'

'Is she? If she is, I don't know her. I've burned those

drawings; no one should be allowed to see things like that. I can't sleep for thinkin' about her and him. It makes me sick.'

Margaret sits down next to Hywel and puts her hand on his arm.

'I'm really sorry, Hywel. I can't begin to explain or excuse what happened between them, but don't cast her out.'

'I didn't, she went of her own accord. And what about Tom? He's my best friend.'

'I know, it's an awful situation. But Bronwyn will need help. She's gone through hell as well.'

'Serves 'er right. She's a slut; there's the truth of it. No decent girl would do what she got up to with Davies. Tom's disappeared. Geraint and Morgan 'ave had to leave the town and 'ave gone to join up. They'll probably get killed in the war. I'm left to try an' hold this place together. I 'ave to go into Knighton to get what I need, because I'm too embarrassed to show my face in Presteigne.'

'I'm so sorry for all that has happened. But I have to ask if you have any idea where she is?'

'No, I don't, and I don't want to know.'

'Hywel, she'll need help, believe me! If you think you're going through hell, she will be feeling just the same – if not worse. Only another woman can understand what she's going through. If you know anything, please tell me.'

Hywel relents.

'Clara Davies 'as got the solicitors on to me. She's after the money Davies was sending Bron. It's not really the money, of course – she's got plenty o' that – she just wants revenge. The solicitor's man said Bron's been seen in Cardiff, in Tiger Bay, working the pubs.'

'As a barmaid?'

Hywel looks at Margaret with a laconic smile, then spits out an answer.

'No, Margaret, she's a "floozie", a "good-time girl" – whatever name you want to put on it. My little sister is a whore to sailors and drunks and anybody else with two bob in his pocket!'

Margaret shudders in disbelief.

'I must find her.'

'Don't bother! If that's how far she's sunk, there's no way back. Tiger Bay is a hell on earth.'

'I'm going to find her. If I do, will you take her back?'

Hywel takes a long time to answer. But when he does, it is with a chilling finality.

'No.'

Margaret gets up to leave.

'Aren't you forgetting your side of the bargain?'

'There's not much to say. Captain Philip Davies died in my arms from his wounds. He was brought to me in Bavay, a small town in France, about the same size as Presteigne. He was a brave man and, if it's of any comfort, he loved your sister. I was with an officer from the Cameron Highlanders and Philip asked him if he would give your sister a letter and a small memento when he was next on leave. The Camerons' officer has picked up a wound himself and has been sent home to Scotland, which is why I'm here.'

Hywel walks over to the window and looks out over the farm.

'I'm glad he's dead. Because I'd decided that, when he came home, I'd put a pitchfork through his guts.'

Margaret looks at Hywel and has not the slightest doubt that he means what he said. Hywel turns to look at Margaret.

'All of a sudden, prices are going up because of the war. I was thinking of letting the farm to one of our neighbours and joining my brothers with the Welch. What's it like out there?'

'Stay here, Hywel; it's a slaughterhouse.'

'Sounds about right to me. I'd rather die a quick death for

King and country out there than die a slow one here, wallowing in my own shit.'

'Don't imagine they're all quick deaths; many are not. Stay in Wales.'

'I think I might risk it.'

As Margaret prepares to leave, Hywel turns away from the window.

'Thank you for coming such a long way.'

'Don't go to the war, Hywel. Find yourself a local girl, stay here and raise Swaledale sheep and a family of your own.'

New Street Station, Birmingham

It has been a hectic few days for Britain's First Lord of the Admiralty. On Monday, Winston spoke at an all-party recruiting rally in Liverpool. As usual, his powerful oratory struck a chord with the audience. But his remark that, if the ships of the German Fleet continued to hide in their ports, they would be 'dug out like rats in a hole', although generating rapturous applause on Merseyside, brought extensive criticism in the Conservative press. It also earned a fatherly rebuke from Asquith, who said that his words had upset the King and were hardly dignified for a Cabinet minister.

When Winston hears of the reprimand by telegram, he is travelling back to London with his friend F. E. Smith. They are eating lunch between trains at Birmingham's New Street Station.

'FE, much as I admire the Old Block, I sometimes wonder whether he realizes what we're up against in this war. Bless him, he means well, but we have to stir up the British fighting spirit.'

'I agree, Winston, but he's your leader, not mine. Don't you think his time's up? He's too much of a gentle pacifier; you need Lloyd George in Number Ten. He'll stiffen our sinews. On the other hand, you might also consider making a run for the highest office?'

'Too many enemies, including the King – who does not care for me – but you're right about LG; it's only a matter of time.'

'Excuse me, sir.'

John Gough, Winston's Special Branch protection officer, comes to the table and hands Winston another telegram, which he opens carefully.

'Oh dear, FE, it's bad news.'

Winston pauses to reread the telegram. A flash of anger darts across his face.

'What in God's name were they doing there!'

FE picks up the telegram. It reads:

Engagement at Broad Fourteens, close to Dutch coast, early this morning. Three cruisers sunk. *Cressy, Hogue, Aboukir* hit by German submarine torpedoes. 60 officers and 1,400 men believed lost.

'Weren't they the cruisers from the victory at the Heligoland Bight?'

'Yes, they were. Fifteen hundred men lost! Heads will roll, FE. I met with all my senior men on Jellicoe's flagship, the *Iron Duke*, only last week, when we were briefed about the submarine threat in the North Sea. I immediately issued a note ordering that patrols close to the German and Dutch coasts should cease. They've not taken a blind bit of notice of me!'

'Do you want me to leak the memo to the press? You'll get the blame otherwise.'

'Tempting, FE, but we must appear to be united. I'll take the bullet; it will only be a flesh wound.'

'Yes, but it'll sting like buggery.' FE hands Winston his copy of *The Times*. 'Look, Winston, it's a poem from a chap called Laurence Binyon. How beautifully put!'

Winston reads the poem out loud, raising his voice so that others nearby can hear. He finishes it in tears.

> They went with songs to the battle, they were young.
> Straight of limb, true of eye, steady and aglow.
> They were staunch to the end against odds uncounted;
> They fell with their faces to the foe.
>
> They shall grow not old, as we that are left grow old:
> Age shall not weary them, nor the years condemn.
> At the going down of the sun and in the morning,
> We will remember them.
>
> They mingle not with their laughing comrades again;
> They sit no more at familiar tables of home;
> They have no lot in our labour of the daytime;
> They sleep beyond England's foam.

There is silence from those who have been listening, except for one man, who asks a policeman who Winston is. When he is told, he walks up to Winston and shakes his hand.

'God bless you, Mr Churchill. We're all right behind you. Give 'em hell!'

Applause breaks out all around. Winston acknowledges the support.

'You see, FE, this is different. This is not a war of governments and generals, it is a war for the hearts and minds of people. It touches our very souls.'

'Do you really think it so different? The Napoleonic Wars were fought between Revolutionary France and ourselves, trying to protect our ancient monarchy.'

'Perhaps, but let me quote some figures: four hundred and seventy thousand men have joined up for Kitchener's volunteer army. That's nearly half a million men in just six weeks.'

'But they're amateurs. They are being sent to face a professional army that has been decades in the making.'

'Agreed, but this is a citizen army. And if it maintains its belief in its cause, it will be formidable. Take Glasgow: a whole battalion raised from men who work on the buses and trams, and another from former members of its Boys' Brigade. Working-class men who care about their King, their country and their empire. I would wager that, with appropriate training, they will soon be the equal of the Hun, especially given the heinous behaviour of some of the Kaiser's men.'

'Winston, you are an incurable romantic! But I admire you enormously and feel privileged to know you as a dear friend.'

'Thank you, dear boy. Stay close to me over the coming months.'

When the two men are on the train to London, Winston opens a letter from Clemmie, who is close to giving birth to their third child. He has seen little of her or his children in recent days, so her words of love and support are a great comfort to him. One section, the final paragraph, makes him glow with pride.

> *Asquith relies on you more and more. You and LG are the only dynamic ones he has.*
>
> *Don't hang back. You rule our mighty navy with such vigour and wisdom – a navy which will surely decide the fate of this, the greatest war in all history.*
>
> *I am so proud that you are in thick of it.*
>
> *Your ever loving,*
> *Clemmie*

Winston immediately puts pen to paper himself.

> *Darling one,*
>
> *I am enjoying FE's company, as usual. Last night's meeting was full of British Bulldog spirit from FE's excellent Merseyside constituents – who, I believe, call themselves 'Scousers'. A fine lot. I*

asked FE what 'scouse' means. Oddly, it means at least three things: a cheap Irish stew they eat; the name of their distinctive accent; and their name for themselves. How strange! FE mimics their accent wonderfully, in which book becomes 'bewk' and cook is 'cewk'. He tells a wonderful story at the expense of his homeland.

St Peter is at the Pearly Gates of Heaven to greet a group of Scousers. As he has not met many Scousers before, he disappears to check their credentials with God. God agrees the Scousers can be admitted to Heaven, and Peter goes to give them the news. But he soon returns, looking shocked.

God asks him, 'What's wrong?'

'They've gone!' says St Peter.

'The Scousers?'

'No, the Pearly Gates!'

I thought you would enjoy the story; it made me smile, as FE always does.

Darling, I feel I am in my prime. No Black Dog in weeks. I go to France tomorrow to pep up the Royal Marines. A new phase of the war is emerging; we need to secure the Channel at our backs. Winter will soon be with us and we need to be mindful of the long term. I have been studying the maps; the city of Ypres could be the key. I will talk to John French about it.

Tell Goonie that I will also see Jack, who is with the hussars in the area. I have sent them some Admiralty 8-ton trucks to help with logistics in their support of our marines.

I think of you and the kittens every day. Kitten Number 3 will soon be with us, what a delight!

Tender love, dearest one
W

The next day, Churchill is in Dunkirk, the first of several visits to France over the coming days when, to the annoyance of many in the armed forces and the Cabinet, he takes a central role in the war on land as well as at sea and in the air.

He urges his Marine Brigade to maraud around the Belgian border area to convince the German High Command that it is a much larger force than it actually is, and to give encouragement to the local population. He orders air attacks on the Zeppelin sheds in Cologne and Düsseldorf. He also tries to persuade Sir John French to allow the army to use six-inch naval guns on the battlefield, a suggestion that the Commander-in-Chief rejects out of hand.

Winston knows the nature of warfare is changing. The intensity of the fighting and the killing power of the weaponry diminishes significantly any semblance of a code of chivalry between soldiers. As military theorist Karl von Clausewitz said it would, war has become 'absolute' and unrelenting, involving all the resources of the nations involved, including its innocent civilians.

After German air raids on civilians in Ostend, the Cabinet discusses the possibility of retaliating against German cities but, for the time being, rejects the idea. However, Asquith orders the mining of major parts of the North Sea, instructing: 'Make provision on a Napoleonic scale to deploy those infernal devices freely and even lavishly.'

Reports also come in of German infantry units using white flags of surrender in order to entice British units out of their defensive positions before firing on them. Churchill is incensed and issues an immediate order to the Grand Fleet.

All transports believed to be conveying German troops are to be sunk at once by gunfire or torpedo. No parley with or surrender by a transport on the high seas is possible.

He later adds more instructions to the order.

There is no obligation to recognize a white flag. Sir John French has found it necessary to order instant fire to be made on any German white flag, experience having shown that the Germans habitually and systematically abuse the emblem. Consequently, any white flag hoisted by a German ship is to be fired upon as a matter of principle.

Chancellor of the Exchequer David Lloyd George delivers a chilling speech at the Queen's Hall in London, one that he discusses with Winston beforehand.

'Should I be so bold, Winston?'

'Yes, they will listen to you. You will make the nation think. It needs to think long and hard about what we face in the coming months and years.'

Lloyd George takes Winston's advice and makes his speech. One passage, in particular, sends shock waves across the land – especially among those who have lived with years of prosperity and privilege.

A great flood of luxury and sloth, which has submerged the land, is receding and a new Britain is appearing.

We can see for the first time the fundamental things that matter in life and that have been obscured from our vision by the tropical growth of prosperity.

Thursday 24 September

Mary Broxup has lost a lot of friends since Tommy decided to volunteer for the army, and it has been the same for Cath Kenny, Mick's wife.

When the recruiting office opened, 104 men enlisted in just three hours. Many more failed the minimum requirements: men have to be at least 5 feet 6 inches tall, in good health, aged between nineteen and thirty-five. Old soldiers are accepted up to the age of forty-five, which can be extended to fifty for experienced NCOs.

Over 50 per cent of those who tried to enlist were below the height requirement, or had poor teeth or eyesight. Significantly, many showed signs of rickets, or were undernourished. The examining medical officer was shocked by the number of skin diseases he saw, particularly impetigo, and the number of men with various venereal diseases.

Burnley signed up fourteen men, including Thomas John Broxup, Michael Ciaran Kenny, Vincent Michael Sagar and Nathaniel Mordecai Haythornthwaite, all of whom passed their medicals with ease. Vinny (still smarting from his rejection by Burnley Football Club) and Twaites (loyal, as ever, to his pal) are both just shy of their eighteenth birthdays, but were allowed through as they scored highly on the physical tests.

At the recruiting office the four met local legend John-Tommy Crabtree, steward at the Keighley Green Club. Although beyond the age limit by several years, he had been nodded through on the basis that he would be an inspiration for future recruits and good for battalion morale. He lied about his age, saying he had never had a birth certificate, and told the recruiting officer he was only forty-one when, in truth, he is forty-six.

Feeling a sudden shiver of autumnal air coming from the broken window above the sink, Mary now moves on to Tommy's chair and snuggles up to him.

'How's General Kitchener's finest recruit?'

'Don't ask, lass.'

'Same old routine?'

'Aye, we spent t'mornin' marchin' up an' down Fulledge Rec. No sign of uniforms or kit, an' no rifles. One of t'lads said we'd get rifles next Sheffield Flood, an' another said we'd get uniforms next Preston Guild. I reckon they're reet. We're like little lads laikin' at soldiers, we 'ad to pretend we 'ad rifles, usin' broom 'andles an' bits o' wood. Lads an' lassies on t'way to shifts at Rawlinson Street Mill gee' us some reet mockin'. We deserved it, I reckon. Only thing kept us goin' were t'company paymaster; he arrived t'day from Accrin'ton. We get paid t'morn.'

'That's a relief! We're dead skint.'

Tommy frowns and looks at Mary despondently.

'Are we doin' reet thing, lass?'

'Aye, I think so; but I'm in a reet moither abaht it every day. I need to get mesen some work.'

Tommy is reluctant to mention a possibility he heard about today. He knows Mary is proud to be a four-loom weaver, a position of some esteem among fellow workers, especially as a woman.

'How abaht pot washin'?'

'Where?'

'Spoke to Old John-Tommy Crabtree t'day. He said he could get thee some work washin' pots at Keighley Green.'

Mary smiles broadly.

'Tell 'im I'll tek it; I'm not above washin' a few ale pots.'

'Reet, I'll sort it tomorra. I thought tha might not fancy it.'

'I'll do any kind o' work. When can I start?'

'Weekend, I should reckon.'

Tommy and Mary cuddle up closer together, relieved that some money is coming into the house. Tommy smiles to himself.

'Reet funny do t'day wi' t'volunteers. This officer appears, must be fifty-five if he's a day, from down south, calls 'issen a "colour serjeant". He walks on t'Fulledge Rec in full khaki uniform wi' brass buttons, peaked cap an' shiny boots tha could see thy face in. He starts bellowin' at t'lads, "*Get fell in!*", "*One two, one two!*" and all that baloney. He says 'is name is Colour Serjeant Severn and he's 'ere to turn us into proper soldiers.

'So after a bit, he sees Jimmy Dowd grinnin' – yer know, that lad we 'ad a set-to wi' at t'Keighley Green – an' 'e shouts: What are you laughin' at?

'Jimmy says: Nowt, Serjeant.

'Serjeant then says: Can't yer speak the King's fuckin' English? What's 'nowt' mean?

'Jimmy says: It means "nothin'"', Serjeant.

'Serjeant says: Non-commissioned officer on parade, say, "Nothin", *sir!*

'So Jimmy starts to grin again an' says: Sorry, *sir.*

'Serjeant says: Do yer often laugh at nothin', yer daft northern bastard?

'And so it goes on an' on, til t'serjeant, who's 'alf a heed shorter than Jimmy, says: Listen, you big ugly twat, I've taken on thick-necked Boers twice your size. How old are you?

'Jimmy says: Nineteen, sir.

'Serjeant says: By your age I'd fought in the Zulu Wars and had an assegai in me ribs.

'So Jimmy grins again an' says: What's an assegai, sir?

'Lots o' t'lads start laughin'. Serjeant's grey tash twitches like a little 'edgehog an' 'is eyes bulge. His face goes as a red as a beetroot an' he leans for'ard an' sticks his nose in Jimmy's mush an' says: It's a spear, you cheeky bastard, and Zulus are twice the men you'll ever be!

'He then grabs Jimmy's bollocks an' squeezes 'em. Jimmy goes to lamp 'im one, but the serjeant lays his nut on 'im an' knocks 'im reet on 'is backside. He then shouts out: Any more comedians or 'ard cases with something to say?

'Then, some silly bugger from t'back shouts: Tommy Brox and Mad Mick Kenny, sir!

'So he calls out us names an' tells us to step for'ard.'

Mary pushes herself up from Tommy's embrace and stares at him.

'Don't tell me, tha's thumped 'im?'

Tommy adopts a solemn look, suggesting that he has. Then he pauses, and smiles.

'Course not! I knows I'm daft, but I'm not that bloody daft. Serjeant spoke to Mick first: So you're a "Mad Mick", are yer, lad?

'Mick says: It's a nickname I've picked up, sir.

'Serjeant says: So are yer going to be a "Mad Mick" in my company?

'And Mick says: No, sir, only wi' t'Germans.

'Serjeant says: Good lad, that's what I want to hear. Then he turns to me and says: What about you, Tommy?

'So I says: Same as Mick, sir. I'm here to fettle t'Germans.

'By then, Jimmy Dowd is pickin' 'issen off t'floor. He's got a reet shiner on 'is forheed an' is still rubbin' 'is bollocks. Serjeant says to 'im: See, Jimmy, these two hard cases have got a brain to go with their brawn. See if you can work out where yours is!

'So that's our new gaffer; an 'ard little bugger. Me an' Mick'll 'ave ter think on an' keep our heeds down. We're off on a route march in t'morn; through Brierfield an' Nelson an' then o'er Trawden way an' across Widdop.'

'But that's miles, Tommy!'

'I know; tell yer what, we're gonna be as fit as whippets when we feight t'Germans.'

Docklands, Tiger Bay, Cardiff

It takes Margaret two days to travel to Cardiff from Pentry Farm. By the time she arrives in the docklands area it is nine thirty in the evening and Tiger Bay's pubs are crowded. The throng heaving in the fug of tobacco and perspiration is a mix of the least wholesome of the indigenous Welsh inhabitants of the host city and a similar residue of its many migrants and visitors. There are numerous merchant ships anchored in the bay – many more than usual – as war is good for business and trade.

Tiger Bay is a fascinating racial cocktail of the poor and dispossessed. There are the locals, many of whom are themselves second- or third-generation sons and daughters of those who have sought refuge on Welsh shores. Then there are the myriad sailors – including Somali, Yemeni, Greek, Irish, West African, Norwegian and legion others.

Crimes of all sorts are commonplace, but the perpetrators are rarely caught, as most of them are already at sea by the time their misdemeanours are discovered.

Using the disguise of being a member of the Band of Hope, Margaret persuades the desk serjeant at the local police station to check on the new recruits to Tiger Bay's 'ladies of the night', saying she is looking for a girl of eighteen, long black hair, very pretty.

'This is Cardiff, miss, most of the girls have long dark hair and look pretty – at least, at the start.'

'She comes from a small town on the English border, so perhaps her Welsh accent is not that strong.'

The serjeant looks at his log book.

'There is one very pretty lass; she's been arrested twice in the last month, name of Alice.'

He also tells Margaret which of the local pubs 'Alice' has been seen in. But he finishes with a note of caution.

'Be careful, miss, it's not the sort of area you should be going into alone.'

Margaret, now feeling distinctly uncomfortable in the neat and prim clothes of a middle-class lady, manages to make herself heard above the multilingual din of the Bute Dock Hotel, West Bute Street. She asks the barman if he knows a girl called Alice.

'No one of that name here, miss.'

Margaret slips a twopenny piece into the barman's palm.

'If you see her, can you tell her that a good friend wants to speak to her?'

'Don't know the lady, miss.'

Margaret is convinced that she is in the right place and decides to bide her time. She orders a gill of milk stout and a glass of port. They are the tipple of the local girls and, although a little incongruous for a woman of her status, the alcohol helps her fit in with the crowd and its potency soon makes her feel better.

After about twenty minutes, during which Margaret has to fend off several admirers who feel certain that she is a well-to-do lady looking for a 'bit o' rough', a young woman appears at her shoulder.

'I hear . . . you . . . you're . . . a friend . . . o' mine?'

Bronwyn's speech is slurred and she seems to have aged ten years. She has lost a lot of weight and her once shiny black locks are lank and knotted. The flawless pale skin of her face has become dappled and acned. Her eyes are blood-shot, her clothes grubby and she has the seedy aroma of destitution about her.

'I need to talk to you privately.'

'Are you . . . the Sally Army?'

'No.'

Margaret notices that the landlord is staring at the two of them very intently.

'Can we go somewhere?'

Bronwyn smirks at Margaret.

'Is that what yer after? I've 'eard 'bout women like you. It'll cost yer five shillin'.'

Margaret has to think quickly, the landlord is on his way over to them.

'Agreed, but four shillings.'

'Give it t' George . . . the landlord. Wait five minutes, then . . . come up.'

When Margaret hands George two florins, he grasps her wrist tightly.

'I 'ope you're not one of them do-gooders lookin' for "fallen women". Because if y'are, I'll come up an' fuck you myself. It looks like you could do with it.'

Margaret pulls her hand away and gives him a withering look.

'Take your money and get out of my way.'

When Margaret enters Bronwyn's room, the girl has already stripped to her petticoat and chemise; her skirt and bodice are discarded on the threadbare carpet. The bed is unmade, the sheets stained and the room reeks with an unpleasant mingling of cheap scent and human body odour. Bronwyn starts to unbutton her chemise, but is finding it difficult in her drunken state.

'What's yer name?'

'Margaret.'

'Come here . . . Margaret . . .'elp me wi' these.'

'You can stop undressing. I'm here with some things from Philip Davies.'

Bronwyn's fingers stop fumbling. She glares at Margaret and tries to clear her head.

'I don't know anyone called . . . Philip Davies.'

'Here's a letter from him.'

As Bronwyn accepts the letter from Margaret's hand, she collapses to the floor in a heap and begins to sob uncontrollably, her tears only adding to her pitiful appearance. Her hands shake as she tears open Philip's letter. It takes her several minutes to read the three pages of small, precise handwriting.

Margaret watches the girl closely. She does the mental arithmetic on the timing of Bronwyn's descent and shivers when she realizes how dramatically sudden it has been – just a few short weeks. She is worried about drug use of some sort in addition to the girl's palpable drunkenness. She looks around the room and notices a squat brown bottle of Papine on the mantelpiece, a well-known opiate used by doctors to treat pain but also in widespread use in the opium dens of Britain's docklands.

Her other concern is the likelihood that Bronwyn has contracted at least one venereal disease. If she has, she hopes that it is something treatable, like gonorrhoea, which she sees regularly in her army patients, rather than something like syphilis, which she sees more rarely and for which the treatment is prolonged and usually unsuccessful.

Bronwyn has finished reading Philip's letter and is crushing it into the palm of her hand. She has her eyes squeezed tightly shut, as if trying to purge her memories.

'We need to get you out of here.'

Bronwyn opens her eyes. They are just red-rimmed pools of tears. She looks totally devastated.

'And go where? I belong here. Philip's wife was right, I'm just a whore.'

'No, you're not. You've just been knocked down by some terrible events. We can get you back on your feet.'

It takes a long time for Bronwyn to answer. She is rocking herself and shaking her head; her tears are still flowing down her cheeks, blurring her make-up.

'You don't know what I did. If you knew, you would agree with Clara Davies!'

'Listen, you are not the first and you won't be the last woman to have gone through what you've experienced. You need to be strong. If you are, you can get over this.'

'Leave me be! There's no way back for me. When I left Presteigne, I walked and walked, until I couldn't walk any further. I had no money, so I stole food and milk, anything I could find. I was at my wits' end. I managed to get to Brecon, sleeping rough. I must have looked dreadful; dirty clothes, hair all over the place. It was late and I was exhausted –'

'You don't have to tell me this.'

'I do; I want you to understand what I've become.'

'You haven't "become" anything. You're just a little girl lost.'

'I'm not a "little girl" any more! Philip Davies saw to that. And then the landlord at the Boar's Head in Brecon . . . It's by the river. I was going to throw myself in, but I couldn't do it. I ended up sleeping in the pub doorway. He found me the next morning, said I could trust him. He gave me money, cleaned me up. But, of course, he wanted something in return. First with him, then his regulars.

'When I'd saved a few bob, I ran away and got the bus to Cardiff. But it was the same there. I had nowhere to go, but I knew what to do. It didn't take long to find Tiger Bay. It was horrible, but the gin helped, and then my little bottle of Papine. So you see, that's what I've become!'

'Bronwyn, I'm a nurse, nothing shocks me. I've been in France with the army. Philip died in my arms. I know what happened between you. And your brother told me about what happened at Pentry. As for the shame in what you did, it's a guilt you share with thousands of women. Including me.'

Bronwyn turns to stare at Margaret. Her words have made a connection with her.

'You didn't do what I did, end up shaggin' men, an' worse, for two bob!'

'I'll tell you what I did . . . one day. But for now, we need to get you out of here.'

'Was Philip badly injured?'

'Yes.'

'Was he in pain?'

'Yes, he was, but he was very brave. His final words were for you.'

'What did he say?'

'He asked me to tell you that you made him very happy and that you should take wing and fly.'

'What does that mean?'

'I think he meant that you were capable of doing good things, or important things. And that you should try to achieve them.'

Bronwyn begins to heave with more sobs. Margaret takes advantage of the moment and grabs the bottle of Papine. She empties its contents out of the window, then does the same with the gin flask standing next to it. Finally, she pulls Bronwyn up and steadies her.

'Is there a back way out of here?'

'Yes, but George will see us.'

Margaret looks at her fob watch; it is turned 10 p.m. She hopes the landlord is going to be busy at the bar.

'Come on, let's go. Do you have many things?'

'They're in a bag under the bed. I have fourteen shillings in my purse; it's all I have.'

Margaret helps Bronwyn to get dressed, then manoeuvres her down the stairs to the carriage she has asked to wait for her.

The cab driver is suddenly roused from his sleep, his horse from its nosebag.

'I nearly gave you up, miss. Is this the young lady you were looking for?'

'Yes, and I'm very relieved you're still here. Take us back to my boarding house, please.'

As the carriage pulls away, Margaret looks back to the Bute Dock Hotel. The light from its windows is spilling on to the pavement outside, where dozens of men are drinking and smoking. She can hear English and Welsh but also several languages that she has never heard before, spoken by men who seem to represent all the nations of the earth. She turns to Bronwyn, who has closed her eyes and is resting her head in the corner of the carriage.

Although she has tried to reassure Bronwyn, she reflects on how far and how disastrously the girl has fallen: a young and innocent farm girl from a quiet valley in Radnorshire just a few months ago, and now a two-bob whore in Tiger Bay. Getting Bronwyn's life back to even a semblance of normality is not going to be easy.

When they reach Margaret's room close to Cardiff Castle, she gets to work with her usual expert efficiency. Bronwyn's clothes are discarded and she is deposited in the boarding house's bath for a prolonged soak. She washes her thoroughly from head to toe, brushes and combs her hair and then checks for lice. Fortunately, although there are a few nits, Margaret doesn't find the infestation she had feared.

When she gets the girl to bed, she gives her a small sip of laudanum to help her relax and then sits with her until she falls asleep – probably the first decent night's sleep she has had in a long time. Margaret smiles to herself. Bronwyn already looks more like a young farmer's daughter than a docklands' tart.

Margaret watches over Bronwyn until the early hours. After a while, the temptation to read Philip's letter becomes too strong. She rescued it from Bronwyn's grasp in her grimy room earlier and put it in her handbag.

It begins not unlike many soldiers' letters to their sweethearts. She has read several; men in her care will often ask her to proofread their stilted prose. Some even dictate to her what they want to say to wives and girlfriends back home because they cannot write themselves, either as a result of their injuries or through a lack of education.

Philip's immaculately penned letter is, at first, written in the formal Edwardian style of the day, almost as if composed by a town clerk, telling of the Welch Fusiliers' journey to France and what they have been doing since. But then, towards the end, the language changes. Margaret guesses the latter part might have been written on the eve of battle, or after witnessing the death of a comrade. The final passage makes her weep.

I know not what will become of me. This war is becoming a hell on earth and I fear many of us will not survive it. But what will be, will be. Far more important is what will become of you. I readily admit that my initial attraction to you was born of lust, which then became an infatuation of blissful proportions. However, I want you to understand that everything changed. I fell in love with you, and I'm still in love with you – a deep and abiding love that will never go away. You have a wonderfully inquisitive mind, a strong will and a shrewd intelligence – so much so that there is little you couldn't do if you put your mind to it –

The letter ends at that point. Philip must have intended to write more, but his wounds at Mons prevented it. Margaret eventually falls asleep in her chair as Bronwyn continues her deep slumber.

The next morning, wearing Margaret's clothes and make-up and with her hair brushed to restore a semblance of its dark lustre, Bronwyn could easily pass as her nursing colleague.

'Are you ready for this, Bronwyn?'

'No, I need a drink and a smoke.'

'Sorry, you're off the booze and cigarettes – and anything else you've been using.'

'But I can't cope without them.'

'Yes, you can; you have to. If it gets too bad, there is something I can give you.'

'What?'

'A little laudanum. But in decreasing doses.'

Bronwyn answers like a forlorn child.

'I'll try . . .'

In contrast, Margaret responds like a stern headmistress.

'You had better! If you let me down, I'll let you go. You must understand that, Bronwyn.'

Bronwyn composes herself and smiles at Margaret.

'Please call me Bron. And tell me one thing: why are you doing this for me?'

'Because of the promise I made to Philip. And because of what you have had to suffer.'

'Doesn't what we did disgust you?'

'No, it doesn't.'

'And what about what I've become?'

'That doesn't disgust me either. But that was yesterday. Today is a new beginning for you.'

'I can't believe what's happening to me.' Bronwyn embraces Margaret and clings to her. 'Is it really true?'

'Of course it is. Come on, let's get moving.'

'Where are we going?'

'To Hereford General Hospital. I can get us into the nurses' quarters there, where you can be looked after.'

Bronwyn recoils.

'What does that mean?'

'Bron, I have to be blunt with you. You have head lice and, from the look of your pubic area, you have gonorrhoea and vaginal warts at least; you may have caught other things as well. You have a bad cough from smoking and drinking, and we have to get you off that Papine you've been taking. It's liquid opium, highly addictive.'

Bronwyn looks devastated.

'One more thing; we need to make sure you're not pregnant.'

'I know I'm not pregnant.'

'How?'

'I lost Philip's baby two weeks ago.'

Margaret pulls the girl more tightly to her.

'You poor thing. Let's get going, so that we can make you better.'

Friday 25 September

Boughton House, Kettering, Northamptonshire

Kitty Stewart-Murray has spent the month of September organizing concerts and generally supporting Bardie as he prepares his Scottish Horse in Dunkeld for the long journey to France. However, in late September, the true horror of the Great War reaches the grandeur of Blair Atholl.

When the old duke hears of Hamish's wound and the ominous disappearance of Geordie, he retreats to the bosom of his mistress, Mrs Maud Grant, who lives in a small estate cottage high up Glen Tilt, leaving Lady Helen to run the house and the estate. Several Blair families, estate workers and people in the household have already lost loved ones. Of the reservists who were summoned to their regiments two have been killed, six wounded and two more designated missing. Everyone remarks that Scotland has not lost so many men since it fought the English hundreds of years ago.

When Bardie's Scottish Horse is sent south to new barracks at Kettering, Kitty travels with him. When he subsequently hears that Hamish is on his way home from France to recover from his wound, he calls for a family gathering in Kettering.

Fortunately, the Stewart-Murrays do not have to accept accommodation that is any less luxurious than Blair Castle. Indeed, in many ways their surroundings for the latest gathering of their clan are even more sumptuous.

Old family friend William Montague Douglas-Scott, the 83-year-old 6th Duke of Buccleuch, has made his Northamptonshire home, Boughton House, available to them. Boughton's

Georgian splendour is grander and on an even larger scale than Blair. Situated only three miles from the Scottish Horse's improvised, ramshackle Kettering barracks and stables, it is a world away from the awful reality of the war that is currently unfolding along the French-Belgian border.

William Douglas-Scott is immeasurably rich – one of the wealthiest British landowners – and the Stewart-Murrays feel at home. In more normal times, the Friday dinner before a country-house weekend of much eating, drinking and debauchery would represent an enticing aperitif. But the Stewart-Murray gathering comprises only a small group of close family, and its mood is made sombre by the shadow of war.

With the Duke of Buccleuch ensconced in his London home – Montague House, in Whitehall – Bardie and Kitty act as hosts for the weekend at Boughton. Hamish hobbles in, protecting his lame thigh. Lady Helen brings her 'friend' David Tod, about whom the rest of the family are highly dubious because of his middle-class origins, calling him 'Edinburgh egghead' and 'lowly salesman'. Lady Dorothea, 'Dertha', is with her husband, Colonel Harold 'Harry' Ruggles-Brise.

Harry is the only member of the family with something to celebrate. He has been given command of 20th Brigade, composed of the 1st Grenadiers, 2nd Scots Guards, 2nd Gordon Highlanders and the Border Regiment, and will soon depart for France. He is in two minds. Partly exhilarated at the prospect of command, he is an accomplished soldier and musketry training expert who should be looking forward to his army pension, but now faces a long cold winter on the front line. He puts on a brave face.

Bardie proposes a toast.

'To Harry, congratulations and bon voyage!'

Lady Helen then adopts the role of the surrogate Duke of Atholl. Despite being the heir to the dukedom, Bardie accepts her suitability as titular head of the family with equanimity. Helen stands with her back to the fire, as her father would.

'Well done, Harry. I've also got good news from Evelyn. She has written a brief note to Father. Her apartment in Malines was ransacked when the Germans took the town, but she and her companion managed to get away to the coast with all their valuables intact. However, she did leave them some presents. She cooked a dozen steak and kidney pies and left them in her larder, but laced them with so much pepper that they were inedible. She also left two carafes of wine on her dining-room table, but half filled them with balsamic vinegar!'

Evelyn's antics raise a smile among the assembled company, but Helen's mood then changes and she begins to make circles on the top of her wine glass.

'Hamish, what do you make of the reports about Geordie?'

'I have taken care to be positive in my letters to Father, but I fear the worst. For there to be no word of him, or those around him, suggests that a shell may have burst close by. There were also reports from men of the Black Watch I spoke to, confirming that the Germans executed anyone they found on the battlefield.'

Lady Dorothea is visibly upset.

'Hamish, *please* –'

'Dertha, I'm sorry, but I'm afraid the truths of a cruel war are brutal.'

'I know that, but Father is worried sick. None of us like it when he goes running off to Mrs Grant, but it is his way of dealing with distress. He can't bring himself to show his emotions to us, so he goes to her. She mothers him, I think.'

Bardie mutters under his breath, 'Among other things!' but only Kitty hears him.

Helen asks for a few moments of silent prayer for

Geordie's safety, after which Kitty changes the subject and tries to inject some levity into the gathering.

'I have been given an onerous commission of my own.'

David Tod embraces Kitty's tactful diversion with an enthusiastic response.

'For which I am sure you are eminently suitable, Lady Katharine!'

'You're so kind, David. Do call me Kitty. Well, I'm delighted to tell you that as well as my work for the Voluntary Aid Detachment, my new contribution to the war effort is going to involve legions of knitters! As you all know, Scottish regiments go to war in their kilts, with not a lot of warmth beneath their pleats of Highland cloth, substantial as these are. General Sir John Cowan, our army's outstanding Quartermaster General, has asked me to produce fifteen thousand hose tops to warm the knees of our Scottish boys this coming winter.'

Bardie smiles. This is a family gathering, so unnecessary propriety is eschewed.

'The truth of it is, knees are not the nub of the issue!'

Kitty continues without the slightest embarrassment.

'Quite what part of the male anatomy is at risk has not been discussed. Regardless, "fifteen thousand hose tops" is the order of the day.'

Dertha's husband, Harry, the only non-Scot present, is curious about the mysteries of the dress of the 'True Scot'.

'Come on, Kitty, are they long socks or long johns?'

'Harry, I can tell you categorically, they are hose tops and extend only to the top of a man's thigh, but they will still take some knitting. As I'm sure you know, a Scotsman's thigh is a fine example of the male anatomy.'

Everyone laughs at Kitty's wit. She takes their evident enjoyment as encouragement.

'My sister, Imogen, who is an accomplished knitter, has provided the template. She told me that she had to carry out some detailed research in order to do so . . .' She pauses, enjoying the innuendo. 'Please note, Imogen is a spinster of mature years, so I refrained from asking how the research was done.'

There is more laughter.

'In any case, General Cowan has approved the design, so I've enlisted Gwendoline Macbeth, Bardie's secretary, who is an organizational whizz, and all the wives of the Scottish Horse, who are now knitting feverishly. Unfortunately, there is not enough khaki wool to knit them all in battlefield colours, so we're using various coloured wools that match regimental tartans. We've got a team of scrutinizers to inspect the finished garments. Any that are too big are being sent to the navy, to be worn in their sea boots; any that are too small are being sent to the Indian Army, whose knees, God bless them, are more used to tropical climes and have arrived in Europe several inches below their short trousers.'

There is a further round of applause from Kitty's audience, who are eager to restore the good humour of the evening.

'And I can assure you that the order will be complete by the end of October; well before the winter's chill swirls around the sporrans of our brave lads!'

An even bigger bout of enthusiastic applause and laughter ensues, which is followed by as convivial a dinner as worries about Geordie's well-being allow.

When Monday morning arrives, and the Stewart-Murray weekend gathering comes to an end, they will all realize that this is the last occasion they will spend together for some time. Nothing is said explicitly – that would be tempting fate – but the embraces and farewells are long and heartfelt.

Monday 28 September

While Bronwyn is taken care of by Margaret's nursing friends at Hereford General, she travels to the Midland Bank in Ludlow to retrieve the contents of the safety-deposit box that Philip has left for Bronwyn.

Inside is a small intricately inlaid walnut box containing a large collection of jewellery – rings, brooches, pearls and earrings – a few gold coins, which Margaret thinks must be Greek or Roman, and a roll of crisp white £5 notes, worth £150 in total. By the look of the cache, Bronwyn is not going to be immensely rich, but she is certainly no longer poor.

There is also a letter. It has no envelope and bears no date.

Darling Bron,

That you are opening this box means one very sad truth – my demise has come to pass. Perhaps it is for the best! I sincerely hope that my end has been swift and relatively painless.

Rushing off to the Welch Fusiliers and leaving you behind was the worst day of my life, but at least we had that last magical afternoon together. I hope you remember it as fondly as I do. Contained herein are a few things that I hope will allow you to pursue the life you deserve to enjoy. I'm sorry about Tom. He's a good man and I hope he finds happiness with someone else. As for you, please choose your men carefully. Few will be worthy of you.

Finally, I have a confession to make about those drawings that seemed to add so much excitement to our time together. You often said that you felt guilty about initiating our relationship and that you weren't sure that a 'decent' girl should enjoy the feelings you experienced.

First of all, I must tell you that I was the seducer. I deliberately left those so-called lewd images around in the hope that they would entice you. I wove the web that entangled you. I have no regrets; it brought me the greatest pleasure of my life. I hope the same is true for you.

As for your feelings, the fact that you feel them so readily and in such abundance is not a sign that you are not a 'decent' woman, but that you are a real woman. Always remember that. And during your long and undoubtedly successful life, think of me from time to time.

With all my love for ever and a day,
Philip

♥

At the bottom of the box, there is a small lithograph signed with Philip's initials and a short message: 'Remember me, x'.

When Margaret looks at the print, she is shocked at the explicitness of the image. She immediately understands the intensity of the relationship between Philip and Bronwyn, and why the girl now feels so tormented by guilt.

When Margaret returns to Hereford General, she finds Bronwyn looking much better. She has been well taken care of by the nurses and has been seen by a consultant venere-ologist, who has begun a course of treatment for her. Thankfully, she does not have syphilis. He has also confirmed that she has recently suffered a miscarriage.

Margaret now has a dilemma. She needs to complete her recruitment drive around the hospitals of the West Country. Even more importantly, she needs to return to France to continue to care for the thousands of dying and wounded young men on the battlefield. However, Bronwyn has had almost no time to regain her health, to come to terms with her guilt or to regain her self-confidence.

That evening, they discuss the problem together. It causes Bronwyn immediate distress.

'Please don't leave me, Margaret! I don't have anywhere to go. And I'm not strong enough to get by on my own yet.'

Margaret knows that Bronwyn is right. She also knows that she cannot ask the Hereford nurses to take care of the girl indefinitely. She is at a loss for a solution, until Bronwyn makes an audacious plea.

'Take me to France with you. I'll scrub floors, make beds, mop up the blood; anythin' you want me to do.'

It is a radical suggestion. But Margaret knows that so dire is the situation in France, no one will care where Margaret's recruits come from.

'Bron, you will see terrible things; you can't imagine how distressing it will be for you, especially on top of your own problems.'

'But it will help me! I won't have time to think about my own worries.'

Margaret is unsure. She needs time to consider.

'Let me think about it. We can talk in the morning.'

'How much is what Philip left me worth?'

'Well, there's the money, and probably the same again in jewels and coins, if not more.'

'Then I can make my own way to France.'

Margaret smiles. Bronwyn is finding her feet already.

'You could, but you should really put it in the bank. Bron, please let me think about it. I'm an army nurse, with professional responsibilities.'

Sensing that Margaret is not prepared to discuss the matter further, Bronwyn abruptly changes the subject.

'Did you see the drawin' Philip left for me?'

'Yes.'

'Do you think I'm wicked?'

'No, you're just a woman, like the rest of us. We all have secrets and dark thoughts.'

'Is that really true, Margaret?'

'It is for those of us who are prepared to admit to them.'

'It's really important for me to know that.'

'Don't worry, you are no more wicked than the rest of us –'

'So have you done things you regret?'

'Of course.'

'Can I ask you about them?'

'Not yet; maybe one day, but not yet. Who knows, when we get to France . . .'

Bronwyn's eyes light up. Her face glows, and she beams like a child.

'Does that mean you're going to take me?'

Margaret smiles. She can see why Philip could not resist this young girl; she is adorable.

'Yes, but don't let me down.'

'I won't, I promise.'

'I have three more hospitals to visit, one of them in Birmingham. I think we should sell the jewels and coins there and open a bank account for you.'

'Thank you, Margaret, I'm so grateful.'

'One more thing, Bron.'

'Whatever you want.'

'Let's burn that print. You need to bury that part of your past.'

Bronwyn smiles before taking a last look at one of the images that led to the agony and ecstasy of recent months.

She then folds it neatly and throws it on to the fire.

PART FIVE: OCTOBER
Race to the Sea

Friday 2 October

Life has become a little easier for the small group of friends sitting together at Burnley's Keighley Green Club. The men's army pay is being delivered weekly by D Company's paymaster, and Cath has begun to help Mary washing pots behind the club bar in the evenings and cleaning the club rooms in the afternoons.

As it is only 6.30 p.m. and the Friday night rush has not yet begun, Mary and Cath are relaxing with Tommy, Mick, Vinny and Nat before their shift starts at 7 p.m. Although not as well off as they were when they had regular employment, they are not suffering the hardship they faced a few weeks ago.

Former club steward John-Tommy has put on his old apron and is helping his successor get to know the locals. The club looks like it did a generation ago. It is as if nothing has changed, but much has – some things profoundly. There are still vast amounts of beer being drunk and tobacco smoked. Billiards and three-card brag are being played, with extravagant amounts of money changing hands in gambling and challenge matches. As always, there is good humour, plus occasional flashpoints of antagonism and the usual end-of-evening fisticuffs. But there is also lots of talk about the war, with debate focused on its morality, and much reflection on the way the fighting is touching so many people.

Although the radical pre-war discussions about votes for working-class men, trade union rights and the rights and wrongs of the suffragette movement have become less vocal, people are still talking openly about the future and what will happen when the war is over. It is as if the conflict in Europe has created a new national debate about a whole range of issues, but mostly with the presumption that change is no longer a desire, more an inevitability. The national and local press are central to the discussion, but so are people like Mary and Cath, whose opinions are being listened to more and more.

Cath has been asked to speak at a British Socialist Party meeting in Great Harwood Town Hall, which will take place in ten days' time, but she is terrified about speaking in public and does not want to accept. Mary is trying to persuade her to change her mind.

'Y'll be fine. I'll 'elp thee write it, then we can rehearse together until tha can all but recite it parrot-fashion.'

'No, lass, I can't. Henry Hyndman'll be there. I can't speak in front o' 'im. What wi' my accent an' all; they'll think I'm stupid.'

'Well, think on it. I'll 'elp thee wi' it, if tha wants.' Mary glances at the clock behind the bar. 'Come on, look at t'time. We've got work to be doin'.'

As Mary and Cath begin their night's work, the men begin drinking in earnest. Their talk is all about the trials and tribulations of their training with the Accrington Pals. Vinny's major gripe is the route marching.

'If I sken another track up fuckin' Pendle, I'll shoot mesen.'

'Tha can't shoot tha'sen; tha's not got a rifle!'

Nat's smart remark makes them all laugh but, as Mick points out, other than marching, they are not doing much that will prepare them as soldiers.

'No boots, no uniform, no weapons! It's just daft, innit?'

Tommy is philosophical about it.

'Aye, but we're gettin' paid; dunno abaht you lot, but I can cope wi' doin' bugger all.'

'Twenty-five-mile hikes are not "bugger all", Tommy.'

'Stop yer moitherin', Vinny, an' get some more ale in.'

Mick is reading Cath's newspapers.

"As tha seen this in t'*Accy Times*? Some lad's saying that Local Master Tailors are up in arms cos old Harwood 'as given t'uniform contract to a Leeds firm. That's not reet, is it? Can't 'ave Tykes makin' uniforms fer a Lanky battalion!'

A batch of obsolete Lee-Metford training rifles arrived for the battalion in the middle of the week, but only 350 of them, and they all went to the two Accrington companies, much to the dismay of the Burnley lads. There has also been disquiet in the week about pay, initiated out of the blue by a recruit who wrote an anonymous letter to the *Burnley Express*, which was published in its midweek edition.

The gist of the letter suggested that the Accrington Pals are being paid 5d a day less than other pals battalions – notably the men of the Manchester City Battalion, who are receiving 3s 11d per day – and that their clothing allowance is much less than other battalions.

To everyone's surprise, the letter produced an immediate response. Honorary Battalion Captain John Haworth, the Mayor of Accrington and founder of the battalion, appeared on Fulledge Recreation Ground just this morning, in the middle of drills, and announced that he knew nothing of the discrepancy, but that it had clearly been an error. He declared that pay would be increased to match the sum paid to the Manchester lads and that it would be backdated to the day of joining up. He also said that the clothing allowance would be increased to match other battalions.

He finished his short speech with a blunt statement: 'Gentlemen of North-East Lancashire, you have answered the call to defend your country; now your country must respond in kind, and I'm going to make sure it does!'

His words produced a wave of cheers and applause. Most of the men were astonished. They were used to having to fight their employers tooth and nail for even minor concessions in pay and conditions, and now a single letter to a newspaper had produced an immediate response. There was much excited talk among the men: perhaps this really was going to be the beginning of a new kind of citizen's army and a new kind of country, where ordinary people matter. That afternoon, D Company ran up Deerplay Moor with an enthusiasm not seen before.

Mick has put his newspapers down.

'What do yer reckon to our new officers, Tommy?'

'They're alreet. I thought they'd be reet posh, but they're not bad lads, especially Riley. He's a good 'un, I reckon – plays a bit o' cricket, likes an ale – he'll do fer me.'

Lieutenant Henry Davison Riley was the first man in Burnley to react positively when John Harwood began his campaign to raise a local pals battalion. It was Riley's advertisement in the *Burnley Express* in September that led to the beginnings of the Burnley contingent of the Accrington Pals.

Riley is a 33-year-old local businessman with a finger in several commercial pies, notably his family's Fancy Cloth business in Colne. He spends his spare time trying to create opportunities for local youngsters, especially the provision of sport and evening educational classes. He began Burnley Lads' Club in 1901 and many of D Company's recruits are from the club. He is also a leading light in the Industrial School Movement and the Discharged Prisoners Aid Society.

Vinny and Nat know Riley from Burnley Lads' Club, but they also know another recent officer recruit – local cricketer and footballer Fred Heys.

'He's a good lad an' all; Nat an' me's laiked wi' 'im many a time. He can bat a bit and 'as got a beltin' off-break.'

Frederick Arnold Heys is a 26-year-old solicitor from Oswaldtwistle and, like Henry Riley, throws himself into the local community at every opportunity. He is secretary of Calder Vale Rugby Club and Burnley's Clarion Club for working-class enthusiasts of the new sport of cycling. Because most members have left-leaning tendencies, the cycling club, like many others in the country, took its name from Robert Blatchford's left-wing newspaper, the *Clarion*. Heys, himself a man of socialist principles, is an avid thespian and member of the Burnley Light Opera Society.

Mick likes D Company's CO, Captain Ross, largely because both men have a passion for boxing, which they talked about when Mick joined the battalion. Both men are huge admirers of British champion Bob Fitzsimmons.

'Any man who can list all Bob's fights an' knows in which rounds he knocked out 'is opponents is alreet wi' me.'

Raymond St George Ross is an analytical chemist in Burnley and was asked by his good friend Henry Riley to become the borough's recruiting officer for the Accrington Pals. Another local man of diverse talents, being an accomplished flautist, chorister and amateur thespian, he has been a territorial soldier for several years and brings some military experience to D Company.

The company's complement of officers is finalized by the arrival of a man who is Tough by name and tough by nature. Arnold Bannatyne Tough, one of six brothers and sisters, is a 24-year-old dentist from Accrington. His father is a general practitioner in Accrington and a stalwart of the local community. A renowned local pugilist who, like his friend Raymond Ross, is an admirer of boxing legend Bob Fitzsimmons, Arnie Tough is a big man who does not readily suffer fools and enjoys exercising in the boxing ring at Burnley Boys' Club. None of the local lads can better him in the ring. Although they are probably better street fighters – where few rules apply, and sometimes none – in the ring, under the Marquess of Queensberry's rules, Tough is beyond equal.

Although most of D Company's officers have served as volunteer territorials, most of the military know-how in the company emanates from retired regular army NCOs. They have been brought in to 'put some backbone into scrawny weavers and some discipline into headstrong miners', as they are inclined to repeat at every opportunity. As well as Colour Serjeant Jimmy Severn, whose sharp tongue and even sharper forehead they have already met, there are another two who are just as formidable.

Andrew Muir is fifty-five years old and from Maryhill, in Scotland, but he was brought up in Clayton-le-Moors and became an apprentice calico machine-printer. He joined the territorials as a young man and rose through the ranks to become a colour serjeant before being discharged because of his age, in 1910. Sadly, Muir has recently received devastating news and has been given fourteen days' compassionate leave. His son, Rifleman John Muir of the 1st King's Royal Rifle Corps, died of his wounds in France, having been badly injured at the Battle of Mons.

Three years younger than Muir, George Lee from Widecombe, in Devon, left a farming community at the age of sixteen to join the 24th Regiment of Foot, the South Wales Borderers. He fought in the Zulu Wars in its last battle, at Ulundi, in July 1879. He subsequently rose to the rank of colour serjeant and became a drill instructor.

Like Jimmy Severn, both men have now been brought out of retirement to get the Accrington Pals ready for war.

The battalion is to be commanded by an old friend of John Harwood, 64-year-old Colonel Richard Sharples, an Accrington solicitor and territorial soldier of many years' service. His adjutant and senior captain is another Accrington solicitor, 48-year-old George Nicholas Slinger.

It did not take long for Lieutenants Tough and Ross to notice Mick and Tommy's significant physiques and to hear the stories of their prowess as street fighters. They struck an immediate rapport with the two men and tried to persuade them to put on gloves and transfer their bare-knuckle skills into the 'noble art' of the ring and to eschew the use of their hob-nailed clogs in a contest.

Finally, Tommy and Mick did climb into Burnley Lads' Club's boxing ring for some sparring. Although they performed well against the other lads in the battalion, putting all-comers on the seat of their pants, they fared less well when they boxed against Colour Serjeant Jimmy Severn. He fought for his regiment as a young man and proceeded to give them a stark lesson in ring craft.

With Vinny and Nat looking on, both Tommy and Mick struggled to lay a glove on the veteran soldier, despite towering over him, having a much longer reach and being less than half his age. Each of their wild swings was avoided with a duck or a sway. Every punch was blocked by raised arms or gloves, before being bettered with disguised, short, sharp counter-punches. Mick soon had a bloody nose and welts under each eye. Tommy's lip was badly cut, leaving him with a mouthful of blood, and he had to suffer a succession of body blows to his ribs that made him bend double in pain.

In awe of the colour serjeant's skills, both men shook hands with Severn after their three bouts, each lasting three minutes, and thanked him for his boxing lesson. While they got their breath back and came to terms with the brutal exposure of what they thought were their pugilistic talents, Tough and Ross sat down next to them. Ross was grinning.

'Well, gentlemen, there's the difference between fighting and boxing.'

Mick was still shaking his head.

'I don't think I landed a dacent punch on 'im, sir.'

'But you're strong, Kenny. He hit you very hard, but you didn't back away. You have a strong chin and you are a mountain of a man. We can make you into a good boxer, as well as a good fighter.'

'Thank you, sir.'

Tough turned to Tommy.

'The same goes for you, Broxup. You're strong and have very quick hands. You just need to learn how to use them with a thoughtful cadence, rather than with a rush of blood.'

Tommy looks at Mick, curious about what Tough means by 'thoughtful cadence'. Mick just raises his eyebrows; he has no idea either. Tough realizes that he has baffled his men and grabs Tommy's wrists to show him how to punch in combinations: in twos, threes, fours; upper body, lower body. And how, at the same time, to duck and sway and anticipate one's opponent's punches.

Tommy smiles appreciatively.

'Where didst tha learn how to box, sir?'

'At school; I went to Giggleswick School, where boxing is taken very seriously.'

Tommy is amazed.

'By 'eck, when I were at t'elementary school, sir, t'teachers ollus tried to stop us feightin'!'

Tough smiles back warmly.

'Giggleswick is a four-hundred-year-old private school for young gentlemen, not far from here, beyond Skipton. I had to board, in dormitories like an army barracks. No mother to comfort us, teachers who would beat us at the drop of a hat and prefects who treated us like slaves. Cold water, early morning runs in the snow, all designed to toughen us up for a life of service to our King and country. It did us the power of good!'

Ross then described his school.

'I went to Sedbergh, up in the Dales. Same kind of regime, except we'd say it was tougher than Giggleswick, our big rivals. Our school motto was *Dura Virum Nutrix*, which means "Stern Nurse of Men".'

Mick, Tommy, Vinny and Nat have no idea about the world of the men they have always been told are their 'betters', but they are beginning to realize it is not quite as they thought. They know that the well-to-do boys of their town go to Burnley Grammar School, the local school for those more fortunate than themselves, or for a few poor lads who are exceptionally clever.

They have also heard of those who are the sons of the aristocracy and go off to posh schools in the south, where they are waited on by servants and taught to be 'proper gents'. Only three families in the Burnley area are in that league – the Towneleys of Towneley Hall, the Shuttleworths of Gawthorpe Hall and the Asshetons of Downham House – all ancient families who most people believe are a different breed, born to rule.

But local northern schools, with rigours like Giggleswick and Sedbergh, are news to the pals. They hang on Ross's every word as he continues to describe a whole new world.

'As well as cricket, rugby and football, we were taught boxing, fencing and horse-riding to equip us as soldiers who would spread Christianity and the British way of life throughout the Empire. Every year, we did the Wilson Run, ten miles over the moors; that sorted the men from the boys.'

Tough then interrupts Ross.

'I suppose you won it in your time?'

'Yes, I did, twice. And I hold the record: one hour, fifteen minutes and twenty-three seconds.'

'Hmmm, thought you might have, not that you're one to crow about these things!'

'Course not, old man.'

The four Burnley lads realize that, behind the education and privilege of their officers, these are men just like them and that their lives are not quite as they had imagined. Mary and Cath have told them stories about the top hats and tails at Eton and Harrow, and have tried to persuade their menfolk that it is not a matter of breeding, simply of privilege. The four friends are not sure they understand the difference. Nevertheless, they do not feel antagonistic about the backgrounds of their officers, more intrigued, especially by schools like Sedbergh and Giggleswick, which seem to be for men not unlike themselves who come from their own communities.

The four new recruits to the Accrington Pals continue their Friday night drinking session, but they drink less than usual and avoid any provocations that may lead to an end-of-evening fist fight. Their journey to becoming professional soldiers has begun in earnest.

Victoria Station, London

Winston is rushing from his Admiralty car to catch a train from Victoria to Dover. He is on his way to France to see why the Royal Marine Brigade has withdrawn to Dunkirk. He is late for the departure, but John Gough, his Special Branch protection officer, accompanied by two burly Royal Marines, has gone ahead to hold the train. Thus, it is departing ten minutes late. The passengers are restless and the driver is anxious to get moving, but the two marines on his footplate persuade him to stay where he is.

When Winston gets to the platform, he is intercepted by a marine serjeant with an urgent message from Lord Kitchener, the Minister for War. Winston is summoned to Kitchener's house in Carlton Gardens; he must go immediately. The trip to France will have to wait. Winston gathers John Gough and dashes across the station concourse, past the Friday evening commuters, leaving the Dover train driver cursing, 'Bloody politicians!'

Waiting for Winston in Carlton Gardens with Kitchener are Sir Edward Grey, Foreign Secretary, Prince Louis of Battenberg, First Sea Lord, and Sir William Tyrrell, Eddie Grey's private secretary. Winston is given a whisky by Kitchener's butler and listens intently as the Minister for War outlines the grave situation in Belgium.

'Winston, we think Antwerp is about to fall, which could mean our attempt to create a bulwark for the Channel ports is in peril. Zeebrugge will be exposed, and a German advance along the coast to Calais would be difficult to stop.'

'How much time do we have?'

'Very little. There are reports that two of the city's defensive forts have already fallen. The Belgian Army is on its knees; the country's politicians and generals are beginning to wilt.'

Winston rises to his feet. There is a gleam in his eye.

'Where's the PM?'

'On a train to Cardiff for a recruiting rally.'

'May I suggest I send the Royal Marine Brigade to the Belgians? Immediately!'

All in the room nod, and Winston dictates a telegram to be sent from the Admiralty. As the courier leaves, he passes another with a telegram from the French government in Bordeaux. It brings good news. The French are to send two territorial divisions to support the defence of Antwerp. They are also to launch a major offensive near Lille to distract the German High Command.

'*Vive la République!* That's excellent news.'

Winston is in his element. The others in the room look at him, in awe of his unbounded spirit.

'I'll go to Antwerp to put some starch in their collars. I know the King, and he'll feel better with a British minister in his city.'

Eddie Grey looks doubtful.

'Winston, it's a good idea, but we know how much you relish a scrap. We mustn't lose you to a German bullet, or to one of their prisoner-of-war camps.'

Winston gets to his feet, swallows what is left in his tumbler of whisky and makes for the door.

'Eddie, I can't guarantee the trajectories of bullets, but I can assure you that I will not be taken prisoner. I was once a POW of the Boers. I managed to escape and I promised myself never to let it happen again.'

Winston's march to the door effectively pre-empts Kitchener's decision about the First Lord's visit to Antwerp. His irrepressible vitality has made up Kitchener's mind for him. He and Grey both shake Winston's hand and wish him well.

While Winston travels to the coast by car, Eddie Grey sends a telegram to Sir Francis Villiers, the British minister in Belgium.

> First Lord of the Admiralty will be at Antwerp between 9 and 10 tomorrow. It is hoped that he may have the honour of an audience with the King before a final decision as to the departure of the Government is taken.

Delayed by German artillery threats between Ostend and Antwerp, Winston does not arrive in the city until after lunch on Saturday. He immediately hastens to reassure Charles, Comte de Broqueville, the Belgian Prime Minister, of the sincerity of British and French intent.

Later that day, the Royal Marines begin to arrive.

The following morning, Winston goes on a tour of the city's defences and conducts an inspection of the beleaguered Belgian troops. He is with Admiral Horace Hood, his naval secretary.

'They look broken, Horace.'

'They do, sir.'

'I need to take charge of our marines and get them into positions that will show the Belgians we mean business.'

Winston calls over a stenographer and dictates a telegram back to the Admiralty in London. He orders a vast array of materiel for the defence of the city. The scale of the order causes consternation among Admiralty staff, including Prince Louis; they are worried that their First Lord is 'playing soldiers' again.

Winston is exhilarated by being at the forefront of the defence of the ancient city and, at last, able to direct military strategy on the ground. However, realizing that his duty should take him back to London, he sends an outrageous telegram to his Prime Minister.

If it is thought by HM Government that I can be of service here, I am willing to resign my office at the Admiralty and undertake command of defensive forces assigned to Antwerp, provided that I am given necessary military rank and authority and full powers of a commander in the field.

When Asquith receives Winston's offer, he is dismayed. He regards the suggestion as ridiculous; it is typical of his extraordinary First Lord but, all the same, preposterous. That morning, he does Winston no favours by revealing the contents of his telegram to several cabinet colleagues. In doing so, he uses the damning phrase, 'After all, he would be a Lieutenant of Hussars commanding two major generals!' These are words that begin to circulate around Westminster.

When Winston hears of the rebuke, he is, not surprisingly, livid.

Asquith declines Winston's offer, insisting that he is needed at home. However, Winston decides to stay in Antwerp, at least until more reinforcements arrive, thus fulfilling his promise to the Belgians.

The situation deteriorates: French reinforcements in the form of a Marine Fusilier Brigade are delayed, as are British reinforcements under the command of General Sir Henry Rawlinson, which are detained in Bruges.

That evening, Winston attends a meeting of the Belgian Council of War, presided over by King Albert. After it ends, he sends a message to Kitchener: 'All well. I have met King Albert and his Ministers in Council, who resolved to fight it out here whatever happens.'

With still no sign of Rawlinson and his British reinforcements, nor of the French, Winston takes personal charge of Antwerp's defences. The Royal Marines continue to hold out in their hastily dug trenches around the city.

The following day, General Rawlinson arrives, but without his army of 40,000 men, who are still on their way.

With Rawlinson now able to take charge, Winston feels he is able to withdraw to London, where several political enemies are already discrediting his efforts, pouring their words into the ear of the King and on to the pages of Fleet Street's newspapers. Undaunted, Winston continues to badger Asquith for direct military command in France and goes to Downing Street, where he berates the Old Block for over twenty minutes.

That evening, Asquith writes to his mistress, Venetia Stanley. His letter contains a vivid description of Winston in his pomp.

> *Having 'tasted blood', he is ravenous for more and begs for command. His mouth waters at the thought of K's new armies, these 'glittering commands'. I much regret that no shorthand writer was there to get down some of the phrases, which were priceless. He is a wonderful creature, with a curious dash of schoolboy simplicity and what someone once said of genius: 'a zigzag of lightning in the brain'.*

The Cabinet is split about Winston. Half, including Kitchener, Lloyd George, Grey and Lord Haldane, the Lord Chancellor, think he is a political and military prodigy. Most of the others, largely lesser men, jealous of his talents, see him as a dangerous maverick.

*

On 8 October, the French decide to halt their reinforcement of Antwerp. General Rawlinson asks for permission not to commit his British reinforcements and to withdraw the marines from their trenches around Antwerp. Winston is furious, but he is powerless to prevent the inevitable outcome.

Without the French, and with Rawlinson unwilling to commit his men, Antwerp falls to the German Army on 10 October. Fifty-seven marines are killed in defence of the city, with hundreds more taken prisoner. The British press round on Winston, with headlines that scream: 'The Antwerp Blunder!'

Asquith does little to defend his First Lord. For the first time since the beginning of the war, Black Dog pays Winston an unwelcome visit and he descends into a deep depression.

That evening, F. E. Smith arrives at the Admiralty with a car and with an antidote to Black Dog. He has already spoken to Kitchener, who has cleared the plan with Asquith. Lord Louis of Battenberg will take charge at the Admiralty for a few days, while Winston takes a break and spends a long weekend with his family at Blenheim Palace.

It is where he was born, the home of his first cousin, Charles 'Sunny' Spencer-Churchill, the 9th Duke of Marlborough, and the place where, as a little boy, he first vowed to emulate the glorious deeds of his ancestor at the Battle of Blenheim.

On 7 October, Clemmie gave birth to Sarah Millicent Hermione Churchill, the third kitten in the Churchill litter. She was born in the First Lord's flat at the Admiralty but, because of the Antwerp crisis, Winston has hardly seen his new daughter.

It has been a grim time for all of them. Clemmie had to endure the last days of her pregnancy while Winston was embroiled in Belgium and had to suppress her own grave concerns for his personal safety. Now, he is being pilloried in the press for a debacle that, at worst, he managed to prevent happening for over a week entirely through the strength of his personality.

As FE's driver takes them through a wet and squally night to Blenheim, Winston's friend tries to cheer him by reading aloud a note recently sent to Clemmie by Eddie Grey.

'Listen to this, old chap: "I am sitting next to Winston in Cabinet, having welcomed him back from Antwerp. I feel a glow imparted by the thought that I am sitting next to a hero. I can't tell you how much I admire his courage, gallant spirit and genius for war. It inspires us all."'

Winston smiles at FE, but only thinly, and grasps Clemmie's hand.

'Eddie is very kind; *you* are kind, FE, to do this for Clemmie and me. I am in my cups, I'm afraid. Give me a little time, old friend.'

Both Clemmie and FE know that now is not the time to challenge Winston's assessment of his own well-being. It is better to give him time to wrestle with Black Dog in his own way. The rest of the journey to Oxfordshire takes place in silence, as Winston broods, staring fixedly through the car window at the wind and rain of the passing night.

Monday 12 October

Great Harwood's new town hall, only completed ten years ago, is packed. It is a special meeting of the British Socialist Party, called to air opinions about the war. The room is full for two reasons. First, leading socialist Henry Hyndman is the main speaker, and he always pulls a large crowd. And second, the debate about the war has reached fever pitch in recent weeks as more and more join up for Kitchener's Army and ever more bodies return from France.

After much cajoling from Mary, Cath has agreed to speak at the meeting. She is petrified. After several local speakers have addressed the meeting, Henry Hyndman, as usual, gives a typically rousing speech in support of socialist principles but, to the consternation of many in the audience – a few of whom boo the speaker – he also articulates a powerful defence of Britain's war effort. His closing words bring the majority of the audience to their feet.

'Comrades, our boys at the front are fighting a just war against an enemy bent on a new imperialism. The bloodlust of the Kaiser must be defeated. I know that our own leaders are hardly radicals, as we use the phrase, but the unity that we now see in Britain will bring inevitable change. Our servicemen are fighting for freedom in France and Belgium, a freedom that cannot be denied them when they return home. Until that time, we must do all we can to support them.'

The time has come for Cath to speak. She is the first woman to be invited to speak at any of the local Lancashire branches, an honour accorded her following the recommendation of several Burnley members. She is introduced by the Chairman of the meeting.

'Comrade Catherine Kenny, a weaver from Burnley. Welcome, Cath.'

Cath's heart is pumping so fast, she can hardly breathe. The fact that she is almost seven months pregnant is not helping; neither is the fact that, in the last couple of weeks, the baby's little flutters of movement have been replaced by easily discernible kicks.

Mick is in the front row with Mary and Tommy. Nat and Vinny are at the back of the room with other friends who have travelled from Burnley to listen to her speak in public for the first time. Lieutenant Heys is there to hear her with several members of the Burnley Clarion Club who, of course, have cycled the six miles to Great Harwood.

Mary and Cath have abandoned the dowdy Lancashire shawls worn by the local working-class women, an attire that makes them look like impoverished nuns, and are wearing smart pleated skirts and blouses, like well-to-do ladies. Mick and Tommy are very proud; their lasses look very fetching indeed. The men are looking exceptionally neat and tidy: they sport short-back-and-sides military haircuts, clean-shaven faces, well-brushed Sunday best clothes and highly burnished boots. They look quite the part.

Henry Hyndman, seeing how nervous Cath seemed, took her on one side before the meeting began and gave her some simple advice: 'Be yourself, be true to what you believe; you'll be fine. They will love your honesty.'

The silence is deafening as her trembling fingers try to flatten her speech on to the lectern in front of her. She looks up and peers through the town hall's window just as the clock on Mercer's Tower nearby is about to strike eight o'clock. Cath sees the minute hand move, prompting her to begin, her voicing cracking with apprehension.

'Good evening . . . Comrades . . .'

Then, as if on cue, the clock strikes with a loud clang. It stops Cath in her tracks and makes the audience laugh. Mercer's Clock Tower was built by his daughter in memory of John Mercer, one of the giants of the cotton industry and the inventor of 'mercerized' cotton. An impoverished child, who never attended school, he taught himself to read and write and to understand the basics of chemistry. He would eventually be admitted to the Royal Society and become a juror at the Great Exhibition of 1862. Cath knows the story of John Mercer well. He is one of her heroes. As she continues to fumble with her speech, she remembers Henry Hyndman's words of encouragement.

As the clock booms its seventh strike, she decides to heed Hyndman's advice and, despite the hours of writing and rehearsing, abandons her scripted words and lays them to one side. She looks at Mick, who is as nervous as she is. But, as Mercer's clock strikes its last chime, she smiles and thinks to herself: *If little John Mercer can do what he did and transform the cotton industry, I can make a little speech.* The weight of fear lifts from her shoulders. She rests her hands on the side of the lectern and begins.

'It's 'ard to foller a lad like Mr Hyndman. 'E's cleverer than me and 'as 'ad a proper education. But I'm goin' to try because 'e's been an inspiration to me an' lots o' t'people in this room. Like John Mercer, whose loud clock is reet outside that yonder window, he's an example to all on us.'

Cath begins to flow. For over fifteen minutes, she describes her childhood in the squalor of a cellar dwelling in Brierfield, a suburb of Burnley, the daughter of Irish immigrants, and how she struggled to learn to read and write. She speaks with an easy fluency, full of humorous detail about the delights of long-drop lavatories and carbolic soap, of visits from the schools' nurse, 'Nitty-Nora, the Bug-Explorer', and tide-marks around children's necks who are only able to swill their faces before going to school.

She describes the early socialist meetings she attended and her gradual conversion to the cause of equality for all. Her ancient East Lancs dialect is understood perfectly by the locals and even those who are not familiar with its nuances understand the greater part of it and enjoy its peculiar charm. Mick smiles broadly, proud of his wife. Henry Hyndman nods appreciatively as she gets to the nub of her proposition, one that is not in direct opposition to his, but more a cry from her heart.

'I got t'sack fer picketin' at Howard an' Bullough's strike, so did me 'usband, Mick, and me friends Mary an' Tommy. We ended up wi' no job and blacklisted in t'mills an' t'pits. We 'ad nowt, an' no prospects of owt. So Mick an' Tommy an' their mates Nat an' Vinny joined up. Not because we 'ad a choice, but because we 'adn't!'

A round of applause echoes around the room from those who think she is going to support the anti-war position. But they are to be disappointed.

'Now we're committed to Britain's war effort, there's no goin' back. There's lads' lives at stake – one in, all in! Colliers, weavers, posh lads, poor lads, they all bleed!'

A much louder roar of approval reverberates around Great Harwood Town Hall. If Mercer's Tower Clock were to strike again, it would not be heard.

'So I 'ave no argument wi' Mr Hyndman's opinion o' t'war. Like 'im, I support this war because it'll bring change, an' it'll mean that when our lads come 'ome, it will be to a land fit for heroes!'

Cath's closing remarks bring the entire audience to its feet. Mick jumps onstage to give his wife a warm embrace. Then Henry Hyndman does the same.

'Comrade Kenny, that was an excellent speech. You are a natural; you should have no fears about speaking in public. I loved your closing line, "to a land fit for heroes". Do you mind if I steal it?'

'Do what tha wants wi' it, Henry; I'm just glad it's over!'

Lieutenant Heys appears at Mick's shoulder.

'Good evening, Mick!'

'Even', sir.'

'Call me Fred; no formalities here, not at a meeting of socialists. Please introduce me to your formidable wife.'

'Cath, this is Lieutenant Heys. 'E's in charge o' t'platoon.'

'Rousing words, if I may say so, Mrs Kenny.'

'Thanks, Lieutenant.'

'I think you and Mr Hyndman are right, this war will herald a new order in Britain.'

Cath frowns.

'Aye, mebbe . . . Just bring 'em 'ome in one piece.'

Later, back at Keighley Green Club, Tommy and Mick are enjoying a drink.

'So, your Cath did alreet t'neet.'

'She did that; I'm reet proud on 'er.'

'Yer know what, Mick?'

'What's that, Tommy?'

'We gonna 'ave to start listenin' to our Cath an' Mary; they're cleverer than we are.'

'I reckon tha's reet, Tom lad.'

Saturday 17 October

Herlies, Nord-Pas-de-Calais, France

The 4th Battalion Royal Fusiliers reach the small town of Herlies at dusk on 17 October. They are now only twelve miles south of the Belgian border at Armentières. Herlies occupies a strategic position on the main road between Béthune and Lille.

Since their bloody encounter at Maison Rouge Farm at Vailly-sur-Aisne, over a month ago, the 4th Fusiliers have moved north in stages by train, French Army transport and on foot. On occasions, there have been four or five days of fifteen-hour marches. Even the most inexperienced soldier knows that both the Allies and the Germans are trying to gain the strategic advantage of controlling the Channel ports.

For Maurice and Harry, life has been quiet. Since Harry's mental aberration in Vailly and his fortunate disciplinary reprieve by Major Ashburner, he has been subdued. His usual happy-go-lucky demeanour and his eye for a pretty girl – or any girl, for that matter – have only been glimpsed on rare occasions. Maurice is worried about him.

The general strategic position in France continues to be dire for both the Germans and the Allies. After the heroic victory on the Marne, the priority for the French has been consolidation; for the British it has been to make certain that there is a route home across the Channel. Ominously, when the victorious German Army marched through Antwerp on its victory parade, it took them five hours to pass and their ranks were made up of 60,000 men. The Germans have already occupied the key city of Lille after a huge artillery bombardment. Then, only two days ago, Ostend fell.

With more German advances come more atrocities, adding significantly to the level of hostility at the front and at home in Britain. Tens of thousands of Belgians are pouring into London and the South of England, all with horrendous stories of acts of German cruelty.

Along a line almost forty miles long, German, French and British units have been clashing in a series of light to medium skirmishes. Casualty levels are rising inexorably. Both sides are beginning to come to terms with the awesome power of the machine gun and the value of the well-protected infantry position, where highly trained marksmen can have a significant impact on advancing troops across open ground.

The use of heavy concentrations of artillery is also proving deadly. But both sets of High Command are still scratching their heads, trying to absorb as quickly as possible the consequences of these changing patterns of warfare. All of their senior men served in a different age and went to Staff College in an era dominated by memories of massed ranks of infantry, of dashing cavalry attacks, when artillery fired shrapnel weapons, not explosive shells. While they develop new strategies to meet new times, men die in droves.

To the south of the fusiliers' latest position, the 1st Dorsets and 1st Bedfords suffer major losses close to Givenchy, three miles east of Béthune. The Bedfords lose almost all their officers. To the north, the 1st Royal Warwicks are mauled at Méteren, losing over 250 men in a single encounter.

For the fusiliers, a night behind hastily arranged cover in and around Herlies beckons. There are Germans all around the small town, many in sniping positions, and there is the constant 'ping' of bullets hitting hard objects. Sometimes, the bullets strike flesh and the noise is altogether different — as are the cries of the stricken men.

There are also frequent bursts of artillery fire, which are reducing most of Herlies's buildings to rubble. When a shell finds a human target, the victim is often incinerated or blown to pieces. The men have already realized that it is often better to be killed instantly in such an attack than to survive in unbearable pain, only to die days later in a body shattered beyond repair.

Nights are drawing in and it is becoming colder and wetter, making life for the soldier even more onerous. Not only that, all know that winter is yet to bite with its inevitable ferocity and that there is no prospect of an end to hostilities in the foreseeable future.

Maurice and Harry's platoon has taken up positions beneath and around the ruined walls of the Eglise Saint-Amé, which has neither roof nor spire intact. It is not clear which army inflicted the damage or when, but, like its church, the village is also devastated, its inhabitants long gone.

'What a bloody mess, 'Arry.'

'Too true, Mo. The whole fuckin' thing's a mess.'

With six men for company, the two veterans have been ordered to form a battle outpost at the corner of Saint-Amé, using the rubble of its nave for cover. A German attack could come at any time or, using the cover of darkness, exploratory skirmishers could suddenly appear out of the gloom. On the other side of the road sits another outpost and, behind them, the rest of the platoon and its machine gun are scattered along the road's drainage ditches. The men of the forward outpost take it in turns to keep watch.

The night passes uneventfully, but they do hear artillery and rifle fire from both their right and left flanks. Unfortunately, just before dawn, it begins to rain heavily, making life even more miserable. The men of the 4th Battalion were promised winter greatcoats over a week ago, but they still have not appeared.

Just after a damp and cold dawn, Maurice is the first to hear the beginning of the German attack.

''Arry! Cavalry! Look, right down the middle of the fuckin' road, dozens of 'em.'

The platoon springs to life. Lieutenant Mead, a newly arrived officer from the 1st Battalion, shouts orders to the men. Captain Leicester Carey, the recently promoted replacement for James Orred, who was killed at Maison Rouge, is fifty yards further back sending a messenger to Major Ashburner to inform him of the attack.

Mead, a man of no more than twenty-five, is in his first battle. Harry claims that he knew the lieutenant was what he called a 'weekend soldier' as soon as he met him.

'I can sniff out the amateurs. They smell nice an' clean; they don't 'ave the whiff of muck and bullets abaht 'em.'

Maurice smiles and thinks to himself: *Good old 'Arry, never one to make a considered judgement when a first impression will do.*

Bullets begin to pepper the remnants of the nave of Saint-Amé behind them. A German machine gun has opened to their right and sniper fire is finding targets all around them. One or two men are hit; one is dead for sure, his head like a crushed melon.

Lieutenant Mead can just be heard, bellowing, 'Pick your targets! Commence firing!'

Several men have already got off rounds before Mead gives his order. The massed ranks of the German cavalry are now within 300 yards and advancing at a gallop.

'What're our machine-gun boys' doin'? They should be mowin' 'em down like fuckin' daisies!'

Harry is angry, swearing and cursing as he lies in a prone position, firing rapidly.

'Come on, Mo, target practice! Yer can't miss!'

Maurice adopts the same pose. Harry is right, it is harder to miss a target – whether man or horse – than to hit one.

The broad chests of the oncoming horses are the easiest mark, so many riflemen aim for those. But there is more satisfaction to be had in taking a man clean out of his saddle – and, besides, it grants the marksman another notch on his rifle's stock. Accurate British musketry is already inflicting crippling losses on the pure-black steeds of the approaching cavalry, but they keep coming on relentlessly.

The men approaching at speed are no ordinary troopers. They are the rigorously chosen elite of the Imperial Guards Cavalry Division, the *Gardes du Corps*. They were first raised as the personal bodyguard of the Kings of Prussia by Frederick the Great, in 1740. The troopers are hand-picked from all over the German Empire for their horsemanship, fighting ability and endurance. The officers, selected with equal sternness, are exclusively from the German aristocracy, mostly Prussian Junkers.

Their uniforms are more sea blue than the German Army's standard field grey, and they are shod in fine, pale leather, highly polished cavalry boots. The flowing pennons on their lances are halved in black and white and decorated with the Black Eagle of Prussia. Although the troopers are wearing standard-issue pickelhaube helmets, not so the senior officer in the middle of the front rank. He is sporting an eye-catching, lobster-tail dress helmet of polished tombac brass, topped with a huge eagle grasping its prey.

The man beneath the ostentatious headdress sits tall in his stirrups, his square jaw giving a firm anchor to the helmet's lamellar chinstrap, his blond moustache almost matching the golden hue of his helmet.

Harry spots the prize immediately.

'Mo, look at the Granny Grunt in the middle! He's mine, I'm 'avin' that 'elmet!'

Harry fires two shots in quick succession. The first misses the German's head by a whisker, the second hits the rider next to him in the shoulder and catapults him from his horse.

'Fuck!'

Harry's target disappears from view behind a group of riders, and the opportunity passes.

The covering fire from the German positions ceases as the Prussian cavalry close in at breakneck speed. Despite heavy losses, they keep close formation. When they reach the fusiliers' positions, they break off into small groups and use their lances and swords to launch a ferocious attack. Several dismount and begin to use their G98 rifles. A fierce firefight ensues with much hand-to-hand combat.

Lieutenant Mead, despite Harry's assessment of him, does it by the book: he orders the men around him to fix bayonets and form small squads to advance at a run and take on the dismounted Prussians at close quarters. The scene is reminiscent of a medieval battle, with men in very close proximity trying to hold their ground. Bayonets and sabres clash violently; rifles and pistols exchange fire at close range, inflicting terrible damage; and men wrestle one another to the ground in individual duels to the death. Every available weapon – conventional and improvised, including knives, clubs, feet, fists and teeth – is used to maim and kill one's opponent.

Bodies fall to the ground, men shout in German and English, but their screams are the same in both languages. Blood spews in all directions and washes over the ground. There is no mercy; the killing is bestial.

Maurice, now standing in the middle of the road, senses movement behind him and turns just in time to avoid the arc of the sabre wielded by the grandiose officer on whom Harry had earlier trained the sights of his rifle. The Prussian's mount rears, almost unseating him, but knocking Maurice to the ground with a thump. Harry rushes forward and grabs the horse's bridle to pull it to the ground.

'Got you, Fritz. I'm 'avin' your 'elmet, golden boy!'

But the Prussian turns athletically in his saddle and slashes at Harry's left arm with his sword. Harry manages to get the barrel of his rifle in the way, just in time to deflect the blow. Nevertheless, the blade bounces off the rifle and slices into Harry's arm, causing a deep gash just below the shoulder. He falls backwards, but as he does so, he gets off a shot from his Lee-Enfield, hitting his adversary full in the throat. The bullet's impact makes a sound like an apple being squashed; blood spurts in all directions. It exits at the back of the man's head, flipping his flamboyant helmet over his face and on to the ground.

'Gotcha, yer bastard!'

The stricken man slumps forward and drops his sword, blood streaming down his tunic. His horse runs off in panic before depositing its lifeless rider in a field fifty yards away.

Despite the wide gouge to Harry's upper arm, his only concern is the prize lying on the ground in front of him. Maurice, still shaken, is getting up from the road.

'Quick, Mo, get that 'elmet for me. You can 'ave the sword.'

Maurice picks up the helmet and sword and runs back to help Harry to the safety of their rubble-strewn entrenchment by the church, where he hides their booty under their knapsacks. The fighting all around them is still intense, although there are now more men on the ground dead and dying than are on their feet still fighting.

'Come on, 'Arry, let's drop back down the road.'

He grabs Harry's good arm but, as he does so, a German bayonet enters his back just below his ribs. The cavalryman must have been hiding in the church. The bayonet is quickly withdrawn, ready for another strike, but Maurice reels round and knocks the German's rifle to one side with his own before shooting him square in the chest.

To his surprise, Maurice does not feel as much pain as he thought he would. He has been knicked by a blade twice before, once in India and once in South Africa. Neither was a serious wound, but both felt worse than this.

Suddenly, the 4th Fusiliers' machine gun opens up, making everyone scatter for cover.

'Abaht fuckin' time! Bet the tosser got it jammed again!' Harry then shouts at Maurice, 'Come on, Mo! Fritz's infantry's comin' across the fields!'

As they both get down behind the rubble, dozens of field-grey uniforms stream across the open ground on the other side of the road. Harry peers over the top of the stones.

'We're in a bit o' bovver, Mo.'

'Not 'alf! How's the shoulder?'

'Stings like buggery, but it's only a flesh wound. How's the back?'

'All right, I think, mate; it don't 'urt that much.'

Harry's concerned. Although it might not hurt now, there is certain to be internal bleeding.

'Do we stay 'ere, or scarper?'

All around them are dead and wounded from both sides. One or two of their platoon are still behind the rubble, firing at the enemy, but most are either dead or have made a run for it.

'I think we should leg it, 'Arry.'

'Well, if you can run, I can. Let's go, but I'm not going without my 'elmet.'

Both grab their spoils. Harry manages to get the helmet in his knapsack and Maurice wraps his sword in his groundsheet. They decide to take a quick look at their surroundings before making a dash for it. As they do, they see Major Ashburner running down the road to their right, followed by at least sixty fusiliers, including Captain Carey and Lieutenant Mead. They take up positions in the ditches on the far side of the road and unleash several volleys of fire, which halts the German infantry in its tracks. Almost all the men in the front ranks fall immediately, while those further back run for the cover of a copse of trees to the right.

Ashburner orders his men to charge and the fusiliers chase the Germans into the copse, where a ferocious fight ensues.

Almost all of the cavalrymen who attacked them are now either dead or have retreated, leaving Maurice and Harry alone with the dead and dying of the encounter.

Harry helps his friend to his feet.

'Come on, let's go, while it's quiet. You're bleedin' like a stuck pig.'

The back of Maurice's tunic is soaked in blood and the wound is beginning to hurt him far more than when it was first inflicted. The two men begin to stagger across the ruins of Saint-Amé, back towards the centre of Herlies. They step over the rubble on the other side of the nave and into a small yard at the back of the village, which seems deserted. Maurice begins to stumble, so Harry helps him through the back door of a small house.

It is the middle of the day, the sun has begun to shine. Although it is autumn, the sun is warm. They enter a small kitchen. A table still sits in the middle of the room, but one of its legs is broken. The chairs that belong to the table are scattered around the room; they are all broken. Nothing else remains. The family which would usually be sitting there enjoying a leisurely French Saturday lunch has long gone.

Maurice and Harry slump to the floor. Maurice is very pale and Harry's concerns for him are deepening. His friend has lost a lot of blood. He decides to give him a breather for five minutes before trying to get him back to the battalion dressing station. However, despite heavy gunfire not very far away, they are both overtaken by fatigue and fall into a deep sleep.

Twenty minutes later, they have a rude awakening. A group of Prussian cavalrymen, survivors of the gruesome encounter nearby, stumble into the room. Three of them are wounded; three are unharmed, but exhausted.

The noise of the German arrival wakes Harry and Maurice but, by the time they reach for their rifles, it is too late. Several German rifles are pointing directly at them.

Then, in excellent English, one of the men addresses them calmly, 'Good afternoon, gentlemen.'

Recognizing the man as a Rittmeister, a cavalry captain, by the two pips on his epaulettes, Harry thinks quickly. The fighting between them was so intense barely half an hour ago, and there have been so many stories of German atrocities, but these men seem like proper soldiers who follow the old code of discipline and honour.

Harry salutes and prompts Maurice to do the same.

'Good afternoon, sir. You speak good English, Captain.'

'Thank you, Serjeant, I lived two years in London. I was fencing coach at London Fencing Club with the famous maître, Leon Paul.'

Harry tries to get to his feet and help Maurice do the same.

'It is not necessary to stand; you are wounded. Please stay on the floor.'

'Thank you, sir. My friend 'as a bayonet wound through his ribs. He needs to see a medic.'

'Yes, of course, but we need to get back to our lines. If we do, we will take care of you and your friend. But I am not certain where are our comrades. At this moment, you are our prisoners, but we may soon be yours. I think we are closer to your position than to ours. I have sent two men to find out what is the situation. Please be patient.' The Rittmeister smiles. 'I liked London but, under these circumstances, I do not think it would be wise for me to go back.'

The Germans light cigarettes and pass them around. Maurice refuses; he is in considerable pain and looking very pale. The Rittmeister kneels down to look at Maurice's wound.

'It is clean; I don't think it penetrates organ. But it needs strapping.'

'Are you a doctor, sir?'

'No, but I have seen many sword wounds; this is not too deep.'

Maurice grimaces.

'It were a bayonet, sir.'

The German helps Maurice take off his tunic and shirt.

'Ah, yes, the crude hole of bayonet; not neat like sword.'

He then takes a clean white, neatly folded handkerchief from his pocket and begins to rip Maurice's shirt into strips.

'I am sorry, but I'm sure your Lord Kitchener can buy you another one. This will hurt, but it must be done.'

He clicks his fingers and a German serjeant produces a small pewter hip flask.

'Marillenschnaps, Austrian apricot brandy. It is good for drink and good for wound.'

He takes a swig before pouring a liberal amount on to the handkerchief and applying it to the wound, which he secures with strips of Maurice's shirt.

'*Das ist gut*, now you need rest. Here, drink schnapps.'

'Thank you, sir.'

The captain inhales from his cigarette with relish.

'We allow ourselves five cigarettes a day. This is our second.' He turns to Harry. 'What is your regiment, Serjeant?'

'The 4th Battalion Royal Fusiliers, sir.'

'How very appropriate; London men. From where?'

'Leyton, sir, in the East End.'

'Ah, yes, I coached at City of London School, Blackfriars. I used to watch the Thames rise and fall on tide; fascinating. We do not have this on our rivers so much. My name is Carl von Tannhausen, my family home is in Eberswalde, in Brandenburg.'

Harry is watching one of the Rittmeister's men very closely. He has noticed the hilt of the 'confiscated' Prussian sword sticking out from beneath Maurice's groundsheet. The burly German, who looks uncannily like the beastly

'Hun' depicted in the British newspaper cartoons, suddenly leans forward and pulls the sabre from its hiding place.

'*Mein Gott, Rittmeister! Der Säbel von dem Major!*'

The German strikes Harry a heavy blow across the face with the back of his gloved hand and points the tip of the sabre at Maurice's throat.

'*Du Bastard!*'

'*Nein!*' von Tannhausen bellows at his man. '*Sie würden das gleiche tun. Es ist eine Kriegstrophäe.*'

The German serjeant lowers the sword and relents. Harry breathes a huge sigh of relief.

'Thank you, sir. What did you say to 'im?'

'I told him that he would do the same. It is what I think you English call "spoils of war".'

'Well, sir, we're sorry. But we didn't steal it.'

'I understand. You should know that the men were very fond of Major von Mecklenberg. His family has been part of the *Gardes du Corps* since its formation.'

Harry feels a strong sense of remorse, an emotion he has never felt before.

'Sir, I think I'd better tell yer that I've got 'is 'elmet in my knapsack.'

Von Tannhausen smiles.

'I am not surprised. I was told that you boys – Cockney boys, am I right? – are very light with fingers. Do I use the right expression?'

Harry looks appropriately sheepish.

'Almost, sir, but I know what you mean.'

'I think, Serjeant, you perhaps should give the pieces to me so that they can be returned to the major's family. My men will feel happier then.'

'Very good, sir.'

Harry retrieves the gleaming eagle helmet from his knapsack and hands it to his captor. Von Tannhausen then collects the sword from his serjeant.

'Beautiful, isn't it?'

The Rittmeister turns the sabre in his hands. Heavily gold-plated, its hilt is inlaid with ivory. Its guard spews from the mouth of an eagle, which forms the weapon's pommel. The guard covering the blade hides a small compartment that is home to a tiny, but perfectly matching, skinning knife.

'To prepare the animal for the fire, Serjeant.'

Harry is fascinated; he has never seen a weapon so beautifully made. The blade of the weapon, almost two feet long, shines like mirrored glass, and on it are delicately etched hunting scenes of boar, deer and bear. Like the master swordsman he is, the Rittmeister then slashes the sabre through the air, making a soft 'whoosh' of sound no harsher than the merest breath of wind.

'You could cut a man in half with this.'

Harry thinks back to his encounter with the weapon and realizes how lucky he has been.

Just at that moment a German corporal bursts into the room.

'*Rittmeister, Englische Infanterie in der Straße!*'

There is a sudden panic in the room as, hearing that British soldiers are in the street, the Germans spring to life. But their response is too late. There is a burst of gunfire from the kitchen window above where Maurice and Harry are sitting. Three of the Germans are flung backwards by the impact of bullets at close range. Harry shouts at the top of his voice.

'*No!* Cease firing! They're our prisoners!'

But his plea cannot be heard. The kitchen door bursts open and another hail of bullets sends more Germans sprawling, their blood splashing on the wall behind them. Rittmeister von Tannhausen is hit in the chest and thigh; he falls against the wall and slides down it until he is sitting like a rag doll propped up in a child's playroom. He looks at Harry, with half a smile and half a grimace of pain on his face.

'Perhaps I would have been safer in London after all –'

He barely finishes speaking before two more bullets thud into his chest, making his body jerk. His eyes close and his chin drops on to his chest.

And yet, still more rifle fire fills the room; more bullets slam into the bodies of the already dead Germans.

Harry jumps to his feet.

'*Enough!* They're fuckin' dead!'

Men of his own platoon edge cautiously into the room, emerging through the shattered doorway; they did what they thought was best and are shocked at Harry's response.

'Sorry, Sarje, we thought it was the right thing to do.'

'Never mind, Corporal; help me get Serjeant Tait to the dressing station.'

One of the platoon picks up the Prussian helmet, while another picks up the sword.

'Cor blimey! Take a butcher's at these, must be worth a fuckin' fortune.'

Harry turns on the two men.

'Listen, you two arseholes, them things belong to me and Serjeant Tait. If they're not with our kit when we've 'ad our wounds dressed, I'll skin you alive! When I'm outta this shit'ole, they're goin' back to Germany where they belong. We took them off a brave man to stop twats like you gettin' 'old of 'em!'

The fusiliers look at Harry. Out of earshot, one of them mutters, 'What's got into 'im? Looks like 'e's goin' doolally tap!'

Harry's wound needs several stitches, but he will be able to resume duties after a few days. Maurice's injury is much more serious, but he has been very fortunate. The bayonet puncture has missed both his lung and kidney on his left side, but it is a deep laceration and he will be sent to a rear field hospital in Boulogne to recover.

Both Major Ashburner and Captain Carey have been

injured in the battle at Herlies, but not seriously enough to take them out of action for long. However, Lieutenant Mead will not be going anywhere. Like thousands of others, he will be buried nearby, or at least those pieces of him that can be retrieved from where a shell exploded just next to him.

Maurice's departure and the heavy fusilier casualties in the encounter – five officers and 150 men killed, missing or severely wounded – only worsen Harry's disposition, already melancholy after the melee at Vailly. The loss today of so many comrades, and the unnecessary death of Rittmeister von Tannhausen, a man who treated him with kindness and respect, have left Harry with much to ponder. And his thoughts serve only to darken his mood even more.

The one positive thought that stays with him is his resolve to return the Prussian helmet and sword to the family of the man he killed.

Sunday 18 October

The Royal Welch Fusiliers' austere nineteenth-century cas-tellated Hightown Barracks is more like a prison block than a home from home for the Thomas boys. Used to their iso-lated cottage at Pentry Farm, amidst the rolling hills of Radnorshire, life in a large barracks room with scores of other men is alien to them; as are military discipline and rou-tine. They do not find the regime physically demanding, but its rigidity and mind-numbing repetition is psychologically exhausting. Even so, they are exemplary soldiers.

Geraint and Morgan have been here since joining up at the beginning of September, in the aftermath of the scan-dalous revelation of their sister's relationship with Philip Davies. Their older brother, Hywel, followed them to High-gate when he joined up later in the month, following Margaret Killingbeck's visit to Presteigne in search of Bronwyn. Her visit partially rescued him from his melancholy, and he did what he said he would do: he closed up the cottage, let the land to a neighbour and joined Kitchener's Army.

The 1st and 2nd Battalions Welch Fusiliers, which have been in France since August, have seen little action and suf-fered almost no casualties, other than the ill-fated Captain Davies. In stark contrast to so many other regiments, their only hardship has been the many pairs of blistered feet caused by ill-fitting new boots.

A draft detachment of around 100 reservists is being pre-pared at Hightown for the long journey to reinforce the 1st

Battalion. They are the pick of the men in training; not only are they fit and ready to fight, their departure will create space for the new volunteers who are flocking to the recruiting offices.

The draft will be led by 2nd Lieutenant Francis Orme, a gangling 23-year-old from a renowned military family, who has only recently passed out of Sandhurst.

As news of an imminent departure for France spreads around the barracks, the three Thomas boys are summoned to the Regimental Adjutant's office. With the senior officer are Colour Serjeant Major John Hughes and Lieutenant Orme.

The three boys march in smartly and salute. The adjutant smiles at them.

'Stand at ease, Fusiliers. How is your training going?'

Hywel answers.

'Very well, thank you, sir, but I'm a little behind my brothers.'

'Well, all three of you are doing exceptionally well.' He looks down at various sheets of paper in front of him on his desk. 'You are physically strong, and your scores on the range are outstanding – especially yours, Fusilier Thomas, H. Your scores are as high as we've ever seen from a novice; you are a remarkable marksman. Indeed, were it not for the small matter of the war in France, we would be preparing you for the Regimental Shooting Championships at Bisley.'

Hywel looks distinctly self-conscious.

'Thank you, sir. I've always enjoyed shooting on the farm.'

'Now listen; you will have heard that Lieutenant Orme here is taking a detachment of men to France next week, probably on Wednesday. Altogether, one hundred and nine men have been chosen, all with some experience as reservists. All, that is, except six recent volunteers, all of whom show great promise. We have spoken to the other three, Fusiliers Jones, G. and Jones, E. and Fusilier Bennett.'

The Thomas brothers look at one another in amazement; they know what is coming next.

'Yes, we have chosen all three of you to be part of Lieutenant Orme's detachment.'

All the Thomas boys thank the adjutant in unison; there are smiles all round.

Before CSM Hughes dismisses them, Lieutenant Orme offers them some warm words of encouragement.

'Delighted to have you in my detachment, Fusiliers Thomas, Thomas and Thomas. It will be my first posting as well. Perhaps we can help one another?'

Appreciative of the lieutenant's words, Geraint answers this time.

'Thank you, sir, we'll do our best.'

CSM Hughes then takes them to the Regimental Quartermaster's store, where they are issued with weapons and kit. It is a proud moment for them, and they find it hard to stop grinning during the whole process.

Finally, they are taken to the Orderly Room where their details are checked by the Regimental Clerk, a punctilious serjeant, who fires questions at them.

When it comes to the question about their next of kin, there is a difference of opinion. Initially, Hywel answers for all three of them.

'None, Serjeant, both our parents are dead. There are just the three of us.'

Morgan disagrees.

'I have a twin sister, Bronwyn.'

The serjeant looks puzzled.

'Make your minds up. If one of you has a sister, then you all have a sister! Unless you breed differently in Presteigne. What's her address?'

'Don't know, Serjeant.'

'Then it isn't much bloody use me putting her down, is it?'

The boys look at one another. They do not know how to answer.

'Look, if you cop a Jack Johnson in France and you all go up in smoke, we have to send a telegram to someone. I need a name and address.'

Geraint, never afraid to ask an obvious question, asks the one that both his brothers want to ask.

'What's a "Jack Johnson", Serjeant?'

The serjeant smirks.

'It's an exploding shell that gives off shitloads o' black smoke.'

The boys still seem none the wiser.

'Don't you have newspapers in Presteigne? Jack Johnson is World Heavyweight Champion. He's a bloody darkie, black as the ace of spades! Anyway, I need a name.'

Hywel comes up with a name.

'The Reverend Henry Kewley, the Vicarage, St Andrew's Church, Presteigne. Thank you very much, Serjeant.'

'That'll do. Now off with you! And try not to get in the way of a Jack Johnson in France . . . or a whizz-bang.'

'What's a "whizz-bang", Sarje?'

'Fuck off, you cheeky little bugger!'

That night, the Thomas boys are allowed to leave Hightown Barracks and go into Wrexham to celebrate their deployment. They do not go very far, just to the King's Mill, a Banks's pub a few hundred yards down the road. It is very much a soldiers' haunt. Many men come up to them to shake their hands and congratulate them, and a few even buy them jugs of ale.

As they talk, Morgan takes the opportunity to get something off his chest.

'Hywel, I know your opinion of Bron, disownin' her an' all that. But when it comes to our next o' kin, shouldn't she know if we get blown up by one of those Jack Thompsons?'

'Jack Johnsons!'

'Yeah, one of those.'

'I suppose so. But what do we give as her address? A dockside whorehouse in Tiger Bay, Cardiff?'

'Perhaps that nurse who came to Pentry has found 'er and straightened 'er out?'

'Not much chance o' that, Morgan. There's no way back from bein' a tart in Tiger Bay.'

Geraint changes the subject.

'I wonder what Tom's up to?'

Hywel misses his boyhood friend. Tom has not been seen since the trauma over Bronwyn.

'If he's got any sense, he'll be a long way away from Presteigne and will never go back.'

Morgan looks into the fire glowing in the hearth, then stares at the chestnut-coloured brew in his jug.

'Bet they don't 'ave Banks's Mild in France.'

Hywel looks at his younger brother. Although he has felt much better since following his brothers and joining the Welch Fusiliers, he is still very raw after the ordeals of the summer. But he is putting on a brave face in front of Geraint and Morgan.

'I'm sure they 'ave beer in France. And I'm sure it will 'ave the same effect as Banks's.'

'I 'ope so, Hywel! I do 'ope so, with all those darkie bombs goin' off.'

Hywel smiles pensively and also stares into the fire. He is still thinking that a quick and painless death in France will be an appropriate end to a life full of sadness and with no prospect of respite.

Sunday 25 October

The constant series of attempts by the German and Allied armies to outflank one another all along the French-Belgian border goes on relentlessly. The loss of life increases alarmingly by the day.

The war, initiated by rulers whose motives are akin to the vainglories of medieval kings and princes, is, despite the impressive resolve of its generals and soldiers, impossible to win, at least in the short term. All the while, the new technologies of transportation and weaponry are enabling millions of young men to be sent to the battlefield, where they are being killed on a horrifying scale by increasingly lethal modern armaments.

The British Expeditionary Force, the greater part of Britain's small but outstanding army, is being destroyed. Of the BEF's original strength of eighty-four infantry battalions just two months ago, each of which comprised about 970 men, only nine have between 350 and 450 survivors. Thirty-one are down to between 200 and 300, and eighteen have fewer than 100 fit men ready for action. The most severely depleted of all, the 1st Loyal North Lancashire, is a battalion in name only as it now consists of one officer and thirty-five men.

Besides the obvious bullet wounds, shrapnel injuries and the mutilations caused by artillery shells, a new malady is beginning to emerge. There are more and more reports of less tangible symptoms after combat, including tinnitus, amnesia, headache, dizziness, tremors and hypersensitivity to noise. What puzzles the medical staff is that men often present with these ailments even when they have not been in close proximity to an explosion. There are also increasing numbers of men who appear 'lost' or 'disorientated'. Fellow soldiers coin a new term for their condition: 'the thousand-yard stare'. The medics begin to use the term 'shell shock'.

Many suffer from 'nervous disorders' that some call 'fear of battle' and others call 'cowardice in the face of the enemy'. For the men of High Command, 'shell shock' and 'nerves' pose a major dilemma, one that they choose to ignore. After all, what is the difference between conditions caused by the psychological stress of battle and the 'cowardice' exhibited by men who do not have the stomach for the fight? Few senior commanders allow themselves to show much sympathy for men who are described as 'shell-shocked' or suffering from 'nerves', even though there is much evidence that the phenomenon extends to the very top of the military hierarchy.

As in France and Germany, the personal tragedies of the death toll reach into every corner of Britain, including the homes of the ruling class, whose sons in the officer corps are dying in staggering numbers. Prince Maurice of Battenberg, the nephew of Winston Churchill's First Sea Lord, Louis of Battenberg, and a grandson of Queen Victoria, dies at Ypres serving with the King's Royal Rifle Corps. Winston's cousin, 2nd Lieutenant Norman Leslie, the son of Lady Randolph's sister Leonie and her husband, Sir John Leslie, is killed with the Rifle Brigade at Armentières.

It is also a bleak time for the Stewart-Murrays of Blair Atholl. There is still no word from or sighting of Geordie. It is now six weeks since he was last seen in action with the Black Watch near Vailly.

Eton College, perhaps the one school that most typifies the noblesse oblige of the British aristocracy, and the Stewart-Murrays' Alma Mater, will send 5,629 Old Etonians to fight in the Great War. Of these, 1,157 will be killed, another 1,460 will be injured and 130 will be taken prisoner. Those who are born to lead must expect to bleed.

The telegrams begin to arrive at remote farms, village cottages, detached and semi-detached suburban homes and terraced houses all over the country. For the time being they are delivered to the families of professional soldiers and army reservists, but that will soon change, as will their volume and frequency.

The Ypres Salient remains the critical fulcrum of the war in the autumn of 1914. For British forces, the fighting is being concentrated into an increasingly confined area along a line between Lille and Béthune in the south, and between Ypres and Armentières to the east.

But the whole of the front line extends much further. North of Sir John French's BEF at Ypres, between his soldiers and the coast, the Allied line is held by French and Belgian troops who are resolutely defending their position west of the Yser River under the direct command of Albert, King of the Belgians. To the south of Béthune, the defensive bulwark is held by General d'Urbal's 8th French Army, which continues to fight with great tenacity. Facing the Allies are two entire German Army Groups: the 4th, under General Duke Albrecht of Württemberg, and the 6th, under Crown Prince Rupprecht of Bavaria. In total, Allied forces number just over 350,000, while the two German armies can muster well over 500,000.

French colonial troops from Morocco have already acquitted themselves well in the fighting. Newly arrived British Empire troops from the Meerut and Lahore Divisions of the Indian Army will soon perform with equal distinction, despite having only meagre supplies, few munitions and no winter clothing.

Significantly, the events in and around Ypres in the autumn of 1914 are to offer a salutary lesson: in the battles of the Great War, it is far easier to defend a position than to attack one. Both the Allies and the Germans are running short of food, clothing, medical supplies and materiel. Shells and bullets are being rationed and transportation is becoming a major headache. The railway systems are in chaos and the roads are blocked by shell holes, broken-down vehicles and endless streams of civilians seeking refuge from the fighting.

Bicycles become a godsend for messengers and reconnaissance; dogs are used as pack animals for machine guns and small mortars. Horses are put to use in the more mundane role of beasts of burden, rather than as cavalry chargers, and aerial scouting from the sky becomes vital to strategic planning.

There is many a nostalgic sighting for British men far away from home when huge fleets of buses arrive, still painted in the liveries of the bus companies belonging to the towns and cities of their origins. They include over 300 red and white 'Old Bill' London buses requisitioned from the London General Omnibus Company. Each BEF brigade is allocated thirty buses, manned by their own volunteer drivers, who are given uniforms and rifles. Stories soon circulate, apocryphal or otherwise, that men are being driven to the battlefield by bus drivers who previously drove them to work in Civvy Street.

Serjeant Harry Woodruff and what remains of the 4th Battalion Royal Fusiliers arrive at Pont Logy, 1,000 yards due west of Neuve-Chapelle, early in the afternoon of 25 October.

Neuve-Chappelle is a village of little distinction eight miles north-east of Béthune and sixteen miles south-west of Lille. Like so much of the ground over which the opposing armies have fought since the war began, the landscape is monotonously flat, with only the occasional church spire to break up the otherwise tedious horizon. Well-engineered French rural roads criss-cross the terrain in almost endless straight lines and disappear to a vanishing point, their drainage ditches offering the only cover between huge open fields of crops.

The fusiliers can see the houses of Neuve-Chappelle in the distance. They are occupied by men of Germany's 158th Infantry Regiment (7th Lotharingians) from Paderborn in Westphalia. The Londoners are told that the order to attack is imminent and that they must stand to.

Harry looks round at his platoon. Most are new reservists, recently arrived from hasty preparatory retraining at Albany Barracks. He wishes Maurice was here, but it has only been eight days since his bayonet wound at Herlies. At least Captain Carey is nearby; both he and Major Ashburner have recovered from the flesh wounds they received in the skirmish.

There has been no replacement for Lieutenant Mead, killed at Herlies, and no new company serjeant major to replace Billy Carstairs, killed at Vailly.

An hour passes and there is still no order to attack. The only movement is the appearance of a bicycle at about 3 p.m., hurtling towards them down Rue du Grand Chemin from the direction of Battalion HQ. It carries a fusilier, peddling frantically, as if in possession of an urgent message. But when the rider comes to a halt at the side of the road, it is not a messenger but Platoon Serjeant Maurice Tait.

Harry is open-mouthed.

'What the fuck are you doin' 'ere?'

'I've come to keep an eye on you!'

'Thought you was gonna be banged up in 'ospital.'

'The nurse I saw was a right Miss Fitch, and the Doc said I'd be as right as ninepence in a fortnight, so I fucked off!'

'How did yer get back?'

'Hitched a lift wiv some Cherry Bums, 4th Hussars, on their way down 'ere.'

'Hussars! "Whose-arse" tonight, you mean! Not gone queer on me, 'ave yer, Mo?'

'Fuck off, 'Arry! They were good lads; their officer gave me a packet of fags.'

'He sounds like an iron hoof to me. Didn't tell yer to bend over and tie up yer shoelaces, did he?'

Maurice just grins, ignoring Harry's taunting. So Harry changes the subject.

''Ave yer seen Ashburner?'

'Yeah.'

'What did he say?'

'He said, "Fusilier Tait, you are a very ill-disciplined soldier and deserve to be sent straight back to the hospital and punished for insubordination." Then he stood up, smiled at me and said, "But we need men like you here. Very good to have you back. Your platoon is at Pon Loggy" – or something like that – "so see if you can get up there. A little skirmish is in the offing."'

Harry smirks.

'Little skirmish! Take a butcher's: a thousand yards of open ground, and Fritz is in every birch an' broom in them 'ouses over there. Some tosser at HQ 'as looked at a map and said, "Jolly easy stroll to the German positions, no problem for our lads!" Well, he don't 'ave to fuckin' walk it, do he?'

Maurice realizes that Harry's mood is no calmer than when he left.

Five minutes later, the order passes down the line and hundreds of Cockneys in khaki begin to move across the broad fields of Neuve-Chapelle; to the right are the Northumberlands, to the left the Lincolnshires. They are a comfort to the London boys. They have given stern support whenever it was needed in the past; today they will have to do so again.

The first men begin to fall at about 700 yards. The toll

grows exponentially with every yard thereafter. There is no cover, and no evasive action is available; survival is a lottery, determined by the aim of the German marksmen, or the breaths of wind that make bullets veer away from their intended victims. Who would send men across open ground into repetitive hailstorms of bullets unleashed from lethally accurate modern rifles and machine guns? The answer is tragically simple: generals who have no other strategy, because none has yet been thought of.

The fusiliers, like all the other men on the battlefields on both sides of the Great War, know that the only combination that will unlock the secret code of victory in this diabolical conflict is simple: whoever is prepared to sacrifice the most men, the most resources and has the strongest stomach for the fight. All any man can hope for in the numbers game of the Great War is that his name, in the final reckoning, will be added to the list of survivors rather than the toll of the dead.

Harry and Maurice, in the absence of a replacement for Lieutenant Mead, are de facto commanding officers of their platoon. They have survived over 800 of the 1,000 yards to Neuve-Chapelle when they hear Captain Carey's order: 'Fix bayonets!'

Instead of running pell-mell towards the German positions, Maurice and Harry order their men to crouch down and take a breath as they fix their bayonets. It is a shrewd decision; fusiliers around them take the brunt of the final frantic volleys of the German defenders, loosed before the hand-to-hand fighting begins. When the hail of bullets recedes, Harry orders the platoon to charge. With the two serjeants leading the assault, they identify a single modest house in Neuve-Chapelle and storm into it.

Their platoon is now only a dozen strong – half the number which, only minutes ago, started the 1,000-yard walk – but there are only a handful of Germans in the house. After five minutes of primordial killing by bullet and bayonet, all the Lotharingians, the sons of Paderborn's tailors, clerks and artisans, are dead. Four fusiliers are also dead. Blood covers the walls and floor; crumpled bodies have fallen in distorted heaps in the corners of the room or lie sprawled across the meagre peasant furniture. Patches of German field-grey uniforms have turned ruby and circles of British khaki have become brown, darkened by the cherry red of men's blood.

There is a sudden eerie silence, except for the deep breathing of men recovering from the exertion of a fight to the death. Of the twenty-six men who began the attack at Pont Logy with Maurice and Harry, only eight are still standing.

Harry issues a stark command.

'Make sure all these German bastards are dead. If they're not, slit their fuckin' throats.'

His emotion is in stark contrast to his benign attitude towards his German adversaries only a few days ago in Herlies.

But that is the terrible dichotomy of men's appetites in wartime.

Wednesday 28 October

Even for Winston Churchill, a senior aristocrat and member
of the British Cabinet, and Harold Asquith, an urbane and
wily old Prime Minister, an audience with the King is a daunting experience, especially if it takes place at Windsor Castle.
The oldest inhabited royal palace in the world, it is a long
drive from London. Its Upper Ward, where the Royal Apartments are located, is approached by passing a collection of
buildings that represent 900 years of British history, from
the time of William the Conqueror.

Winston spent much of his childhood amidst the splen-
dours of Blenheim Palace but, as the two men walk into the
Royal Apartments, even he marvels at the almost endless
procession of gilded rooms leading to the White Drawing
Room, where the King will see them.

After being shown in, the two men are left alone for a
while. The room is full of mahogany trays piled on several
tables, on desks and even on the floor. Each tray is full of
stamps from every part of the Empire and every nation on
earth. Shooting, at which he is an excellent marksman, naval
history, about which he has a profound knowledge, and phil-
ately, on which he spends a fortune, are the King's greatest
and only passions.

Exactly on the stroke of 11 a.m., George Edward Ernest
Albert – His Majesty George V, by the Grace of God, of the
United Kingdom of Great Britain and Ireland and of the Brit-
ish Dominions beyond the Seas, King, Defender of the Faith,

Emperor of India – walks in, accompanied by Colonel Arthur Bigge, Lord Stamfordham, his private secretary and most trusted courtier. Stamfordham has devoted his life to the Royal Family and was previously private secretary to the King's grandmother, Queen Victoria.

Although the King is kindly, unassuming and somewhat open-minded compared to many in the higher echelons of the nobility, Stamfordham is highly conservative and distrusts Asquith's liberality. As for Winston, he dislikes him intensely and is probably jealous of his flair and ability – and perhaps, more particularly, of his nobler origins. Arthur Bigge is from a wealthy Northumberland family that has fallen on hard times; he is the son of the humble vicar of Stamfordham, a small village ten miles east of Hexham. As a career soldier, he rose to the rank of colonel in the Royal Artillery before being appointed to the Royal Household in 1895. His peerage as Baron Stamfordham was granted as recently as 1911.

Both visitors bow and say in unison, 'Good morning, Majesty.'

'Prime Minister, Mr Churchill, please sit. Some tea?'

A footman appears, as if from nowhere, pours the tea and then makes an unobtrusive exit.

Stamfordham sits to one side. He will scrutinize every word, gesture and nuance and will later commit all his recollections to paper for the King's records. Much of the private bile and public vitriol that has been recently directed at Winston has been filtered to the King through Stamfordham. Those with an axe to grind know that he is the route to the King's ear. Those in the navy – of which King George is very fond, having served in it for many years – who dislike Winston's meticulous approach to even the smallest detail of naval affairs, use Stamfordham as a conduit to the King.

The King Emperor begins the formal meeting.

'Prime Minister, before we begin the business of the day, I have a slightly parochial matter to raise with Mr Churchill.'

The King looks stern. The rays of the sun suddenly burst into the room, making his thick brown beard and waxed moustache glow. His worsted morning coat and waistcoat look immaculate, as if they have never been worn before; his grey silk cravat, the gold Albert chain of his pocket watch and his bulldog-toed shoes, the latest fashion in men's footwear, gleam in the bright light. He is an impressive, fatherly figure, much loved by his people, as is 'May' – his imposing wife, Queen Mary.

Winston knows that the King does not hold him in high regard – their personalities being almost polar opposites – and that he disapproves of his mother, Lady Randolph, especially in view of the rumour that she was one of his father's many mistresses.

'It is by way of a small request. Iain Stewart-Murray, Duke of Atholl, is a good friend of both of us, I believe.'

'Indeed, sir, but I know his son Bardie far better.'

'Good, because my request is about Bardie. Atholl was at Balmoral shooting the other day. He's in very low spirits, poor old boy. All three sons are in the army. One's been wounded and is at home recovering, and he fears he's lost his middle boy, who's not been heard of for several weeks. They hope he may be a prisoner; but it's not looking likely, as the Germans usually make a fuss if they capture a titled soldier.'

The King leans forward and takes a cigarette from the case in front of him. He offers the case to the others, who all refuse. The same footman makes another fleeting appearance to light the King's cigarette and retreats once more.

'Anyway, I gather Bardie and his fellow investors, Bendor Grosvenor, that Rothschild chap and others, have developed a flying apparatus.'

'They have, sir, with a Mr William Dunne, a very accomplished aeronautical engineer.'

'Is that what they call them? Well, Atholl thinks he's as

mad as a hatter. So, what about his contraptions? Are they any use to us?'

'I'm afraid not, sir, both the Naval Air Service and the Flying Corps have tried them. They are not sturdy enough for the battlefield.'

'I see. Will you then put him out of his misery?'

'I will, of course, Your Majesty. I have spoken to Lord Kitchener, who is very fond of Bardie and his Scottish Horse. He has asked him to come down to the War Office to talk about the future deployment of his regiment, and I will use that opportunity to give him the bad news face to face.'

'Very good, Mr Churchill; I'm delighted that you plan to tell him in person. Thank you for your consideration, and forgive me for indulging in what might seem like a bit of nepotism on my part. But I don't want Iain worrying about a flying contraption when he has three sons in the midst of war.'

'The duke is fortunate in having so thoughtful a friend in Your Majesty.'

The King smiles for the first time.

'Now, to the matter in hand. Prime Minister?'

Asquith draws a noticeable breath.

'Indeed, sir, the Admiralty; Mr Churchill would like to make some changes and has some recommendations with which, I have to say, I concur.'

'Very well. Mr Churchill?'

'Sir, I feel I need to move Lord Louis on as First Sea Lord. The constant pressure from the press and others, some within the navy itself, regarding his German roots is undermining his ability to think clearly and act decisively. He is wonderfully loyal and a talented naval man, specifically recommended by Jacky Fisher when he retired, but the idle chatter in the military clubs in St James's is vile, especially the poison that has been spat out by Admiral Lord Charles Beresford.'

'The man's a fool! Surely you can tell him to keep his opinions to himself?'

'He is, sir, and rest assured I have told him to hold his tongue. But the damage is done.'

The King's unsympathetic demeanour returns.

'And with whom will you replace Prince Louis?'

'Jacky Fisher, sir . . .' Unusually, Winston pauses to gather himself. 'And I would also like to bring back Arthur Wilson.'

'Good heavens, they are both in their seventies!'

John Arbuthnot, Admiral of the Fleet, the Lord Fisher, is widely credited as the architect of the modern Royal Navy. A rabid reformer and mastermind of the dreadnought battleship, he is hugely respected. But he has been retired for over three years and his irascible personality does not endear him to everybody, especially not the King, who once had to ask him to stop waving his clenched fist at him during an otherwise amiable discussion.

Sir Arthur 'Tug' Wilson, equally abrasive, is a man in Fisher's mould and very much the kind of energetic character Winston needs. The holder of a VC from the Mahdist War of 1884, he is an uncompromising, hard-nosed veteran. But he is also retired, and the King thinks him 'uncouth'.

The King gets up from his chair and wanders over to the window. As if on cue, Lord Stamfordham speaks for the first time.

'Mr Churchill, how is your brother, Jack? I believe he is with the Oxfordshire Yeomanry in Dunkirk, part of what I believe the press is calling, and I quote, "Churchill's Dunkirk Circus, a gimmick of comically armoured Rolls-Royce cars and an excuse for a bit of sport for the Lord of the Admiralty's little brother."'

Winston is livid that Stamfordham should repeat, word for word, a line from the *Morning Post*, but he knows he must avoid the man's deliberate attempt to provoke him.

'Stamfordham, how kind of you to inquire about Jack. He is doing very well, as is the Yeomanry, who are helping King Albert keep the Germans on the far side of the Yser River. Indeed, Jack saw the King only the other day, who made a point of expressing his gratitude to us for all our support in Antwerp and along the coast.'

Mention of the King of the Belgians makes King George turn his head back to the conversation momentarily. Asquith is not sure if it is true that Jack saw the Belgian King. Nevertheless, it is a shrewd riposte by Winston. However, Stamfordham is not finished. As the King then pretends to be distracted by one of his trays of stamps, his private secretary continues to taunt Winston.

'His Majesty understands that Lord Kitchener is very agitated about the threat of an invasion and has questioned whether the navy is fully prepared for such an eventuality.'

Winston's neck reddens visibly, and he shifts uncomfortably in his chair. But before he can answer, Asquith responds firmly.

'Lord Kitchener has twice raised this subject in Cabinet. His views have been well aired and discussed, and Mr Churchill gave a very eloquent outline of the navy's strategy in the event of an attack. I am happy that our fleet is well prepared for any eventuality with respect to the German Grand Fleet, and that there is no imminent danger of an invasion.'

Now that the Prime Minister has taken the sting out of Stamfordham's scorn, Winston feels uninhibited in his response.

'Howell Gwynne of the *Morning Post*, whose views are, let me say, not admired for their broad-mindedness, and a few of the less intelligent Tory press – which is, by definition, most of them – have their hooks into me, but I'm used to that. If they were not so inclined, I would have to conclude that my actions were somewhat misguided.'

Winston knows that Stamfordham is a Tory sympathizer

who, like most of the Conservative Party, has never forgiven him for crossing the floor of the House to join the Liberals ten years previously.

It is now the King's private secretary who is discomfited, but he knows that propriety demands that he must not rise to Winston's adroit rebuff. Now that Stamfordham's baiting of Winston is over, the King returns to his chair.

'Mr Churchill, tell us about the *Audacious*. I believe she has gone down, but that the sinking will be kept secret. Is that wise?'

'That is a good question, sir. She finally went to the bottom last evening, a victim of a mine off the Irish coast. She is a major loss, but everyone on board was taken off. Militarily, we should deny the Germans any good news and do all we can to avoid damaging the status of our fleet. On the other hand, it is always difficult to deny the public information they should rightly have; indeed, Lloyd George is of that view. However, the Lords Jellicoe and Kitchener are adamant that the news should be suppressed.'

'I am not surprised by the incorrigible Mr Lloyd George's opinion. What is your view, Prime Minister?'

'I agree with my generals and admirals, sir.'

'Always wise, Prime Minister.'

The King smiles again and, in a gesture of friendship, addresses Winston by his first name.

'Tell me, Winston, what of your future? The Prime Minister informs me you are anxious for a military command.'

Winston beams.

'Your Majesty, nothing would enliven me more. May I be frank, sir?'

'Of course.'

'The stark truth is that while we have the German Grand Fleet confined to their ports and our imperious fleet remains on station, impregnable and magnificent, the Admiralty is an increasing tedium for me – especially when I hear, day after day, of the awful situation around Ypres.'

'What role would you want?'

'Well, sir, my French is passable; they have a regard for me, as I have for them. And Sir John French is well disposed towards me. I could envision a role on his staff, perhaps with a command to the south, next to the bulk of the French Army.'

'As a general, of course.'

'Of course, Your Majesty.'

The King looks amused; Asquith smiles benignly.

'Your Majesty, there is no limit to the ambition and resolve of the First Lord of the Admiralty. He is a warrior, as in times past. However, I need him in London, where there is a paucity of men of his breed.'

'Quite so! I agree, Prime Minister. Winston, if ever, God forbid, my cousin's Prussian Grenadiers come marching up the Long Walk to Windsor, I would feel very much safer if you were to take charge of the castle's defences.'

'Your Majesty, you honour me greatly with your kind remarks. Worry not, if your security is ever threatened, I will be at your side, my life at your disposal.'

The two men smile at one another warmly before Asquith brings the discussion back to the question of Fisher and Wilson at the Admiralty.

'Sir, will you approve the appointments Mr Churchill requests?'

'Prime Minister, the two of them are argumentative with everyone and behave like cantankerous bullies to many. They are retired men in their seventies; the whole experience could kill them!'

As quick as a flash, Winston seizes the moment.

'But, Your Majesty, I cannot imagine a more glorious death!'

All four men smile at the kind of quick-witted remark for which Winston is becoming renowned.

That afternoon, King George V signs the official announcement of the appointment of Lord Fisher as First Sea Lord and agrees that Sir Arthur Wilson may rejoin the Admiralty as a special adviser to the First Lord. Winston is then left with the onerous task of asking Prince Louis of Battenberg to resign. However, the 'blond, blue-eyed little German Prince', as Asquith describes him, is more relieved than sad when he hears the news. He will retire to the tranquillity of the Isle of Wight, where the jealousies of his fellow naval officers and the cruel comments of a xenophobic press are a long way away.

Winston is delighted that he now has Fisher and Wilson where they are needed, keeping the Royal Navy on an even keel. He is buoyed by the King's effusive comments, which do much to send his recent Black Dog back to its kennel.

Thursday 29 October

Reform Club, Pall Mall, London

The Coffee Room of the Reform Club is, as usual in the middle of the week, full for luncheon. The Club Trolley of traditional roast rib of beef is the choice of most members, but Lamb Cutlets Reform, the invention of the club's legendary chef, Alexis Soyer, is also very popular, as is his equally renowned Club Trifle for pudding. Not that either dish is all that remarkable in concept or execution. Lamb Cutlets Reform is simply lamb cutlets in breadcrumbs with an onion sauce. Club Trifle is typical English trifle, but with an inordinate amount of cream and lashings of sherry-soaked sponge. The members of the Reform may have sophisticated, radical principles, but their culinary tastes are distinctly gauche.

As Winston is taking luncheon in the bastion of liberalism with the son of a duke, who is also a Tory MP, he does not receive quite the same welcome as when he is with Lloyd George. Also, his star has waned a little, even among fellow liberals, since recent attacks in the press about his handling of the Admiralty and his involvement in the defence of Antwerp.

Winston is not looking forward to his meeting with Bardie Stewart-Murray, so he girds his loins with a stiff drink beforehand and paves the way by ordering a claret that is far too expensive for a midweek lunch. Bardie notices both and braces himself for bad news.

'So, Winston, how is Clemmie and your third child – Sarah, I think?'

'Yes, Sarah; both are well, thank you, Bardie. They are with me at the flat at the Admiralty, which is very satisfactory. I am sorry to hear about your brothers. I was with the King on Wednesday and he told me that your father is not taking the news too well.'

'No, he's pretty glum about it all, but I've kept the worst bit from him. I have had a letter from a Captain Marinden, an officer in the Black Watch, Geordie's regiment, which is not the best of news. He said that he had met a man in Dalmeny Hospital, in Lothian, the other day, who told him that Geordie was severely wounded at the Battle of the Aisne. His men dressed his wounds but were driven back by an enemy attack and had to leave him under cover in a quarry. The men said they had little hope that he could survive his injuries.'

'I'm so sorry, Bardie, I'm afraid it doesn't sound too promising. Don't you think you should tell your father? It will be for the best in the long run.'

'I know, and I intend to tell him when I next go to Blair. Hamish will be there, which will help. My sisters have had a bit of a scare too. Evelyn, who lives in Belgium, just managed to get out of Malines before the Germans ransacked her apartment. And Dertha's husband, Ruggles-Brise, got a bit too close to a German whizz-bang and is in hospital in Boulogne.'

'How's he doing?'

'All right, I think; Dertha's with him. His shoulders have been peppered with shrapnel, but he's in one piece, and they think he'll be up and about in a month or so.'

'And Helen?'

'She's well, but she's another source of concern to Father. She runs the house and estate, as you know, and Father relies on her so much. But she's taken up with an Edinburgh chap who is not to Father's liking.'

'Let me guess: not aristocratic, perhaps even middle class, and a bit of a liberal?'

'Yes, all of those things! A businessman and a sculptor of

some renown, apparently, who plays opera all the time on one of those new Tournaphones.'

'Oh dear, Bardie, he sounds like an absolute cad!'

At first Bardie is not sure if Winston is serious. But when his luncheon companion smiles at him mischievously, he realizes the remark was said tongue-in-cheek. Winston steers the conversation towards its intended destination.

'I hear you've seen Lord K. What are his plans for your Scottish Horse?'

'Well, they're infuriating, to be truthful. Kitchener seems very agitated about an invasion on the east coast and has said that he is drawing up plans to use the Scottish Horse for coastal defence duties for the time being. The bugger is, I'm now at brigade strength, with three regiments raring to go. So I asked him to send at least one to France. He said no, categorically, but to be patient, my time will come.'

'I'm sure it will, Bardie. K is a little preoccupied with this invasion threat he's got into his head, no matter what I say to convince him otherwise. Is Kitty with you at Kettering?'

'She is; we're staying at Boughton House, near Kettering, courtesy of Billy Douglas-Scott. Now, you'll be amused by this; she's organizing the knitting of thousands of hose tops for the Scottish regiments.'

'Very thoughtful of her; we can't have the Scots boys feeling the bite of winter's wind around the Trossachs! And how is Kitty?'

'Thriving. As you know, she's into everything. She wants to go into Parliament, and I think she will one day.'

'But I thought you told me she was opposed to the suffragettes?'

'She is!'

'How strange is the female mind, Bardie. I think they're cleverer than us, but just have strange ways of showing it.'

As the banter continues, Bardie is led to reflect on the recent improvement in his relationship with Kitty. However, it has only got better after initially getting much worse. Following the violent row and sexual frisson at the end of July, at Eaton Place, which sparked a new passion between them, Kitty heard rumours from a girlfriend that Bardie is the father of another illicit child, this time a boy, slightly older than Eileen Macallum, his child by his mistress in Mayfair. The boy's mother is from the Scottish lesser-gentry and lives in Ayrshire.

Following the news, Kitty immediately went to London to speak to her mother's lawyer – not to ask for a divorce, but to seek a way to formalize a new arrangement for their marriage. Her terms were very simple: Bardie has to make an annual payment to each child of £150. Although the children will always be welcome at Blair Atholl, the two mothers will not be and their names are never to be mentioned in his wife's company. Bardie may carry on seeing both women, but only in circumstances beyond Kitty's awareness and only infrequently.

As for the two of them, they will continue to live together as man and wife, but in separate bedrooms and without conjugal rights. Should there be any other mistresses or children, the same rules will apply. It is also stipulated that Kitty will be free to pursue her own 'friendships', should she wish to.

An appropriate document was drawn up, which Bardie has signed, and has now been deposited in their lawyers' safes. Although it has taken time to adjust to the new arrangement, their marriage is now maturing into a long-term friendship and both are happy with the outcome. It is a state of affairs perhaps helped by the fact that, while they have been staying at Boughton House, it has been difficult for Bardie to visit either Ayrshire or Mayfair. However, now that he is in London, and close to the Curzon Street home of his London mistress, he will be paying her a visit, a temptation he cannot resist.

Winston, having got all the way to cheese and an accompanying glass of port, cannot avoid the main reason for the lunch any longer.

'Bardie, old boy, I need to give you a little more bad news.

I'm sorry that it coincides with a difficult time for your family.'

'Winston, I think I can spare you the details. The Dunne prototypes don't pass muster, do they?'

'I'm afraid not, Bardie. They are very clever, ideal for civilian use, and may well make excellent training aircraft. But in a war zone, they are not sturdy enough.'

'I understand, and I think Dunne has already come to the same conclusion. But he just can't bring himself to say so.'

'I know I made you some promises when I came to see you at Blair Atholl. But my engineers are adamant; it's a very manoeuvrable light aircraft, but it's not a warplane. I can't go against their advice.'

'I understand. These decisions have to be taken on their merits. We're at war, there is no room for sentiment or favouritism.'

'Look, if it makes any difference, I'd be happy to have Dunne and his engineers at Farnborough. They would make a genuine contribution.'

'Thank you, Winston, that may well help; Dunne's a funny chap, but very clever. His latest theory is that time isn't chronological, but that the past, present and future all exist at the same time. He claims that sometimes he has dreams that happen in the future.'

'Really! Well, that could be bloody useful, especially if he can tell Kitchener what the Kaiser's going to do this winter.'

Both men laugh loudly.

The lunch has gone far better than Winston thought it would, and he is grateful for Bardie's generosity of spirit. He walks the short distance back to the Admiralty, feeling far better than when he left.

As for Bardie, he can look forward to the comforts to be had in Curzon Street this evening.

Friday 30 October

Poperinghe is one of only two Belgian towns still not under German occupation. It is eight miles west of the fighting at Ypres and only seven miles from the French border. The centre of Belgium's hop-growing industry and famed for its excellent beer, its Grande Place is crammed with troops and military vehicles.

The hotels, bars and shops that form the perimeter of the cobbled square are doing a roaring trade, particularly the *estaminet* La Maison de Ville, which serves the cheapest beer and is frequented by the most raucous British soldiers. It also serves the beers brewed by the Trappist monks at the nearby Westvleteren Monastery. Its 'light' blond beer is much stronger than an English ale and its 'extra' dark brew is almost three times the strength. The former is bottled with a green cap, the latter with a blue cap, and the men have already coined the phrase 'to go on a greeny', which is to get drunk, or a 'bluey', which is to get blind drunk.

The town has already earned the moniker 'Pop' and a reputation for having no shortage of girls willing to offer their favours to any 'Tommy' with one franc to give the madam and two francs to give to the girl. Pop has two official brothels, *maisons tolérées*, sanctioned and inspected by the medical officers of the French Army, and dozens of unofficial street-walkers and backstreet cathouses. Hundreds of girls have flocked from Paris and Brussels to reap the rewards.

On busy nights, queues of men form. Young waiters serve them beer as they wait their turn. Of course, appropriate military distinctions apply: the men go to 'red light' establishments while the officers frequent 'blue light' institutions, where the furnishings and fittings are a little more salubrious, the girls slightly younger and, perhaps, more fetching.

Pop is also the location of several British field hospitals. They occupy two schools, long since abandoned by their pupils, and a lace factory that closed down at the outbreak of war. One of them is the workplace of Sister Margaret Killingbeck and nursing auxiliary Bronwyn Thomas.

Margaret is relieved to have a semi-permanent home. She, her patients, staff and beds have moved multiple times since they arrived one month ago. They have been here for a week. Bronwyn's health and demeanour are much improved and she has been true to her word; she spends her days changing beds, cleaning wards and emptying bedpans and urine bottles.

Margaret and her nurses are lodging in a small hotel just behind Pop's Grande Place, where she allows Bron one glass of beer and one glass of wine every evening. Her drug habit is over, she no longer needs laudanum and her gonorrhoea is responding well to treatment.

Men and sex have proved to be no temptation for Bron – at least, as far as Margaret knows. She did engage in a brief sexual liaison of sorts with a guardsman who was severely wounded by a shell and had lost both his arms above the elbow. He was high on morphine and feeling frisky and asked her if she would oblige him and 'give him relief' before he died. She did so without hesitation, and thought nothing of it, regarding it simply as a gesture to comfort a dying man.

She then gave him a kiss. She did not tell anyone about it: what was the point? The young man died the next morning and Bron went to his bed again to give him another kiss, this time on his now icy-cold lips.

Bron often watches Pop's street girls with a mixture of

emotions. Sometimes she shivers, when a memory of a particularly unpleasant encounter comes into her head, but mostly she feels concerned for the welfare of the girls and often tries to speak to them in their limited English, but also in French, which she is trying hard to learn.

Bron, Margaret and the rest of the girls on their shift have finished for the day. They began at 6 a.m, and it is now six in the evening. They are sitting at a table outside the Maison de Ville. It is unseasonably mild, making it possible to sit in the open air. The nurses are watching the commotion of intense military activity going on around them. Later, the bar will be full of drunken soldiers looking for girls or trouble – or both – but for now it is relatively calm. There are a few wolf whistles and a little banter is directed at them, but it is all good humoured. Some of the nurses have developed relationships with soldiers billeted nearby and are engaged in hushed or animated conversations with them.

Then, from inside the *estaminet*, comes the evening's first rendition of the soldiers' version of 'Mademoiselle from Armentières'.

The polite version begins:

Mademoiselle from Armentières, parlez-vous?
Mademoiselle from Armentières, parlez-vous?
Mademoiselle from Armentières
She hasn't been kissed in forty years.
Hinky, dinky, parlez-vous.

Oh farmer, have you a daughter fair, parlez-vous?
Oh farmer, have you a daughter fair, parlez-vous?
Oh farmer, have you a daughter fair
Who can wash a soldier's underwear?
Hinky, dinky, parlez-vous.

The officers get all the steak, parlez-vous,
The officers get all the steak, parlez-vous,

The officers get all the steak
And all we get is the bellyache.
Hinky, dinky, parlez-vous . . .

But the soldiers' far more vulgar version begins:

Three German Officers crossed the Rhine, parlez-vous,
Three German Officers crossed the Rhine, parlez-vous,
Three German Officers crossed the Rhine
To fuck the women and drink the wine.
Hinky, dinky, parlez-vous.

They came to the door of a wayside inn, parlez-vous,
They came to the door of a wayside inn, parlez-vous,
They came to the door of a wayside inn
Pissed on the mat and walked right in.
Hinky, dinky, parlez-vous.

Oh landlord, have you a daughter fair, parlez-vous?
Oh landlord, have you a daughter fair, parlez-vous?
Oh landlord, have you a daughter fair
With lily-white tits and golden hair?
Hinky, dinky, parlez-vous.

My only daughter's far too young, parlez-vous,
My only daughter's far too young, parlez-vous,
My only daughter's far too young
To be fucked by you, you bastard Hun!
Hinky, dinky, parlez-vous.

Oh father dear, I'm not too young, parlez-vous,
Oh father dear, I'm not too young, parlez-vous,
Oh father dear, I'm not too young,
I've just been fucked by the blacksmith's son.
Hinky, dinky, parlez-vous . . .

After which there are many more even more explicit and
even more anti-German verses. The nurses are not in the

slightest discomfited; they have heard it many times before and, compared to the horrors of a field hospital, a few crude words are of no consequence.

Margaret is watching Bron closely, delighted that she is doing so well. Having her accepted into the Queen Alexandra's nurses, even as an auxiliary, has not been easy. Emma McCarthy, the Australian-born matriarch of the service, is Matron-in-Chief of the entire British Expeditionary Force and in charge of over 600 nurses in France. She would only permit Bron to stay as a personal favour to Margaret, and only after she revealed to her Bron's personal circumstances.

Matron McCarthy is old-fashioned. She thinks it dangerous to recruit young women who are attractive, saying that girls who have not been blessed with an appealing face – and certainly not with an ample bosom – are the best choices. She admits that, although pretty faces and a fulsome figure are not, of themselves, barriers to being a good nurse, they invariably lead to men being difficult patients. She is happy to take ageing spinsters, saying that, at a certain age, women no longer incline men to suckle at their breasts and instead inspire men to treat them like their grandmothers.

McCarthy is an ideal candidate for her own selection criteria. Never married, she is fifty-five years old, slight of frame, with the severe appearance of a serjeant major, and runs a very tight ship of healing. One of only six nursing veterans of the Boer War, she was a founding nurse in the Queen Alexandra's Service and has been the army's senior matron for over ten years. She was on the first ship carrying the BEF across the Channel on 14 August.

Bron is smiling, something she has begun to do more and more in recent days, and is watching intently as a column of marching men comes into view. They are typical of new recruits. It is always possible to spot the new arrivals from Blighty; they are smartly dressed, clean-shaven, singing and smiling, and certainly do not look like lambs being led to the slaughter. Farmers will tell you that animals always know when they are on their way to the slaughterhouse, but human beings seem to have lost that instinct. These new lads, like all before them, look like schoolboys on their way to an exciting new adventure with the Boy Scouts.

This group, about 100 strong, are wearing hackles, the headdress that marks them as fusiliers. The hackles are white, which signifies they are men of the Royal Welch Fusiliers. Bron thinks the white hackles look familiar, but is not sure why, until an inebriated soldier nearby shouts in Welsh, '*Croeso mawr i chi, Ffiwsilwyr Cymreig!*' which Bron knows means a warm welcome to France for the Welsh boys.

It is Philip's regiment. Bron jumps to her feet in the hope that he will be at the front of the column, leading his men. He is not, of course. Bron sits back down; she looks at Margaret with tears in her eyes. Margaret smiles at her warmly and leans across to kiss her on her cheek.

'I think we should order a bottle of red. You look like you need it.'

'But that will put me over my limit.'

'I know, but you've been so good, one night won't do any harm.'

Bron turns to look back at the Welshmen marching towards her. Now that they have an audience in Pop's Grande Place, they are singing '*Sosban Fach*' in fine Welsh voice. Suddenly, Bron's face becomes a fixed stare, as if she has been momentarily cast in stone. She then turns her head to one side, as if trying to hide herself from view.

'What's the matter, Bron?'

For the briefest of moments, Margaret wonders if Bron has, after all, seen Philip Davies.

'Margaret! It's the boys; my brothers! There, on the far side, at the front; all three together, behind the serjeant. Oh God! Don't let them see me.'

Margaret looks across and sees a boy who, from his

likeness, is clearly Bron's twin. Next to him is her younger brother, Geraint, and on the other side, Hywel. She hardly recognizes him: he is clean-shaven, with his hair cropped short, and looks much more wholesome than when she met him at Pentry Farm.

Bron is still hiding her face as the fusiliers' colour serjeant major orders them to salute as they pass the tables of the Maison de Ville. The men salute and turn their heads. Realizing that Hywel might well remember her, Margaret abruptly turns away. But it is too late; Hywel does see her and keeps his head turned towards her long after the rest of the Royal Welch have reverted to eyes forward.

'Did they see me?'

Bron's heart is racing; she has suddenly become the bewildered, petrified girl from the summer. Margaret thinks it wise not to mention that Hywel has almost certainly recognized her.

'No, don't worry; even if they looked this way, they would only have seen the back of your head.'

'I couldn't bear it, if they knew I was here. I'm not ready to see them; I may never be.'

Margaret picks up their bottle of wine and takes Bron inside the *estaminet*, where she finds a quiet corner.

'It's unlikely they'll be billeted nearby. I'm sure they'll be gone in the morning. There are tens of thousands of men along a line that stretches for many miles.'

'I hope so, Margaret. I know it seems odd, but the only way I can cope at the moment is not to feel anything. I switch off my feelings when I'm tending the wounded; I imagine I'm a vet, treating simple creatures, not human beings.'

'We all have to do that, Bron.'

'I bury my memories, and I try to feel numb towards everything, but they come back. Life was so simple at Pentry. Tom was a good boy; we could have been happy. You know, sometimes I hate what Philip did to me, taking my innocence, making me feel things that I may never feel again. Other times, I think I can't live without him and I want to feel those things again. Do you know what I mean?'

'Of course I do; you're no different from the rest of us.'

Bron rests her head on Margaret's shoulder and begins to cry; not in great lurches of anguish, but more like the whimpering of a distraught child. Margaret cradles her head and rocks her gently.

'Come on, let's get you back to your room. We can drink our wine there, and you can get some sleep.'

They finish the bottle in Bron's room, after which, with Bron feeling distinctly tipsy, Margaret helps her get into bed. As she pulls up the bedclothes, Bron grasps Margaret's hand.

'Will you stay with me until I go to sleep?'

'Of course.'

She rests her hand on Bron's brow. The girl closes her eyes and, for the first time since her brothers' sudden appearance, looks at ease. She keeps her eyes closed, but after a few moments asks Margaret the question she has been wanting to ask since they arrived in France.

'Do you remember when you told me that you had secrets of your own that helped you understand what I was going through with Philip?'

'Yes, I remember. I certainly know what it means to feel guilt.'

'Will you tell me about it? It will help me to know that someone as strong as you has dark secrets as well. One of the girls said you were seeing an officer – a toff. Is he your dark secret?'

'Hamish Stewart-Murray? He was the officer at Philip's bedside when he died. No, we've never even kissed; he's not my type. I think he's very keen, and he's certainly charming, but he's a posh rascal, only interested in going to bed with me.'

'Aren't they all!'

'I suppose so. But I carry no guilt about him.'

Bron opens her eyes and stares at Margaret pleadingly.

'Oh, please tell, Margaret.'

'I can't, Bron; it may harm our friendship.'

Bron puts her arm around Margaret's neck and smiles at her.

'But it might make it stronger.'

Margaret pulls away gently, but maintains her resolve.

'No; like you, I have to bury the past in order to cope. Now, let's both get some sleep, and I'll see you in the morning.'

Graveyard of the Old Contemptibles

Wednesday 4 November

Saturday 31 October became the critical day of the First Battle of Ypres. The German High Command, dismayed that their 4th and 6th Armies had failed to break through enemy lines, despite launching relentless infantry attacks and pouring murderous fire into the Allies' defensive positions, developed a new plan.

Using fresh troops transferred from the south, a new Army Group was formed under the command of General Max von Fabeck, a respected infantryman. While the two existing Army Groups continued their attacks in their present positions, von Fabeck was ordered to throw his six divisions, over 60,000 men, at a point which Erich von Falkenhayn, the German Commander-in-Chief, thought was the weakest in the entire Allied line. He chose a position only six miles wide, between Ploegsteert Wood and Gheluvelt, just four miles west of Ypres.

Von Falkenhayn, notoriously demanding and uncompromising, insisted that his men strike a 'hammer blow' to the British defenders, pushing them back, taking control of the Messines Ridge and thus opening the door to Ypres.

Von Fabeck's Order of the Day could not have been more explicit, nor laden with more scorn.

> We must and will conquer and settle for ever the centuries-long struggle. We will finish the French, British, Indians, Moroccans and other trash. They are feeble adversaries, who surrender in great numbers if attacked with vigour.

To help ensure success, von Fabeck was given 260 heavy guns and almost 500 smaller-calibre pieces. The British defenders, on the other hand, had far fewer artillery resources and were having to ration shells.

The German onslaught began at 4 a.m. that morning, without a preliminary artillery bombardment, thus catching the British unawares. Ferocious battles raged all along the six miles of the attack until daylight allowed some sense to be made of the situation. The morning was damp and foggy with visibility poor. At one point, in the village of Beccelare, a mile north of Gheluvelt, defended by the 1st Battalion Scots Guards, a gust of wind cleared the fog to reveal an entire regiment of German infantry just eighty yards away. To their right, just three diminished companies of the Black Watch and the Coldstream Guards faced three battalions of seasoned Bavarians.

As the British positions began to weaken against over-whelming numbers, General Haig asked for help from General Joseph Dubois, commander of the 9th Corps of the French 8th Army, who readily sent a brigade of cuirassiers and three infantry battalions. But still, the sheer weight of German numbers was beginning to overwhelm the British positions.

The road to Ypres was full of artillery pieces being rushed out of danger; hundreds of wounded men were limping and shuffling westwards. A gap appeared at one section in the line – right in its centre, close to Gheluvelt – leaving barely 1,000 battle-fit British troops standing between Ypres and the massed battalions of Fabeck's army.

With just two of his staff officers for company, General Haig rode up to assess the situation. Immaculately turned out as always, he sat calmly on his conspicuous white horse and gave encouragement to his men as shells burst all around him. Despite his presence, the day looked lost; a miracle was needed. But, in an action typical of many such acts of heroism in the Great War, a miracle did happen.

Just at the moment of imminent defeat, Major Edward Hankey of the 2nd Battalion Worcesters, an Etonian and a veteran of the Boer War and the Sudan, was ordered to attempt an audacious counter-attack.

The Worcesters had already been involved in heavy fighting throughout October and had suffered severe casualties. But they were the only unit not already committed to the battle. As Hankey prepared for his attack, he counted just seven officers and 357 men. They off-loaded their packs, ate a tin of hot stew, quaffed a rum ration and were given extra ammunition. As they sat on the ground, the major spoke to them only briefly.

'These are our orders: "The 2nd Worcesters will take Gheluvelt." We can and will do it. Good luck to you all.'

They had to cross 1,000 yards of open ground in front of them, just beyond a line of trees. As they emerged from the treeline and looked around, every other British and French soldier was moving in the opposite direction, towards Ypres.

Hankey turned to his regimental serjeant major and asked quietly, 'Are they up for it, Sarn't-Major?'

'All up for it, sir,' was the immediate response.

Hankey then bellowed his order.

'*Officers to the front; advance at the double!*'

In the few minutes it took the Worcesters to charge across the muddy field of stubble, they lost over 100 men – almost a third of their number – in a hail of fire so intense that some men said they could see bullets in the air like waves of rain in a storm. When they eventually reached a copse next to Gheluvelt Château, Hankey ordered bayonets to be fixed before his men emerged from the trees to confront over 1,200 Germans in the process of looting the château. Fierce hand-to-hand fighting followed; miraculously for the

Worcesters, their opponents were novices from a Bavarian reserve battalion, who soon scattered in disarray.

Hankey ordered his men to spread out left and right. They soon made contact with remnants of the Scots Guards on one side and the South Wales Borderers on the other. Thus, the line was restored before the German commanders could take advantage of the breach.

At the end of the day – a day which saw ferocious fighting, as intense as any since the beginning of the war – von Falkenhayn decided to retreat to lick his wounds.

As the men of the 4th Battalion Royal Fusiliers gather in the village square at Merris, a small village nine miles north of Armentières, on the morning of 4 November, all the talk is of the heroics around Ypres and, in particular, of the amazing counter-attack by the Worcesters – an action that it is now being talked of as the charge that saved Ypres and the Channel ports.

The success helps disguise the sorry state of the Royal Fusiliers' own battalion. Since the costly bayonet charge at Neuve-Chapelle on Sunday 25 October, they have suffered three more days of close-quarters fighting, during which they had to be supported by two companies of French Chasseurs Alpins, the elite mountain troops of the French Army, who were a very welcome sight and came to their aid just in time.

The fusiliers were taken out of the line on the 29th and marched to Merris, taking a route via Vieille-Chapelle and Doulieu. When the roll is taken at Merris, only eight officers and 350 men have survived the ordeal. Captain Leicester Carey has fallen, shot through the head by a sniper, and almost all the NCOs have perished. Harry and Maurice are among the lucky few.

They have spent the morning cleaning their uniforms, kit and rifles and, having been inspected by General Horace Smith-Dorrien, Commander II Corps BEF, are standing to attention to listen to him address them. Harry and Maurice are not keen on listening to addresses, especially not from generals.

'Stand at ease, men. I will make this brief, as I know you would prefer some well-earned rest rather than listening to me. I just wanted to say that I cannot find the words that adequately express my admiration for the way in which your regiment has behaved. All through the campaign, you have had it the hardest of any regiment in my Corps and I can safely say there is no better regiment in the British Army than the Royal Fusiliers. I can assure you that when this war is over, you will be treated as heroes at home. Thank you on behalf of everyone at HQ and everyone at home. I can't promise you it's going to get easier; it isn't. You will be back in the trenches very soon, and winter is approaching quickly. However, I am not concerned, because I know you men will stick it out better than the Germans. Until we meet again, brave Fusiliers!'

An appreciative cheer goes up from the ranks of men. Maurice looks at Harry quizzically.

'Thought you said he'd be a tosser like all the others?'

'No, I didn't.'

'You bloody did!'

'Well, the exception proves the rule.'

'Which is?'

'All top brass are wankers!'

'Well that one's got a DSO on his ribbons, so at one time he must have done more than give speeches.'

Not long after Smith-Dorrien leaves, Harry and Maurice hear that, having been promised eight days' rest out of the line, they will be going back in just forty-eight hours.

Harry is furious.

'Fuck a duck, at this rate none of us'll be left by Christmas!'

Maurice is much less perturbed.

'The adjutant says we're replacing the 1st Dragoons, who are worse off than us.'

Harry's ire rises another notch.

'Fuckin' Cherry Bums! I bet they get their eight days off, while we get our arses blown off for 'em.'

'Come on, 'Arry, you need a tiddly; let's get into that gaff opposite the church before the other lads drink all the pig's ear.'

The prospect of a beer calms Harry down. He decides to let Mo in on something that has been bothering him lately.

'Mo, what are we gonna do wiv that German officer's clobber?'

'Dunno, we can't carry it around for ever.'

'Let's bury it.'

'Where?'

'Someplace where we're sure to be able to find it again. But nice an' deep, where no bastard comes across it by mistake.'

Two hours and four strong Belgian beers later, Maurice and Harry, using a yew tree as a base point, have paced out a spot that is twenty strides into a farmer's field. They have spent many hours in recent weeks preparing endless trenches, so digging a deep hole for their captured Prussian sword and helmet does not take them long, especially when fortified by the extra flagons of beer they have brought with them.

When they are finished, Harry proposes a toast. He is drunk and the words do not come easily.

'To Herr Fritzy Mecklenberg . . . and his mate, Tannhausen . . . may they rest in peace.'

'Amen.'

'Mo, do me a favour; if I cop it, promise me you'll get this loot back to that bloke's family?'

'Course I will.'

Both men, still swigging from their brown ceramic

flagons, stagger back to the road and into the village's tiny café. The bar owner is trying to remove the last few fusiliers, who are much the worse for wear. It has been a long night for him. The village has seen troops pass through before, but this is the first time any have been billeted there, and it is his first experience of British drinking habits and the raucous behaviour it produces. Both his serving girls left halfway through the evening, no longer able to cope with having their arses tweaked and their breasts squeezed.

Harry notices some of the men giving the owner a hard time and bellows at them.

'*Right, you lot, fuck off! Now!*'

No one messes with Serjeant Harry Woodruff and his order has the desired sobering effect. He then turns to the diminutive bar owner and waves his empty flagon at him, as does Maurice.

'*Non, messieurs, s'il vous plaît, le café est fermé.* Finish!'

Harry waves his flagon again and attempts some of the French he has picked up.

'*Non . . . ouvrez!*'

Harry's intimidating demeanour has the same effect on the little Frenchman as it does on his men and he fills both flagons with beer. He refuses to take money for them, but pushes both serjeants out of the door and gestures to them to sit at the outside tables.

'*Pas de chants, pas de cris, s'il vous plaît;* no sing, no shout!'

With a hasty flourish, he then closes and bolts his door. The bar lights go out seconds later, leaving Maurice and Harry illuminated only by the glow of the cigarettes they are smoking. Harry is still feeling morose over the incident with the Prussian Guards.

'Them German toffs we killed.'

'What abaht 'em?'

'Well, they're rotting in the ground, just like any other boys.'

'Once we're in the earth, we're all the same, 'Arry. Worms don't know a toff from a barrow-boy.'

'Except for their families, they'll soon be forgotten.'

'That's the way of it, 'Arry.'

Harry pauses, pulls on his cigarette and takes a deep draught of beer.

'We're gonna end up the same before long, ain't we?'

'S'pose so; we're all gonna cop it sooner or later, the way this is goin'.'

'Who'll remember us?'

'We should've got 'itched an' 'ad kids, like other blokes.'

'What, an' leave 'em with no fathers? Not on your Nelly!'

Maurice does not respond. Like Harry, he knows that, other than the fading memories of their ageing parents, and their scant regimental records, no one will regret their passing, or remember who they were or what they did. Almost everyone they have served with over the years is dead, or has been invalided back to Blighty. There is silence between them for some time. Another cigarette is lit and more beer drunk. Then Harry resumes his melancholic reflections. Maurice cannot see them, but there are tears running down his friend's cheeks.

'This new army Kitchener's makin'.'

'What abaht it?'

'Two-thirds of the battalion's gone, Mo: top soldiers, pros. The new recruits are kids: poor farm boys from some shit'ole in the middle o' nowhere; city boys who think they're Jack the Lads. They 'aven't a fuckin' clue. Poor sods! If only they knew.'

Maurice grabs Harry's arm.

'Come on, let's get our heads down; the war can wait til the mornin'.'

Early the next morning, too early for Maurice and Harry, they are ordered to Battalion HQ at Bailleul, two miles away.

Major Ashburner has been badly wounded and has gone home to England, so they have been summoned by Colonel McMahon, the new commanding officer. The two serjeants have managed to smarten themselves up a bit, but are still very bleary-eyed. McMahon has just been promoted to brigadier, but has not yet received the extra pip on his epaulettes. He will soon be transferring to the newly arrived 10th Brigade's HQ, removing the last veteran senior soldier of quality from the 4th Fusiliers' line officers.

'Are we gonna get a bollickin', 'Arry?'

'Dunno, don't see why we should; unless it's a bollickin' fer survivin' this far!'

'What abaht last night?'

'Nah, no one seen us.'

McMahon is a tall, lean man with a bald pate and heavy moustache. His cavalry boots and spurs gleam in the weak autumn sunlight. But their lustre is not his work; it's the product of the elbow grease of his batman.

Battalion HQ is an abandoned barn next to a large manor house where the officers are billeted. Trestle tables are covered with maps; messengers and junior officers, looking stern, scuttle around with purpose. Behind the barn, the officers' horses are stabled. Mounts long since abandoned as chargers are now used to carry messages.

McMahon smiles at Harry and Maurice.

'You look worn out, Serjeants. Is that last night's R and R, or last week's fighting?'

Maurice looks a little discomfited, but not Harry.

'A bit of both, sir. Serjeant Tait and I did enjoy a couple o' beers last night. First in a while, sir.'

'Very well done. I was also celebrating my promotion to Brigade last night. I hope you are feeling a little better than I am.'

'Congratulations, sir.'

'Well, I think it most appropriate if you enjoy a little more beer this evening. We are adding a crown to your three stripes, Colour Serjeants Tait and Woodruff. Very well done!'

Harry and Maurice look at one another. They are delighted to be promoted; it means extra pay and a better pension. But it also means they are unlikely to stay together in the same platoon.

Then, to their relief, McMahon continues.

'We are expecting a large contingent of at least three hundred reservists from Albany in about three weeks' time, so you will be staying with C Company for the time being. But with our current shortage of officers, a great burden rests on your shoulders as senior soldiers. The men will look to you for leadership, and your new officers will need your help and advice. Please continue the sterling work you have been doing.'

'Thank you, sir; we'll do our best.'

Taking their commanding officer at his word, Maurice and Harry enjoy a little more beer in celebration that night, and are soon to be found back in the bar in Merris. There is no shortage of beer for them as almost every man in the bar places a jug in front of them. As they do, most salute mockingly, some bow and a few even attempt curtsies.

'Well, Colour Serjeant Tait, whadda yer reckon?'

'Not bad, Colour Serjeant Woodruff!'

'Might still be goners next week, though. A little cloth crown on our arm ain't gonna stop a German bullet.'

'S'pose that's one way of lookin' at it, 'Arry, you miserable fucker!'

'Only jokin', Mo; come on, we've got about forty pints o' pig's ear to drink before stop-tap.'

The following day, on the night of 6 November, the 4th Battalion moves back into the line east of Hooge, on the south side of the Ypres–Menin road, where C Company forms a defensive position on the edge of Herenthage Wood. To its left are French Algerian Zouaves, unmistakable in their bright-red baggy pantaloons and navy-blue jackets, and to its right are the far less ostentatious Northumberland Fusiliers.

Maurice and Harry have decided that Geordies are worthy of respect after all, given that the Northumberlands have fought with them for three months and have twice helped get them out of a tricky spot. As for the North Africans, they are not so sure.

'Bloody Nora, Mo; look at that lot! They look like fuckin' circus clowns.'

'I 'ope they fight as well as they look!'

It is not long before the 4th Fusiliers are welcomed back to the conflict with the most intensive artillery barrage they have faced since they arrived in France.

It begins in the morning and lasts all day.

By the late afternoon, Harry and Maurice's platoon – all but two of whom are new men assigned from other depleted platoons – have had three near misses. Nerves are frayed and Harry is on edge. Maurice can always tell because he is even more aggressive than usual, which is saying something.

'This is bollocks! Fuckin' lyin' here, takin' a pastin'. Why don't we attack the fuckers?'

'Cos we'll get mown down by their Mausers, 'Arry.'

'Better way to go than waitin' for one of their Jack Johnsons to blow yer Tommy Rollocks off.'

Maurice suddenly opens fire.

'Here they come! Fuck me, it's nearly dark; cheeky buggers.'

Harry shouts orders to the platoon, which still does not have an officer attached to it.

'Fire at will! Make sure of your targets.'

Harry dashes to the far left of the platoon's position to make sure they are in good spirits. When he gets there, he looks over to the Zouaves. He struggles to see many men still alive. Their positions have received several direct hits and it is now difficult to tell where the bright red of their pantaloons ends and the blood they have shed begins. All their French officers and senior NCOs appear to be dead, and the men look to be in disarray. Fortunately, the Germans have not yet realized that the French-Algerian sector of the line is all but undefended.

Harry shouts to Maurice.

'Mo, I'm takin' 'alf the boys to cover the 'ole on our left!'

With only a dozen men at his disposal, Harry takes control of a position previously occupied by two companies, comprising over 150 men. He immediately rallies the Zouaves' survivors and places fusiliers at intervals along their line. Within moments, having now seen how meagre are the numbers facing them, the Germans close to within yards of them. Fortunately, Harry's cry, '*Fix bayonets!*' works equally well in French and English.

A lethal assault begins by the 106th Royal Saxons from Leipzig, who pour into the position like a swarm of ants. Maurice, whose own position is being overwhelmed by the same German regiment, looks across but cannot see British khaki or Zouave red for German field grey.

While Maurice, leading by ferocious example, tries valiantly to hold together his half of the platoon, Harry rallies the Algerians in a murderous close-quarters encounter against overwhelming odds. The position appears hopeless until, just at the point where only a few of the defenders remain on their feet, a support company of fusiliers – D Company, barely seventy strong – led by Lieutenants Stapleton, Bretherton and Jackson, appears out of nowhere and rushes the Saxons. The men from Leipzig panic and begin to retreat before D Company head off in pursuit of the fleeing Germans.

Almost all are never seen again; sixty-two men and all three officers do not come back. But their sudden appearance has saved the day for the Zouaves and for the exhausted men of C Company.

In pitch darkness, Maurice and Harry gather the remnants of their platoon, just seven survivors, and take charge of a mere eleven Zouaves. They share their rations, which are hardly enough to sustain a family, let alone twenty men. But one of the Algerians produces a bottle of cognac – from where beggars belief – and hands it to Harry, whose uniform drips with sweat and blood. Fortunately, the former is his, but the latter is not.

'*Pour vous, mon brave!*'

Harry thanks the Moroccan, whose face looks like it has been carved from the rock of the Atlas Mountains, and passes it around the group. Now confident that he has grasped the enormity and beauty of the French language, he says to his comrade-in-arms:

'*Mercy, Monsewer.*'

Two days later, Colour Serjeants Tait and Woodruff will be summoned to Battalion HQ. They are now the only senior NCOs to have survived this far into the war. They are part of an ever dwindling elite. There are only six officers left from the original roster who sailed from Southampton, and only a quarter of the men remain.

However, the two doughty survivors are about to receive some heartening news from the battalion adjutant.

'Gentlemen, following your action the other day at Herenthage Wood, Colonel McMahon has recommended you both to Brigade for gallantry awards. Colour Serjeants Tait and Woodruff, you are both recommended for a Distinguished Conduct Medal. Now, I must stress that a recommendation is not an award. But given the detail of the citation that has been sent to Brigade, I don't think there's any doubt. Congratulations!'

Harry and Maurice have been given another reason to celebrate, but neither feels particularly excited by the news. They feel honoured, of course, but the loss of so many comrades, and the dire circumstances and exhaustion of three months of warfare, are taking their toll.

That night, they do have a beer or three to lighten their mood. Maurice tries to cheer up Harry, but he uses the wrong words and only makes matters worse.

'S'pose it's somethin' to leave for the grandchildren.'

'You ain't got any bloody kids yet, never mind grand-children!'

'I know, but I'm gonna fix that when we get 'ome.'

Harry explodes and throws his beer across the bar.

'For fuck's sake, Mo; we aren't goin' 'ome. Ain't you realized that yet!'

Maurice tries to stop him, but Harry rushes out, pushing men out of the way as he goes.

Sunday 8 November

Zwarteleen, West Flanders, Belgium

The three Thomas boys are a long way from home. Before they sailed for France two weeks ago, the furthest they had ventured from Presteigne – apart from Hightown Barracks, in Wrexham, the dreary home of the Welch Fusiliers – was Hereford in England and Builth Wells in Wales.

They have seen Birmingham, London, Southampton and Paris, admittedly only through the windows of their railway carriage, and are now staring across the monotonously flat landscape of Flanders. But Belgium is not offering much of a greeting.

By the time Lieutenant Orme's detachment joined the 1st Battalion at the end of October, they found it had all but been destroyed in an engagement at Zandvoorde, a hamlet six miles south-east of Ypres, where, unbeknown to them, they faced German regiments which outnumbered them six to one. During the fighting, 276 officers and men were killed and fifty-four taken prisoner. By the end of the encounter, only eighty fusiliers remained.

The new arrivals from Wrexham, who were supposed to be a small supplement to the original battalion, outnumber the old. Not only that, the survivors whose ranks they have joined look as if they have been to hell and back. It is a cruelly inauspicious start for 109 young men from North Wales who have never been to war before.

The second Sabbath of November has dawned much later than it should because a dense fog hangs over the ground. It is also cold; a damp, clinging cold, not unlike the Welsh weather they are used to. Contrarily, the English inhabitants of Presteigne call this kind of weather 'typically English', but the Welsh residents insist it is 'typically Welsh'.

They are crouching in a deep drainage ditch on the Ypres side of the road to Zandvoorde, 1,000 yards south of Zillebeke, at a small hamlet called Zwarteleen. Ypres itself is less than three miles away. It is 6.15 a.m. The severely depleted Royal Welch has been amalgamated with the Queen's Regiment, 1st Royal West Surreys, also much reduced in number by the severity of the fighting. They are supported by the South Staffs boys, with the 2nd Warwicks in reserve.

Although the British troops are in Belgium, where the population speaks a language distinctly alien to them, the four regiments preparing to attack have, like many British Army brigade groupings, distinctive dialects so different from one another that comprehension is often a challenge and a source of much banter.

They are to attack a line of trenches just ahead of them in order to push back a previous German counter-attack. As one of the West Surreys said earlier, the war is becoming a bit of a merry-go-round: one side digs a trench, the other side attacks it and takes it, then the other side counter-attacks and takes it back. 'Then we start all over again – bloody daft!'

Hywel, Morgan and Geraint and the other 106 new arrivals from Wrexham still look pristine in their uniforms. Their faces, despite the foul conditions, still glow with enthusiasm. However, as the time for the assault draws closer, some faces begin to be etched with anxiety. Lieutenant Orme, who is also a novice, walks among the men with his serjeants, calming any nerves. When they reach the Thomas boys, Orme stops to speak to Hywel.

'Private Thomas –'

'Sir!'

'I have been hearing about how good a shot you are. The adjutant tells me that you are the best he's ever seen, a born sniper. I want you on top of that barn over there. As soon as we attack, I want you to target their machine-gunners. For every one you eliminate, you'll save ten lives.'

'Very good, sir.'

As soon as Orme has gone, Hywel turns to his brothers, smiling.

'Hey, boyos, no pressure then! Listen, you take care of yourselves out there.'

'We'll be fine, Hywel; we can run faster than you!'

The order to attack comes at 6.30 a.m. sharp. There is no artillery barrage to soften up the German opposition; the Royal Field Artillery in this sector has no shells. The German trenches are only 150 yards away and are not taken by surprise.

As soon as Lieutenant Orme raises his pistol and his men appear in the open, beginning to cross the road, a fusillade of bullets cuts through the air like rapiers. For those who are experiencing it for the first time, it is utterly terrifying. For those who have experienced it many times before, it is just as frightening. In some ways, it is even more difficult for the experienced men because they know what a high-velocity bullet can do to a man. Several men do not make it across the road; they die in the first moment of their first battle.

As his comrades-in-arms rush across the open fields, Hywel climbs to his sniping position, a lofty perch at the apex of a Zwarteleen barn, one of the few buildings in the area still standing, He begins to pick out his targets. He has never shot a man before and winces every time a German body recoils hideously after being struck.

He makes a decision there and then never to keep a tally, something he relished doing on the farm when competing against his brothers at shooting pheasant. He has been given enough ammunition to slaughter a regiment and carries on firing until his fingers ache and his barrel is too hot to handle.

Every now and then he pauses, to see if he can measure

the progress being made by his brothers. But they become lost in a sea of khaki uniforms set against Flanders mud.

Lieutenant Orme's men make it all the way to the German trenches, where bayonets are fixed and a quick flurry of excellent British close-quarters battle training scatters the Germans far and wide. Hywel can hear cheering from the Fusiliers and the Surreys. However, that soon subsides as enfilade fire pours in from cleverly disguised German machine guns. They have a line of fire along the length of the trench, exposing the Welsh and Surrey boys to bullets thudding into the walls and even the floor of the trench in repetitive waves.

Men fling themselves against the walls, trying to find a hollow that will hide them from the deadly onslaught. Several crumpled khaki heaps lying in the bottom of the trench shudder as they are hit over and over again. Thankfully, they are already dead.

Hywel is still trying to locate his brothers, but he cannot identify them. As he strains to see them, he feels what seems like a breath of wind by his ear and realizes immediately that it is a passing bullet. He quickly slides down the barn roof and on to the ladder he used to get into position. Bullets follow him, smashing roof tiles and timber. At least one German sniper has found him.

He was warned about the high quality of German sniping and the fact that some are using newly developed telescopic sights, which improve accuracy significantly. When he sees how accurate their fire is, he vows to himself that he will move heaven and earth to hit an enemy sniper and take his rifle and scope. But, for now, his priority is to find his brothers.

As long as he uses the barn for cover, he is safe from snipers. But between him and the captured trench where his brothers and their comrades are pinned down, there is 150 yards of open ground. As a single target it would be impossible for him to cover such a distance without being shot. All he can do is wait.

He looks at his watch; it is still only mid-morning. Machine guns and snipers are still firing on the boys in the trench. Then he notices a broken slat in the wooden wall at the back of the barn. If he can prise open the gap a little more with his bayonet, he can use the opening as a sniping position that his German adversaries would find very difficult to pinpoint.

He is soon in position with the muzzle of his rifle protruding from the wall of the barn and picking out targets. His first priority is the machine-gunners. They are a relatively easy target as they have to put themselves in such prominent positions in order to fire. He picks out one with ease, but the second one's crew is protected by a wall and he can only see the fat barrel of their MG 08.

So Hywel turns his attention to the snipers. They are much more difficult to find as they are not only expert shots but are also trained to camouflage themselves and use well-protected positions. Nevertheless, after several hours, he has pinpointed three and dispatched them. The hour is now drawing late and the light beginning to fade.

The men in the trench are still trapped and under fire, but at least some are firing back, confirming that several are still alive. Then, out of the corner of his eye, he notices movement in a small coppice of trees to his left. It is a German sniper taking up a new position. He is only sixty yards away and Hywel can clearly see the long thin outline of the barrel of a telescope sight on top the of his Mauser rifle. It is a prize too good to miss. As the German marksman gets into a prone position at the base of a tree, Hywel puts two bullets into him before he can raise his rifle. All he has to do now is wait for darkness to retrieve his reward.

When dusk falls, pandemonium breaks out in the trench, as a massed German counter-attack overwhelms the beleaguered men of the Royal Welch and the West Surreys. It is now too dark for Hywel to help, so he has to stand there and listen to the appalling sounds of hand-to-hand combat. The worst of all are the cries of anguish from the youngest voices, high-pitched and clear, the voices of boys whose throats are not coarsened by tobacco and hard liquor.

The battle lasts until total darkness descends, when all goes quiet. Hywel is then able to cover the sixty yards between him and his sharpshooting trophy. When he reaches the coppice, it takes him a while to find the dead German. But when he does, he retrieves the rifle from the man's hands, which still clutch it tightly. Hywel lights a match. The German is an older man, perhaps in his late thirties, the first enemy he has seen up close. He is certainly not the Hun of the propaganda posters. Dressed in field khaki, he could easily be a Welch Fusilier – indeed, a man you could pass in the streets of Presteigne.

He lights another match because he has seen something interesting. On the German's left sleeve is a small cloth badge depicting a hawk framed by two oak leaves. It is his sniper's insignia, the perfect complement to the booty of the man's rifle and scope. Using the tip of his bayonet and the illumination provided by several more matches, he unpicks the badge and puts it in his pocket. He then raises the match to blow it out. As he does so, he feels a searing pain burn through the palm of his right hand and the thump of a bullet embedding itself into the tree behind.

It is as if a crucifixion nail has been hammered into his palm. He can feel blood flowing down his fingers and excruciating spasms of pain running up his arm. He quickly undoes one of his puttees and uses it as an emergency bandage to strap his hand. None of the fingers of his smashed hand responds, so he has to grasp one end of the puttee between his thumb and his palm, a procedure that produces yet more pain, and wrap it around as tightly as he can, which ratchets up the agony to yet another level.

Sweat is pouring down his face and his heart is pumping

like a steam engine. He tries to calm himself, taking deep breaths, comforted that at least the sniper can no longer pick him out in the darkness. He thinks back to his naivety. Why strike so many matches in a dark wood? He had been the canny fusilier who sniped the sniper; now he has been sniped in turn. How careless is that?

The pain subsides a little and his breathing eases. He begins to think about the perverse reasoning that brought him to France. Joining up was an expedient escape from unbearable adversity; now things are even worse. Both his brothers are probably dead in a trench just fifty yards away. He has not been granted the quick death he had hoped for. And now that his hand is shattered, a return to the life of a farmer is well-nigh impossible. Similarly, his recently discovered talent as a marksman is ruined.

He begins to think about his wound and the fact that he needs medical help. That reminds him that he saw Sister Margaret Killingbeck in Poperinghe – which, in turn, makes him think about Bronwyn. Was it wrong of him to think so badly of her? He feels sure Sister Killingbeck would not have been able to find her. His anguish makes him conjure up dreadful thoughts about his little sister. Is she still in some fleapit in Tiger Bay, sucking off fat Greek sailors or being fucked by big buck niggers? He begins to cry. Did her big brother let her down by not rushing after her and bringing her back to Pentry? He thinks he did; he feels ashamed of himself.

His Lee-Enfield is by his side. Even with one hand, he could use it to put an end to his misery and join his brothers in peace. It is unlikely anyone would realize that he had shot himself, and he would have the quick and noble death he wished for. An eerie silence begins to settle across Flanders' battlefields as a dark night subdues the fighting. There is some noise from distant artillery, which echoes around the boundless fields like rolls of thunder.

Hywel decides it will be his death knell. He reaches for his rifle with his good hand and turns it so that the muzzle is in his mouth. He reaches for the trigger and inhales a huge lungful of air.

But his concentration is broken by rustling in the under-growth and whispered, anxious voices. Hywel immediately swings his rifle around in the direction of the noise. He cranes his neck to see if the whispers are in Welsh or English, or the alien tongue of the German enemy. Seconds later, it is clear that the voices are mostly English, a few with a strong Welsh lilt. Some are even speaking Welsh.

Hywel gets to his feet and collects his two rifles. Thwarted in his attempt to end his wretchedness, he now thinks only of his brothers. His eyes are fully adjusted to the darkness; he can see shadowy figures stumbling towards him. There are some singletons, but most men are in pairs, or trios, help-ing one another to get back to the positions they started out from this morning.

Hywel joins his comrades and shuffles with them back to Zwarteleen. When they arrive at a ruined farmhouse on the Zandvoorde Road, they find it is an impromptu Battalion HQ. There is light from tilley lamps; there are cups of hot tea, and even warm food.

Men are helped to sit on the floor all around the farm-house. Young boys, all bright-eyed and smiling with bravado this morning, are not boys any more; they are broken men. Lieutenant Orme is not in the farmhouse, neither are Ger-aint and Morgan. Hywel begins to cry again.

An arm wraps itself around his shoulders while the hand of the other arm proffers a mug of tea. It is CSM John Hughes, a face Hywel has not seen since Wrexham.

'Colour Serjeant, what are you doing here?'

'What do ya think, son?'

'But I thought you stayed behind in Wrexham –'

'I did, but I arrived yesterday with another three hundred likely lads. How's your hand?'

'Got a bullet through it; it's not a lot of use any more.'

'Well, it's your passport home, then. It could be a lot worse. Where're your brothers?'

'In the bottom of a German trench.'

'Are you sure?'

'Think so.'

'Come on, let's get you into an ambulance and have the medics sort out that hand. By the way, one of the officers back here had his field glasses on you during the day. He said he'd never seen marksmanship like it. Well done, lad.'

'Thanks, Colour Serjeant.'

Hywel's polite words belie the desolation he feels at the end of a day that has changed his life.

Of the 109 Royal Welch Fusilier reservists who took part in the attack at Zwarteleen, only seventeen have made it back unharmed. Eight more are wounded, but managed to get out alive. The rest are assumed to have perished. Of the six recent volunteers to the regiment who were chosen to accompany the reservists, only Hywel has made it back. Lieutenant Francis Orme, the eldest son of an old Anglo-Irish landowning family from County Mayo, was killed right at the end of the day's fighting. He fought courageously all day, organizing his dwindling numbers with calm authority and encouraging any who faltered. Having decided to use the gloom of dusk to fall back, he was the last man to leave the trench. As he did so, he was shot in the back by a single sniper's bullet. He was twenty-three years old.

No one could recall seeing either Morgan or Geraint Thomas fall, but it was thought that no one was left alive when the trench was evacuated. Morgan was eighteen, Geraint seventeen. Today would have been Morgan's nineteenth birthday. Hywel has a packet of five Wild Woodbine cigarettes in his knapsack. It was to be Morgan's birthday present.

Monday 9 November

The British Army's main field hospital in Flanders occupies all three floors of the old Provoost Lace Mill in Poperinghe. It houses over 600 men in beds so close together that there is only just room to pass between them. Matron-General Emma McCarthy visited the hospital yesterday and declared that she was very satisfied with the way it is being run.

Margaret Killingbeck, one of three ward sisters, is in charge of Ward 1 on the ground floor. She is mightily relieved, knowing what a tartar McCarthy can be. British sappers have been able to restore the mill's ancient steam-powered lifts so that the worst cases, those who have no need of the ground floor operating theatres and who are likely soon to die from their wounds, can be kept in the relative calm of the top floor.

It is a relief to the medics, nurses and orderlies that they have a relatively permanent base in Pop, given that they have moved all their patients and equipment five times since arriving at the Front.

Despite the immaculate cleanliness and organizational efficiency of the hospital, and the elevated tranquillity of the top floor, it is a grim place. It is, after all, an old lace mill, not a hospital. Painkilling drugs are in short supply, there are not enough surgeons, and sheets and blankets are hard to keep clean. On Ward 3, at the top, although there is mostly silence from the men slowly losing the struggle for life in semi or total unconsciousness, some are fighting their battle noisily, unable to deal with the dreadful ordeal of their pain, or unable to accept that death is close.

Hywel Thomas is allocated a bed on the ground floor, the area reserved for men who may not need to be sent home to Britain and could go back to active service. He is a borderline case. The injury to his palm has badly damaged his right hand, but he is still mobile. And his state of mind has improved. The desire for revenge has overcome the self-pity he felt in the coppice at Zwarteleen.

When the senior surgeon, Surgeon-Captain Noel Chavasse, a man just twenty-nine years old, examines Hywel's mangled right hand, he concludes that the bullet has shattered metacarpals two and three, the bones that control his two central fingers – the middle finger and the ring finger.

Hywel's first question is to ask whether he will still be able to anchor his rifle. The surgeon furrows his brow.

'You won't be using a rifle any more, Fusilier. You're going home. Your regiment won't take you back in your condition.'

'But, sir, I'm the best shot in the battalion. They've made me a sniper.'

'But it's your right hand –'

'I'm left-handed, sir.'

'I see, let me have another look.'

Chavasse spends several minutes carefully examining the wound and talking to his juniors, who are gathered around Hywel's bed.

'It's a clean hole, but the metacarps are beyond repair. There will be extensive nerve damage, and the healing time will be months.'

'Please, sir, I have no family to go home to. My parents are dead, and both my brothers were killed yesterday.'

Captain Chavasse is stunned. He can see the desperation on Hywel's face.

'I'm sorry . . . that's very unfortunate. Please accept my

condolences.' The surgeon examines the hand once more. 'What is your name, Fusilier Thomas?'

'Hywel, sir.'

'Look, Hywel, it could take three or four months to heal. To be blunt, the army is not going to feed and house you for that length of time in the unlikely hope that you are going to be able to shoot again.'

'Sir, I only need my right hand to rest my rifle on. I'm a quick healer, and while it's getting better I can work here at the hospital.'

'With one hand?'

'Yes, sir.'

'Doing what?'

Hywel looks around at the frantic activity of the nurses and orderlies.

'Most of what they're doing, sir. I have a strong left hand.' Chavasse smiles.

'Let me talk to your CO.'

'He doesn't know me, sir. I only arrived from Wales last week. Our officer was killed yesterday; the only one who knows how good I am is Colour Serjeant Hughes.'

'Very well, where is he?'

'At the Front, I think, sir – the other side of Wipers.'

'Well, I think he may be a little preoccupied at the moment.'

Chavasse smiles again and looks at his juniors next to him. They stand in respectful silence, waiting to see what he will decide to do. His smile breaks into a mischievous grin.

'Very well, I'll take your word for it that you're a top marksman. I'll operate this afternoon and will see what we can do. You'll need a reinforced glove, but I know where we can get one.'

Chavasse's juniors look puzzled; this is the first they've heard of such a thing.

'Desoutter Brothers in London, a new company set up by Marcel Desoutter. Eighteen months ago, he was badly injured in a flying accident. I had to take his leg off. Not satisfied

384

with the wooden leg he was fitted with, he and his brother designed a new artificial limb made out of duralumin, an alloy of aluminium. They have now started a new company making artificial limbs.'

One of Chavasse's juniors cannot resist making an acerbic quip.

'From what we've seen in the last three months, sir, they'll soon be rich men.'

'Quite! I'll get them to make a reinforced glove for Fusilier Thomas, designed to help the hand in supporting a rifle. It'll be a good challenge for them and an interesting case for us.' He then turns to Hywel. 'You make sure you bag plenty of the Hun to justify all this.'

'Don't worry about that, sir. There is a German sniper I need to nail for Lieutenant Orme and for popping my hand. He may as well pay for my brothers too.'

'That's the spirit! I should warn you, you'll have no flexibility from your middle fingers, but your little finger, your index finger and your thumb should, with a bit of luck, hard work and a following wind, function as they do now.'

'Thank you, sir.'

'You will be in pain for several weeks and should only undertake light duties for three months after that. Then we'll put you on the range and see how you get on.'

'Don't worry, sir, I'll take the eye out of a sparrow at three hundred yards.'

'I'm sure you will. Nurse, would you tell Sister Killingbeck to get this man ready for surgery after lunch?'

Hywel's euphoria at the news about his hand is dramatically dissipated on hearing Margaret's name. His eyes follow the nurse. As they do, he sees a nursing auxiliary appear from the sluice room, where the bedpans and urine bottles are dealt with. It is another blow to his elation of only moments ago. The auxiliary is the sister he has disowned.

Bronwyn looks pristine in her pale-blue uniform, white

apron and cap. In fact, Hywel thinks she looks even prettier than the sweet Welsh lass he remembers from happier days at Pentry before the trauma of the summer. Bronwyn does not notice Hywel as she walks past the end of his bed.

He is distraught; his eyes begin to fill with tears. He does not know what to say or do. His instincts tell him to run away, anywhere, but he has no clothes, bar the hospital gown they have given him. He also wants to have his operation so that he can fulfil his newly found purpose in life: to avenge Lieutenant Orme and his brothers by killing more Germans.

Bronwyn has gone out of sight, further down the ward, but she soon appears again, carrying a bedpan, and walks back past Hywel's bed. He calls out in Welsh, wishing her a happy birthday.

'*Penblwydd hapus, cariad.*'

Bronwyn lets out a squeal and drops the enamel bedpan and its contents all over the ward floor. She turns towards Hywel, screams again and rushes out of the ward. As she does so, she pushes past Margaret, who is carrying the notes of 'Fusilier Thomas, Royal Welch Fusiliers'.

Guessing immediately what has happened, Margaret brings to bear all the discipline and self-control of her training.

'Nurse Henderson, sort out that bedpan.' She then calmly walks over to Hywel's bed. 'Good morning, Fusilier Thomas. How are you feeling?'

'I've felt worse, Sister, but only just.'

'Well, let's get you operated on so that you can start to get better.'

Then, as she goes around his bed tucking in his sheets and arranging his pillows as nurses do, she speaks again, but in a whispered tone that no one else can hear.

'You are looking a lot better than when I saw you at Pentry.'

'Thank you . . . Can I call you Margaret?'

'Of course, but only in private.'

'How did you find Bron?'

'It wasn't difficult. She was where you said she would be.'

'Doing what I told you?'

'Yes.'

'And?'

'She's fine. Can't you see that?'

'How did you do it?'

'I'm a nurse . . . and a woman. She saw you in Pop when you arrived.'

'I saw you, but not Bron. Was she with you?'

'Yes.'

'Then she saw Geraint and Morgan as well?'

'Of course; it was quite a shock for her.'

'Not as big as the one she's got coming. I don't know how I'm going to tell her.'

Margaret stops fiddling with Hywel's bedding, a look of horror forming on her face as she sees the pained expression on Hywel's.

'They're both dead. We got cut to pieces yesterday. I was lucky; I was sniping behind the attack. So few of the boys came back.'

Margaret cannot hold the tears in check. Despite all her resolve, they begin to spill down her cheeks and her chest heaves involuntarily.

'Look, Hywel, I must go and find Bron. I'll get a staff nurse to cover for me for an hour, she'll get you ready for the op . . .' She pauses, remembering her duty. 'Are you all right?'

'Yes, you go. I'm not feeling like I did when we met before. I've found something I'm good at, and I want to recover for my brothers' sake. I also want to make it up to Bron for not looking after her.'

Margaret puts her hand on Hywel's shoulder and then rushes away to the nurses' quarters, where she finds Bronwyn curled on her bed, sobbing. Margaret sits on the edge of the bed, pulls Bronwyn towards her and cradles the girl's

387

head in her lap. She begins to stroke her hair, but does not say anything.

Several minutes pass before Bronwyn speaks.

'What's wrong with him?'

'He's been shot in the hand.'

'Which one?'

'The right.'

'Thank God for that small mercy; he's left-handed.'

'Don't worry, they're going to patch him up. He'll be fine.'

'He said "happy birthday, lovely girl".'

'Why didn't you tell me it was your birthday?'

'I'd forgotten. And besides, I can't remember what day it is, let alone the date.' Bronwyn sits up and shakes her head, as if to clear her thoughts. 'Do you think he's forgiven me?'

'Yes, I think he has.'

'I'm sorry I dropped the bedpan; he gave me such a fright.'

'Don't worry about that.' Margaret takes a deep breath. 'Bron, you know I said I would tell you my dark secret one day?'

'I remember; I've been hoping you'll tell me ever since we got to France.'

'Well, I think I should tell you now. But I want to say something first . . .' She takes another deliberate breath. 'I love you, Bron.'

Bronwyn smiles, her tears gone.

'And I love you, Margaret; you have saved my life and been so kind to me.'

'But it is more than that; I *really* love you.'

Bronwyn looks puzzled.

'That is my dark secret. I like women; I'm ashamed to say I'm physically attracted to my own sex.'

Bronwyn is shocked, motionless. Margaret stands up and straightens her crumpled uniform.

'There, I've said it. I've wanted to tell you for weeks, but I was terrified that you would reject me. I don't want us to be lovers, but I wanted you to know. I think you are so brave, dealing with everything you've had to endure. I watch you every day, putting up with all the drudgery on the ward, and you never complain; you are so strong.'

Bronwyn has regained a little of her composure.

'Margaret, I don't know what to say –'

'Don't say anything. I just wanted you to know so that we can be honest with one another. I know all your secrets, and now you know mine.'

'Have you had many lovers?'

'Just two. A girl back home – you know, in the village I told you about in Swaledale? She was the vicar's daughter, from two villages away, down in the valley. She was full of life, very clever; they were happy days together.'

'What happened?'

'We got caught in her bed by her mother. She told her parents that we were in love and she was going to run away with me. All hell broke out. She was sent to her mother's sister somewhere – they wouldn't tell me where, for obvious reasons – and my parents threw me out on the street.'

'What did you do?'

'Worked in pubs, did cleaning; whatever I could, just to get by.'

'You didn't do what I . . . ?' Bronwyn cannot bring herself to put it into words.

'No, but I sank pretty low. I tried men, lots of them, looking for the one that would release me from my "illness". That's what they say, you know, that it's an "illness". That's why I said that I understood what you were going through.'

'How did you become a nurse?'

'Study, hard work, just like you're doing now.'

'What about your other lover?'

'A nurse, like me, at Guy's, where I trained. She was very precocious and very sexually aware, which is why I understood what happened between you and Philip. And why I am so certain there is nothing peculiar about you.'

'Bloody hell! I wish you'd told me all this ages ago; it would've helped a lot.'

'I'm sorry, but it's not an easy thing to talk about.'

'And your boyfriends?'

'Most were young, immature and, you know . . .'

Bronwyn smiles – a warm, sympathetic smile.

'I know! They're big, 'airy, smelly things, aren't they?'

Margaret smiles back, but then stops herself. She sits down next to Bronwyn again.

'Bron, I told you I love you and bared my soul so that you know how much I care about you, because I think you're going to need me. There's something else.'

'Oh God, Margaret, your face!' Bronwyn begins to shake her head wildly. 'Not one of the boys? Not Geraint or Morgan?'

Margaret is struggling to maintain her composure. Bronwyn stares at her friend's now stern demeanour and begins to scream.

'No! No! Please don't tell me. *Please!*'

'Bron, Geraint and Morgan are dead. They were both killed yesterday, in the same attack in which Hywel was injured. Few of the Welch Fusiliers survived. I'm so sorry.'

Bronwyn howls in a fusion of anger and sadness.

'Why our family? Look at what's happened to us! Ma an' Da gone, two brothers dead, another injured. And me, a so-called redeemed whore who spends her days emptyin' tins o' shit, moppin' up blood, an' pickin' up bits of bodies.'

Margaret lets Bronwyn wail for a while. She longs to comfort her friend, but is afraid any gesture on her part may be misconstrued.

'Morgan and I were so close as kids. We even knew what the other was thinking. And Geraint, well, he was my baby brother; no more than a child, really.'

Margaret feels inadequate in the face of such grief and attempts to put her arms around Bron, but the girl recoils and pushes her way.

390

'No! No! And on top of everything else, my best friend's a fuckin' fanny-licker!'

Margaret swings round and runs out of the room in floods of tears. She keeps going, even though she can hear Bronwyn calling after her, shouting that she is sorry.

Margaret does not reappear on the ward until over an hour later, when Dr Chavasse is just finishing his second round of the day. He notices immediately that Margaret has been crying.

'Sister, are you all right? You've been away rather a long time.'

'Sorry, Captain, I've just been telling one of the nurses that she has lost two brothers, one of whom was her twin. And it's her nineteenth birthday today.'

'Oh, I see, how very distressing for you. And for her; poor girl. Do I know her?'

'Yes, I think so, her name is Auxiliary Thomas. She happens to be Hywel Thomas's sister, as well.'

'Oh dear, what a terrible business all round. She's the pretty little Welsh one; the one who's caught the eye of several of my juniors.'

Margaret winces.

'Yes, she's a pretty little thing; I'm sure all the young men are after her.'

'Her nineteenth birthday, you said? How did she become a nurse so quickly?'

'It's a long story.'

Chavasse changes the subject and brings them back to the unintentionally callous cataloguing of injury, healing, infection and death; the daily routine of the Royal Army Medical Corps.

'Sister, most of today's operations have gone reasonably well. We lost four men in theatre, but they were pretty irretrievable. The rest are a mixed bag.'

Chavasse begins to hand notes to Margaret, who keeps them carefully in order.

'These are two amputees above the knee, and three below the knee. They are in good shape, but they'll have to go upstairs to Ward Two to recover before being sent home. I have three for the top floor. Grimwood: I'm afraid his lungs will not recover, he's going to need morphine and will spit blood until he dies. Matthews: I've stitched up his stomach, but there's nothing further I can do for him; just give him enough morphine to take the edge off, but he won't survive the night. And this poor sod, Macpherson: he must be as strong as an ox, he should be dead already; give him a lot of morphine, he deserves it.'

'What about Hywel Thomas, Captain?'

'Ah yes, he's with this lot' – Chavasse hands several more notes to Margaret – 'all fit enough to stay downstairs and convalesce before going up the line. Thomas begged to stay here, said he had scores to settle. I've patched up his hand. I think he'll retain feeling in his thumb, and perhaps his index finger, but the rest will be useless. Infection is the problem with him. Try and get him to behave himself. One of my lads has telegraphed London to see if we can get him a reinforced glove.'

'Why, Captain? Surely he's no use to the infantry with one hand?'

'Apparently he's a crack shot. An officer came over about an hour ago, an odd fellow, wearing a Stetson cowboy hat. He looked like a big-game hunter, called himself Major Hesketh-Prichard. He said Thomas was the best shot the Royal Welch has ever had and that his scores on the range broke all British Army records. They're going to make him a serjeant when he recovers and get him to help train others to shoot.'

Margaret goes to Hywel's bedside before she goes off duty that afternoon to reassure him about his hand. He has already been seen by Major Hesketh-Prichard and is ecstatic about the news.

'What did the major tell you?'

'He wants me to join this training unit he's startin' up, to improve our snipin'. Apparently, our average soldier is a much better shot than the average Fritz, but their snipers are much better than ours. I did a deal with him.'

'Really?'

'He agreed I could go back to my battalion for three months to pop that Hun who plugged Lieutenant Orme.'

'How will you find him?'

'If his unit is still here, I'll find him. Then I told the major I'd nabbed a telescopic sight off the sniper I shot. I thought he was goin' to kiss me! He's taken it off to be tested.'

'That's excellent news. Well done!'

'So, how's Bron? Did you tell her about the boys?'

'Yes, I did.'

'Is she in a bad way?'

'I'm afraid she is, Hywel; she's going to need you to lean on.'

'Please ask her if I can come and see her. The Doc said I can get up in a few days, if I wear a splint.'

'I will, Hywel. I've given her some time off, but I hear they're expecting another big battle later this week, when I'll need her back. Why not wait until Thursday.'

'Thanks, Margaret.'

Margaret makes her way back to the nurses' quarters, where she finds Bronwyn waiting for her in her room.

'Margaret, I hope you don't mind me being in your room, but I didn't want to miss you.'

'Of course not. How are you feeling?'

'A little better, but still very raw. Listen, I'm sorry about what I said. I was upset.'

'Don't be sorry, it was a crude way to put it, but I've heard worse. So now you know, you're not the only one who has to live with guilt. You said you thought you weren't normal; well, how many women do you know who are lesbians?'

'Is that what you're called?'

'Yes, "lesbian" describes what I am, but most people use expressions like the one you used.'

'Oh, Margaret, I'm so sorry, I didn't mean it.'

Bronwyn embraces her, but this time Margaret is the one to reject the approach.

'No, Bron; if we're going to stay close, you can still treat me like a friend but you can't be intimate with me.'

'Oh, I see, but I liked our cuddles together.'

'So did I, but they were also an agony for me, because I so wanted them to go further.'

'I understand; it must have been awful for you. Let's go out for a drink in the Maison de Ville tonight. After all, it *is* my birthday!'

'Are you sure? What about your brothers, isn't it in poor taste?'

'It might be, but me an' the boys always had a drink together – in good times and bad – so let's go an' have one for them.'

'All right; you know, Bron, you are so strong. I just don't know how you do it.'

'I do it thanks to you.'

'Come on, I think we both need a drink.'

Forty-five minutes later, having taken a bath and changed their clothes, Margaret and Bron have toasted Geraint and Morgan and are sitting in the Maison de Ville, in Pop's Grande Place.

Neither one says much to the other; they are both deep in their own thoughts. So much has happened to them in the space of just a few months. There is so much pain and suffering all around them. Their emotions are strained almost to breaking point, and yet, they are sitting in a bar enjoying a drink. After a while, Bronwyn utters a long tortured sigh.

'If I was at home now, I'd be dressed in black, sittin' by the fire. No one would say anythin'; all the men would look grim, the women would wail. But look at us, drinkin' wine!' She looks around the room with a wry smile on her face. 'And look at this lot, all drinkin', laughin', lookin' for a quick one with any old tart. What's the war doin' to us?'

Margaret has her own thoughts. Other than the lover she had at Guy's, she has not talked to anyone about being a lesbian since she left Swaledale. She is still not reconciled to her sexual feelings and spends many hours hoping that, miraculously, she will revert to 'normal'. The trouble is, to her, her feelings *are* normal. She has not really heard what Bronwyn said.

'Margaret?'

'Sorry, I was daydreaming.'

'I was saying, the war is turning us into thoughtless, cruel creatures.'

'Yes, I suppose it is. We talk about the men like a vet talks about cows: put this one with the poor milkers; this one can go to the knacker's yard . . .'

As she continues, the two nurses suddenly hear the crisp tones of an aristocratic male voice.

'Good evening, Margaret, I was told I would find you here. How are you?'

It is Hamish Stewart-Murray. He is back from Blair Atholl; his wound has healed and he is rejoining the Camerons, who are billeted near Ypres. Margaret is flustered and, not helped by the red wine, her cheeks glow a rosy red.

'Hamish, good heavens . . . er, I'm fine. Please sit down; have some wine.'

'That's most kind, thank you. But only if I'm not intruding?'

'No, no, not at all. And how about you; your wound is healed?'

'Yes, it's fine. I'm going up to Ypres tomorrow, back to the Camerons.'

Hamish looks at Bronwyn and smiles.

'Oh, sorry; Hamish, this is Bronwyn Thomas. We nurse together.'

Margaret realizes at once that she should not have mentioned Bronwyn's first name, thus revealing who she is.

'Bronwyn, what a lovely name . . .' He pauses as he

remembers where he has heard the name before, but manages to stop himself saying so.

Bronwyn realizes who Hamish is.

'It's all right, Margaret, Hamish. This is a day for shocks. You must be the officer who was there when Philip died. I hope you don't think me too wicked, sir.'

'Not at all, Bronwyn, and please don't call me "sir"; it's Hamish, this is Civvy Street.'

Bronwyn has a mischievous look on her face.

'Well, Hamish, I think you should take Margaret out to dinner and buy her the best bottle of wine in Pop. She needs cheering up.'

Hamish's face transforms itself into a broad grin.

'That was exactly my plan, Bronwyn; how astute of you. Would you like to join us?'

'That's very kind, but three's a crowd.'

Hamish's grin gets broader still. But Margaret is looking less than pleased.

'Hamish, you're so kind, but I have to be on duty at –'

Bronwyn interrupts her.

'Margaret, don't be a spoilsport! Hamish has come all the way to Pop to see you; you can't stand him up.'

Bronwyn is right, and Margaret knows it. Her face softens.

'Yes, of course . . . Hamish, that would be lovely.'

An hour and a half later, Margaret is enjoying herself. She and Hamish have both heard that the Germans are likely to make one last attempt to break through at Ypres before winter finally takes control. There will be no time for relaxation for many days to come, so, despite her initial reluctance, she is now grasping the opportunity with increasing relish.

She has been treated to the best food and wine in Poperinghe, at a small, inconspicuous family restaurant behind the Grande Place. Somehow, it manages to provide the local senior French and British staff officers with fare on a par with the giddy heights of Parisian cuisine.

'Hamish, that was astonishing food, better than anything I've ever had in London. Thank you so much. How do they do it?'

'They always find a way to serve fine food here, even in the most trying circumstances.'

Their conversation flows.

Margaret tells Hamish a little of Bronwyn's story and of her life amidst the horror surrounding Ypres. It is good therapy for her.

Hamish tells her about his family problems, Geordie's likely death, and his father and brother's indiscretions.

'And what about yours, Hamish?'

'There have been a few, but not with the same consequences as Bardie's.'

'I should hope not!'

'And what about yours?'

Margaret's mood changes and becomes sombre again.

'There haven't really been any – at least, none I care to remember.'

Hamish seizes the moment.

'Would you like to change that?'

Margaret takes a while to answer. She is on the horns of a dilemma. She had so hoped that Bronwyn might reciprocate her feelings, but it does not look like she will. Perhaps she could love a man, after all, and find satisfaction with him? Hamish is not like the other men she has met. He seems kind and gentle, and she is sure he is an experienced lover.

'Where are you staying?'

'Here; they have a small apartment upstairs. Very cosy, very private.'

Margaret is tempted. She can feel the beginnings of a sexual frisson – perhaps this time? She takes his hand.

'Hamish, if I stay with you, will you be gentle with me?'

'Of course, like a butterfly on gossamer.'

Wednesday 11 November

Hooge, West Flanders, Belgium

The first snow of winter has been falling on the fields of Flanders. For a fleeting moment the endless soft white blanket makes the flat landscape look almost appealing, rather like looking down from above and seeing a vast expanse of pure white clouds. But only for a moment; the hideous reality of what the pristine snow temporarily disguises soon returns as drizzle replaces snowflakes.

As if everyone has not suffered enough already – soldiers and civilians alike – winter's true viciousness has arrived. Temperatures have dropped significantly and those in the open are not only wet, hungry and miserable but are now also shivering from cold. The last thing anyone wants, especially the beleaguered Allies who have steadfastly held their ground against repeated German attacks, is another battle. But that is exactly what Erich von Falkenhayn has planned; one last throw of the dice before the depths of winter change the game.

He has been carefully husbanding men and materiel: shells, rifle and machine-gun ammunition, winter boots, gloves and greatcoats. He has also been looking at the skies. He thinks that, although cold weather is a nightmare for any soldier, it is less arduous for his elite Bavarians and Prussians, who are more used to the icy temperatures of the heart of Europe, than for his French and British enemies, who come from more maritime climes. So, for him, the first snow of winter provides the ideal moment to attack.

Von Falkenhayn has created yet another army group to

add to Army Group Fabeck, which he created at the end of October. He chooses a 64-year-old Prussian warhorse, General Alexander von Linsingen, to lead the attack and gives him the cream of the German Army. Pomeranians, West Prussians, the pick of the Kaiser's beloved Guards: the 1st and 3rd Foot Guards, and the 2nd and 3rd Guards Grenadiers. Each is formidable, but together they represent a fearsome challenge.

On the other hand, facing them are three all-but-spent Allies.

The remnants of the Belgian Army in the north are fighting valiantly for the last western fringes of their homeland. Thankfully for them, German attention is now focused further south.

The French, proud and brave, are exhausted. They still go to war as Napoleon did, with pomp and bravado, but there is a limit to how many men in splendid uniforms they can sacrifice to protect their Republic. The generals still have the resolve, and their men the stomach, but for how much longer without stockpiles of shells and ammunition?

The British are in an even worse position. The British Expeditionary Force, which was the major part of the British Army, is almost destroyed. Inexperienced reservists, few with serious combat experience, are just about keeping it alive, but its death knell may sound within days.

There have been a few days of relative calm, only interrupted by two unpleasant instances. Two days ago, a Belgian farmer was discovered illicitly supplying the Germans with meat, even though he had a contract with the British Army. He was tried and found guilty by a military court. When he was executed by firing squad, Brigade HQ insisted that every resident of the man's village over the age of fifteen stand in the village square to witness the event, ensuring that he died in front of all his relatives and friends. The incident did little for Anglo-Belgian relations.

The following evening, during a night-time skirmish with

what was probably a German reconnaissance patrol, three members of the 4th Battalion Fusiliers' Number 3 Platoon heard voices behind their trench. Suspecting that the Germans might have outflanked them, they called, 'Halt! Identify yourselves!'

No response was forthcoming, so the fusiliers opened fire. Then came an impassioned cry.

'Fuck! You've shot my officer.'

'Why didn't you answer?'

'I'm the platoon serjeant. We were three yards apart in the dark. I couldn't see him. He thought I was going to respond, and I thought he was. Then you opened fire.'

'Serves you right, then, don't it?'

The two men were Royal Engineers, running a telephone line to the 4th Fusiliers' trench. The officer had been shot through the jaw and his side. The stretcher-bearers took him back to Battalion HQ, but his prospects did not look good. No one mentioned the incident again and no disciplinary action was taken, nor was it even considered, the consensus being that the two sappers had been bloody fools.

With the snow turning to rain in the middle of the night, and the temperature rising slightly, dawn beckons with a dank, cold mist to add to the misery of the scene.

The German assault is presaged by the most intense artillery bombardment since the beginning of the war. It begins at 6.30 a.m on Wednesday 11 November. It does not stop for two and a half hours and is targeted at a small area between Zonnebeke in the north and St Eloi in the south, an area just seven miles wide, barely four miles east of Ypres. The ground shakes beneath every building in the town, an indication of how awesome the impact is on the front line.

The 4th Battalion Royal Fusiliers is dug in at Hooge, at the epicentre of the bombardment. For newly decorated and promoted Colour Serjeants Tait and Woodruff and the men of their Number 2 Platoon around them, it is an assault that even the most seasoned veterans of the British Army find hard to bear. At times, the ground beneath them rises like a wave crashing on to a beach, before it drops them back down with a shudder. Sometimes, they are covered in showers of earth from an impact nearby. Inevitably, many men are injured, shredded or totally obliterated. That is horror enough, especially if the remains of friends and comrades fall on you like gory rain. But then there is the even greater horror of contemplating death by an unseen missile which is going to do to you what has just happened to your neighbour.

The deafening noise is relentless. A few minutes are just about bearable; but for two and a half hours, it is a hell on earth.

In order to say anything, even to the man next to you, you have to shout in his ear. Beyond that distance, hand signals are the only option. Maurice and Harry are curled up together in a foetal position on a dry platform at the bottom of the trench, hoping and praying that they are not about to receive a direct hit. Like others who have experienced heavy shelling before, they are using cotton-wool earplugs to deaden some of the unrelenting din.

Harry signals to Maurice to pull out one of his plugs for a moment.

'Fuck me, Mo, this is beyond a joke!'

'I know, this is the worst one ever. You all right?'

'Not really, Mo. I'm gettin' the willies. I'd rather have a fourpenny one than put up wiv this much longer.'

Maurice looks at Harry and points to tell him to put his earplug back in. Harry is sweating profusely and his hands are trembling. He has never liked being under a barrage of shells and this one is far worse than anything they have experienced before. As Harry closes his eyes to try to obscure what is happening to him, Maurice puts his arms around his friend and holds him tightly.

Some of the young reservists nearby notice what is happening. Maurice smiles and nods at them to reassure them. They smile back. Strangely, they do not seem to sense weakness in their colour serjeant by witnessing Harry's predicament. Every man there, young or old, novice or veteran, is feeling the same thing – utter terror. Each is fighting his overwhelming instinct to flee and is praying for his deliverance from the ordeal.

A direct hit into a trench kills most men in the vicinity; it is a quick death. Two things are worse: to be some distance away and be hit by shrapnel, which takes off a limb or disembowels you; or to be cowering in a trench when a shell explodes just in front or behind it, so you are then buried alive. With more shells falling and the ever-present sniper fire, it takes a huge amount of courage for your comrades to dig you out before you choke to death. Most do not try.

The 4th Fusiliers' Number 2 Platoon has taken one direct hit, obliterating the trench and replacing it with a deep crater. It leaves no trace of the three men who stood there. It also suffers one near miss, about twenty yards from Harry and Maurice. Three men have shrapnel wounds, one serious, and are withdrawn.

Respite from the bombardment arrives at 9 a.m. when the trajectory of the shells rises towards the rear, where it is intended to soften up the reserves. Everyone knows that the infantry assault is imminent. Maurice looks at Harry. His face is contorted, as if in great pain. He is holding his rifle close to him, his knuckles white with tension. Maurice taps him on the shoulder and helps him take out his earplugs.

'It's all right, Harry; it's over. Fritz will be here soon. Come on, eyes front.'

Harry opens his eyes. As he does so, he notices that many of the men are looking at him.

'What the fuckin' Ada, what are you lot starin' at? I just

don't like loud noises. Any of you tossers got a problem wiv that? Look to your fronts, you bunch of arseholes!'

The men of Number 2 Platoon are relieved. Good old 'Arry, the 'Leyton Lash' – which they call him when he is not listening – is back to his old self, the toughest NCO in the regiment. They regard Maurice differently. Calmer than Harry, he listens more; you can go to him with your problems. But do not get on the wrong side of him; he can be just as hard as Harry, if he needs to be.

Number 2 Platoon is in the centre of the 4th Battalion Fusiliers' position. Its new officer, Captain Reginald Harold Routley, has recently arrived from India, all his fighting having been done on the North-West Frontier. It is hard to imagine what he makes of the shelling and the rain and mud of Flanders.

Now that the worst is over for Harry, Maurice goes to the far left of his platoon's trench to stiffen the boys. Captain Routley is at the other end, with Harry in the middle.

When the elite German Guards attack, it is as if they have forgotten the lessons of Mons. Perhaps the elan of these old regiments demands that they attack as they always have done. They come on in tight formations, their officers with swords drawn. They could be Napoleon's legendary Old Guard making its final, futile attack in the fading light at Waterloo a hundred years earlier. They too were cut down in droves by lethal British musketry.

The Germans emerge out of the heavy mist at 9.45 a.m. precisely; there are 17,500 of them along a line just seven miles wide. That is equivalent to a man and a half for every yard. Facing them in their trenches are just 7,800 defenders.

Advancing directly in front of the Fusiliers' centre is the 4th Battalion, Queen Augusta's Guards Grenadiers, men from Berlin, one of the elite regiments of the old Prussian Army. Even over the din of gunfire, the Fusiliers can hear the Guards Grenadiers singing their regimental song '*Die Wacht am Rhein*' as they approach. They look very impressive, tall men, immaculately turned out, their field-grey uniforms looking distinctive, even at a distance and even in the gull-grey murk of a November morning.

Although Royal Field Artillery is rationing shells, the fusiliers have good stocks of small-arms ammunition. With clear orders to keep the men supplied, Maurice and Harry have put the two youngest reservists in charge of boxes of ammunition. The company's quartermaster serjeant has also been able to find a supply of rifle oil and cleaning rags, so their rifles are in pristine condition – about the only things they possess that are.

When the Germans come within range, Captain Routley issues the order to fire, a command repeated by Maurice and Harry. It is target practice again, just like Mons, and the Guards Grenadiers fall like tin soldiers in a fairground shooting stall. But they keep coming on; there seems to be an endless supply of them. By now, there is firing all along the seven-mile front, and the great battle is fully engaged; the noise is almost as deafening as the early morning artillery bombardment.

Return fire begins to wreak havoc among the Fusiliers. The Germans have brought snipers with them across the open ground and they are picking targets from concealed positions.

To the defenders' amazement, and despite appalling losses, some of the Germans make it all the way to within twenty yards of the trench. Harry looks to his right. Routley should have given the order to fix bayonets by now, but he has not. Harry sees why; he has been wounded in the head and one of the medics is dressing it. He seems to be conscious, but blood is pouring down his face. Harry gives the order as loudly as he can.

'*Fix bayonets!*'

Within moments there are Germans jumping into the trench. Harry swings round to see that there is a Guards Grenadier on either side of him. As they both lunge at the same time, one screams something incomprehensible in German; the other shouts, 'Take this, Tommy!' in perfect English. But Harry is too good for even these elite Berliners. He deflects one bayonet with the butt of his rifle and the other with his own blade. He then grabs one of the Mauser's barrels and pulls the man holding it towards him. As the man tumbles forward, Harry crashes his elbow into his face, smashing his nose and making him reel backwards into the bottom of the trench.

The second man tries to fire his Mauser, but Harry flicks its muzzle upwards, directing the bullet harmlessly into the air. Harry pulls his trigger in the same moment, the impact of the bullet at close range throwing the man backwards like a rag doll.

Harry then turns to the other grenadier, who, despite being almost submerged in the muddy water at the bottom of the trench, is trying to get a shot away.

Harry is soon on top of him with his boot on his chest. He raises his bayonet to strike.

'Take this, Fritz!'

Harry plunges his bayonet deep into the man's chest and uses his boot to lever it out again. As he does so, a fountain of blood rises a foot into the air.

There are hand-to-hand battles all along the trench. Worryingly, there seem to be more men in field grey than khaki. Fighting with an extraordinary ferocity, Harry decides to move towards Captain Routley. All the tension created by the morning's bombardment is leaving him like steam from a pressure valve. He kills several of the enemy in quick succession, encourages his men as he passes them and picks some up from the bottom of the trench and gets them fighting again.

Using bayonet thrusts and bullets, fierce kicks with his boots and bludgeons from his rifle butt, he finally reaches Routley, who has managed to get to his feet. His medic is dead, slumped against the side of the trench, with a bullet through his heart.

Harry looks around. There is now more khaki alive in the trench than field grey, and there do not seem to be any more Germans closing in from the open ground. For a brief moment he clambers on to the trench parapet from where he can see to the far end of the trench, where the survivors from Maurice's section seem to be more numerous than in his own section. Maurice is unharmed and appears to be in control of the situation.

Those few Germans who are not dead begin to run back from whence they came. Most of them make it, largely because the Fusiliers are too exhausted to raise their rifles. Harry turns his attention to Captain Routley.

'Are you all right, sir?'

'Yes, thank you, Colour Serjeant, a bit dazed. I think the bullet has taken off quite a big bit from the corner of my eyebrow, so I won't be winning any beauty contests in the future.'

'No, sir, but I think you should sit down. You're losin' a lot o' blood.'

'Thank you, most thoughtful of you.'

'What are your orders, sir? I think Fritz is scarpering.'

'Is he? Very good. I'm afraid I can't see very well out of my left eye and my right is pretty hazy. Before he died, this poor medic told me that I've got some bone splinters in my eye. So I won't be chasing the Hun for a while. You and the men have done enough for one day. Let's get some rest. We'll hold our ground until we hear from Colonel McMahon.'

'Very good, sir. With your permission, I should go and check on Colour Serjeant Tait's section.'

'Carry on, man. By the way, the colonel tells me that a DCM is on its way to you.'

'Yes, sir.'

'Well, I think you've earned a bar to your medal today. Bloody good show. I will be recommending you.'

'Thanks very much, sir.'

Before Harry can reach Maurice, Colonel McMahon appears from behind the trench. He is leading about fifty fusiliers he has gathered from various platoons along the line.

'Number 2 Platoon to me, please! Colour Serjeant Woodruff, get your platoon organized. Where's Captain Routley?'

'Wounded, sir; he's over there.'

McMahon sends over a medic to see to Routley.

'Where's CSM Tait?'

'Over the other side, sir.'

'Bring his men in as well. We're going after the enemy.'

'Is that wise, sir?'

The colonel does not answer but stares at Harry in a way that makes it very clear that his question is not appropriate.

'Very sorry, sir.'

'Carry on, Colour Serjeant.'

Harry's heart sinks. McMahon's got itchy feet, he obviously fancies a whiff of glory before he goes off to Brigade, but it is the last thing Harry wants to do. Moments later, over eighty men have gathered behind the colonel, who leads them out beyond the trench. He and his adjutant, Captain George O'Donel, who is back at Battalion HQ, are the only officers from the entire battalion still able to fight.

McMahon jumps up on to an ammunition box.

'Fusiliers, there is a farm a hundred yards to the north-west. That is our objective. Follow me, and let's show Fritz what Royal Fusiliers are made of!'

Despite sniper fire, and the attentions of a distant machine gun, most of the eighty men make it to the farm. The colonel was possibly right to try to claim it. It is on higher ground and is a much better defensive position, but his worthy ambition has cost him his life. Halfway across open ground, a young corporal next to him fell to the ground mortally wounded. McMahon knelt down to help him; as he did so, the leather of his cavalry boot seemed to explode as he was shot through his lower right leg.

Maurice, who had resumed his position at Harry's side, shouted, 'Sniper!'

Harry was indignant.

'Bloody madness! Out here with a colonel's crown an' pips on his shoulder. He's a sittin' duck!'

Harry was right, Colonel McMahon was too obvious a target for a hawk-eyed sniper. While he tried to get to his feet to pull his boot off his stricken leg, two more bullets hit him almost at the same time. One ripped into his right shoulder, momentarily spinning him to the left, before the other hit him in the left side of his abdomen, twisting him the other way. He fell to the ground slowly, trying to hold on to consciousness, but his resistance lasted only a few seconds before he collapsed in a heap.

Colonel Norman Reginald McMahon DSO from Farnborough in Hampshire, forty-eight years old and a veteran of the Burma Expedition and the Boer War, never received the extra pip to signify his new promotion to brigadier. Much loved by his fusiliers, he led from the front and embraced the realities of modern warfare much more readily than most of his contemporaries. He tried to insist that every battalion in the army had six machine-gun crews, but he was ignored. Now, along with tens of thousands of others, he is dead in the mud of a Flanders field.

The remnants of the 4th Fusiliers, who have managed to make it to the farm to secure McMahon's forward position, try to collect their thoughts. Maurice and Harry, two lance corporals, a corporal and sixty-seven men are holding a farm a hundred yards beyond their trench of this morning. The Germans seem to have retreated, and the firing is dying down all along the line. As far as the two colour serjeants can tell from the direction of fire, it looks like the huge German offensive has been repulsed.

'What should we do, 'Arry?'

'How long to dark, Mo?'

'Two hours.'

'Then let's post lookouts. Put some boys on the roof and make a perimeter.'

'I'll go an' get McMahon when it's dark and quiet.'

'All right, I'll get the boys organized. Well done today, mate –' Harry doesn't finish his sentence; something is bothering him. 'You've got a good memory, Mo. What did old McMahon say to us at Southampton when we left Blighty?'

'Funny, I was thinkin' abaht that. He said, "A Royal Fusilier does not fear death. He is not afraid of wounds. His only fear is disgrace. I look to you not to disgrace the name of the Regiment. God speed, brave Fusiliers."'

Harry bites his lip. He is nearly in tears.

'Top man, McMahon . . .' His eyes filling, he pauses and looks at Mo. 'It's not bollocks, is it, Mo?'

'What's not bollocks?'

'All that regimental honour and disgrace pony?'

'I hope not, 'Arry; men are dyin' for it.'

'Fuckin' right, Mo. Thanks for lookin' after me this mornin'.'

'Don't mention it.'

'I went fuckin' berserk later. Dunno what got into me. I took out abaht ten of 'em!'

'You're just a good soldier, 'Arry. A bit mazawattee, but a fuckin' good Tommy. I'm glad you're on my side!'

General von Falkenhayn's final throw of the dice at Ypres has failed. With increasing pressure on the German Army from setbacks on the Eastern Front, he knows that any attempt to crush France in the short term will never happen. He now realizes, as do most of the astute generals, that a relatively small number of well-armed, resolute defenders can hold back a far superior force of attackers. It is a grim lesson learned at a terrible cost. In the First Battle of Ypres, he has lost over 50,000 men, killed or missing, with another 84,000 wounded.

The British Expeditionary Force has been destroyed. The statistics are horrifying. Most of the battalions that arrived in France at the end of August were composed of, on average, between 900 and 1,000 men, with an officer corps of approximately thirty. By the middle of November, the number of fit men, able to fight, averages thirty, with only one surviving officer per battalion.

In all, in just six weeks from 14 October to 30 November, the BEF loses 58,155 men: killed, missing or wounded.

Ominously, the end result of this mass slaughter is not victory for either side, or even the prospect of victory. The end result is stalemate along a huge meandering line from the Channel to the Alps.

Sunday 29 November

Belcaire, Lympne, Kent

November has not been a good month for Winston Churchill
and his family. After seeing the King at the end of October,
who was kind enough to compliment Winston's tenacious
warrior spirit, his mood improved. But it darkened again
shortly afterwards, largely as a result of yet more sniping from
the press and another naval disaster, the first defeat in a full
naval encounter for the Royal Navy for over a hundred years.

On 1 November off the Pacific coast of Chile, at Coronel,
a Royal Navy squadron under the command of Rear Admiral
Sir Christopher Craddock, comprising the *Otranto*, *Monmouth*,
Good Hope and *Glasgow*, engaged a German squadron under
the command of Vice Admiral Graf Maximilian von Spee.
Craddock had left his battleship, the *Canopus*, in Montevideo
to guard his coal ships and was ordered by Admiral John
Fisher, First Sea Lord, not to engage von Spee's squadron
without her.

For reasons not altogether clear – but more likely a product of his renowned bravery than wilful disobedience or
stupidity – he ignored the order and attacked. He was
out-gunned by the enemy, and his ageing, slower vessels were
manned by inexperienced crews that consisted largely of
reservists. *Good Hope* and *Monmouth* were sunk. A total of
1,570 men went to the bottom, Craddock included; he was
accompanied by his dog, which he always took to sea with
him. Von Spee's squadron was unscathed.

Although Craddock had disobeyed his orders, the circumstances of the encounter were not revealed publicly and

Winston took the blame for the ignominious defeat. Thankfully, Asquith and the War Cabinet were supportive. Later, the Prime Minister suggested to Winston that the navy needed to 'break some crockery and make a lot of noise doing it'.

Winston and Jacky Fisher immediately ordered the battlecruisers HMS *Invincible* and HMS *Inflexible* to sail south, despite the fact they were still undergoing repairs in Devonport Dockyard. When Winston heard that dockyard workers still needed to finish work on *Inflexible*, he ordered the cruiser to sail forthwith and take the men with her. Support ships were sent south to rendezvous with *Invincible* and *Inflexible* to create a powerful squadron. The orders were simple: find and destroy von Spee's squadron.

Only a day after news of the Coronel fiasco, Winston was further perturbed when he heard that, because of the heavy losses suffered around Ypres, the Oxfordshire Hussars, his brother Jack's regiment, would be going into the front line. Jack was likely to be under fire very soon. His anxieties for his brother were exacerbated on 6 November, when he learned of the deaths of two close friends.

Following the loss of his entire family fortune and the severe wounding of his twin brother, Francis, at Mons – for which he was awarded the Victoria Cross – Riversdale Grenfell was killed in action near Vendresse. Winston was very close to both men.

Major Hugh Dawnay of the 2nd Life Guards was the same age as Winston and had been at Sandhurst with him. They served together in South Africa, where he was awarded a DSO, and in the Sudan, where they fought together at the Battle of Omdurman. Dawnay was killed in action near Harlebeke on 6 November. He left four sons. Winston cried openly when he heard the news.

Winston received the only good news of the month on 9 November, when a letter arrived from Jack, telling him that he had been taken on to Sir John French's staff at British Expeditionary Force HQ and would thus be coming out of the front line.

Although it was one piece of good news, Winston's Black Dog still snapped at his heels. Clemmie, who had been having a difficult time since the birth of their daughter Sarah, went to stay as a guest of Sir Philip Sassoon at his new house, Belcaire, at Lympne on the Kent coast. Her absence became a major factor in Winston's depression, and even the letters between them became few and far between. He received one on 19 November that initially cheered him, but in which Clemmie mentioned that she was paying a mountain of household bills. That only served to remind him of their parlous personal finances.

She also mentioned that it was snowing heavily on the Kent coast. This made him very morose as he thought about the terrible conditions the men were facing in the trenches in Flanders.

During the month, Winston also crossed swords with both Lord Kitchener and Sir John French several times over his 'Dunkirk Circus' of armoured cars and the activities of his Royal Navy Division and Royal Marines on the French coast. They complained that he was continuing to interfere in army matters, when he should be concentrating on the navy. The Prime Minister was, on the whole, supportive. But being a consummate politician, he was prone to blow in the wind if it suited him.

On 25 November Asquith called a meeting of the War Council. Only the most senior members of the Cabinet were there: David Lloyd George, Chancellor of the Exchequer, Sir Edward Grey, Foreign Secretary, Lord Kitchener, Minister for War, and Winston, First Lord of the Admiralty. Arthur Balfour, former prime minister and now a senior member of the Conservative Opposition, was also invited as an elder statesman.

In answer to provocative probing by Balfour, Winston gave a bold and breathtaking account of Britain's naval defences against a German invasion. After the meeting, Asquith said of him: 'He has the glow of genius about him.' But Winston left the War Council as disconsolate as when he arrived.

However, waiting for him in Downing Street was his friend F. E. Smith, with a summons from Clemmie, a three-line whip insisting, regardless of naval matters or crises at the Front, that Winston must join her at Belcaire on the evening of the 29th because the next day, Monday 30 November, will be his fortieth birthday.

Entering his forties is not a rite of passage he particularly relishes. His father, Lord Randolph Churchill, fell from grace dramatically at a relatively early age and died at the age of forty-five. Winston has always firmly believed it unlikely that he will live longer than his father. Nevertheless, even if he contemplated it, FE would not permit him to decline Clemmie's summons.

Belcaire, Sassoon's new house, is only just completed. It has been built in Cape Dutch style, full of avant-garde art, and is surrounded by Italian terraced gardens. The lavish paintings and decor are not to Winston's taste; when he arrives, his mood darkens rather than lightens and he pronounces the place, 'Vulgar!'

To make matters worse, that morning he received a letter from his friend Valentine Fleming about conditions in Flanders. He read it in his car on the way to the Kent coast; its contents made him weep. Fleming wrote of a strip of land ten miles wide, stretching from the Channel to the Swiss border, littered with the rotting dead bodies of soldiers. He described in the most vivid terms the shapeless heaps of blackened masonry that once were farms, homes and churches, the repulsive distortion and dismemberment of horses, cattle and sheep, and the lines of men coated with mud, unshaven, hollow-eyed, unable to cope with the relent-less barrage of inhuman missiles from the sky.

While they are dressing for dinner, Winston begins to sob. Clemmie rushes to his side to console him.

'Darling Pug, whatever is the matter?'

'What do you think?'

'Black Dog?'

'Of course. They're trying to drive me out of the Admir-alty, I've fallen out with Kitchener and French, and I'm responsible for our first naval defeat since the war of 1812. Not only that, I'm lonely in Whitehall without you.'

'I know, darling, but I had to get away with the kittens. It's not good for them to be cooped up in Westminster with nowhere to play. Besides, I've been having rather a bad time of it myself.'

'Yes, of course; I don't mean to sound selfish. You were quite right to bring them down here. But listen, I've had a letter from Val Fleming. It's very morbid, but may I share it with you?'

Clemmie takes the letter and reads it with increasing dismay.

'How dreadful! It's hard to imagine.'

'I know, the world has never seen anything like it before –'

He stops himself and looks Clemmie in the eye. His boy-ish face looks even younger as tears stream down his cheeks.

'– and warmongers like me are responsible!'

Clemmie stiffens herself and adopts the tone of a scold-ing mother.

'Winston, you don't start wars, you win them. Pull your-self together!'

Clemmie hands the letter back to him. He notices that he had scribbled a note on it in the car, a thought that had sud-denly occurred to him: *What would happen, I wonder, if all the armies suddenly and simultaneously went on strike and said some other method must be found of settling the dispute?*

Clemmie's rebuke and the scribbled thought give him the stick with which to chase the Black Dog from his consciousness. He reasons that, if men like him buckle, enjoying the comfort and security of home and hearth in Britain, what chance have the poor buggers who are wet, cold and fighting in fear of their lives in Flanders.

He wipes the tears from his eyes, tugs at his waistcoat and pulls back his shoulders.

'Come on, Cat, I need a glass of champagne. I'm bloody well going to be forty tomorrow, so I'd better get on with sorting this bloody mess out. Oh, and remind me to tell Philip that my lobby porter at the Admiralty has more taste in interior design than he has!'

Over the next thirty-six hours, within the bosom of family and friends, Winston goes some way to clearing the murky shadows from his mind. Clemmie and Philip Sassoon have produced the ideal guest list for Monday evening's birthday celebrations.

Jack's wife, Goonie Churchill, is there with the children, Johnnie and Pebbin, as are F. E. Smith and his wife, Margaret. Eddie Marsh, Winston's private secretary, is also a guest, along with Winston's cousin Sunny, the 9th Duke of Marlborough, with his wife, the American Vanderbilt heiress, Consuelo. It turns out to be a most enjoyable evening of excellent food and wine, and even better company.

The next morning, refreshed and reinvigorated, Winston pays his host, Philip Sassoon, an unusual compliment.

'Dear boy, your taste in decor is hideous. But in every other respect, your worth is inestimable. Thank you so much.'

PART SEVEN: DECEMBER
Christmas Truce

Tuesday 8 December

HMS Inflexible, *Falkland Islands, South Atlantic*

Tom Crisp is leaning on the rail and looking over the port side of HMS *Inflexible*, staring at the bleak and rugged landscape of the Falkland Islands. It is midsummer in the South Atlantic, but the cold black sea heaving beneath him and the heavy rain clouds over the desolate islands remind him of Britain in winter. Not that he is too familiar with Britain's coastal waters. Before he left Presteigne, at the end of August, he had never seen the sea before.

The ordeal of his fallout with Bronwyn, when her relationship with Philip Davies was revealed, proved too much to bear. The despair he was feeling about her betrayal, and the inevitable humiliation that would follow both within his family and among his peers, made life in the small community impossible.

He packed a few things in a canvas bag, collected his tools from his employers and left Presteigne on the same evening as the shocking encounter at Pentry between Bronwyn and Davies's wife, Clara. He did not tell his parents what had happened, but left them a short note saying only that he had to get away and that they would soon hear why. He promised that he had not done anything wrong, that he was fit and well and would write to them when he was settled.

Fortunately, he had his carpentry skills to fall back on and was able to find work in Hereford for a couple of weeks. He then trusted in his hunch that there would be lots of work for skilled craftsmen in and around the military establishments. He found some work at Bovington Infantry Camp, in

Dorset, where he heard that the Royal Navy's dockyard at Devonport was desperate for skilled craftsmen of all kinds.

When he arrived there, he simply gawped at the gigantic scale of the Royal Navy's warships. By some distance, they were the biggest objects he had ever seen. He was put to work on HMS *Inflexible*, a giant over 170 yards long and weighing over 17,000 tons, with 6-inch-thick armour plating. He tried to picture what her size would mean to people back home. He concluded that she would not fit into Presteigne's narrow High Street, but could just about wedge herself in between the buildings of Broad Street. She would fill it from one end to the other and would be three times the height of the Shire Hall, its tallest building. She carried almost 1,000 officers and men, the same number as the whole of Presteigne and its surrounding parish.

Tom watched in amazement as the dockyards' stevedores carried aboard new provisions. He had never seen so many boxes, sacks and barrels, in addition to the armaments, hoisted aboard by cranes. There seemed to be endless numbers of cases of ammunition for her fixed machine guns and her company of Royal Marines. Then came hundreds of gigantic Lyddite shells, each one painted canary yellow with a red ring below the nose to warn that it had been filled with explosive.

Despite her colossal weight, he was told she was capable of over 26 knots – which meant nothing to him whatsoever – but when it was explained that this was equivalent to 30mph, he found it impossible to believe. Built by John Brown on the Clyde only seven years earlier, she was a new innovation, a 'greyhound', as quick as a cruiser, but armed like a battleship.

Her hull had already been repainted in dry dock on orders from the Lord of the Admiralty himself. She was a sight to behold. Every shade of grey imaginable, from gull grey to coal black, ran across her in bizarre patterns of swirls and stripes.

The dockyard painters said it was called 'camouflage' and had been designed by a chap from London who arrived in an Admiralty Rolls-Royce, complete with easel, and was dressed in a paint-stained smock. The men were distinctly unimpressed by his bohemian appearance, and especially by his name, Solomon Solomon, which caused much amusement and soon became 'Solly Solly the Silly Sod'! However, their opinion soon changed when, in less than two days, he reproduced *Inflexible* in his sketches in the most wonderful detail. He won them over even more when he sketched several of the men's portraits, signed them and gave them as gifts.

A week later, his designs arrived; 'battleship grey' was a thing of the past, and the painters had to spend days mixing colours to match Solomon's new colour palette. Four-letter expletives and the word 'gimmick' were much in evidence during the entire process.

Men swarmed all over her, replacing rivets, refurbishing boilers, painting her decks and interiors. Spanners clanged, hammers thumped and the painters sang and whistled as they made her gun turrets and funnels match her variegated hull. Particular attention was paid to her gunnery, which had been stripped and was being reassembled and calibrated.

Her sixteen 4-inch Mk III guns can hurl a 25lb shell 9,000 yards. Housed in four huge hydraulically powered double-barrelled gun turrets, her eight 12-inch Vickers Mk X goliaths can launch an armour-piercing Lyddite shell weighing 850lbs over fourteen miles. She also carries seven Maxim machine guns and five 18-inch Mk VI compressed-air torpedoes, which have a range of 4,000 yards. *Inflexible* is a leviathan, an awesome machine of war.

Tom fell in love with her as soon as he saw her.

He spent most of his early weeks below decks working with a team of men under the supervision of *Inflexible*'s Chief Ship's Carpenter, William 'Billy' Cawson. A Cornishman from Stratton – not far from the sea, near Bude, but a long way from anywhere else – he has completed thirty years' service in the navy, having joined at the age of fifteen. He should have retired in the summer, to run the Port William, a pub in Tintagel, which he has had his eye on for years. But, with the outbreak of war, his captain, Richard Phillimore, asked him to stay on 'until Christmas'.

Then, on 10 November, Billy heard that orders had arrived from the Admiralty that *Inflexible* and her sister ship, *Invincible*, being repaired in the dock next to her, were to set sail the following morning. So his retirement would have to wait.

When Tom and the other civilian craftsmen on board heard the news, they made the obvious point that their work had not yet finished. To which came the blunt reply that Mr Churchill, First Lord of the Admiralty, had ordered that any civilians with work still to complete must sail with the ships and finish their tasks in transit. Needless to say, there was great consternation, but the men's employers had already bowed to the inevitable and thus the men had to stay or lose their livelihood.

To make matters worse, their destination soon filtered down below decks. Chief Artificer Engineer Charles Richard had been told to get up steam for a fifteen-day, 15 knot marathon voyage south; first stop, Montevideo.

Most of the men had never heard of it. When they were enlightened, they all dashed home to their wives and families. Some called into church to pray; a few wrote wills on scraps of paper, or whatever they could find. And all the men – bar a couple, who had 'taken the pledge'– got drunk.

In a role that harks back to the days of timber ships and canvas sail, as Chief Ship's Carpenter, Billy Cawson is also a warrant officer, the navy's equivalent of an army serjeant. Apart from the engine room, steering, weapons and wireless, he is responsible for all structural and maintenance issues on board. He has a crew of thirteen: a mate, a blacksmith, two plumbers, two painters, an electrician, a cooper and five artisan mates. They look after the integrity of the ship, especially emergency repairs to any breaches of the hull or damage on deck. The loading and securing of the ship's cargo and dunnage is under Billy's charge, as is the maintenance, dropping and raising of the 150 tons of her anchor and chain.

Tom's work on *Inflexible*'s interior, especially the repairs and alterations to the wardroom and to Captain Phillimore's quarters, was completed just four days out from Devonport, after which he asked to join Billy's team. He discovered he had good sea legs – even in the bowels of the engine room, where even the most experienced men often submit to sea sickness – and found the work absorbing. The residue of pain from the memories of Bronwyn and Presteigne was still considerable, but his new life at sea did much to help him push it to the back of his mind. He had little time to brood and the further from home they travelled, the better he felt.

There has been so much to learn about the life of a 'Jack tar', most of it fascinating, some of it bizarre, and a few things offensive. Tom is amazed to discover that some of the junior midshipmen in the Gunroom – called 'wonks' by their superiors, who treat them with varying levels of degradation, including beatings and verbal humiliations – are only fifteen. Instead of going from Osborne House, the junior Royal Naval College, to Dartmouth to complete their officer training, they have been sent to sea.

While at Devonport, Tom soon heard the common naval expression, 'Ashore it's wine, women and song; aboard it's rum, bum and concertina.' Or alternatively 'rum, bum and baccy' or 'rum, bum and the lash'. At sea, he has become aware that behind the amusing ditty there are still some unfortunate practices. He has witnessed several incidents.

In one, the Gunroom President, the most senior of the three sub lieutenants, or 'subs' – called 'snotties' by the rest of the ship's company – assigned to the Gunroom, was feeling bored. Possessed of a vindictive streak, he shouted: 'All the young men are getting slack; half a dozen all round!'

After which, all six wonks were beaten across the bare arse with the Gunroom Punishment Stick and their chastisement recorded in the Punishment Book, a large leather tome with all the wear and tear of frequent use. One wonk, a lad scarcely fifteen years old, received six beatings before they got beyond the Canaries, the last one because some beard fluff had appeared on his chin. Sadly, because he had never shaved, he had not realized; nor did he have a razor with which to scrape it off.

On another occasion, the cry 'Uttings!' was heard. Despite the fact that it was not the name of any of the wonks, they had learned that they must respond immediately. The nearest one did so at the double.

'Yes, sir!'

'What use are you, Uttings?'

'No use at all, sir. None, absolutely bugger all. Sweet FA, sir.'

His prescribed response, which had to be repeated verbatim every time he was summoned, made the subs howl with laughter. The silly catechism of 'jolly japes' was repeated several times a day throughout the entire voyage.

When Tom got to know some of the boys, he discovered that most were from modest middle-class backgrounds. To his amazement he learned that, because they are still officially undergoing training, in order to supplement their meagre salary of 1s and 9d a day, their parents have to pay the Admiralty £50 a year. Tom wonders what will happen should the young boys be killed in a forthcoming battle.

Wonks are not permitted to smoke or drink spirits, but they are allowed a 10s wine bill each month. With port or sherry costing only 2d a glass, they soon acquire the habit of consuming large quantities of alcohol.

But the midshipmen wonks will, one day, be officers. Many

will go on to be commanders and captains with their own ships, and a few will even be admirals of the fleet. Not so, the junior ratings. On the early days of the voyage, Tom watched wide-eyed as boys of the same age as the midshipmen, some looking even younger, and certainly smaller, scurried around the decks going about their work. Many were barefoot, their trousers rolled up to their knees, looking for all the world like street urchins, which is what they were before being picked up off the street after some minor transgression and given the choice: 'The spike or the navy?'

Tom asked one, who looked no more than twelve and whose feet looked particularly raw after spending days scrubbing the decks in the wind and rain, why he did not wear shoes or boots.

'Never 'ad none, Mister.'

'Where are you from, lad?'

'Rotherhithe, Mister.'

'Do your parents know where you are?'

'Ain't got none, Mister. Am I in botha?'

'No, no, carry on.'

Young ratings on *Inflexible* carry the rank 'boy' and are, in effect, ship's servants until they are older and are given the rank of 'ordinary seaman'. There are nine boy telegraphists, five boy signallers and thirty-four boy seamen on HMS *Inflexible*.

Floggings in the Royal Navy were abolished in 1879, but the aura of rigid discipline is still present, and navy life is rich in curious rituals, peculiar phrases and odd behaviour. Tom finds it all intriguing. Although he has had to go through a highly disciplined and exploitative apprenticeship, he finds the navy's traditions unnecessarily harsh. But few of the older men on board agree with him, saying that the system instils discipline and, indeed, made them the men they are today.

As for the 'bum' and 'buggery' of naval ditties, nothing is ever said. As far as Tom can tell, there is no evidence of the ship's boys providing sexual gratification, willingly or otherwise, to the older men. However, the wonks and boys are also known as 'peg boys', and 'pegging' is an old-fashioned euphemism for fucking.

Eventually, on a sultry night near the equator, by which time Tom knew Billy Cawson much better, he asked him directly.

'Mr Cawson, if I may ask?'

'Ask away, laddie.'

'Well, I've enjoyed the rum, and I've seen the boys thrashed black and blue, but what about the buggery?'

'What about it?'

'Is it true, Mr Cawson, that the wonks are bum-boys?'

Billy laughed loudly.

'Look, lad. I've known it 'appen. Every ship's got a few pansies an' little lads who take it up the arse – probably got a likin' for it at school – but no more than on Civvy Street. You put a thousand men on a ship for six months, with no women for company, and some will end up shaggin' the ship's cat, let alone one another. Truth of it is, it is against King's Regulations and if ye're caught, ye're for the high jump.'

Tom thinks Billy's response is a very considered reply; he suspects this is not the first time Billy has been asked the question.

'Besides,' Billy continues, 'as I've always said, if a man's been caught buggering the boys, he's sent to a naval prison in Blighty, where he'll get right royally buggered 'imself. Serves the bastard right!'

Tom smiles, thinking this is an even better answer that obviously reflects Billy's true feelings on the matter.

And so, a few days after taking on coal at Montevideo, Tom is staring at the metropolis of Port Stanley. Billy Cawson joins him. It is 9.45 in the morning.

'Bloody hell, Tom, it looks worse than the Outer Hebrides – an' a godforsaken place that is!'

'There's no mistakin' it's a long way from Radnorshire too, Mr Cawson.'

Port Stanley is no more than a few streets with rows of small wooden houses covered by corrugated iron roofs. The only buildings of substance are Government House, with its quaint green roof, and the newly rebuilt, neo-Gothic Christ Church Cathedral.

Inflexible has taken on coal and is getting up steam. There is a sudden flurry of activity on deck, alerting Billy.

'Come on, lad, I think we're off!'

The Battle of the Falkland Islands is about to commence. Admiral von Spee's squadron has taken on coal at Picton Island from a captured British collier, but he is short on shells, having used a large part of his arsenal at the Battle of Coronel. For reasons unfathomable by his own senior officers, and despite being out-gunned by the British ships and slower than the 'greyhounds' *Invincible* and *Inflexible*, he decides to attack. His senior commanders advise him to make a run for Germany, but he chooses to ignore them.

He commands two armoured cruisers, *Scharnhorst* and *Gneisenau*, and three light cruisers, *Nürnberg, Dresden* and *Leipzig*. Besides *Invincible* and *Inflexible*, the British squadron consists of armoured cruisers *Carnarvon, Cornwall* and *Kent* and the light cruisers *Bristol* and *Glasgow*.

The day has improved; there is good visibility, the sea has become placid and the sun has broken through. As the mighty warship pulls away from Port Stanley, Tom and Billy go below decks to their battle station next to the engine room. Tom has never felt or heard the engines at full speed. It is like being in the belly of a giant beast as it digests its prey, the rhythm of the engines like the monster's beating heart. The heat becomes intense; the air thick with a heady mix of oil, coal and human perspiration.

At about 13.00 hours, the ship suddenly lurches to port,

throwing men off balance and sending anything not lashed down flying in every direction. Billy shouts at Tom.

'Brace yourself!'

Within moments there are two huge explosions, and the ship shudders. Tom's face becomes a picture of terror. He thinks *Inflexible* has been hit.

'It's all right, laddie, that's our big Vickers fartin'!'

The explosions then come in pairs at regular intervals. It is like being in the barrel of a gun, with every recoil juddering *Inflexible*'s superstructure as if it were in an earthquake.

'Jesus, Mr Cawson, it's like being in a biscuit barrel with a packet of 'apenny bangers!'

'Just say a prayer to thank him upstairs that you're not on the receivin' end!'

Von Spee's flagship takes extensive damage; its funnels are flattened and it begins to list. She sinks at 16.17, taking von Spee and his two sons with her; there are no survivors. *Gneisenau* sinks at 18.02, *Nürnberg* at 19.27 and *Leipzig* at 21.23. Two of the vessels produce multiple explosions as their armaments magazines go up. There are only 215 German survivors; a total of 1,871 men perish. The Royal Navy squadron loses ten men, killed in minor damage to the *Invincible*.

Tom goes up on deck to help the German survivors come aboard. Some are smooth-chinned boys, no older than the wonks and boys on *Inflexible*, but most are gnarled veterans of the Kaiser's marine: cooks and wardroom waiters, gunnery artificers and able seamen. In fact, the men of the two navies could be interchangeable.

Then the wounded German sailors are helped aboard. Some are badly burned, their clothes ripped off by explosions, their skin blackened like overcooked meat. Bright-red blood oozes from the worst burns, making them look like hot embers in a hearth. Lifeboats are lowered to help the worst cases. Bodies are pulled up to check if there is still life in them; if there is not, they are put back like the unwanted catch from a fishing net.

Tom has not been sick for the entire trip, but he is now. He has never seen anything like it.

Inflexible's Ship's Surgeon and his Sick Berth Stewards are going to have a busy night. But no matter how hard they try, they are unlikely to be able to save the worst burns cases as they will not be able to prevent infection. Those who die on board will be buried at sea in the time-honoured naval tradition, sewn into sailcloth, weighted with whatever is to hand and cast overboard. In Nelson's day, the dead were sewn up in their hammock, with the last stitch through their nose to make sure they were dead rather than unconscious, then a couple of round shot at their feet to take them to the bottom.

The German dead are blessed just like British tars with the immortal words used on such occasions.

We therefore commit his body to the deep, looking for the general Resurrection in the last day, and the life of the world to come, through our Lord Jesus Christ; at whose second coming in glorious majesty to judge the world, the sea shall give up her dead; and the corruptible bodies of those who sleep in Him shall be changed, and made like unto his glorious body; according to the mighty working whereby He is able to subdue all things unto himself.

It has been Tom's first experience of war, but he witnessed the battle in semi-darkness, miles from the focus of the action. Not a single bullet, nor an explosive shell, came anywhere near him, and yet he feels exhausted and troubled as if he has been in the thick of it.

Billy Cawson consoles him.

'Tom. We don't live or die like soldiers, who fight face to face with the enemy. We die with our ships; if our ship survives, we all live; if she goes down, we all go with her, or we end up like these poor sods.'

After the Battle of the Falkland Islands, raids on commercial shipping around the world by the Kaiserliche Marine, the Imperial German Navy, cease. Britain's naval supremacy across the world's oceans is restored.

Tom Crisp soon gets over his first experience of war and settles into life on board HMS *Inflexible*. Although he needs a little more time before he is certain, he is confident that when they next reach a British port, he will ask Billy Cawson to take him on permanently as part of the ship's company.

Wednesday 23 December

Tommy and his fellow volunteers Mick, Vinny and Nat feel much more like real soldiers and much less like the Boy Scouts they were accused of being in November. The taunts that greeted them from less than generous observers as they marched past have stopped.

Uniforms of Kitchener's melton blue, rather than khaki, arrived early in December and the volunteers thought they looked very smart, positively handsome, in their matching side caps worn at a jaunty angle. Some young girls even wolf-whistled as they passed. Rifles arrived two weeks later, as did horses for the officers, most of whom had to learn how to ride them and also find somewhere to stable them.

With appropriate military paraphernalia came proper training. Range practice began on Hambledon Moor, as well as proper military exercises, including manning outposts and picketing. Lectures and demonstrations were given in rifle maintenance and map reading; in many instances, lessons in the basics of reading, writing and arithmetic were needed. Route marches became longer and more arduous, the worst being what the lads called the 'Witches' Marathon' – thirty-five miles over the Nick O' Pendle and back through the haunts of Pendle's famous witches, Old Mother Demdike, Anne Chattox and Alice Nutter.

The route took them past Nat Haythornthwaite's front door, in Sabden, where 'Mrs Twaites' invited Nat and his mates in for a cup of tea and a rest. They managed to drop out without being seen and rejoined the column on its return. However, someone must have snitched on them and they each got one week's field punishment, which was ordered to be a timed, six-mile march every morning at 6 a.m., including Sunday.

The excursions of C Company on the moors above the town have led to some amusing incidents.

During one exercise, Tommy's platoon was high on a moorland road, doing a picketing exercise. He and Mick, who were acting corporals, sent Nat and Vinny to a remote spot miles from anywhere, where they were told to close the road to anyone unless they used a password. They saw no one all morning and were freezing cold as biting Pennine winds blew sleet and snow all around them. Then, early in the afternoon, an old farmer appeared through the snow with his sheepdog. Vinny asked him where he was going.

'None o' thy business,' was the abrupt reply.

Vinny tried to assert his authority.

'Well, tha'll need t'password when tha comes back, old fella.'

'Will I now?'

'Aye.'

'So what's t'password?'

Vinny realized that Tommy hadn't told them what password to use, but Nat came to his rescue and made one up.

'Dirty Gertie!'

Vinny could not believe the name Nat had chosen. The old farmer looked stunned.

'Don't be bloody soft, I'm not sayin' that,' he muttered, and wandered on his way.

Two hours later, the old man returned, bow-legged and wizened, with his white muffler wound tightly around his neck and his clogs jangling along the road. When he was challenged, he ignored the two men in blue and walked past.

Nat looked at Vinny.

'What do we do now?'

'I think we're s'posed to shoot 'im.'

'We can't do that.'

'Why not?'

'Cos all our bullets are blanks!'

'Well, should we at least tell 'im 'e's been shot?'

'Might as well.'

Vinny shouts after the old farmer, who has, by now, almost disappeared in the swirling snow.

'Eh, old fella; tha's been shot!'

'Nay, lad; tha's missed!'

On another occasion, a platoon would not let a delivery lad from Oddies' Pies pass their checkpoint unless he handed over a tray of pies 'for t'ungry lads defendin' King and country', or so they said.

Oddies complained to Captain Slinger, the battalion adjutant, and the miscreants all received one week of field punishments. The price of the pies was deducted from their pay.

As well as the four 'Accrington Pals', several others in Burnley's Keighley Green Club are in uniform. Because John-Tommy Crabtree, the former steward at the club, is a Pal, the Club has become D Company's main watering hole. John-Tommy is there with some older men. Cath and Mary are also there; it is their night off from washing pots. Cath is huge; she has still not given birth, although the midwife thinks she is at least two weeks' overdue.

They had invited their Burnley officers to join them, but army protocol demands that officers and men do not fraternize openly. The Thorn Hotel, only 200 yards from Keighley Green, Burnley's oldest tavern, and situated in the middle of the town amidst its better shops, has become D Company's unofficial officers' mess. The Thorn has several luxuries not typical of most of the town's public houses. One of them is fitted carpets, even in the bar, another is bar food and a third, perhaps the most radical, is no spittoons.

Tomorrow will be Christmas Eve and everyone in the Keighley Green Working Men's Club is in festive mood.

The Pals are having a late drink, having been at Accrington Town Hall for a battalion Christmas concert. It was a great success, and all the acts were performed by the officers and men. There was good humour between the battalion's companies from different towns: A Company (Accrington lads), chided D Company (Burnley lads), while B Company (from Blackburn) did the same to C Company (from Chorley).

John Harwood, Mayor of Accrington and founder of the battalion, gave a speech before the concert. He spoke well and with considerable East Lancs pride in what has been achieved. He also talked with some pathos about the casualty figures from France and about the plight of men at the Front shivering in their trenches. He knew that none of it would discourage the 900 men in front of him; quite the reverse, they are made of sterner stuff.

C Company's contributions to the concert included Captain Raymond Ross and Lieutenants Riley, Heys and Tough singing – reasonably melodiously – extracts from *HMS Pinafore* by Gilbert and Sullivan, although Fred Heys clearly had a much better voice than the other three. CSMs Severn, Muir and Lee played the spoons and brought the house down. Not only were they dressed in Egyptian fezzes and caftans, which seemed to have no relevance to a rendition of spoon harmonies, but their playing was neither tuneful nor in unison.

Hoots of laughter rolled around the town hall as the three hard men, a Cockney, a Scot and a Devonian, who had spent the previous two months berating the inadequacies of their Lancastrian charges, turned a musical routine into a comedy act. It was hilarious and convinced those present, who had begun to wonder, that their company serjeant majors were human after all.

During the concert interval, presents were distributed. Each man went onstage to collect a neatly parcelled gift of two pairs of socks from the officers' wives and from Elizabeth Sharples, the wife of Battalion CO Colonel Sharples. A boxed, initialled silk handkerchief was also given to each of the officers, including the colonel, who looked more delighted than anyone else, leading everyone to the conclusion that he was not used to receiving presents from his somewhat severe-looking wife.

At the end of the evening, Colonel Richard Sharples addressed the men. He droned on a little but, right at the last, produced the biggest cheer of the night.

'Ladies and gentlemen, I am delighted to be able to tell you this evening that, two days ago, we heard from the Ministry of War that the 11th Battalion East Lancashire Regiment will go to barracks in Caernarvon, North Wales, to complete their military training in early February next.'

At long last, the tedium and discomfiture of playing at soldiers in their own backyard will be coming to a definite end. The men had begun to think that they would never leave their hometowns and that the war would be over before they had a chance to prove their mettle.

John-Tommy Crabtree comes over to Tommy and Mick's group.

'Alreet, Mary; Cath, that's a reet lump tha's got there, when it's due?'

'Dunno, John-Tommy, feels like it shoulda been born a week last Christmas!'

'So what are you two gonna do while these daft apeths laik at soldiers in Caernarvon?'

'Mary an' I reckon we're gonna go down south an' drive ambulances.'

'Can you drive?'

'No, but one o' t'lads at Trafalgar Mill said he'd teach us on mill's lorry.'

'But how will yer find a job?'

'Easy, Henry Hyndman said he get us sorted. Mary winked at 'im. He fancies Mary does old Henry.'

'What about t'child?'

'I'll take it wi' me.'

John-Tommy then turns to the quartet in blue.

'Hey up, Tommy, an' what dost reckon to thy lasses runnin' off down south?'

Mick smiles mischievously.

'They can suit th'sels, they ollus do. Me an' t'lads'll be chasin' them Caernarvon lasses around.'

Cath clips Mick around his ear.

'If you go anywhere near 'em, I'll 'ave yer knackers off an' I'll put 'em in a jam jar on t'mantelpiece. So think on!'

John-Tommy quickly changes the subject and turns to Nat and Vinny.

'So it's off to Caernarvon fer us. Yer know they 'ave a different language yonder?'

Nat is perplexed.

'But it's in England, in't it?'

'Nah, lad, it's in Wales; they're Welsh.'

'So what do they speak, John-Tommy?'

'Welsh, Nat.'

'Are they on our side?'

There is laughter all round, but Cath's swipe at Mick has stirred her loins. She suddenly grasps her abdomen and lets out a moan of pain.

John-Tommy is the first to react and tells Mick and Tommy to help Mary get Cath to the club office. He looks at the big clock above the bar. It's almost midnight. He smiles at Cath reassuringly.

436

'Looks like tha's gonna 'ave a Christmas Eve baby, our Cath.'

Cath is too preoccupied to notice John-Tommy's words. By the time she is helped into the office she has almost given birth. John-Tommy pushes Mick into the office with his wife and Mary and gets everybody else out. He then grabs Vinny.

'Go an' get old Ma Murgatroyd! Number 8, Parker Street, just round t'corner. Run, lad!'

Ma Murgatroyd, who used to be a midwife, is fast asleep when Vinny hammers on her door, and she takes a while to get dressed. By the time they get to the club, they are too late.

The baby, a boy, has been born.

But there are no celebrations, no cries from the little infant. The lad is stillborn and nothing can be done to help him.

Ma Murgatroyd confirms that he is dead and that he almost certainly died some time ago in the womb.

Cath and Mick are inconsolable; it will be a very sad Christmas for the Burnley Pals.

Friday 25 December

Blair Atholl Castle, Perthshire

From the outside, Blair Atholl Castle on Christmas Day 1914 looks much as it has always done. With fresh, thick snow on the ground and no overnight visitors to spoil the virginal blanket on the drive, the white stucco walls blend perfectly with the landscape of the estate and the glens all around. Only the grey slates of the conical roofs of its turrets and its many windows break up the pure white panoply.

But much has changed at Blair. It is the quietest Christmas celebration in living memory. The pipes and drums of the duke's private army, the Atholl Highlanders, are silent. Many of its men have volunteered for the army; as for the rest, the duke has asked them to stay away. There will be no piper playing from the battlements today. There have been too many deaths in France of men from the estate and the local community. Although not yet in mourning, the duke is sure that his middle son, Lord George, 'Geordie', is dead.

More bad news arrived at 6 p.m. on Christmas Eve, courtesy of a willing young lad who brought the telegram from the village post office in the middle of a snowstorm. After spending several weeks at Blair recovering from his infected leg wound, Hamish returned to his regiment in France, the Cameron Highlanders, early in November. However, his company did not see action until 20 December, when he led them in an attack on German positions at Givenchy, near Ypres. The attack was a success and the German trench was

438

taken. But late that night, while reconnoitring his defences with a small patrol, he was ambushed. Two of his men were killed. The telegram was brief and to the point.

> Regret to inform, Major Lord James Stewart-Murray, 1st Battalion Cameron Highlanders, taken prisoner, enemy forces, Givenchy, 20 December 1914. Whereabouts unknown. Reported unharmed and safe.
>
> Kitchener.

The old duke, having been locked away with his mistress in her cottage in Glen Tilt for most of the winter, had dragged himself away to host Christmas lunch for his immediate family. Already desperately morose about Geordie, the telegram from the Ministry of War was too much for him and he immediately took to his bed, refusing all visitors. Lady Helen decided that she had no choice other than to send for his 'lady friend', Mrs Grant, who promptly took him back up to her cottage. He was in tears as he left.

There will not be the usual houseful of guests at Blair this year; there will be none of its renowned gaiety, and certainly none of its notorious debauchery. Lady Helen has given most of the servants the week off. She has invited her friend from Edinburgh, David Tod, and Bardie and Kitty have travelled up from England. Lady Dorothea, 'Dertha', and her husband, Harry Ruggles-Brise, who is still recovering from his shrapnel wounds, have also arrived from England, but only late last night, delayed by the snow.

So the family gathering is just six. They have all risen late and taken a very sombre breakfast, coming to terms with the news of Hamish. They decide to exchange presents before lunch and then to sit down together for the best Christmas fare Blair Atholl's vast estate and fine kitchen can muster. There will be beef, goose and turkey, all Blair meat, and the vegetables will be those grown on the estate and in the kitchen gardens and greenhouses. Mrs Forsyth, the butler's wife who runs the kitchen with a rod of iron and is never addressed by any other name, even by her husband, has made the stuffing, pudding, cake, mince pies and sorbets.

It is also agreed to plunder the cellar for the 7th Duke's favourite Bollinger and three bottles of 1900 Château Petrus, the finest vintage in a generation. Bardie asks Forsyth to bring up some Monbazillac for pudding and a Grande Champagne cognac for the men with their cigars. He means to ensure that some kind of Christmas cheer comes to the Stewart-Murrays, even if it has to be induced by alcohol.

Bardie says grace before lunch and asks everyone to think of Geordie, in the hope that he has managed to survive, of Hamish, hopefully not too cold or miserable in a German prisoner-of-war camp, of poor old Father, heartbroken about what has happened to his family, and of Evelyn, about whom nothing has been heard for some time.

After Bardie has finished, and the servants begin to serve lunch, Lady Helen produces a surprise.

'Amidst the gloomy reports, I have some good news. I have just received a letter from darling Evelyn.'

She begins to read as, for the first time since they arrived, everyone is able to smile.

Dearest Father,

I have taken a little cottage in the woods near Spa. Very quiet here, no hint of fighting. My rooms in Malines are just about in one piece, but the damage is extensive. Like the rest of the town, windows are gone, blinds are rags, china smashed to dust, furniture in splinters. I doubt I will ever return.

But I am well, and my faithful companion is so kind to me.

Please send my love to all at Blair at Christmas,

Evelyn

David Tod offers a thoughtful response.

'All of us here, safe in Scotland, let us give thanks.'

'Hear, hear!' is the response from everyone.

Harry Ruggles-Brise, shifting uneasily in his chair as his shoulder injury makes him wince, makes polite conversation.

'So, Kitty, what have you been up to?'

'Well, I go to London on VAD business once a week. But it's a long way from Blagdon; it's a bit of a bore, really.'

'Blagdon?'

'Blagdon Hall, Matty Ridley's home. He's a Tory MP and Colonel of the Northumberland Hussars –'

Bardie breaks in and takes over Kitty's account.

'Kitchener is still bothered about the east coast and has ordered me up to Northumberland at the beginning of the month.'

'With the whole of the Scottish Horse?'

'Yes, three battalions of us. Wouldn't let even one battalion go to France.'

'Bloody stuff and nonsense! There's no possibility of a German invasion. I don't often agree with Churchill, but in that respect, he's spot on.'

'Harry, strictly on the QT, I spoke to Kitchener the other day. Churchill and Lloyd George are cooking up a scheme to launch a spring offensive in the Dardanelles to get the Central Powers fighting on another front. He told me he's earmarked the Horse for the campaign.'

To the annoyance of the two soldiers at the table, who cannot understand how an Edinburgh merchant with a part-time line in sculpting can possibly have an opinion about war that is worth listening to, David Tod offers his view.

'A wise strategy, it seems to me. If there's a stalemate in France and Belgium, another front makes sense.'

Bardie shrugs off David's opinion.

'Whether it does, or it doesn't, is neither here nor there. I'll leave that to Kitchener and French. But if it gives my boys a chance to fight, then I'm up for it.'

Harry then chips in.

'I have to say that, although Churchill has some military experience, he has never been in a position of high command; after all, he's a bloody politician, for God's sake! And now we've got that odious little Welshman sticking his oar in.'

Helen draws a line under the conversation.

'Kitty, Dertha, shall we withdraw?'

The three ladies of Atholl settle in the drawing room. Unbeknown to the men, who are happily drinking cognac and smoking the finest Bolivar Cuban cigars, Helen has secreted a bottle of Bénédictine, her favourite tipple, under her chair.

'Ladies?'

An increasingly intimate conversation ensues as the liqueur bottle empties. Eventually, Kitty's relationship with Bardie comes up.

Helen is blunt.

'So, Kitty, how have you persuaded Bardie to keep his trousers on?'

'I haven't. He can do what he likes with his trousers. But now we're on an equal footing, which means other men's trousers are within my compass once more.'

Dertha is impressed.

'Well done, Kitty. I'm pleased to say that I don't think Harry has the imagination to stray. What about you, Helen, are you going to take the leap with your sculptor? He seems very sweet.'

'I think I might. Father will be upset, but he's now got other things on his mind . . .' Helen's eyes fill with tears. 'Everything is changing. What will become of us?'

Kitty takes the question to another level.

'I worry for Bardie and for the family. When he inherits the title, will it mean anything? Old Europe is dying, and I

fear Old Britain is dying with it. All those men being slaugh-
tered at the Front! Will the survivors come back and accept
the world they left behind? I doubt it. You know I don't agree
with the suffragettes, but do we really expect to deny working
men the vote when they're dying in multitudes for a country
they have no say in running?'

Dertha is shocked.

'Really, Kitty, you sound like a communist! Harry says, if
we give everyone the vote, we will be under socialist rule
within five years.'

'He may be right. But it may not be possible to stop it happening. And it may not be right to do so.'

Helen is less shocked than Dertha, but is still surprised.

'Kitty, you sound just like David; he says much the same.
You should go into politics.'

'Perhaps I should.'

The conversation gradually becomes less and less erudite,
the mood more and more solemn, until Christmas Day
1914 at Blair Atholl ends in a drunken haze. Everyone fears
for the future and knows that the carefree days of the past
are probably gone for ever.

At the stroke of midnight, after consuming the greater
part of a bottle of Glenmorangie, the 7th Duke of Atholl
cries himself to sleep in the arms of Mrs Maud Grant in her
modest Glen Tilt cottage.

British Army Field Hospital, Provoost Lace Mill, Poperinghe, West Flanders, Belgium

A British Army field hospital in one of the most dangerous
zones of the Great War is not an ideal setting for a Christmas
celebration. Neither are the hospital's celebrants in the best
of spirits. Many are badly wounded, some are dying; all would
rather be anywhere else. Back in the trenches with their

mates, no matter how wet and cold, would mean that at least they are fit and well. Home would be perfect, but they know that is not going to happen.

In addition to those with war wounds, there are plenty of men with infectious diseases, respiratory problems and a growing number with an ailment the doctors are struggling to define. Some call it 'nervous fatigue', others call it 'mental exhaustion' and a few – those of less generous spirit – call it 'malingering'. The latest description, which attempts to relate it to its most obvious cause, is 'shell shock'.

The milder cases wander around aimlessly in a world of their own, their eyes lost in the 'thousand-yard stare'. The worst cases find corners in which to hide, where they shiver and convulse like sick dogs. Some shout and scream, and a few become violent and have to be restrained. In fact, Surgeon-Captain Noel Chavasse has insisted that Brigade assigns a squad of infantry to the hospital to help with recalcitrant patients.

Because 'hospital' is '*hôpital*' in French, it has not taken long for the field hospital in Poperinghe's old lace mill to be called 'Pop-Hop'.

Sadly, Christmas Day did not start well at Pop-Hop. Two men died of their wounds on Christmas Eve, and when Margaret arrived for duty early on Christmas morning she found the night staff searching frantically for a missing man. A Coldstreamer from Berwick, he talked the night before about not being able to bear the thought of Christmas. Already missing his left arm, he had been told he would have to lose his right because gangrene had set in. He was found an hour later in an outbuilding. He had cut the wrist of his offending arm and bled to death.

The doctors, nurses, auxiliaries, orderlies, stretcher-bearers and ambulance drivers are all exhausted, but they are trying hard to make the day as enjoyable as possible for the sick and injured.

Hywel Thomas, his hand in a sling, is doing sterling work, helping men eat and drink and talking to them to boost their morale. His new purpose in life has given him a vitality that inspires many of the patients and is also often a boost to the demoralized staff. His reconciliation with Bronwyn has grown stronger by the day, and they have helped one another come to terms with the loss of their brothers.

Hywel's reinforced glove has arrived from London and Captain Chavasse allows him to wear it for an hour a day when his sling and bandages are removed to clean his wound. He is fortunate that his hand has remained free from infection and that he has good movement in his thumb and some feeling in his index finger. His glove is a very simple but clever device. An extra-large, officer's black cavalry glove, it has been reinforced by sewn-in, bendable copper rods that allow Hywel to position his fingers to help him secure the barrel of his rifle.

Thoughtfully, Desoutter Brothers have also sent the other glove of the pair. He wears both when he is practising holding his gun outside the hospital, as it means that he gets the same feeling in both hands. He is soon christened the 'Black-Handed Assassin' by the other patients. Understandably, he is impatient to fire his rifle, but Captain Chavasse has expressly forbidden it for the time being and insists that he only rests the rifle gently on his injured hand.

Major Hesketh-Prichard has visited Hywel twice to discuss the training programme for the army's new School of Sniping. On his second visit, he brought Hywel's new serjeant's stripes with him which, much to Hywel's amazement, also included a crown.

The major explained.

'We thought we might as well make you a colour serjeant, as you may well be teaching other serjeants how to shoot!'

'But, sir, I've only just turned twenty.'

'I shouldn't worry about that! There are shave-tail

officers younger than you who are on the front line leading thirty men.'

'Well, thank you, sir.'

Smiling proudly, the major then handed Hywel a pair of small brass lapel pins, sporting a design of crossed rifles topped by an 'S'.

'The new insignia for all who pass through the new School of Sniping. Yours is the first pair.'

'Major, they look very well. I'll treasure them, but I think I might put 'em in my pocket when I'm out snipin'. I've been sniped by a fellow sniper once before, and I don't intend lettin' it 'appen again.'

The major then produced a gleaming new rifle from its canvas bag.

'I have another present for you. I have spent many days at the Royal Small Arms Factory in the Lea Valley, in London, working with its armourers. This is the experimental P13, intended to replace the standard-issue Lee-Enfield. It has a Mauser-type action and has been fitted with a new telescopic sight based on the one you took from the German at Zwarteleen. The primitive long-range sights used by British snipers in the Boer War have remained largely unchanged. Thanks to you, these are much better. The Ministry of War has approved an order for an initial production of three hundred and fifty sights.'

'When will we get them, sir?'

'Hopefully, in time for our first recruits in the spring. Let me know what you make of the rifle and the sight.'

He then asks his batman to bring over a large box of rifle ammunition.

'I've brought you a box of the latest .303 Green Spots to practise with when your hand is healed.'

Hywel still has revenge on his mind but, bolstered by his serjeant's stripes, he is beginning to channel it into the zeal of a professional soldier.

'So I still 'ave time to get back to my battalion, sir?'

'Yes, I'll give you a month. In the meantime, I need to find three more training officers and ten NCOs.'

While things are beginning to improve for Hywel, Bronwyn is still emptying bedpans and mopping floors. But her recovery seems complete and her youthful vitality has returned. She is very much a favourite among patients, doctors and any male visitors to the ward. She has had to learn to live with all kinds of banter, innuendoes and overt propositions. Being a lot worldlier than they know, she is able to deal with almost anything. A typical situation was witnessed by Hywel, who was about to rush to her aid when he realized that she was more than capable of taking care of herself.

A precocious young Scouse gunner from the Royal Artillery, who had lost two fingers in a gunnery accident, suggested he needed help from Bronwyn.

'Nurse, can I 'ave a bottle?'

Bronwyn hurried away, came back with an enamel urine bottle and handed it to the now grinning gunner.

'Can you 'elp me with it, gorgeous?'

Bronwyn did not bat an eyelid, but lowered her voice seductively.

'Do you mean, help you put your . . . er . . . artillery piece in the neck of the bottle?'

The young lad leered.

'That's right, darlin'. An' you can give it a tug while you're at it.'

Bronwyn leaned forward, by which time every soldier on the ward was hanging on her every word.

'Well, if you can get your little weapon in there, I'm not interested. I prefer real men with ten-inch howitzers!'

The Scouser was duly admonished as hoots of laughter reverberated around the ward. Bronwyn's crude rejoinder became the talk of Pop-Hop for days.

Bronwyn and Margaret are in their usual haunt, Pop's

Maison de Ville. It is the end of a long day, made even longer by the staff's attempts to provide a semblance of Christmas joviality, including a lunch of roast pork. It was cooked by Pop-Hop's cooks, who butchered a pig caught near the Front by an eagle-eyed and fleet-footed gunner on Christmas Eve.

The women's relationship is still close but, other than work matters and pleasantries, little has been said between them since, some weeks ago, Margaret confessed to her love for Bronwyn.

Bronwyn sees that Margaret is deep in thought.

'Are you all right?'

'Yes, just tired.'

'Come on, Margaret, what's the matter?'

Margaret's eyes redden; she throws her head back.

'It's Hamish; I heard yesterday from an officer in the Camerons that he was taken prisoner a few days ago.'

'I'm so sorry. He seemed like a nice man.'

'Yes, he is – a bit of rogue, but nice with it.'

'Have you fallen for him?'

'Not really, but I'm very fond of him. And now I won't see him until the end of the war, if ever.'

'I'm sure you will. Try not to worry, you'll see him again.'

Bronwyn scrutinizes Margaret as she stares into her empty wine glass. She fills it with more of Maison de Ville's cheapest *vin de table*, which, over the weeks, seems to have become less and less cheap and more and more unpalatable.

'I never asked, but how was your dinner with Hamish?'

Margaret smiles.

'The dinner was wonderful. But that's not what you meant, is it?'

'I suppose not; so, how was your *night* with Hamish? Did he "make a woman of you"?'

'Bron, that's unkind.'

'Sorry, it was. You've been so wonderful to me; I just want you to be happy.'

Margaret takes a quaff of her wine and follows it with a cavernous breath.

'I had a nice time with Hamish; he was very sweet and gentle. I tried, Bron.'

Bron reaches out and touches her hand. Margaret smiles, but tearfully.

'The truth is, I am what I am.'

'Oh, Margaret, it's hard for me to understand. Don't you enjoy men at all?'

'Bron, it's hard to answer questions like that.'

'Remember, it's me! You know all my little secrets and have taught me not to be ashamed.'

'I feel some things, but it's not the same. The truth is, I'm queer; a freak!'

Bronwyn pushes Margaret's glass away and puts her arm around her.

'You're nothin' of the sort; you're a wonderful woman, my saviour. I love you so much. And I don't care that you prefer women, I still love you. Come on, let's go home; we both need some sleep.'

Bronwyn leads Margaret away, in a tender reversal of their roles when Margaret rescued Bronwyn in Tiger Bay. When they get back to Margaret's room, Bronwyn helps her undress and puts her to bed.

As Margaret rests her head on the pillow, the tears of the woman who runs her ward like Florence Nightingale – proud, dignified and supremely professional – run down her cheeks and soak into the rough cotton sheeting.

Bronwyn strokes her brow.

'I love you, Margaret.'

Margaret opens her eyes.

'Bron, do you remember that night when you asked me to stay with you? When you were very upset –'

'Yes, I do.'

'Will you stay with me tonight?'

'Of course.'

Bronwyn slips off her dress and climbs into bed with Margaret, where she holds her like a mother would cradle a child. Margaret's tears subside and her anxiety diminishes.

'Thank you, Bron.'

Margaret closes her eyes and is asleep very quickly, leaving Bronwyn to reflect on their strange circumstances. She feels so much love for Margaret, but no hint of arousal by being close to her. She realizes how hard it must be for Margaret to live in a world where emotions she cannot prevent herself from feeling are regarded as so wrong.

She also knows that, sooner or later, she is going to meet a man who will help her regain her own sexual feelings. And when that happens, it will be very difficult for Margaret to deal with.

10 Downing Street, Whitehall, London

A reinvigorated Winston Churchill, for once in receipt of modest praise following the navy's victory in the Battle of the Falkland Islands, has spent most of December feverishly looking for ways to break the impending stalemate on what is becoming known as the 'Western Front'.

'The Balkans!' he would cry. Or, 'The Baltic!', 'The Caucasus!' He has written memos, harangued his friends and lectured his War Cabinet colleagues: 'We must strike at the Turks!', 'Russia: how can we help the Czar to hit harder in the East?'

With the passionate, mercurial but vastly experienced Jacky Fisher at the Admiralty, Winston has been able to concentrate on the broader canvas of the conflict. Inevitably, it has led him into clashes with his colleagues and the renewal of denunciations by the Tory press.

Sadly, as the circumstances of the war have worsened

towards Christmas, the men in charge of its execution, normally shrewd and considered, broad-minded and wise, have begun to lose sight of even the most obvious circumstances, and have started bickering like juveniles.

On 17 December Winston wrote to Asquith, asking if he could go to France to see for himself what his 'Dunkirk Circus' of planes, marines and armoured Rolls-Royces was up to. He also wanted to use the opportunity to see Sir John French and boost his morale. Asquith's reply insisted that Winston seek the approval of Lord Kitchener before going. When he duly did so, instead of replying, Kitchener went to Asquith to complain that the First Lord of the Admiralty was, yet again, interfering in the strategic business of the army.

Winston was furious that Kitchener had gone to the Prime Minister instead of replying directly to him, and a series of sternly worded letters followed. Ultimately, it was agreed that Winston could go to France for his inspection, but not to see John French. Winston resented the snub bitterly.

Similarly, as many had predicted, and especially Clemmie, Jacky Fisher's volatility was becoming as much of a burden as a bonus. Letting his temperament get the better of him and seemingly unable to differentiate between his laudable forcefulness and his sheer bloody-mindedness, he was rapidly making enemies. Many in the Admiralty and the Conservative Party began to say that the only difference since Fisher's return to the Admiralty has been that it is now ruled by two Churchills, when one was already too much to bear.

By Christmas Day, the spat among Britain's war leaders has calmed down as they prepare to spend Christmas with their families, and as the press and MPs do the same. It is not so in the trenches, where the rain, mud and cold pay no heed to Christian feast days. At least the Germans are Christians, so the shelling and sniping have become more and more sporadic.

Herbert Asquith has spent Christmas Day with his family – his second wife, Margot, and his youngest children, both Margot's, Elizabeth and Anthony. But he has now returned to Downing Street, where he knows his private secretary and mistress, Venetia Stanley, will be waiting for him. He has been drinking, even more than his usual prodigious volume, and is feeling amorous. It is six thirty; they will have an early supper and retire to their top-floor love nest for a Christmas night of passion.

As he prepares to sit down and relax, he looks across Horse Guards Parade and sees that the lights are on in the First Lord's office in the Admiralty.

'Bugger me, Churchill's at his desk! Something must be up.'

He looks down at the mound of papers on his desk and sees a large red 'Top Secret' stamped on the memo at the top of the pile. It is a report from Colonel Alfred Knox, British Military Attaché in Petrograd. It is a startling document, describing in great detail the state of affairs on the Eastern Front, where Russian and German forces have been locked in a conflict every bit as gruesome as that on the Western Front. He describes, 'an alarming shortage of rifles', 'men in the front line facing the enemy without ammunition', and quotes the words of a disillusioned general who said that the sturdy Russian infantrymen can scavenge for potatoes and turnips in frozen ground, but that bullets don't grow in fields.

The memo ends with the chilling words: 'I fear an imminent collapse of the Russian Army.'

'Venetia, get Churchill for me. I want him to come over.'

'But, Bertie, it's Christmas Night. What about our supper together?'

'Worry not, the night is young. Where is Lloyd George?'

'He'll be with Frances next door, I should think. I'm sure he said he would spend Christmas Eve and lunch today with Margaret and his family, then come back here this afternoon.'

'Will he be sober?'

'About as sober as you, I imagine.'

'Get someone to go to Number Eleven and ask him to come over for a drink.'

'What's going on, Bertie?'

'A bit of a crisis with the Russians; you can read Knox's memo later. Send someone, Special Branch or a policeman, to fetch Eddie Grey; he'll be at home with Pamela. Then send someone to bring Kitchener; he'll be at Carlton Gardens with one or more of his boys. Hopefully, as it's only six thirty, he'll still have his trousers on.'

By 7 p.m. on Christmas night, Britain's War Cabinet is assembled at Downing Street. Venetia pours whisky for them and Asquith promises that their business will be done by eight thirty, in good time for their private suppers.

Venetia assesses the mood as she carries around the decanter of fifteen-year-old Macallan. Only Winston appears happy to be there. Lloyd George, as eager as anyone to find a solution to the crisis in France, would normally be keen to attend any emergency meeting. But his recent passion for Frances Stevenson, formerly the governess to his youngest child, Megan, and now his private secretary, is a major distraction. Eddie Grey seems impatient, probably feeling guilty about leaving his wife on Christmas night. As for Kitchener, Venetia is not sure what delights he has planned – nor does she want to speculate. She makes her exit, thoughtfully leaving the Macallan behind her.

'Gentlemen, you can thank Colonel Knox in Petrograd for this, and Winston, of course, who spotted it first. Knox says the Russians are on their knees. He fears a collapse, and we all know what that will mean in the west, come winter's end. Now, I know you all have different thoughts, but I think you all agree that we need to open a new front to dilute the Central Powers' military capabilities. Winston, you go first.'

'Thank you, Prime Minister. I will be brief. Nobody here

needs me to reiterate how dire the position is in France, and how long it will be before we can put Lord Kitchener's courageous new army into the field. But, if you will indulge me, I will reiterate one sentiment once more: thank God for the courage and elan of our French friends and for brave little Belgium, who are both holding their ground so fearlessly.'

Even though every man there wants the gathering to be as brief as possible, Winston holds them enthralled for twenty minutes as he not only summarizes the situation but does so with such bravura that he resembles a Shakespearian thespian rather than a politician.

'For my sake, I'm wholly committed to a plan that Jacky Fisher and I have designed – a ferocious, direct attack on Germany from the north-west. First, we will seize the island of Borkum in the North Sea. Then, using Borkum as a springboard, we will hurl ourselves against the foe in vast numbers in Schleswig-Holstein. We will take the Kiel Canal, bring in neutral Denmark and launch a daring naval attack into the Baltic. Finally, with massed ranks of Russian infantry at our side, in the greatest amphibious assault in history, we will put a hundred thousand men ashore on the Pomeranian coast and smash our way through to bring Berlin and the Kaiser to their knees.'

Winston sits down with a self-righteous look on his face, raises his tumbler and takes a deep draught of his whisky. His peers, their faces creased by admiring smiles, are quiet for a moment. They are impressed by the plan, but much more by the way Winston has described it.

David Lloyd George then stands up.

'Winston, you are a hard act to follow. But let me say that, if things get worse and there comes a time when – as Henry V at Agincourt, or Queen Elizabeth at Tilbury – someone has to make a speech to save this nation, then you're the man to do it.'

Lloyd George begins his peroration with a distressing

portrayal of the plight of the men in the trenches, enduring the kind of conditions that 'would destroy the morale of the best of men'. He argues vociferously that the war cannot be won in France without casualties on an as yet unimagined scale. He then describes in detail a 'Southern Strategy', which he finishes with a summary.

'So you see, Salonika is the key on one side, engaging the support of all those who hate the Austrians: Serbs, Montenegrins, Romanians and Greeks. Then, on the other side, Syria, where we strike the Ottoman Turks at their weakest point.'

Kitchener has said nothing. Although he has some sympathy for a southern offensive, he remains convinced that the war will be won or lost on the Western Front, if only because that is where such hordes of men face one another and where the thousand-year rivalry between the Germanic and Gallic civilizations is being played out.

Winston senses the exhaustion in the room, which is not helped by the dwindling contents of the whisky decanter. He sees that both the 'Northern Strategy' and Lloyd George's 'Southern Strategy' have merits.

'Prime Minister, if I may, there is a middle position, which Fisher and I would both support. First, a feint of the kind I have described in the North Sea, with fewer Russian forces, which would disorientate the enemy, followed by another disguise, as David has described, towards Ottoman Syria through Alexandretta. Thirdly, an additional feint attack from the north on Constantinople from Bulgaria and, finally, a major amphibious landing from Greece, Malta and Egypt through the Dardanelles, probably on the Gallipoli Peninsular. From there, Constantinople beckons.'

Following the mention of the evocative name 'Constantinople', a debate ensues, sometimes heated. Reference is made to the traumas of the Crimean War of 1854, and even to the Christian Crusades of 800 years ago.

The name 'Gallipoli' does not strike a chord with anyone, but it soon will.

After the gathering, which does not end until 9.45 p.m., the senior protagonists of Britain's war effort make their way home. Winston goes back to the Admiralty; not to Clemmie, who is still at Lympne, and not to his bed, which will not welcome him for several hours yet, but to the Admiralty Map Room. He gathers two sleepy marines on sentry duty to help him lay out the huge maps of the Eastern Mediterranean. They pin some on the wall before Winston lets them resume their duties.

He then pours himself another whisky – this time his favourite, Glenmorangie – and studies the Bosphorus, especially the landing sites on the western and southern coasts of Gallipoli. After several hours of note-taking, analysis and scrutiny, he marks three crosses on the Gallipoli Peninsula: Cape Helles, Suvla Bay and a small cove north of a headland called Gaba Tepe.

Satisfied that he has done his homework, he retires to bed. It is 3.45 in the morning. As he passes the marines on duty in the Central Hall, he bids them goodnight. They snap to attention.

'Do you need a wake-up call, sir?'

'Yes, thank you; six thirty sharp!'

Kemmel, West Flanders, Belgium

Christmas Day on the Western Front begins inauspiciously. The air is cold, the sky leaden and a haze hangs over the land as if the clouds have descended to drape a dank blanket across the ground. There are patches of snow in places, especially up against trees and hedges, but the immediate landscape is as it has been for weeks, a sea of Flanders mud.

Everywhere and everything is scarred or destroyed. Not a

single building stands undamaged, and most are in ruins. The fields are pockmarked by the impact of shelling, which makes the landscape resemble the craterous surface of the moon – even more so in the silvery glow of the moon itself. Hedgerows are shredded, trees shattered and the deep ruts of artillery gun carriages, ordnance lorries and field ambulances criss-cross between the craters, creating random lines and patterns.

Like rats scampering in sewers, some creatures survive in this wasteland. They live in snake-like scars in the ground, parallel to one another, in separate colonies, competing for territory and the means of survival. They kill their rivals without provocation and in vast numbers and, like lemmings, will occasionally rush at the other's lair in suicidal attacks. These creatures were once ordinary men; now they are part hero, part beast.

The trenches are the worst horror of this wretched environment, where the front-line troops live, eat, defecate and die. It is all but impossible to keep dry, and certainly impossible to keep clean or retain simple human dignities. They are foul places in every sense of the word: a place to eat, but usually standing up; a place to sleep, but only fitfully; a latrine, but with no privacy; and a charnel house, where decaying corpses, or parts of them, protrude from the walls.

The pristine appearance of the professional soldier on both sides of what is now being called 'no-man's-land' has long gone. Every item of clothing has had to be modified or improvised and there is a plethora of garments to insulate or waterproof the body. Following the delayed arrival of greatcoats, sheepskin body warmers have arrived from Britain, as have heavy-duty woollen balaclavas, socks, mittens and gloves. Long johns are a godsend, and most men would prefer a pair of those from the Red Cross than any amount of cigarettes or chocolate.

Indulgences like chocolate are all but meaningless when

hot food and clean water are difficult to find. Scavenging for anything that strays nearby is essential, and Flanders' entire population of domesticated animals was consumed before winter began. Now, nature's larder of rabbit, hare and birds, especially the highly prized pigeon, is diminishing rapidly. The latest source of meat for those with the strongest stomachs – meat that is both the scourge of the trenches, and sometimes its finest delicacy – is roasted rat. At least a consignment of coke braziers has arrived, making it easier to heat food and warm cold fingers.

Lice and sores from a lack of cleanliness only add to the misery. There is also the return of an ailment not seen since Napoleon's *Grande Armée* made its infamous retreat from Moscow. Caused by long-term exposure to wet, cold and unhygienic conditions, the soldiers' feet become sore, infected and even gangrenous. The medics have begun to call it 'trench foot'. Its only cure is to reverse the circumstances that cause it.

Diseases spread rapidly; many bodies still lie in parts of no-man's-land, unburied since they fell, sometimes many weeks ago. So bad is the smell that men wear scarves around their mouths and noses, even when the weather is mild, just to try to keep at bay the stench of open latrines and human putrefaction. A strong wind is like a blessing from heaven. It plays havoc with the accuracy of the snipers and drives away the stink.

All the local civilians have long gone so, around Ypres, where British troops face their German foes, both sets of men are alien to one another, surviving in an alien land without people, which lends yet another surreal dimension to an already bizarre world.

Occasionally, an intrepid soul will wander into the fields of death. A farmer may walk for miles, managing to evade the sentries guarding the roads, to bring a chicken or a piglet to sell for an exorbitant price. Other, less savoury, characters will offer contraband: stolen cigarettes, wine, or various highly intoxicating concoctions produced by home-made stills.

Then there is the 'little chocolate girl', a tiny mite, no more than eleven or twelve, who appears once a week with a knapsack full of chocolate. She will never say who sends her, or where she gets the chocolate from, but does admit that she took the knapsack off a dead British soldier; *'un homme portant une jupe'* she says, whenever she is asked, which at first meant nothing to the soldiers, until an officer explained that it means 'a man wearing a skirt'. Then they realized the dead man must have been from a Scottish regiment.

The chocolate she brings is instantly recognizable to the men: 'Caley's Milk Chocolate, made by A. J. Caley in Norwich', with its emblem of crossed Union Jacks on the wrapper. So it must have come into the possession of her family, or fence, illegally. But it is of no concern to the men as she will exchange a bar for two cigarettes or a couple of coins of any denomination.

It is a mercy that, as winter has bitten ever harder, the clashes between the men in the trenches have diminished. Sniping is still an occasional hazard, and there have been sporadic artillery exchanges, but the will to fight seems to have been dulled on both sides.

That is a blessing in more ways than one, for both sides are desperately short of ammunition and men are finding it hard to clean and maintain their rifles. As a consequence, improvised weapons are commonplace.

Close-quarters encounters have taught men that a long rifle with a bayonet attached is not the most manoeuvrable of weapons. So a multitude of improvised knives, clubs and axes has appeared. A toothed gear from the gearbox of an abandoned vehicle jammed on to a pickaxe handle is a particular favourite, as are various 'trench cleaners', small daggers made from kitchen knives, or farm implements.

Knuckledusters, billhooks and chains are in common use, and some men carry barbed wire to use as a garrotte.

Home-made grenades – 'jam tins', as they have come to be known – where an old ration tin of jam or condensed milk is filled with dynamite, loaded with shrapnel of stones or nails and fused by a roll of gun cotton, prove to be very effective.

However, on the whole, the greater enemies are now mud, lice, hunger and lethargy. Inevitably, morale has plummeted and indiscipline escalated. The annihilation of the greater part of the officer cadre and of the experienced NCOs has left men without leadership. Those officers and NCOs who remain are finding it difficult to maintain basic discipline, let alone preserve the men's willingness to fight.

Harry Woodruff and Maurice Tait have been assigned to separate companies in the 4th Battalion Royal Fusiliers for the first time in their army careers. Maurice has remained in C Company as its colour serjeant, and Harry has gone to be colour serjeant in B Company.

After Colonel McMahon's pugnacious charge in early November at Hooge, they soon had to withdraw from the advanced position they had gained. They ran the risk of being isolated at the small farm they had captured, which was 100 yards beyond the British line, so Harry and Maurice led their fusiliers back. It was a well-executed withdrawal. Even so, it cost six men their lives, and a dozen more were wounded, but it earned them a message of thanks from Brigade HQ.

After resting in dry billets at Festubert for over a week, they have been back in the line at Kemmel, six miles south-west of Ypres, since 21 December. Their two companies are adjacent to one another in the trench, but the men in both are hardly recognizable as those who left Albany Barracks with Harry and Maurice in August. Between them, they can count just eighteen men they remember from those days in the summer.

Harry has been given the bar to his DSM and has become a regimental legend. Maurice is also of legendary status, and the survival of both is thought to be close to miraculous. Needless to say, under their firm rule, both B and C Companies of the 4th Battalion Royal Fusiliers are tight ships with few of the morale and discipline problems affecting so many other battalions.

The new commanding officer, Major John Hely-Hutchinson, is a strong disciplinarian and has immediately imposed his authority on the battalion. Captains Lee, Pipon and Magnay arrived at the end of November. But Lee broke his leg two days later, after falling into a shell hole, and Magnay had a breakdown – an 'attack of the shakes' – during his first artillery bombardment.

Four more officers and thirty reinforcements arrived in Belgium on 11 December, followed by two more young lieutenants on the 19th. Maurice likes his new CO, Captain George Marshall, fresh from duty in Hong Kong. Harry liked his new man, Captain Francis Bovey, but he was killed by a sniper late on the afternoon of the 21st.

Harry was standing next to him and had warned him about putting his head too far above the parapet. He was lying on top of the trench using his field glasses to survey the German position barely 150 yards away. Harry left him to check on the men; when he returned, Bovey was still in the same position. Harry spoke to him, but there was no response, so he pulled him down into the trench.

He was already dead. His face was unharmed, save for a small bullet entry hole above his left eyebrow. But the back of his skull was missing, the shoulders of his tunic drenched in blood. He had been at the front for just seven hours after an eighteen-year career with the Indian Army dealing with civil disturbances and border patrols. Yet again, Harry had no CO and, as its colour serjeant, was temporarily in charge of B Company.

Coming back to a trench after a leave of absence is almost as bad as an extended stay in one. There are the familiar deprivations, filth and lice to deal with but also, at first, the detritus and squalor of other men. The 4th Royal Fusiliers have relieved the Worcesters – good men, heroes of the charge at Gheluvelt – but they are not their own, and it is never the same.

The battalion had been inspected by the King on 3 December, which, apart from the honour, was a major boost to morale as it meant delousing, hot baths, clean shaves, neat haircuts and laundered uniforms. For the first time in many weeks, they looked and felt like proper soldiers. The fusiliers lined up along the Menin Road outside Ypres, but the King kept them waiting for forty-five minutes, in the cold, presumably because he was inspecting several other battalions in different locations. He arrived in a fleet of cars, accompanied by a host of brass hats, and began his inspection immediately. He looked impressive as he walked past in his army greatcoat with its dark-brown fur collar, an added luxury that many men looked at enviously. He nodded appreciatively at the men from time to time. A quick chorus of 'three cheers for the King' was shouted; then he was gone.

It snowed on the 22nd and the men talked briefly about a white Christmas. But then it thawed, and the mud returned.

Harry and Maurice have agreed to meet first thing on Christmas morning at the section where their two companies adjoin in the trench. Dawn has just broken. Each has an enamel mug of tea in his hand.

''Appy Christmas, Mo.'

''Appy Christmas to you, mate.'

'Quiet, ain't it?'

'Too right, 'specially for your Captain Bovey; 'e's gonna be quiet for a long time.'

'Silly bugger, I told 'im to keep his noggin' down! Poor sod, 'e'd only just got 'ere. How you gettin' on wiv Captain Marshall?'

'Oh, 'e's all right, a bit quiet. He's gone off to Brigade, left me in charge, said he'd be back tonight; I reckon he's gawn off to get pissed.' Maurice points in the direction of the German trench. 'Did you 'ear Fritz singin' carols last night? Sweet, it were. Some of our lads joined in; they was singin' "Silent Night" in Fritz, but our lads could follow it and sang along wiv it.'

'You need to be careful, Mo. The boys are s'posed be fightin' the fuckers, not singin' Christmas carols wiv 'em.'

'I know, 'Arry, but it's Christmas.'

'Bollocks, it's no different from any other day. It's dog eat dog, like it's always been.'

Maurice smiles at his friend, good old 'Arry, just the same.

As the two men swig their tea, they hear a distant voice.

'Happy Christmas, Tommy!'

The voice, in heavily accented English, is clearly coming from the German trench.

Harry is immediately alert.

'What the fuck!'

As he throws the dregs of his tea into the bottom of the trench, several young fusiliers come running.

'Colour Serjeant, it's Fritz! They're shoutin' at us all along the line, in English. One of 'em has a Christmas tree with candles on it. 'E's put it on top of the parapet and is sittin' next to it, large as life. What do we do?'

Harry does not hesitate.

'Shoot the bugger!'

He rushes towards where the young soldier came from, pursued by Maurice.

'Fuck a duck! What's goin' on?'

As he runs along, he sees more and more fusiliers sitting on the parapet of the trench.

'Get your heads down, you stupid fuckers!'

Then he sees a lance corporal from Bermondsey, a good lad he has known for years. He is standing in no-man's-land, in full view of the enemy.

''Ere, Sarje, 'ave a butcher's at this.'

He offers Harry his hand to help him up and then helps Maurice up. Maurice smiles, while Harry is open-mouthed.

'Bugger me with a brass rod up a black mountain!'

Through the milky mist, all along the long line of trenches in both directions, German and British troops are in no-man's-land. There are handshakes, smiles and laughter; there is sign language and exaggerated gestures as men try to communicate with one another. Several Germans can speak English and are in great demand as translators.

Harry is ill at ease and looks around anxiously. He is in temporary command of over 100 men, some of whom are very raw recruits. But he is relieved to see through the mist that among the men who are fraternizing together there are several German and British officers.

'I've never seen anythin' like it! What d'ya reckon, Mo?'

'It's a right rum do, I should cocoa! I s'pose we get on wiv it an' shake 'ands wiv a few Fritzes.'

The next hour or so is spent by the men exchanging gifts: beer, wine, cigarettes, chocolate, caps and helmets, badges and insignia. There is also the grisly business of decomposing bodies. Because no-man's-land has been true to its name for many weeks, it is strewn with the corpses of the dead.

Groups are formed, comprising men from both sides, who cooperate together in burial parties and undertake the gruesome ordeal of digging pits for their dead comrades. British and German men are alongside one another and prayers are said by parsons and pastors, sometimes together.

The most senior officer in Maurice and Harry's sector is a

captain they can see in the distance, who is in the Black Watch, but there is no one from Brigade to spoil the party.

There are more German officers around, including several Hauptmanns, the equivalent rank to a British captain, and one very tall and imposing major whose uniform looks immaculate and who wears his leather Prussian greatcoat draped jauntily over his shoulders without putting his arms into its sleeves. He is smoking a Sobranie Black Russian cigarette from an ivory cigarette holder, the business end of which is carved into an eagle's claw.

Undaunted by his striking appearance, and despite the stern look of the two fierce serjeants either side of him, Harry walks up to the tall German and salutes him.

'Excuse me, Major, do you speak English?'

'Of course, Colour Serjeant . . . ?'

'Woodruff, sir.'

'I was at Cambridge before the war, Colour Serjeant Woodruff, where I played football for my college, Pembroke. Do you play football?'

'Well, I did as a lad, sir, for Upton Park in West Ham, a London team.'

'It is a very good game, is it not? Would you like a cigarette? And the other serjeant?'

'Colour Serjeant Tait, sir.'

One of the German's staff serjeants hands around cigarettes from a silver cigarette box.

'Where are your officers?'

Harry has to think quickly.

'Er . . . they're 'avin' a Christmas breakfast at a gaff . . . sorry, at a 'ouse nearby, sir. They've left us in charge, we're old 'ands, see.'

'How very civilized.'

'Sir, will you be here for a while?'

'I don't think so; I will go back to my billet for lunch soon. Why do you ask?'

Harry looks at Maurice. Sometimes Cockney rhyming slang comes in useful, especially in the presence of a German officer who is fluent in Standard English.

'His Majesty's pleasure?'

'You mean those little red riding hoods we put in the safe and sound?'

'You got it, Mo!'

'Good thinkin'! I'm on.'

The German major looks perplexed.

'You are confusing me, gentlemen?'

'Sir, can we be 'onest wiv yer, soldier to soldier?'

'I would be delighted. Honour among soldiers is a rare commodity these days.'

'Well, sir, we took an 'elmet an' sword from a German officer who was killed at Herlies in October. We found out he was called Major von Mecklenberg.'

'A very famous man. I'm sure his sword will be very valuable; you are lucky.'

'Indeed, sir. But you see, there was an incident later, when another officer, Captain von Tannhausen, who told us who von Mecklenberg was, was killed.' Harry looks down guiltily. 'Let's just say he shouldn't 'ave died, sir.'

'I see. So how can I help?'

'Would you take his sword and helmet back to Major von Mecklenberg's family? It's the least we can do for him and Captain von Tannhausen.'

'That is very noble of you, Colour Serjeant. I will gladly do it.'

'But sir, one of us will have to go and get it. And it will take a while.'

'Not to worry. If I'm not here, one of my serjeants will be. This one is Walter and the other one is Fritz. Yes, he is called Fritz. And you are?'

'Harry and Maurice, sir.'

'Very good. How long will you be?'

'Probably well into the afternoon, sir.'

'Try to be back before dark, it will make things much easier. By the way, tell your officers when they have finished their Christmas breakfast that I plan to put an end to this, I suppose we should call it a "Christmas truce", at dawn tomorrow. I will be firing a single shot in the air. Until then, we will honour the ceasefire that has occurred in this sector. I will go to my fellow officer down there and tell him the same.'

'Thank you, sir.'

'No, no, it is a little moment of sanity in a crazy world, so let us treasure it while we can. And thank you for returning von Mecklenberg's belongings. I know his family, they will be very grateful, and I will make sure they know the names of the men who made the gesture.'

'May we 'ave your name, sir?'

'I am Count Christian-Günther von Bernstorff. You may have heard of my father, he is the German Ambassador to Washington.'

While Maurice keeps an eye on the no-man's-land truce, Harry takes his trenching tool and rushes to Merris to retrieve the Prussian helmet and sword. Merris is eight miles away, across the border into France. He is able to hitch a couple of lifts but, even so, by the time he gets back to Kemmel, it is mid-afternoon and the light is beginning to fade.

Maurice then leads Harry to where the two German serjeants, Walter and Fritz, are sitting, smoking cigarettes. The two men jump to attention and salute as the Tommies approach them and the formal handover takes place.

Walter tries to speak in English.

'The major, he say, thanks to you.' He then hands over two bottles of cognac. 'From the major . . .' The serjeant hesitates, then looks at his comrade. '*Frohe Weihnachten*?'

Fritz translates into English.

'Happy Christmas.'

Maurice smiles appreciatively.

'*Fro Vynakten* to you, Fritz!'

The four men shake hands, and Harry and Maurice stroll back to their trench admiring their fine bottles of cognac. They will both have sore heads in the morning.

'Guess what, 'Arry.'

'What?'

'You missed a big international match today.'

'How d'yer mean?'

'We played the Fritzes at football.'

'I 'ope we beat 'em?'

'Nah, but we might 'ave if you'd played. We lost 2-1. They 'ad some good lads. Shame, innit? We'll be shootin' the buggers tomorra.'

As he said he would, at first light the next morning, Major Count Christian-Günther von Bernstorff ordered Walter, his staff serjeant, to fire a single round into the still air. As its echo reverberated across the dreary landscape of Flanders, men on both sides knew that the Christmas truce of 1914 was over.

A brief moment of sanity, and a few expressions of friendship and common humanity, will soon be forgotten as the hatred and carnage resume.

Epilogue

The year on the Western Front ends with a forbidding line of barbed wire and trenches running from the North Sea to the Alps. To establish its meaningless position, over 600,000 men have died. Over 300,000 young Frenchmen are dead, as are 240,000 Germans, not counting another 140,000 on the Eastern Front. Belgian dead number 30,000 as do the number of British dead, all of them experienced veterans of Britain's elite professional army. Yet more horrifyingly, these statistics are only the beginning. Slaughter on an even greater scale is yet to come.

Of the 402 miles of the Western Front, the noble Belgian Army holds the northern 22 miles and the indomitable French Army guards 360 miles to the south. In between, the scant remnants of the glorious BEF form a bulwark of just 20 miles, but it is a vital sector that protects the northern flank of Paris and one that will soon expand. With the Allies digging in deeper and deeper, and more and more elaborately, only yards from where their German enemies are doing exactly the same, the future looks even more desolate than the terrors of the previous five months.

The horrors of 1914 and the extraordinary toll of the dead would surely have persuaded sane men that enough was enough and that reason should prevail.

But wars do not make men more sane, they make them more savage. And the Great War produced savagery on a scale never seen before.

Erich von Falkenhayn, the German Commander-in-Chief, knew in November 1914 that the German High Command's Schlieffen Plan, to strike a quick-fire killer blow to the French, had failed. In addition, the increasing ordeals on the Eastern Front against the Russians were drawing more and more men and materiel away from the west. The two circumstances led him to a profound conclusion: the German cause would, ultimately, be doomed. His homeland would, slowly and inexorably, be bled to death. He advised the Kaiser to sue for peace, but was ignored.

So the Great War will go on. The year 1915 will see the first Zeppelin raids on London and the east coast, and more Royal Navy ships will be destroyed by German U-boats. The passenger ship, RMS *Lusitania*, will be sunk in controversial circumstances off the Irish coast, creating uproar in the USA. It will bring the catastrophe of the Dardanelles Campaign and humiliation for Winston Churchill, as he is made the scapegoat for this sorry episode. Asquith will remove him as Lord of the Admiralty, but offer him the insignificant role of Chancellor of the Duchy of Lancaster.

His political career will appear to be over, and the press will rejoice in the fact. Clemmie will later say that she thought he would die of grief. Churchill will resign from the Asquith government in November and go to the Western Front, where on New Year's Day 1916, he will become Lieutenant-Colonel Winston Churchill, Commanding Officer, 6th Battalion, Royal Scots Fusiliers.

Although Herbert Asquith will continue as Prime Minister, his grip on power will be significantly weakened, caused by the crisis of a catastrophic shortage of shells and the fallout from the Dardanelles debacle. He will form a new coalition government with the Conservative Party. Arthur Balfour will be given the Admiralty, replacing Churchill. Lord Kitchener, popular with the public, but increasingly unpopular with the Cabinet and the army, will be stripped of his powers over munitions, which will be given to a new ministry under David Lloyd George. Lloyd George will emerge as Prime Minister-in-Waiting.

In the country, pre-war tensions over social deprivation, votes for working-class men, women's suffrage and Irish Home Rule will

470

surface again as the social, economic and political impacts of the war begin to hit Britain hard. Lloyd George's new Ministry of Munitions will bring all weapons production under government control and thousands of women will flock into the weapons factories – the Munitionettes – but at wages much lower than men's rates. The Ministry of Agriculture will launch the Women's Land Army – the Land Girls – to help with food production, with the slogan: 'God speed the plough and the woman who drives it.' Women will also begin to move into every sector of industry in vast numbers, including welders, machine operators, stokers, riveters, clerks and civil servants, signalling the beginning of the end of domestic service and fundamental changes in trade unionism.

It will be the year when the new revulsions of flame-throwers and poison gas will be added to mankind's awful catalogue of the instruments of death. There will be a Spring Offensive and an Autumn Offensive, leading to more carnage at the Second Battle of Ypres, and the battles of Neuve-Chapelle, Festubert and Loos.

The Great War will escalate to every continent and the tally of the wounded, missing and dead will add more and more digits. At the end of the year, other than the arithmetic of death, little will have changed on the battlefield.

Another Christmas will pass in abject misery. But, this time, there will be no Christmas truce; hatred will have extinguished all hope of peace.

Acknowledgements

I am indebted to the following primary sources for the factual background to this fictionalized account of the Great War during 1914. Each represents astonishing dedication to the cause of presenting accurate historical detail. Such diligent endeavours are often much more valuable than textbook histories, which usually give only a partial view and are invariably heavily laden with opinion and interpretation. Needless to say, I have used many of them, but they are too numerous to list here. Nevertheless, I am grateful for their insight.

The Community: Presteigne

Glover, Michael & Riley, Jonathon. 2007. *'That Astonishing Infantry': The History of the Royal Welch Fusiliers 1689–2006*. Pen and Sword Books.

Howse, W. H. 1945. *Presteigne Past and Present*. Jakemans.

Laws, Sarah & Purcell, Clare. 1998. *Impressions of Presteigne: An Oral History*. Menter Powys.

Leversedge, Cherry. 1988. *Pictorial Presteigne of Bygone Days*. Leominster Print.

Parker, Keith. 2008. *A History of Presteigne*. Logaston Press.

Royal Welch Fusiliers Museum, Caernarfon Castle, North Wales.

Ward, Dudley H. 2005. *Regimental Records of the Royal Welch Fusiliers (Volume III: 1914–1918, France and Flanders)*. Naval and Military Press.

The Regiment: Royal Fusiliers

Fusilier Museum, Royal Regiment of Fusiliers, Tower of London.

O'Neill, Herbert Charles. 2002 (new edition of the 1922 edition). *The Royal Fusiliers in the Great War*. Naval and Military Press.

The Politician: Winston Churchill

Gilbert, Martin. 2008. *Winston S. Churchill (Volume III: The Challenge of War 1914–1916)*. Hillsdale College Press.

Soames, Mary. 1998. *Speaking for Themselves: The Personal Letters of Winston and Clementine Churchill*. Doubleday.

The Estate: The Stewart-Murrays, Dukes of Atholl

Anderson, Jane. 1991. *Chronicles of the Atholl and Tullibardine Families*. Atholl Estates.

Hetherington, S. J. *Katharine Atholl, 1874–1960, Against The Tide*. Aberdeen University Press.

Katharine, Duchess of Atholl. 1958. *Working Partnership*. Barker.

The Pals: D Company (Burnley Company), 11th Battalion, East Lancashire Regiment, 'Accrington Pals'

Chapman, Tom. 2006. *Old King Coal*. Tom Chapman.

Duke of Lancaster's Regiment, Lancashire Infantry Museum, Fulwood Barracks, Preston.

Haworth, John. 2000. *Another Time, Another World*. Burnley and District Historical Society.

Jackson, Andrew. 2013. *Accrington's Pals: The Full Story*. Pen and Sword Books.

Turner, William. 1993. *The Accrington Pals*. Pen and Sword Books.

Whelan, Peter. 1982. *The Accrington Pals*. Methuen.

I am also more grateful than words can adequately express to all those at Michael Joseph/Penguin Books for their faith in me and their outstanding professionalism.

Finally, to my family and friends – thanks for being so supportive, generous and absolutely wonderful!

Dramatis Personae

(In approximate order of first appearance or mention, using the name by which they are known in the novel.)

The Community: Presteigne

Henry Kewley, 58, born in Ludlow: Rector of St Andrew's, Presteigne.

Aaron Griffiths, 63, born in Radnor: local entrepreneur.

Philip Davies, 40, born in Hereford: auctioneer, Urban District Councillor for Presteigne and Captain, 1st Battalion Royal Welch Fusiliers.

Hywel Thomas, 19, born in Presteigne: farmer, eldest son of the Thomas family of Pentry Farm.

Morgan Thomas, 18, born in Presteigne: farmer, second son of the Thomas family of Pentry Farm.

Bronwyn Thomas, 18, born in Presteigne: farmer and domestic, only daughter of the Thomas family of Pentry Farm, twin sister of Morgan.

Geraint Thomas, 17, born in Presteigne: farmer, third son of the Thomas family of Pentry Farm.

Tom Crisp, 19, born in Presteigne: local carpenter.

Margaret Killingbeck, 24, from Muker, Swaledale: sister, Queen Alexandra's Imperial Nursing Service.

Francis Orme, 23, from Godalming: Lieutenant, 1st Battalion Royal Welch Fusiliers.

John Hughes, 36, from Prestatyn: Colour Serjeant Major, 1st Battalion Royal Welch Fusiliers.

Noel Chavasse, 29, from Oxford: Surgeon-Captain, 10th Battalion King's (Liverpool Regiment, Liverpool Scottish). He graduated with a First Class degree from Oxford in 1907 and ran in the 400 metres for Great Britain in the 1908 Olympic Games in London. He is one of only three men to have won the Victoria Cross twice, the first time on 9 August 1916, at Guillemont, France, and later on 2 August 1917, at Wieltje, Belgium (awarded posthumously).

Dame Emma McCarthy, 55, born in Paddington, NSW, Australia: highly decorated wartime nurse. She received the Queen's and King's Medal (1902), the Royal Red Cross (1902) and a bar (1918), the Florence Nightingale Medal, the Belgian *Médaille de la Reine Elisabeth*, the French *Légion d'Honneur* and *Médaillé des Epidémies* and was appointed Dame Grand Cross of the Order of the British Empire (GBE).

Emma Maud McCarthy left Australia in 1891 to study nursing in England. After qualifying, she was appointed as a sister at the London Hospital and served as Sister-in-Charge at the Sophia Women's Ward during the South African War. This was followed by seven years' service with the Army Nursing Service Reserve. When the Great War broke out, she was posted to the British Expeditionary Force and served in France and Flanders. As Matron-in-Chief, she was in charge of all British and Allied nurses working in the extended region (around 6,000 nurses at its peak).

Major Hesketh Hesketh-Prichard, 37, from Hertfordshire: explorer, adventurer, big-game hunter and marksman who made a significant contribution to sniping practice within the British Army during the Great War. Concerned not only with improving the quality of marksmanship, the measures he introduced to counter the threat of German snipers were credited by a contemporary with saving the lives of over 3,500 Allied soldiers.

During his lifetime, he also explored many remote parts of the world, played first-class cricket (including on overseas tours), wrote short stories and novels (one of which was turned into a Douglas Fairbanks film) and was a successful newspaper correspondent and travel writer. He was an active campaigner for animal welfare and instigated legal measures for their protection.

Solomon Joseph Solomon, 54, from Birchington-on-Sea, Kent: British painter, a founding member of the New English Art Club and member of the Royal Academy. He made an important contribution to the development of camouflage in the Great War, working in particular on tree observation posts and arguing tirelessly for camouflage netting.

William Arthur Cawson, 44, from Stratton, Cornwall: Chief Ship's Carpenter, HMS *Inflexible*.

The Regiment: Royal Fusiliers

Maurice Tait, 34, from Leyton, London: career soldier and Serjeant, C Company, 4th Battalion, Royal Fusiliers (designated 'Z' Company during the Great War).

Harry Woodruff, 34, from Leyton, London: career soldier and Serjeant, C Company, 4th Battalion, Royal Fusiliers.

George Ashburner, 34 from Ashtead, Surrey: Major, Commanding Officer, C Company, 4th Battalion Royal Fusiliers.

Billy Carstairs, 42, from Plaistow, London: career soldier and Company Serjeant Major, C Company, 4th Battalion, Royal Fusiliers.

Maurice James Dease, 24, from Coole, County Westmeath, Ireland: Lieutenant, 4th Battalion Royal Fusiliers. Dease won the first Victoria Cross of the Great War (awarded posthumously). He is buried at St Symphorien Military Cemetery, Belgium; his Victoria Cross is displayed at the Fusilier Museum at the Tower of London.

Sidney Frank Godley, 25, from Willesden, North London: Private, 4th Battalion Royal Fusiliers. Advancing German soldiers captured the wounded Private Godley as he was trying to crawl to safety after making a heroic stand. He remained a prisoner of war in a camp at Dallgow-Döberitz until the Armistice. It was in the camp that he was informed that he had been awarded the Victoria Cross. He received the actual medal from King George V, at Buckingham Palace, on 15 February 1919. He died on 29 June 1957 and was buried with full military honours in the town cemetery at Loughton, Essex.

James Orred, 26, from Blackheath, London: Captain, C Company, 4th Battalion Royal Fusiliers.

Leicester Carey, 28, from Feltham, Middlesex: Captain, C Company, 4th Battalion Royal Fusiliers.

Carl von Tannhausen, 29, from Eberswalde in Brandenburg, Germany: Rittmeister in the *Gardes du Corps* (Guards Cavalry Division), 1st Cavalry Corps.

The Politician: Winston Churchill

Winston Leonard Spencer-Churchill, 39: son of Lord Randolph Churchill (Chancellor of the Exchequer in the 1890s under Lord Salisbury) and Lady Randolph Churchill (the American heiress Jennie Jerome). Veteran of several conflicts around the world, including the Boer War and the Battle of Omdurman. He was Liberal MP for Dundee and First Lord of the Admiralty. He was variously known as 'Pig', 'Pug' and 'Amber Dog' to his wife, Clementine.

Clementine (Clemmie) Churchill (née Hozier), 28: wife of Winston Churchill, familiarly known as 'Cat', 'Kat' and 'Puss'.

Frederick Edwin Smith, 32: lawyer, Conservative MP for Walton-on-Thames, Surrey, lifelong friend of Winston.

Lady Randolph Churchill (née Jennie Jerome), 60: mother of Winston and Jack Churchill and wife of Lord Randolph Churchill, who died in 1895. Lady Randolph married George Cornwallis-West in 1900.

Diana Spencer-Churchill, 5: Winston's firstborn child, known to the family as 'Puppy'.

Randolph Spencer-Churchill, 3: Winston's second child and eldest son, known to the family as 'Chumbolly'.

Sarah Spencer-Churchill: born 7 October 1914, the third of Winston's children (who were often referred to by their father as 'kittens').

John Strange ('Jack') Spencer-Churchill, 34, the younger brother of Winston. Veteran of the Boer War, in which he was badly wounded, he was very close to his older brother.

Lady Gwendoline ('Goonie') Theresa Mary Churchill (née Bertie), 28: Jack Churchill's wife.

Peregrine Spencer-Churchill, 1: Jack Churchill's infant son, known to the family as 'Pebbin' (Winston nicknamed Jack's family the 'Jagoons').

Sir Edgar Speyer, 51: wealthy Jewish banker and philanthropist. Born in New York, he became a British subject in 1892. He was made a baronet in 1906 and a Privy Counsellor in 1909, but was the subject of anti-German attacks in the press after the outbreak of war.

Sir Edward ('Eddie') Grey, 52: British Foreign Secretary from 1905 to 1916. It was Grey who remarked on 3 August 1914, as he stood at his window in the Foreign Office watching the gas lamps being lit: 'The lamps are going out all over Europe. We shall not see them lit again in our time.'

Lord Louis of Battenberg, 60: Churchill's First Sea Lord, a fine sailor with a distinguished career. He was born in Austria (the son of

Prince Alexander of Hesse and by Rhine and Princess Julia of Battenberg); growing hostility after the outbreak of war forced him from office in October 1914 when Churchill, with great reluctance, asked him to step down. The King, conscious of the stigma of German ancestry, asked Louis to change his name to Mountbatten in 1917.

John Gough, 35: Serjeant, Special Branch, Metropolitan Police; Winston Churchill's protection officer.

Harold Herbert Asquith, 61: British Liberal Prime Minister, nicknamed 'Old Block' or 'OB' by Winston.

David Lloyd George, 41: Liberal politician; Chancellor of the Exchequer.

Reginald McKenna, 41: Liberal politician; Home Secretary.

Sir Charles Hobhouse, 42: Liberal politician; Postmaster General.

Herbert Horatio Kitchener, 64: 1st Earl Kitchener, victor of the Battle of Omdurman and hero of the Boer War; Secretary of State for War. 'K' is Winston's nickname for him.

Douglas Haig, 53: veteran of the Sudan and Boer wars; General and Commander, 1st Corps, British Expeditionary Force.

Sir John French, 61: renowned cavalry officer, Boer War veteran and Commander-in-Chief of the British Expeditionary Force.

Horace Smith-Dorrien, 61: veteran of Egypt, Sudan, the Zulu and Boer wars; General and Commander, 2nd Corps, British Expeditionary Force.

John Rushworth Jellicoe, 54: 1st Earl Jellicoe, Admiral of the Fleet; fought in the Egyptian War and the Boxer Rebellion; commanded the Grand Fleet at the Battle of Jutland in May 1916.

Edward Hankey, 39: veteran of the Boer War and the Sudan who served in Egypt as well as being ADC to the Governor of

Western Australia. Brigadier General and Commander, 2nd Battalion, Worcestershire Regiment from September to December 1914. Following his heroics at Gheluvelt, Major Hankey was severely wounded. After recovering from his wounds, he commanded the 3rd Battalion, Worcestershire Regiment from August to November 1915.

Sir Philip Albert Gustave David Sassoon, 25: British politician, art collector and social host, entertaining many celebrity guests at his homes, Port Lympne Mansion (originally called Belcaire), Kent, and Trent Park, Hertfordshire, England. Sassoon was a member of the prominent Jewish Sassoon and Rothschild families; he was a cousin of the war poet Siegfried Sassoon. He was MP for Hythe in Kent from 1912, succeeding his father, initially as the 'Baby of the House'.

Valentine Fleming, 34: son of the wealthy Scottish banker Robert Fleming. He joined the Queen's Own Oxfordshire Hussars (Winston and Jack's regiment), rising to the rank of major.

Sir Edward Marsh, 41: British polymath, translator, arts patron and civil servant. He was the sponsor of the Georgian school of poets and a friend to many poets, including Rupert Brooke and Siegfried Sassoon. In his career as a civil servant he worked as private secretary to a succession of Britain's most powerful ministers, particularly Winston Churchill (1905–1915). Marsh was a discreet but influential figure within Britain's homosexual community.

Charles ('Sunny') Spencer-Churchill, 42: 9th Duke of Marlborough, British soldier and Conservative politician, and Winston's cousin. He was an officer in the Queen's Own Oxfordshire Hussars, fought in the Boer War and was subsequently appointed Assistant Military Secretary to Lord Roberts, Commander-in-Chief of the British forces in South Africa. He returned to active service in the Great War, when he served as Lieutenant-Colonel on the General Staff. Marlborough entered the House of Lords on the early death of his father in 1892 and in 1899 he was appointed

Paymaster-General by Lord Salisbury, a post he held until 1902. He was then Under-Secretary of State for the Colonies between 1903 and 1905. *Consuelo Vanderbilt*, 37: a member of the prominent American Vanderbilt family. Her marriage to Charles Spencer-Churchill, 9th Duke of Marlborough, became emblematic of the socially advantageous but loveless marriages between American heiresses and European aristocrats that were common during America's so-called Gilded Age.

Sir Alfred William Fortescue Knox, 44: a career British military officer and later a Conservative Party politician. Born in Ulster, he joined the British Army and was posted to India. In 1911 he was appointed the British Military Attaché in Russia, where he served as a spy. A fluent speaker of Russian, he became a liaison officer to the Imperial Russian Army during the Great War.

The Estate: The Stewart-Murrays, Dukes of Atholl

John James Hugh Henry Stewart-Murray, 73: 7th Duke of Atholl (known as 'Iain'); Chief of the Clan Murray and Commander-in-Chief of the Atholl Highlanders, Europe's only private army.

John George Stewart-Murray, 43: Marquess of Tullibardine (known as 'Bardie'), eldest son of the 7th Duke; veteran of the Boer War, Conservative MP for West Perthshire and Commander of the Scottish Horse.

Lord George Stewart-Murray, 41: (known as 'Geordie') veteran of the Boer War; a former ADC to Lord Elgin, Viceroy of India, and a major in the Black Watch.

Lord James Stewart-Murray, 35: (known as 'Hamish') veteran of the Boer War and a major in the Cameron Highlanders.

John William Dunne, 39: the son of Irish aristocrat General Sir John Dunne; powered-flight pioneer.

Lady Katharine Stewart-Murray (née Ramsay), 39: (known as 'Kitty') wife of Bardie; accomplished musician and social activist.

Lady Dorothea Stewart-Murray, 49: (known as 'Dertha') the 7th Duke's eldest child; married to Harold Ruggles-Brise, a career soldier.

Lady Helen Stewart-Murray, 47: the 7th Duke's second child; lived at Blair Atholl and acted in the place of her deceased mother, Louisa, the Duchess of Atholl, who died in 1902 in Italy.

Lady Evelyn Stewart-Murray, 46: the 7th Duke's third child and youngest daughter. Emotional problems in her childhood led her parents to send her away to be cared for by a governess; she now lived in Malines, in Belgium, in the company of a companion.

Baron Nathan Mayer 'Natty' Rothschild, 73: banker, politician and senior member of the Rothschild banking dynasty.

Hugh Richard 'Bendor' Grosvenor, 35: 2nd Duke of Westminster; a Boer War veteran and one of Europe's richest men (he owned seventeen Rolls-Royce cars as well as his own private train).

William 'Billy' Wentworth-Fitzwilliam, 42: 7th Earl Fitzwilliam; the owner of Wentworth Woodhouse, the largest private house in Europe.

John Inglis, 40: factor, Blair Atholl Estate.

Jamie Forsyth, 58: butler, Blair Atholl Castle.

Dougie Cameron, 22: first footman, Blair Atholl Castle household.

John Jarvis, 55: butler, Eaton Place, London.

Simon Joseph Fraser Lovat, 42: (known as 'Shimi') 14th Lord Lovat and 3rd Baron Lovat; Roman Catholic Scottish landowner and the 23rd Chieftain of the Clan Fraser. He raised the Lovat Scouts in the Boer War, where he won a Distinguished Service Order.

Eileen Macallum, 8: the illegitimate daughter of Bardie Stewart-Murray; Eileen's mother was thought to be a 'Lady Macallum'.

Angus Farquhar, 38: Company Serjeant Major, C Company, Cameron Highlanders.

John Tovey, 24: Corporal, C Company, Cameron Highlanders.

David Tod, 58: born in Edinburgh; businessman, sculptor and friend of Lady Helen Stewart-Murray.

Mrs Maud Grant, 53: widow and resident of Glen Tilt on the Blair Atholl Estate.

Matthew White Ridley, 39: 2nd Viscount Ridley; British Conservative politician and owner of Blagdon Hall, Northumberland.

The Pals: D Company (Burnley Company), 11th Battalion, East Lancashire Regiment, 'Accrington Pals'

John-Tommy Crabtree, 42, born in Harle Syke: steward, Keighley Green Working Men's Club. Formerly a weaver; retired cricketer and renowned fast bowler for Burnley Cricket Club.

Tommy Broxup, 23, born in Burnley: weaver.

Vincent ('Vinny') Sagar, 17, born in Padiham: weaver.

Nathaniel ('Twaites') Haythornthwaite, 17, born in Sabden: weaver.

Michael ('Mad Mick') Kenny, 25, born in Colne: collier.

Catherine ('Cath') Kenny, 22, born in Nelson: weaver.

Mary Broxup, 22, born in Burnley: weaver.

Harry Hyndman, 72, born in London: radical activist and leader of the British Socialist Party.

John Harwood, 67, born in Darwen: cotton entrepreneur, President of Accrington Stanley Football Club, Mayor of Accrington, founder of the 11th Battalion (Service), East Lancashire Regiment (Accrington Pals).

John Haworth, 38, born in Accrington: Manager, Burnley Football Club.

Jimmy Dowd, 22, born in Armagh, Ireland: weaver.

James 'Jimmy' Severn, 55, born in Bow, London: retired soldier, training NCO, 11th Battalion, East Lancashire Regiment.

Henry Davison Riley, 33, born in Cliviger: local businessman; Lieutenant, D Company, 11th Battalion, East Lancashire Regiment.

Frederick Arnold Heys, 26, born in Oswaldtwistle: solicitor; Lieutenant, D Company, 11th Battalion, East Lancashire Regiment.

Raymond St George Ross, 31, born in Lancaster: analytical chemist; Captain, D Company, 11th Battalion, East Lancashire Regiment.

Arnold Bannatyne Tough, 24, born in Accrington: dentist; Lieutenant, D Company, 11th Battalion, East Lancashire Regiment.

Andrew Muir, 55, born in Maryhill, Scotland: retired soldier, training NCO, 11th Battalion, East Lancashire Regiment.

George Lee, 52, born in Widecombe, Devon: retired soldier; training NCO, 11th Battalion, East Lancashire Regiment.

Richard Sharples, 64, born in Haslingden: solicitor and territorial soldier; Colonel and Commanding Officer, 11th Battalion, East Lancashire Regiment.

George Nicholas Slinger, 48, born in Bacup: solicitor and territorial soldier; Captain and Adjutant, 11th Battalion, East Lancashire Regiment.

Casualty Figures of the Great War

Estimates of casualty numbers for the Great War vary significantly, largely because numbers from the Central Powers and from Russia were not properly recorded, or were lost in the confusion and chaos of the post-war world. The statistics below are drawn from a number of sources, including the following.

- British Empire figures are drawn from The Commonwealth War Graves Annual Report, 2011.
- Official British figures were concluded in a War Office Report of March 1922.
- Estimates of Russian, Greek, Serbian and Montenegrin casualties were presented by journalist Boris Urlanis in *Wars and Population* (Moscow, 1971).
- Estimates of Allied deaths in France, Italy, Britain and Germany were presented in Samuel Dumas's study *Losses of Life Caused by War* (Oxford, 1923).
- Estimates of German and Austrian losses are based on the official German Army Medical Branch war history *Heeres-Sanitätsinspektion im Reichskriegsministeriums, Sanitätsbericht über das deutsche Heer (Deutsches Feld- und Besatzungsheer) im Weltkriege 1914–1918* (Berlin, 1934).

The following are also invaluable sources of information.

- Erickson, Edward J. 2001. *Ordered to Die: A History of the Ottoman Army in the First World War.* Greenwood. (Includes casualty figures for the Ottoman Army.)
- Hersch, Liebmann. 1927. La Mortalité Causée par la Guerre Mondiale. *Metron : The International Review of*

Statistics, Vol 7. No 1. (This study details the demographic impact of the war on France, the UK, Italy, Belgium, Portugal, Serbia, Romania and Greece.)

- Huber, Michel. 1931. *La Population de la France Pendant la Guerre*. Presses Universitaires de France. (This study, published by the Carnegie Endowment for International Peace, lists official data for war-related military deaths and the missing of France and its colonies.)
- Mortara, Giorgo. 1925. *La Salute Pubblica in Italia durante e dopo la Guerra*. Yale University Press. (Lists estimates of Italian casualties.)

The figures in the following table include 6.8 million combat-related deaths as well as 3 million military deaths caused by accidents, disease and deaths while prisoners of war. They include about 6 million excess civilian deaths due to war-related malnutrition and disease that are often omitted from other compilations. The civilian deaths listed below also include the Armenian Genocide (1915), but civilian deaths due to the Spanish flu (1918–1920) have been excluded.

Allied Powers

Country	Population (millions)	Military deaths	Direct civilian deaths (military action)	Excess civilian deaths (famine, disease & accidents)	Total deaths	Deaths as % of population	Military wounded
Australia	4.5	61,966	–	–	61,966	1.38%	152,171
Canada	7.2	64,976	–	2,000	66,976	0.92%	149,732
India	315.1	74,187	–	–	74,187	0.02%	69,214
New Zealand	1.1	18,052	–	–	18,052	1.64%	41,317
Newfoundland	0.2	1,570	–	–	1,570	0.65%	2,314
United Kingdom	45.4	886,939	2,000	107,000	995,939	2.19%	1,663,435
Belgium	7.4	58,637	7,000	55,000	120,637	1.63%	44,686
France	39.6	1,397,800	40,000	260,000	1,697,800	4.29%	4,266,000
Greece	4.8	26,000	–	150,000	176,000	3.67%	21,000
Italy	35.6	651,000	4,000	589,000	1,240,000	3.48%	953,886
Empire of Japan	53.6	415	–	–	415	0%	907
Montenegro	0.5	3,000	–	–	3,000	0.6%	10,000
Portugal	6.0	7,222	–	82,000	89,222	1.49%	13,751
Romania	7.5	250,000	120,000	330,000	700,000	9.33%	120,000
Russian Empire	175.1	1,811,000 to 2,254,369	500,000 (1914 borders)	1,000,000 (1914 borders)	3,311,000 to 3,754,369	1.89% to 2.14%	3,749,000 to 4,950,000
Serbia	4.5	275,000	150,000	300,000	725,000	16.11%	133,148
USA	92.0	116,708	757	–	117,465	0.13%	205,690
Total	800.4	5,712,379	823,757	2,871,000	9,407,136	1.19%	12,809,280

Central Powers

Country	Population (millions)	Military deaths	Direct civilian deaths (military action)	Excess civilian deaths (famine, disease & accidents)	Total deaths	Deaths as % of population	Military wounded
Austria-Hungary	51.4	1,100,000	120,000	347,000	1,567,000	3.05%	3,620,000
Bulgaria	5.5	87,500	–	100,000	187,500	3.41%	152,390
German Empire	64.9	2,050,897	1,000	425,000	2,476,897	3.82%	4,247,143
Ottoman Empire	21.3	771,844	–	2,150,000	2,921,000	13.72%	400,000
Total	143.1	4,010,241	121,000	3,022,000	7,153,241	5%	8,419,533

Neutral nations

Country	Population (millions)	Military deaths	Direct civilian deaths (military action)	Excess civilian deaths (famine, disease & accidents)	Total deaths	Deaths as % of population	Military wounded
Denmark	2.7	—	722	—	722	0.03%	—
Norway	2.4	—	1,892	—	1,892	0.08%	—
Sweden	5.6	—	877	—	877	0.02%	—
Total	10.7	—	3,491	—	3,491	0.03	—

Combined casualty figures

All nations: Allied Powers, Central Powers & neutral nations	Population (millions)	Military deaths	Direct civilian deaths (military action)	Excess civilian deaths (famine, disease & accidents)	Total deaths	Deaths as % of population	Military wounded
Grand total	954.2	9,722,620	948,248	5,893,000	16,563,868	1.75%	21,228,813

British colonies

In addition to New Commonwealth troops listed below, Britain recruited Indian, Chinese, native South African, Egyptian and other overseas labour to provide logistical support in the combat theatres. The Commonwealth War Graves Commission reports that nearly 2,000 workers from the Chinese Labour Corps are buried with British war dead in France.

Colony	Military deaths
Ghana (1914 known as the Gold Coast)	1,200
Kenya (1914 known as British East Africa)	2,000
Malawi (1914 known as Nyasaland)	3,000
Nigeria (1914 part of British West Africa)	5,000
Sierra Leone (1914 part of British West Africa)	1,000
Uganda (1914 known as the Uganda Protectorate)	1,500
Zambia (1914 known as Northern Rhodesia)	3,000
Zimbabwe (1914 known as Southern Rhodesia)	>700

Included with British casualties in East Africa are the deaths of 44,911 recruited labourers.

Ireland

In 1914, the whole of Ireland was part of the United Kingdom; during the Great War 206,000 Irishmen fought for Britain.

Location of war graves

In March 2009, the Commonwealth War Graves Commission produced the following statistics for the resting places of the

British dead in the Great War. The figures include all three services.

- Buried in named graves: 587,989.
- No known graves, but listed on a memorial to the missing: 526,816, of which
  - buried but not identifiable by name: 187,861
  - remains not recovered, therefore not buried at all: 338,955.

The last figure includes those lost at sea. Thus, about half are buried as known soldiers, with the rest either buried but unidentifiable, or lost.

Glossary

Albert chain

An Albert chain is a chain used to anchor a Victorian or Edwardian gentleman's timepiece on to his waistcoat. It was named in memory of Queen Victoria's husband, Prince Albert, who was fond of wearing watch chains with his morning coat and waistcoat. Watch chains worn by women during the period were known as 'Albertina chains'. Both Albert chains and Albertina chains were made of gold or silver. If the watch had a protective cover for the face it was known as a 'hunter'.

Wristwatches did not become widely popular until after the Great War. Prior to that, wristwatches, often sold as bracelets, were designed for women. However, cavalry officers, especially during the Boer War, began to use 'armlet' pocket watches because of the obvious practical advantages. The Great War dramatically changed attitudes towards the man's wristwatch, and opened up a mass market in the post-war era. Service watches produced during the war were specially designed for the rigours of trench warfare, with luminous dials and unbreakable glass. Wristwatches were also found to be needed in the air as much as on the ground, military pilots finding them much more convenient than pocket watches. The British War Office began issuing wristwatches to combatants from 1917 onwards.

Audacious, HMS

HMS *Audacious* was a King George V-class dreadnought battleship of the Royal Navy. The vessel did not see any combat in the Great War, being sunk by a German naval mine off the northern coast of Donegal, Ireland, on 27 October 1914. It took almost twelve hours to sink and there was no loss of life. Most of the crew were taken off by the White Star liner *Olympic*, the sister ship of *Titanic*. The Admiralty and the British Cabinet agreed that the loss be kept secret and so, for the rest of the war, *Audacious*'s name remained on all public lists of ship movements and activities. However, many Americans on board *Olympic* were beyond British jurisdiction and openly discussed the sinking (many photographs, and even a short reel of film, had been taken). On 14 November 1918, shortly after the war ended, the war's worst kept secret was acknowledged by an official announcement in *The Times*: 'HMS *Audacious*. A Delayed Announcement. The Secretary of State of the Admiralty makes the following announcement: HMS *Audacious* sank off the North Irish Coast on October 27th 1914. This was kept secret at the urgent request of the Commander-in-Chief, Grand Fleet and the Press loyally refrained from giving it any publicity.'

Band of Hope

Following the death in June 1847 of a young man whose life was cut short by alcohol, the Band of Hope was first proposed by Reverend Jabez Tunnicliff, a Baptist Minister in Leeds. With the help of other temperance workers, the Band of Hope was founded in the autumn of 1847. Its objective was to teach children the importance and principles of sobriety and teetotalism. In 1855, a national organization was formed and meetings were held in churches throughout the UK. The Band of Hope and other temperance organizations fought to counteract the influence of pubs and brewers, with the specific intention of rescuing 'unfortunates' whose lives had been blighted by drink. 'Signing the pledge' was one of the innovative features of the Band of Hope, and millions of people signed up.

Bar and clasp

In the rubric of military decorations, a 'bar' to an award for gallantry is given if the recipient receives the same award more than once. They do not receive a second medal, but a bar to be attached to the ribbon of their original medal. The bar can be decorated with a crown (as in a Military Cross), or a laurel wreath (as in a Victoria Cross). A clasp is awarded as an addition to a campaign medal and marks the recipient's participation in a specified battle within a campaign. The name of the battle is inscribed on the clasp, which is attached to the ribbon of the medal. Confusingly, 'clasps' are often also called 'bars', but the important difference between the two is that bars only have a design, whereas clasps have the name of the battle inscribed.

British Army School of Musketry

The Army School of Musketry was founded in 1853 at Hythe, Kent. In September 1855, a corps of instructors was added to the establishment, consisting of 100 first-class and 100 second-class instructors who, as soon as they were sufficiently experienced, were distributed to battalions and regiments as required. The use of the term 'musketry' was a misnomer as, by then, muskets (smooth-bore weapons) were being withdrawn from service to be replaced by weapons with rifled bores (rifles).

British Expeditionary Force

Britain's army in 1914 was a volunteer, professional army of great tradition. Although there had been significant nineteenth-century reforms, it was still based on centuries-old practices and prejudices. Most officers needed a private income of at least £250 per year, or £400 for cavalry regiments (which required a man to keep a charger, two hunters and three polo ponies). Some men of the ranks came from long-standing military families, but most enlisted as unskilled labourers. They were largely from poor urban slums, uneducated and often undernourished.

The army medical standard was 5ft 3ins in height, with 33ins chest and 33lbs in weight. Despite these minimal requirements, many applicants failed. Although hardly luxurious, soldiers got regular pay, clean living conditions, adequate food and a rudimentary education. Camaraderie was generally good and professionalism high, especially in basic combat skills and musketry. There was mutual respect between officers and men and non-commissioned officers were drawn from highly disciplined veterans and were of the highest calibre.

In May 1914, British military prowess rested on its immense Royal Navy, the envy of the world. The regular army was small compared to its European counterparts and was 11,000 short of its establishment of 260,000. The number of men under arms on UK soil was 137,000, including recruits undergoing training. The rest were in numerous garrisons throughout the Empire. The BEF sent to France in August 1914 was designated at 48 infantry battalions and 16 cavalry regiments, plus heavy and light artillery and support services. This was many more than the army could muster, so over 70,000 reservists were called to the colours. Although these men had been regular soldiers, most had grown accustomed to civilian life, lacked training and had lost their battle-hardened readiness. Many battalions had to include several hundred reservists to bring them up to strength of around 1,000 men.

Approximately 100,000 strong, the BEF's mandate was challenging: help throw back a German force 1 million strong in cooperation with a French Army equally huge. Its commander, Sir John French, was required to support the French generals, but not take orders from them. However, he had to rely on their goodwill for railway transportation, accommodation and lines of supply. John French was a better fighting soldier than a strategic general. He was liked by his subordinates and had a good reputation within the army, but he was short-tempered and argumentative and suffered from violent mood swings, which veered from overt optimism to deep pessimism. His subordinates – Sir Douglas Haig, who commanded the I Corps, and Sir Horace Smith-Dorrien, who commanded II Corps – were also highly respected, experienced soldiers, but neither had a good relationship with French, especially

Smith-Dorrien, who was appointed against his wishes. Haig was extremely efficient and hard-working, much liked by all around him, but was intensely shy and awkward. Smith-Dorrien was brave and aggressive, but prone to extreme outbursts of temper.

The BEF was to take up position to the east of Cambrai, between Maubeuge and Hirson, on the left flank of General Lanrezac's 5th French Army of 250,000 men. Here it would meet the thrust of the German advance through southern Belgium, led by General Alexander von Kluck's 1st Army, 300,000 strong.

Bulldog-toed shoes

Bulldog-toe button boots (or American boots) and shoes were very fashionable for both men and women from about 1908 to 1920. With their distinctive rounded bulbous toes, they were first popular in North America and then in Europe. The distinctive shape of the toe was considered to be healthy because the toes could move inside the boot, thereby increasing circulation to the foot. Previously, the fashion was for highly restrictive 'toothpick' pointed shoes.

Burnley Lads' Club

The Burnley Lads' Club was formed in 1899 to cater for boys from disadvantaged backgrounds. Many of the original members of the club fell in the Great War, serving with the famous D Company, 'Accrington Pals', along with the club's first leader, Captain Henry Davison Riley. It still flourishes. In 1968 the Lads' Club merged with the Police Youth Club, to create Burnley Boys' Club. The merger enabled the two groups to pool their resources and membership, which included girls, and the club is now called Burnley Boys' and Girls' Club. It is a youth and community centre for young people between the ages of six and twenty-one, irrespective of gender, race and ability. Young people with disabilities are welcome up to the age of twenty-five.

Camouflage

In 1914, British scientist John Graham Kerr persuaded First Lord of the Admiralty Winston Churchill to adopt a form of disruptive camouflage for shipping, which he called 'parti-colouring' or 'dazzle' camouflage A general order to the British fleet issued on 10 November 1914 advocated the use of Kerr's method, which used masses of strongly contrasted colour, consequently making it difficult for a submarine to decide on the exact course of the vessel to be attacked. Artists, known as 'camoufleurs' were employed to design the camouflage of individual ships, some of which were so eye-catching that people would come and gawp at them in dock. It was applied in various ways to British warships such as HMS *Implacable*, where officers noted that the pattern 'increased difficulty of accurate range finding'. However, following Churchill's departure from the Admiralty, the Royal Navy reverted to plain grey paint schemes.

Central Powers/Allied Powers

The Central Powers were one of the two warring factions in the Great War, composed of Germany, Austria-Hungary, the Ottoman (Turkish) Empire and Bulgaria, also known as the Quadruple Alliance. This alignment originated in the alliance of Germany and Austria-Hungary, and fought against the Allied Powers that had formed around the Triple Entente. The members of the Triple Entente were the French Republic, the British Empire and the Russian Empire. Italy ended its alliance with the Central Powers and entered the war on the side of the Entente in 1915. Japan, Belgium, Serbia, Greece, Montenegro, Romania and the Czechoslovak legions (a volunteer army) were secondary members of the Entente.

Cherry Bums

This was a term used by Lord Cardigan for his regiment, the 11th Prince Albert's Own Hussars, which he notoriously led in the Charge of the Light Brigade in 1854, during the Crimean War. The men wore bright-red cavalry trousers in honour of the livery of Prince Albert's House of Saxe-Coburg-Gotha. The term came to be used by infantrymen in sections of the army as a derogatory expression for the cavalrymen in general.

Clogs

There are two explanations of the development of the English-style clog. They may have evolved from foot pattens (soles) which were slats of wood held in place by thongs or similar strapping. They were usually worn under leather or fabric shoes to raise the wearer's foot above the mud of the unmade road (not to mention commonly dumped human effluent and animal dung). Those too poor to afford shoes wore wood directly against the skin or hosiery, and thus the clog was developed, made of part leather and part wood. Alternatively, they have been described as far back as Roman times, and possibly earlier. The wearing of clogs in Britain became more visible with the Industrial Revolution, when industrial workers needed strong, cheap footwear. The heyday of the clog in Britain was between the 1840s and 1920s and, although traditionally associated with Lancashire, they were worn all over the country (for example, in the London docklands and fruit markets, and in the mines of Kent).

Cockney rhyming and other London slang

Barney Moke – poke (sexual intercourse).
Birch and broom – room.
Butcher's (hook) – look.
Cocoa / I should cocoa – I should say so.

Feather-plucker – fucker.

Goose and duck – fuck.

Granny Grunt – cunt.

His Majesty's pleasure – treasure.

Fourpenny one (fourpenny bit) – hit. (A fourpenny bit was an old British silver coin, also called a 'groat', worth four old pennies; it ceased to be minted in 1856.)

Iron hoof – poof / homosexual.

Little Red Riding Hoods – goods.

Mazawattee (potty) – crazy. (Mazawattee was one of the most popular brands of tea from mid-Victorian times onwards. Owned by the Densham family, using tea from the newly established tea plantations of Ceylon, its name is Sinhalese in origin and means 'pleasure garden'. Its growth was helped by the Temperance Movement and the company's clever slogan: 'The cup that cheers but does not inebriate.' The brand was distributed from its warehouse on Tower Hill in London and became a Cockney favourite. The brand declined after the Great War and its Tower Hill warehouse was destroyed during the Blitz in the Second World War. By the 1960s, Mazawattee Tea had disappeared.)

Miss Fitch – bitch.

Pig's ear – beer.

Pony (and trap) – crap (useless / poor quality).

Safe and sound – ground.

Tiddly (wink) – drink.

Tommy Rollocks – bollocks / testicles.

Two and eight – state (as in a state of agitation).

Desoutter Brothers

Marcel Desoutter was one of six children of Louis Albert Desoutter, an immigrant French watchmaker, and Philomène Duret. Learning to fly with the Blériot Company at their Hendon works, he passed the flying tests at the age of seventeen. At the London Aviation Meeting, held at Hendon Aerodrome at Easter 1913, the control stick slipped from his hand while flying his 50hp Blériot Gnome, and the craft dived into the ground at the edge of the aerodrome. Desoutter's leg was badly broken and later had to be amputated above the knee.

He was fitted with the standard wooden leg, but his younger brother Charles used his knowledge of aircraft materials to design a new jointed duralumin alloy leg of half the weight, with which he was able to return to flying. In 1914 the pair formed Desoutter Brothers Limited to manufacture artificial limbs. The firm expanded during and after the Great War, and moved to The Hyde, Hendon, in 1924.

'Die Wacht am Rhein'

This is a German patriotic anthem ('The Watch/Guard on the Rhine'). The song's origins are rooted in the historical French–German enmity, and it was particularly popular in Germany during the Franco-Prussian War and the Great War.

Distinguished Conduct Medal

The Distinguished Conduct Medal (DCM) was, until 1993, a very high award for bravery (second only to a Victoria Cross). The medal was instituted in 1854, during the Crimean War, to recognize gallantry within the ranks, for which it was the equivalent of the Distinguished Service Order (DSO) awarded for bravery to commissioned officers. In the aftermath of the 1993 review of the honours system, as part of the drive to remove distinctions of rank in awards for bravery, the DCM was discontinued (along with the award of the DSO and of the Conspicuous Gallantry Medal). These three decorations were replaced by the Conspicuous Gallantry Cross, which now serves as the second-level award for gallantry for all ranks across the whole armed forces.

Doolally tap

Deolali, India, was the site of a British Army transit camp notorious for its unpleasant environment, and the boredom and psychological problems of soldiers who passed through it. Its name is the origin of the phrase 'gone doolally' or 'doolally tap', a phrase meaning to 'lose one's mind'. 'Tap' may refer to the Urdu word for a malarial fever.

Dunnage

Dunnage is a term with a variety of related meanings but, typically, refers to inexpensive or waste material used to protect, load and secure cargo during transportation. Dunnage also refers to material used to support loads and hold tools and materials up off the ground (such as jacks, pipes) and supports for air conditioning and other equipment above the roof of a building.

East Lancashire, Pennine dialect

Agate – say/said ('be agate' – to say).

Alreet – all right ('reet' – right).

Barm cake – 'barm' is the foam, or scum, formed on the top of the liquor when beverages such as beer or wine (or feedstock for hard liquor) ferment. It was used to leaven bread, or set up fermentation in a new batch of liquor. In parts of the north-west of England, and throughout Yorkshire, a 'barm' or 'barm cake' is a common term for a soft, floury bread roll (on menus in chip shops there is often an option of a 'chip barm'). The term 'barmy' may derive from a sense of frothy excitement.

Best slack – 'slack' is very small pieces of coal, almost coal dust; 'best slack' would be less dust, more small pieces; 'nutty slack' would be bigger, more expensive pieces.

Brass – money.

Childer – children.

Dacent – decent.

Daft apeth – silly person (derived from 'ha'p'orth' – halfpennyworth).

Feight – fight.

Fettle – sort out.

Laik – play.

Lanky – Lancastrian.

Like talkin' to a wood stoop – talking to someone who doesn't listen or can't hear (a stoop is a raised, flat area in front of a door, usually with one or more steps leading up to it).

Lummox – big lump.

Mebbe – maybe.

Mesen – myself ('sen' – self).

Moither – worry.

Neet – night.

Nowt – nothing.

Ollus – always.

Once every Preston Guild – rarely (Preston Guilds take place every twenty years).

Once every Sheffield Flood – very rarely; even more rarely than Preston Guilds. (On the night of 11 March 1864, 238 people were killed, 130 buildings destroyed and 15 bridges swept away in a devastating flood caused by the collapse of the Dale Dyke dam.)

Owt – anything.

Sken – look.

Tha'sen – yourself ('tha' – thou).

Th'eed – the head.

Th'sels – themselves.

T'morn – tomorrow (or tomorrow morning).

Tyke – Yorkshire person.

Yonder – over there or beyond.

The fourth Royal Navy ship to carry the name, the *Enchantress* was a twin-screw Admiralty yacht, launched at Belfast in 1903. Capable of 18 knots, her length, beam and draught were 320ft, 40ft, and 16ft. This ship was the special service vessel, or official yacht, of the Lords Commissioners of the Admiralty.

Enfilade

Enfilade is a concept in military tactics used to describe a formation's exposure to enemy fire. A formation, or position, is 'in enfilade' if weapons' fire can be directed along its longest axis.

Executions

A total of 346 British and Commonwealth soldiers were executed during the Great War. Such executions, for crimes like desertion and cowardice, remain a source of controversy, with some believing that many of those executed were suffering from what is now called 'shell shock'. Between 1914 and 1918, the British Army identified 80,000 men with what would now be defined as the symptoms of shell shock. However, senior commanders believed that if such behaviour was not harshly punished, others might be encouraged to do the same and the whole discipline of the British Army would collapse.

Some men faced a court martial for other offences but the majority stood trial for desertion from their post, 'fleeing in the face of the enemy'. A court martial was usually carried out with some speed and the execution followed shortly afterwards. In his testimony to the post-war Royal Commission examining shell shock, Lord Gort said that it was a weakness and was not found in 'good' units. The continued pressure to avoid the medicalization of shell shock meant that it was not, in itself, an admissible defence.

Executions of soldiers in the British Army were not common-place. While there were 240,000 courts martial and 3,080 death sentences handed down, of the 346 cases where the sentence was carried out, 266 British were executed for 'Desertion', 18 for 'Cowardice', 7 for 'Quitting a post without authority', 5 for 'Disobedience to a lawful command' and 2 for 'Casting away arms'. In some cases (for instance, that of Private Harry Farr), men were executed who had previously suffered from shell shock and who would very likely today have been diagnosed with post-traumatic stress disorder or another psychiatric syndrome, and would not be executed.

Immediately after the Great War, there were claims that the execution of soldiers was determined by social class. During the war, fifteen officers were sentenced to death, but all received a royal pardon. In August 2006, the British Defence Secretary Des Browne announced that, with Parliament's support, there would be a general pardon for all 306 men executed during the Great War. A new law passed on 28 November 2006, and included as part of the Armed Forces Act, pardoned men in the British and Commonwealth armies who were executed in the Great War. The law removes the stain of dishonour but it does not cancel out sentences.

Farnborough

The Royal Aircraft Establishment at Farnborough was a British research establishment, known by several different names during its history, that eventually came under the aegis of the UK Ministry of Defence, before finally losing its identity in mergers with other institutions. The first site was at Farnborough Airfield in Hampshire. In 1904–1906 the Army Balloon Factory, which was part of the Army School of Ballooning, under the command of Colonel James Templer, relocated from Aldershot to the edge of Farnborough Common in order to have enough space for experimental work. In October 1908, Samuel Cody made the first aeroplane flight in Britain at Farnborough. In 1988 it was renamed the Royal Aerospace Establishment before merging with other research entities to become part of the new Defence Research Agency in 1991.

Field punishment

Field punishment was introduced in 1881 following the abolition of flogging and was a common punishment during the Great War. A commanding officer could award field punishment for up to twenty-eight days.

Field Punishment Number One (often abbreviated to 'F. P. No. 1' or even just 'No. 1') consisted of the convicted man being placed in fetters and handcuffs or similar restraints and attached to a fixed object, such as a gun wheel, for up to two hours per day. During the early part of the war, the punishment was often applied with the arms stretched out and the legs tied together, giving rise to the nickname 'crucifixion'. This was applied for a maximum of three days out of four, up to twenty-one days in total. It was usually applied in field punishment camps set up for this purpose a few miles behind the front line, but when the unit was on the move it would be carried out by the unit itself. It has been alleged that this punishment was sometimes applied within range of enemy fire. During the Great War, Field Punishment Number One was issued by the British Army on over 60,000 occasions. Although the 1914 Manual of Military Law specifically stated that field punishment should not be applied in such a way as to cause physical harm, abuses were commonplace (for example, the prisoner would deliberately be placed in stress positions with his feet not fully touching the ground).

In Field Punishment Number Two, the prisoner was placed in fetters and handcuffs but was not attached to a fixed object and was still able to march with his unit. This was a relatively tolerable punishment. In both forms of field punishment, the soldier was also subjected to hard labour and loss of pay. Field Punishment

Number One was eventually abolished in 1923, when an amendment to the Army Act which specifically forbade attachment to a fixed object was passed by the House of Lords.

Fitzsimmons, Bob

Robert James 'Bob' Fitzsimmons was a British professional boxer who made boxing history as the sport's first three-division world champion. He was successively Middleweight, Light Heavyweight and Heavyweight World Champion. Fitzsimmons is the lightest of all Heavyweight Champions, an accolade that, almost certainly, will never be taken from him. Nicknamed 'Ruby Robert' and the 'Freckled Wonder', he took pride in his lack of scars and appeared in the ring wearing heavy woollen underwear to conceal the disparity between his significant trunk and puny legs. He was known for his pure fighting skills and his dislike of training. Fitzsimmons is ranked 8th on *Ring Magazine*'s list of the '100 Greatest Punchers of all Time'.

Gewehr 98 Mauser rifle

The Gewehr 98 (abbreviated G98) was a German bolt-action Mauser rifle firing cartridges from a five-round internal clip-loaded magazine. It was the German service rifle from 1898 to 1935, when it was replaced by the Karabiner 98k. The Gewehr 98 was the main German infantry weapon of the Great War.

Green spot ammunition

Snipers rely on their skill, the quality of their rifle and its sight, but also their ammunition. The first 5,000 rounds out of a new mould are packaged with a green spot so that they can be used by snipers, before the balls of later rounds suffer from minor deteriorations in the ball moulding through wear.

Hackles

These are the long, fine feathers which are found on the backs of certain types of domestic chicken; they are often brightly coloured, especially on roosters. In military parlance, the hackle is a clipped feather plume that is attached to a military headdress. In the British Army the hackle is worn by some infantry regiments, especially those designated as fusilier regiments and those with Scottish and Northern Irish origins. The colour of the hackle varies from regiment to regiment.

Lancashire Fusiliers: primrose yellow.

Royal Fusiliers: white.

Royal Inniskilling Fusiliers: grey.

Royal Irish Fusiliers: green.

Royal Northumberland Fusiliers: red over white.

Royal Scots Fusiliers: white.

Royal Warwickshire Fusiliers: blue over gold.

Royal Welch Fusiliers: white.

Havercake

An oatcake, or type of flatbread, made from oatmeal and sometimes flour, cooked on a griddle or baked in an oven. In Lancashire and Yorkshire, oatcake was a staple of the diet up to the Great War. Oatcakes were often called 'havercakes' (from 'hafr', the Old Germanic word for oats). The word is perpetuated in the nickname 'Havercake Lads' for the 33rd Regiment of Foot (The Duke of Wellington's Regiment, West Riding) and also in the term 'haversack'.

Highgate, Thomas

On 5 September 1914, the first day of the Battle of the Marne, Thomas Highgate, a nineteen-year-old British private, was found hiding in a barn dressed in civilian clothes. Highgate was tried by court martial, convicted of desertion and, in the early hours of 8 September, was executed by firing squad. His was the first of 306 executions carried out by the British Army during the Great War. The only son of a farm worker, Thomas Highgate was born in Shoreham, in Kent, in 1895. In February 1913, aged seventeen, he joined the Royal West Kent Regiment. On the first day of the Battle of the Marne, and the 35th day of the war, Private Highgate's nerves got the better of him and he fled the battlefield. He hid in a barn in the village of Tournan, a few miles south of the river, and was discovered wearing civilian clothes by a gamekeeper who happened to be English and an ex-soldier. Highgate confessed: 'I have had enough of it, I want to get out of it and this is how I am going to do it.'

Having been turned in, Highgate was tried by a court martial for desertion. The trial, presided over by three officers, was brief. Highgate did not speak and was not represented. He was found guilty. At 6.20 on the morning of 8 September, Highgate was informed that he would be executed. The execution was carried out fifty minutes later – at 7.07 – by firing squad. Highgate's name is shown on the British memorial to the missing at La Ferté-sous-Jouarre on the south bank of the River Marne. The memorial features the names of over 3,000 British soldiers with no known grave.

Inflexible, HMS

HMS *Inflexible* was an *Invincible*-class battlecruiser of the Royal Navy, built in 1907. She and her sister ship *Invincible* sank the German armoured cruisers SMS *Scharnhorst* and SMS *Gneisenau* during the Battle of the Falkland Islands.

Jack tar

Jack tar (also Jacktar, Jack-tar or even Tar) was a common term originally used to refer to seamen of the Merchant or Royal Navy, particularly during the period of the British Empire. Members of the public, and also seafarers themselves, made use of the name in identifying those who went to sea. It was not used as an offensive term and sailors were happy to use the term to label themselves. Its etymology is not certain, but there are several plausible possibilities: before the invention of waterproof fabrics, seamen were known to 'tar' their clothes before departing on voyages, in order to make them waterproof; it was common among seamen to plait their long hair into a ponytail and smear it with high-grade tar to prevent it getting caught in the ship's equipment; in the age of wooden sailing vessels, ropes and cables were soaked in tar to prevent them rotting in a damp environment.

Junkers

Members of the landed nobility in Prussia. They owned great estates that were maintained and worked by peasants with few rights. After 1871 they were the dominant force in German military, political and diplomatic leadership. The most famous Junker was Chancellor Otto von Bismarck. Junker is derived from Middle High German 'Juncherre', meaning 'young nobleman', or 'young lord'. Many Junkers took up careers as soldiers, mercenaries and officials. Being the bulwark of the ruling House of Hohenzollern, the Junkers controlled the Prussian Army and their influence was widespread in the north-eastern half of Germany: Brandenburg, Pomerania, Silesia, West Prussia, East Prussia and Posen.

Knur and Spell

An ancient Pennine folk game, akin to the southern English games of trap-ball and probably an ancestor of golf. Often associated with gambling, it was very popular in the nineteenth and early twentieth centuries, especially in the fields around moorland pubs. The object is to hit a 'potty' (knur), sometimes a small piece of heartwood or a small pottery ball, as far as possible with a long flexible club. The longest hit takes the prize. Distances of several hundred yards could be achieved. The game and its name are thought to be Norse in origin.

Lant-trough

A receptacle for collecting human urine. Fermented human urine (lant) was used for various purposes from as early as Roman times. The Romans used it as a cleaning agent for stained clothes and even as a whitener for teeth. The emperor Nero imposed a highly lucrative tax on the urine industry. In nineteenth-century Lancashire, lant was used in the tanning and woollen industries as a cleanser for the removal of natural oils in the production of leather and wool.

Le Cateau, Battle of

The Battle of Le Cateau was fought on 26 August 1914. British General Horace Smith-Dorrien took a calculated gamble during the retreat from Mons, which was against direct orders. Feeling his men were in disarray in a retreat hindered by thousands of French civilians, he decided to fight: 40,000 British troops formed a defensive line just south of the Cambrai–Le Cateau road and just west of Le Cateau itself. Britain suffered many more casualties than at Mons – 7,812 – in a ferocious and hard-fought encounter. It also lost 38 artillery pieces. German losses were much higher, perhaps as many as 20,000. However, Smith-Dorrien's decision meant that the rest of the retreat from Mons could be undertaken with much less arduous harassment and could well have saved a greater part of the BEF from destruction.

Lee-Enfield rifle

The Lee-Enfield rifle was the main infantry weapon used by the military forces of the British Army from the early twentieth century until 1957.

Lee-Metford rifle

The Lee-Metford was a bolt-action British Army service rifle, combining James Paris Lee's rear-locking bolt system and ten-round magazine with a seven-groove rifled barrel designed by William Ellis Metford. It replaced the Martini-Henry rifle in 1888, following nine years of development and trials, but remained in service for only a short time until replaced by the similar Lee-Enfield in 1913.

Lyddite shell

British explosive shells filled with Lyddite were the first British generation of modern 'high explosive' shells. Lyddite is picric acid fused at 280°F and allowed to solidify. The shells detonated and fragmented into small pieces in all directions, with no incendiary effect. For maximum destructive effect the explosion needed to be delayed until the shell had penetrated its target.

Maconochie's and Moir Wilson British Army rations

These were just two of the many manufacturers of Great War army rations. Maconochie's, an Irish stew produced in Fraserburgh and Stornoway in Scotland, was the most popular. Soldiers got a weekly ration of 12ozs of dried 'bully' beef, 1lb 4ozs of bread or flour, 4ozs of bacon, 3ozs of cheese plus sugar, tea, jam, salt, pepper and mustard when available. As in the navy, a 'tot' (half a gill/70mls) of rum was issued daily; double before a battle. Ten thousand copies of the *Daily Mail* were also sent to the Front every day.

Mad minute

This was a pre-Great War term used by British Army riflemen during training at the Hythe School of Musketry to describe scoring a minimum of 15 hits on to a 12-inch round target at 300 yards within one minute using a bolt-action rifle (usually a Lee-Enfield or Lee-Metford rifle). It was not uncommon during the Great War for riflemen to exceed this score. Many could average 30 plus shots; the record, set in 1914 by Serjeant Instructor Alfred Snoxhall, was 38 hits. During the Battle of Mons, there were numerous German accounts of coming up against what they believed was machine-gun fire when in fact it was squads of riflemen firing at this rate.

Marne, First Battle of the

The Battle of the Marne was fought between 5 and 12 September 1914. It resulted in an Allied victory against the German Army. The battle effectively ended the month-long German offensive that opened the war and had reached the outskirts of Paris. The counter-attack of six French field armies and one British army along the Marne River forced the German Imperial Army to abandon its push on Paris and retreat north-east, setting the stage for four years of trench warfare on the Western Front. The Battle of the Marne was an immense strategic victory for the Allies, wrecking Germany's bid for a swift victory over France and forcing it into a protracted two-front war. The Allied armies were over a million strong and faced a German force of over a million and a half.

Allied casualties were over 263,000, of whom more than 81,000 died. German losses were at least 220,000 dead or missing.

Marne taxis

The use of Parisian taxis was the idea of General Gallieni, the military governor of the city. On the evening of 6 September 1914, he requisitioned 1,200 taxis to assemble in the Esplanade des Invalides at 19.00 hours; for the next seven hours they ferried men from their positions on the outskirts of Paris to the front line at Nanteuil (four in the seats, one in the luggage compartment). In all, almost an entire division of 12,000 men was transported. The French Treasury paid the fares according to the standard rate per metre travelled. In all, the bill came to 70,102 French francs (approximately £140,000 today). Taxis were used for the rest of the campaign and became part of French military folklore.

Marquess of Queensberry rules

The code of traditional rules in the sport of boxing is named after John Sholto Douglas, 9th Marquess of Queensberry, who publicly endorsed the code. The Queensberry rules were the first to require the use of gloves in boxing. In popular culture the term is sometimes used to refer to a sense of sportsmanship and fair play. The rules were written by John Graham Chambers, a Welshman, and drafted in London in 1865, before being published in 1867. The Marquess of Queensberry's third son was Lord Alfred 'Bosie' Douglas, the close friend and lover of Oscar Wilde.

Maschinengewehr 08

The MG 08 was the German Army's standard-issue machine gun in the Great War, an adaptation of Hiram S. Maxim's original 1884 Maxim gun. It could reach a firing rate of up to 400 rounds per minute using 250-round fabric belts of 7.92 x 57mm ammunition, although sustained firing would lead to overheating; it was water-cooled using a jacket around the barrel that held approximately one gallon of water. Using a separate attachment sight with range calculator for indirect fire, the MG 08 could be operated from cover. Additional telescopic sights were also developed and used in quantity during the war.

Maxim machine gun

The Maxim machine gun was adopted by the British Army in 1889. In 1912, the army turned to the Vickers gun (see entry below) and then, in 1915, to the lighter Lewis gun (which could be made much more quickly than the Vickers and, although too heavy for efficient portable use, became the standard support weapon for the British infantry).

Melton blue

A blue-dyed version of melton cloth, a heavy, smooth woollen fabric with a short nap, particularly used for army uniforms and overcoats. Its name comes from Melton Mowbray, in Leicestershire, the traditional centre for its production.

Mons, Battle of

The Battle of Mons began on the morning of 23 August 1914 with a heavy German artillery barrage. The men of the British Expeditionary Force, many of whom had only just arrived at the battlefield, were exhausted. They were carrying 80lb packs; many had new boots and were walking on cobbled roads. Nevertheless, they formed up along the Canal du Centre, west and north of Mons, in a defensive position nine miles long. Nine and a half British battalions (10,000 men) held four German divisions (70,000) for most of the day.

The Germans attacked in large numbers, but in close formation, suffering significant casualties from extremely accurate British infantry marksmen. However, by midday large numbers of Germans had crossed the canal and some British units began to fall back. The tactical withdrawal lasted until dusk, but the Germans did not follow in hot pursuit; they had suffered unexpectedly high casualty figures and called a ceasefire to lick their wounds.

British losses on the day were 1,642 killed, wounded and missing. They included 400 from the 4th Battalion Middlesex Regiment and 300 from the 1st Battalion Royal Irish Regiment. German losses were at least 6,000, but could have been as many as 10,000.

Old Contemptibles

Kaiser Wilhelm II of Germany reportedly issued an order on 19 August 1914 to 'exterminate . . . the treacherous English and walk over General French's contemptible little army'. Thus, the regular soldiers of Britain's standing army of 1914, who went to France as the British Expeditionary Force, became known as 'The Old Contemptibles'. However, no concrete evidence has ever been found to suggest that such an order was issued by the Kaiser. It was likely to have been a British propaganda invention, one that has since become accepted as fact and made legend.

Petrograd

During the Great War, the Imperial government renamed St Petersburg 'Petrograd', meaning 'Peter's City', to remove the German words *Sankt* and *Burg*. (In 1924, after the Bolshevik Revolution of 1917, the city was renamed Leningrad; the city became St Petersburg again in 1991, following the end of communist rule.)

Pol Roger

Champagne Pol Roger, founded in 1849, is a notable producer of champagne. The brand is still owned and run by the descendants of Pol Roger. Based around the town of Épernay in the Champagne region, Pol Roger was the favourite champagne of Winston Churchill. After Churchill's death in 1965, Pol Roger placed a black border around the labels of Brut NV shipped to the United Kingdom.

Pompadour

A hairstyle named after Madame de Pompadour (1721–1764), mistress of King Louis XV. Although there are numerous variations of the style for both women and men, the basic concept is hair swept upwards from the face and worn high over the forehead (and sometimes upswept around the sides and back as well). After its initial popularity among fashionable women in the eighteenth century, the style was revived as part of the Gibson Girl look in the 1890s and continued to be in vogue until the Great War.

Primitive Methodists

Primitive Methodism was a major movement in English Methodism from about 1810 until the Methodist Union in 1932. The Primitive Methodists were a major offshoot of the principal stream of Methodism – the Wesleyan Methodists – founded by a Methodist preacher called Hugh Bourne. 'Primitive' was used to clarify their belief that they were the true guardians of the original, or primitive, form of Methodism preached by John Wesley.

Puttees

A puttee (also spelled 'puttie', adapted from the Hindi *patti*) is a bandage for covering the lower part of the leg from the ankle to the knee. It consists of a long narrow piece of cloth wound tightly and spirally around the leg, and serving to provide both support and protection. It was worn by both mounted and dismounted soldiers, generally taking the place of the leather or cloth gaiter. The puttee was first adopted as part of the service uniform of foot and mounted soldiers serving in British India during the second half of the nineteenth century. In its original form, the puttee comprised long strips of cloth worn as a tribal legging in the Himalayas. Puttees were in general use by the British Army as part of the khaki service uniform worn during the Great War.

Race to the Sea

The race began in late September 1914, after the end of the Battle of the Aisne, the unsuccessful Allied counter-offensive against the German forces (halted during the preceding First Battle of the Marne). The route of the race was largely governed by the north–south railways available to each side – the French through Amiens and the Germans through Lille.

In a series of attempts to outflank one another, the race involved a number of battles, from the First Battle of the Aisne (13 to 28 September) to the end of November.

Rittmeister

Rittmeister is German for 'riding master' or 'cavalry master', the military rank of a commissioned cavalry officer in the armies of Germany, Austria-Hungary, Scandinavia and some other countries. He was typically in charge of a squadron or troop, and the equivalent of a captain.

Robert Blatchford and the *Clarion*

Robert Blatchford, the son of an actor, was born in Maidstone in 1851. His father died when he was two, and at the age of fourteen he was apprenticed as a brushmaker. He disliked the work and ran away to join the army, reaching the rank of serjeant major before leaving the service in 1878. After trying a variety of different jobs he became a freelance journalist and worked for several newspapers before becoming leader writer for the *Sunday Chronicle* in Manchester. It was his journalistic experience of working-class life that turned Blatchford into a socialist.

In 1890, he founded the Manchester Fabian Society. The following year, Blatchford and four fellow members launched a socialist newspaper, the *Clarion*. Blatchford upset many of his socialist supporters by his nationalistic views on foreign policy; he supported the government during the Boer War and warned against what he regarded as the German menace.

Royal Army Medical Corps

The Royal Army Medical Corps (RAMC) is a specialist corps in the British Army which provides medical services to all British Army personnel and their families in war and in peace. Because it is not a fighting arm (non-combatant), under the Geneva Conventions members of the RAMC may only use their weapons for self-defence. For this reason, there are two traditions that the RAMC perform when on parade: officers do not draw their swords (instead, they hold their scabbard with their left hand while saluting with their right); other ranks do not fix bayonets. During the Great War, the RAMC lost 743 officers and 6,130 soldiers were killed.

Royal Navy

In 1914 the Royal Navy was by far the most powerful navy in the world. The Royal Navy's basic responsibilities included policing colonies and trade routes, defending coastlines and imposing blockades on hostile powers. The British government took the view that the Royal Navy needed to possess a battlefleet that was larger than the world's two next largest navies put together. By early 1914 the Royal Navy had 18 modern dreadnoughts (6 more under construction), 10 battlecruisers, 35 cruisers, 200 destroyers, 29 battleships (pre-dreadnought design) and 150 cruisers built before 1907. The total manpower of the Royal Navy in 1914 was over 250,000 men.

After the outbreak of the Great War, most of the Royal Navy's large ships were stationed at Scapa Flow in the Orkneys or Rosyth in Scotland, in readiness to stop any large-scale breakout attempt by the Germans. Britain's cruisers, destroyers, submarines and light forces were clustered around the British coast. The Mediterranean fleet (two battlecruisers and eight cruisers) was based in Gibraltar, Malta and Alexandria. These were used during the operations to protect Suez and the landings at Gallipoli. There were also naval forces scattered around the Empire.

The 'dreadnought' was the predominant type of battleship in the early twentieth century. The first of the kind, the Royal Navy's *Dreadnought* made such a strong impression on people's minds when it was launched in 1906 that similar battleships built subsequently were referred to generically as 'dreadnoughts', and earlier battleships became known as 'pre-dreadnoughts'. The dreadnought design had two revolutionary features: an 'all-big-gun' armament scheme, with an unprecedented number of heavy-calibre guns; and steam turbine propulsion.

The 'battlecruiser' was a large capital ship built in the first half of the twentieth century. Similar in size and cost to a battleship, and typically carrying the same kind of heavy guns, battlecruisers generally carried less armour and were faster. The first battlecruisers were designed in Britain in the first decade of the century, as a development of the armoured cruiser, at the same time as the dreadnought succeeded the pre-dreadnought battleship.

From the middle of the nineteenth century, 'cruiser' came to mean a classification for ships intended for scouting, raiding or the protection of merchantmen. Cruisers came in a wide variety of sizes, from the small protected cruiser to armoured cruisers which were as large (though not as powerful) as a battleship.

The 'destroyer' was a fast and manoeuvrable yet long-endurance warship intended to escort larger vessels in a fleet, convoy or battle group and defend them against smaller, powerful, short-range attackers.

Royal Small Arms Factory

The Royal Small Arms Factory was a government-owned rifle factory in the London Borough of Enfield, in an area generally known as the Lea Valley. The factory produced British military rifles, muskets and swords from 1816. The factory was located at Enfield Lock on a marshy island bordered by the River Lea and the River Lee Navigation. (It closed in 1988, but some of its work was transferred to other sites.)

Serjeant

'Serjeant' with a 'j' was the official spelling of 'sergeant' before and during the Great War and appeared in King's Regulations and the Pay Warrant, which defined the various ranks. Even today, Serjeant-at-Arms is a title still held by members of the security staff in the Houses of Parliament. Also, in the newly amalgamated infantry regiment the Rifles (as successor to the Light Infantry, which also used it), the spelling of serjeant is held with the 'j' in place of the 'g'.

Shell shock

See 'Executions' above.

Sobranie

The Sobranie cigarette brand is one of the oldest tobacco brands in the world. Sobranie of London was established in 1879 by the Redstone family, when cigarettes had just become fashionable in Europe. Several generations of the Redstone family blended this tobacco from a secret formula. The original cigarettes were hand-made in the Russian tradition. Sobranie was the supplier to the royal courts of Great Britain, Germany, Spain, Romania and Greece.

Spike

An old English slang word for the workhouse, or a dosshouse for vagrants.

Stew an' 'ard

A traditional dish of North-East Lancashire, especially in Burnley, Nelson, Colne and Barnoldswick ('Barlick'). 'Hard' is the staple of the dish, which are oatcakes made from oatmeal, yeast, sugar, salt and water, made into a pancake batter, then cooked each side on a 'girdle' (griddle) pan, cooled and either used, soft, immediately, or dried to preserve them, leading them to be called 'hard'. The 'stew' would usually be mutton, occasionally chicken and, rarely, beef. The stew would either be poured on to the 'hard' cakes, or they would be used to dunk into the stew.

Stop-tap

An archaic expression for pub closing time.

Subaltern

A primarily British military term for a junior officer. Literally meaning 'subordinate', subaltern is used to describe commissioned officers below the rank of captain and generally comprises the various grades of lieutenant.

Sweet Caporals

Although British soldiers in the Great War thought that Sweet Caporals were French cigarettes, they were in fact produced by the American Tobacco Company, which also produced the Pall Mall and Mecca brands. Caporals were issued to French soldiers and were made from dark tobacco and had a particularly pungent flavour and smell.

Tackler

A tackler was a Lancashire name for a supervisor in a textile factory. He was responsible for the working of a number of power looms and the weavers who operated them. The name derived from the main part of his job, which was to 'tackle' – repair – any mechanical problems encountered with the looms.

Telescopic sight

The first experiments designed to give shooters optical aiming aids date back to the early seventeenth century. The first documented telescopic rifle sight was invented between 1835 and 1840. *The Improved American Rifle*, written in 1844, documented the first telescopic sights made by Morgan James of Utica, New York, based on designs by civil engineer John R. Chapman (the Chapman-James sight). An early telescopic sight was built in 1880 by August Fiedler, forestry commissioner of Austrian Prince Heinrich Reuss. Telescopic sights with extra-long eye relief pieces then became available for handgun and scout rifle use and began to be used by the Austrian and German armies.

Tilley lamp

The tilley lamp derives from John Tilley's invention of the hydro-pneumatic blowpipe, in 1813. In England, W. H. Tilley were manufacturing pressure lamps at their works in Stoke Newington (in 1818) and at Shoreditch (in the 1830s). The company moved to Brent Street in Hendon in 1915 during the Great War and started work with paraffin as a fuel for the lamps.

Tombac

Tombac is a brass alloy with high copper content and between 5 and 20 per cent zinc content. Tin, lead or arsenic may be added for colouration. It is a malleable alloy mainly used for medals, ornaments and decoration. The term 'tombac' is derived from *tembaga*, an Indonesian/Malay word of Javanese origin, meaning 'copper'.

Tournaphone

The Tournaphone was a design of gramophone developed by Pathe in 1906; it played flat records at 90 rpm, starting from the inside and moving to the outside. It was easily changed to play ordinary 78 rpm records (by turning the sound box, and replacing the jewelled stylus with a needle). 78 rpm records continued in use until the 1950s. Tournaphones used a jewelled stylus, not a needle, to play music and audio. The word 'gramophone' was first used by Alexander Graham Bell when he developed a machine using flat records instead of cylinders. Emile Berliner, a German American, first produced flat records that vibrated the stylus from side to side (the opposite of Bell's design).

Uhlans

Uhlans were originally Polish light cavalry armed with lances, sabres and pistols. The title was later used by lancer regiments in the Russian, Prussian and Austrian armies. In 1914, the German Army included twenty-six Uhlan regiments. Because German hussar, dragoon and cuirassier regiments also carried lances in 1914, there was a tendency among their French and British opponents to describe all German cavalry as 'Uhlans'. After seeing mounted action during the early weeks of the Great War, the Uhlan regiments were either dismounted to serve as 'cavalry rifles' in the trenches of the Western Front or transferred to the Eastern Front, where more primitive conditions made it possible for horse cavalry to still play a useful role. All twenty-six German Uhlan regiments were disbanded in 1918–1919.

Under-fettler

An under-fettler is a junior 'fettler' or cleaner. It is a Lancashire name, used in a number of contexts and trades. The verb to 'fettle' variously means to fix, sort or clean; it is also used in the sense of 'sorting someone out'.

Vickers gun

In 1912 the British Army adopted the Vickers as its standard machine gun. Produced by the Vickers Company, it was a modified version of the Maxim machine gun. The Vickers used a 250-round fabric-belt magazine and was regarded as a highly reliable weapon. It could fire over 600 rounds per minute and had a range of 4,500 yards. Being water-cooled, it could fire continuously for long periods.

Voluntary Aid Detachment

The Voluntary Aid Detachment (VAD) was a voluntary organization providing field nursing services, mainly in hospitals, in the United Kingdom and various other countries in the British Empire. It was founded in 1909 with the help of the Red Cross and Order of St John. By the summer of 1914 there were over 2,500 Voluntary Aid Detachments in Britain. Each individual volunteer was called simply 'a VAD'. Of the 74,000 VADs in 1914, two-thirds were women and girls.

At the outbreak of the Great War, VADs eagerly offered their services to the war effort. The British Red Cross was reluctant to allow civilian women a role in overseas hospitals: most VADs were of the middle and upper classes and unaccustomed to hardship and traditional hospital discipline. Military authorities would not accept VADs at the front line.

Katharine Furse took two VADs to France in October 1914, restricting them to serve as canteen workers and cooks. Caught under fire in a sudden battle, the VADs were pressed into emergency hospital service and acquitted themselves well. The growing shortage of trained nurses opened the door for VADs in overseas military hospitals. Furse was appointed Commander-in-Chief of the VADs and restrictions were removed.

Female volunteers over the age of twenty-three and with more than three months' hospital experience were accepted for overseas service. During four years of war, 38,000 VADs worked in hospitals and served as ambulance drivers and cooks. VADs served near the Western Front and in Mesopotamia and Gallipoli. VAD hospitals were also opened in most large towns in Britain. Many were decorated for distinguished service and included well-known women such as Enid Bagnold, Mary Borden, Vera Britten, Agatha Christie and Violet Jessop.

Webley revolver

The standard-issue Webley revolver at the outbreak of the Great War was the Webley Mk V, but there were many more Mk IV revolvers in service in 1914, as the initial order for 20,000 Mk V revolvers had not been completed when hostilities began.

In May 1915, the Webley Mk VI would be adopted as the standard sidearm for British and Commonwealth troops and remained so for the duration of the war, being issued to officers, airmen, naval crews, boarding parties, machine-gun teams and tank crews. The Mk VI proved to be a very reliable and hardy weapon, well suited to the mud and adverse conditions of trench warfare, and several accessories were developed for the Mk VI, including a bayonet and a stock, allowing the revolver to be converted into a carbine (short-barrelled rifle).

'Welch' (spelling)

The spelling of 'Welsh' as 'Welch' is a much-cherished historical peculiarity in the Royal Welch Fusiliers. When the regiment was given its Welsh designation in 1702, the spelling 'Welch' was in common use, and it became a regimental tradition. That is, until 2006, when the Royal Welch Fusiliers merged with other Welsh regiments to form the 'Welsh Regiment'.

Welsh language

Welsh is a Celtic language that emerged in the sixth century and has been spoken continuously throughout recorded history in Wales and along the Welsh border with England. By 1911 it had become a minority language, spoken by 43.5 per cent of the population. There are wide variations in dialect between North and South Wales, as well as variations between counties. As such, there is no standard form of the Welsh language (or 'correct' dialect) to learn.

Bach – little / small.

Cariad – dear / darling / love.

Croeso – welcome.

Cyfarchion – greetings.

Ffrind – friend.

Hapus – happy.

Mam-gu (or *nain*) – grandmother.

Mawr – big / great.

Penblwydd – birthday.

Tad-cu (or *taid*) – grandfather.

Whizz-bang

Although the term was used widely by Allied servicemen to describe any form of German field artillery shells, the 'whizz-bang' was originally attributed to the noise made by shells from German 3-inch field guns. The name was derived from the fact that shells fired from light or field artillery travelled faster than the speed of sound. Thus soldiers heard the typical 'whizz' noise of a travelling shell before the 'bang' issued by the gun itself. Whizz-bangs were consequently much feared, since the net result was that defending infantrymen were given virtually no warning of incoming high-velocity artillery fire (as they were from enemy howitzers).

'Wipers'

The name of the Belgian town of Ypres was difficult to pronounce for the many thousands of British soldiers who were billeted there or passed through, so it very soon became universally known as 'Wipers'.

Ypres, First Battle of

The First Battle of Ypres was fought for the strategic town of Ypres in western Belgium in October and November 1914. The German and Western Allied attempts to secure the town from enemy occupation included a series of further battles in and around the West Flanders Belgian municipality. Ypres was vital to the British need to secure the Channel ports and the army's supply lines. It was the last major obstacle to the German advance on Boulogne and Calais. The Ypres campaign became the culmination point of the Race to the Sea.

The battle highlighted problems in command and control for both sides, with each side missing opportunities to win a significant victory early on. The Germans, in particular, overestimated the numbers and strength of the Allied defences at Ypres, and called off their last offensive too early. The battle was also significant as it witnessed the destruction of the highly experienced and trained British regular army. Having suffered enormous losses for its small size, the 'Old Contemptibles' effectively disappeared after Ypres, eventually to be replaced by fresh reservists who eventually became an army on a scale to match those of its allies and enemies. The recorded casualties were as follows.

French Army: 50,000–85,000 killed, wounded and missing
Belgian Army: 21,562 killed, wounded and missing
British Army: 7,960 killed in action; 29,562 wounded in action; 17,873 missing in action
Total: 126,957–161,957

German Army: 19,530 killed; 83,520 wounded; 31,265 missing
Total: 134,315

Zouaves

Zouave was the title given to certain light infantry regiments in the French Army, normally serving in French North Africa, during the nineteenth century. The chief distinguishing characteristic of such units was the Zouave uniform, which included short open-fronted jackets, baggy trousers (*serouel*) and often sashes and oriental headgear. The Zouaves of the French Army were first raised in Algeria in 1831, initially recruited solely from the Zouaoua, a tribe of Berbers located in the mountains of the Jurjura Range. The four Zouave regiments of the French Army in the Great War wore their traditional colourful dress during the early months of the war. The power of the machine gun, rapid fire artillery and improved small arms would oblige them to adopt a plain khaki uniform from 1915 onwards to reduce their visibility in battle.

Genealogies

The family of Winston Spencer-Churchill

Grandparents

Paternal

John Winston Spencer-Churchill	
(7th Duke of Marlborough)	1822–1883
Lady Frances Vane	1822–1899

Maternal

Leonard Jerome	1817–1891
Clarissa Hall	1825–1895

Parents

Lord Randolph Churchill	1849–1895
Lady Randolph Churchill	
(*née* Jennie Jerome)	1854–1921

Brother

John Strange ('Jack') Spencer-Churchill	1880–1947

Children

Diana	1908–1963
Randolph	1911–1968
Sarah	1914–1982
Marigold	1918–1921
Mary	1922–

The family of the Dukes of Atholl

5th Duke

John Murray   1778–1846
(second son of the 4th Duke; never married)
Siblings
Lady Amelia Sophia Murray   1780–1849
James Murray, 1st Baron Glenlyon   1782–1837

6th Duke

George Augustus Frederick John Murray   1814–1897
(eldest son of James Murray, 1st Baron
Glenlyon)
Spouse
Anne Home-Drummond   1814–1864

7th Duke

John James Hugh Henry Stewart-Murray   1840–1917
(only son of 6th Duke)
Spouse
Louisa Moncrieffe   1844–1902
Children
Dorothea ('Dertha')   Born 1866
(married Harold Ruggles-Brise, 1895)
Helen   Born 1867
Evelyn   Born 1868
John ('Bardie')   Born 1871
(married Katharine ('Kitty') Ramsay, 1899)
George ('Geordie')   Born 1873
James ('Hamish')   Born 1879

Maps

N

SHETLAND IS.

ORKNEY IS.

Scapa Flow

SCOTLAND
Glen Tilt
• Aberdeen
• Blair Atholl
Dunkeld • • Dundee

ATLANTIC
OCEAN

• Edinburgh
Glasgow • • Berwick

North Sea

• Londonderry

• Carlisle

• Belfast

• Middlesborough

IRELAND

Irish Sea

3 4 5 • York
1 • 2 • Leeds
Manchester
• Liverpool • Sheffield

ENGLAND • Overstrand

• Galway   Dublin •

• Wrexham

WALES
• Norwich
6
• Birmingham
• Kettering
7 • Ludlow
• Llandrindod Wells   • Harwich
• Hereford   Blenheim Palace
• Waterford
Cork •
Leyton
• Cardiff   Windsor • London
• Bristol   • Dover
Southampton
• • Lympne
Portsmouth
• Albany
Devonport • Plymouth

St Georges Channel

English Channel

0   100 miles
0   200 km

FRANCE
• Le Havre
• Rouen

Britain on the Eve of War

Europe on the Eve of War

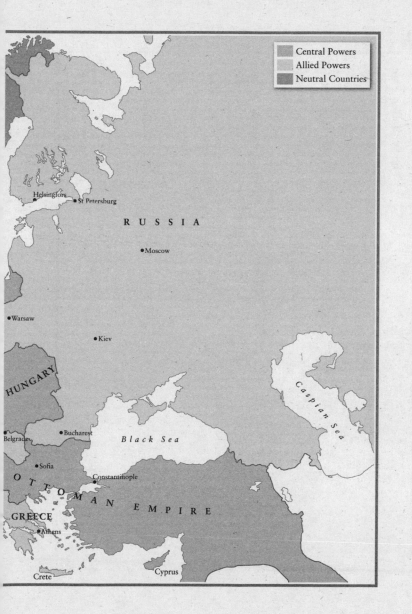

Central Powers
Allied Powers
Neutral Countries

Helsingfors
St Petersburg

RUSSIA

Moscow

Warsaw

Kiev

HUNGARY

Caspian Sea

Belgrade
Bucharest
Black Sea

Sofia

Constantinople

OTTOMAN EMPIRE

GREECE
Athens

Crete
Cyprus

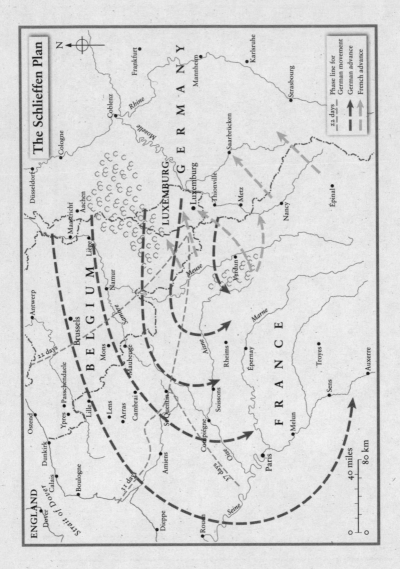

The Schlieffen Plan

N

ENGLAND

Dover
Strait of Dover

GERMANY

Frankfurt

Cologne

Coblenz

Rhine

Moselle

Düsseldorf

Maastricht
Aachen

LUXEMBURG

Luxemburg

Thionville

Metz

Saarbrücken

Mannheim

Karlsruhe

Strasbourg

Epinal

Nancy

BELGIUM

Antwerp

Brussels

Namur

Liège

Sambre

Mons

Maubeuge

Meuse

Verdun

Ypres
Passchendaele

Lille

Lens

Arras

Cambrai

St Quentin

Soissons

Aisne

Rheims

Epernay

Marne

FRANCE

Troyes

Sens

Auxerre

Ostend

Dunkirk
Calais

Boulogne

Dieppe

Amiens

Compiègne

Oise

Paris

Melun

Rouen

Seine

22 days

22 days

31 days

0   40 miles
0   80 km

22 days   Phase line for
           German movement
           German advance
           French advance

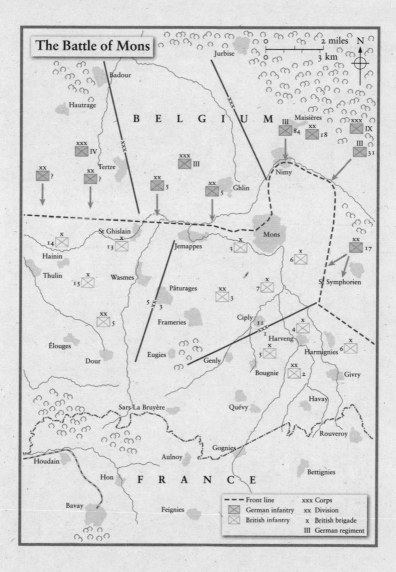

The Battle of Mons

2 miles
3 km

N

B E L G I U M

Jurbise

Badour

Hautrage

Maisières

III 84   xx 18   xxx IX

III 31

xxx IV

Tertre

xxx III

Ghlin

Nimy

xx ?   xx ?   xx 5   xx 5

Mons

St Ghislain

Jemappes

x 14   x 13   x 3   x 6

xx 17

Hainin

Thulin   x 15   Wasmes

St Symphorien

Pâturages   xx 3   x 7

xx 5   5 xx 3

Frameries   Ciply   xxx I   x 4

Élouges   Eugies   Genly   x 5   Harveng   Harmignies x 6

Dour   Bougnie   xx 2   Givry

Havay

Sars La Bruyère   Quévy

Rouveroy

Houdain   Hon   F R A N C E   Gognies   Bettignies

Aulnoy

Bavay   Feignies

– – – Front line	xxx Corps
▨ German infantry	xx Division
▨ British infantry	x British brigade
	III German regiment

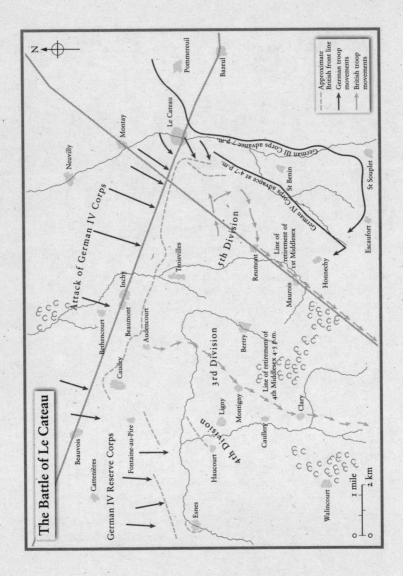

The Battle of Le Cateau

Approximate British front line

German troop movements

British troop movements

N

Pommereuil

Bazeul

Montay

Le Cateau

Neuvilly

German III Corps advance 7 p.m.

St Benin

St Souplet

German IV Corps advance at 4–7 p.m.

Attack of German IV Corps

Thoisvilles

5th Division

Line of retirement of 1st Middlesex

Reumont

Escaufort

Honnechy

Maurois

Inchy

Beaumont

Audencourt

Bethencourt

Caudry

3rd Division

Berry

Line of retirement of 4th Middlesex 4–5 p.m.

Clary

German IV Reserve Corps

Fontaine-au-Pire

Beauvois

Cattenières

Ligny

Montigny

Caullery

4th Division

Haucourt

Esnes

Walincourt

o

1 mile

o

2 km

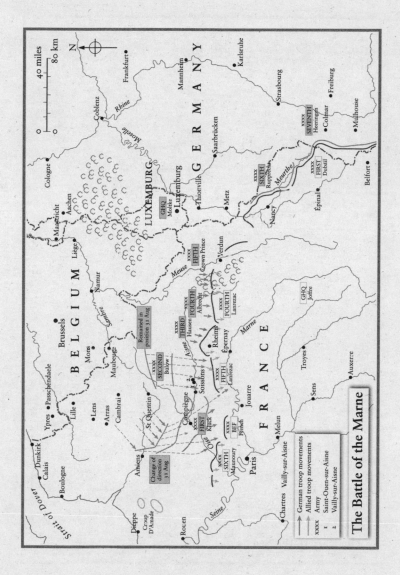

The Battle of the Marne

N

40 miles
80 km

Strait of Dover

Dunkirk
Calais
Boulogne
Dieppe
Group
D'Amade
Rouen
Seine

Ypres • Passchendaele
Lille • Lens
Arras •
Cambrai •
Amiens •
St Quentin

Chartres
Vailly-sur-Aisne

BELGIUM
Brussels •
Mons •
Maubeuge •
Namur •

Maastricht
Aachen •
Liège •
Sambre

LUXEMBURG
Luxemburg •

GERMANY
Cologne •
Coblenz •
Rhine
Moselle
Frankfurt •
Mannheim •
Karlsruhe •
Strasbourg •
Saarbrücken •
Thionville •
Metz •

GHQ
Moltke

xxxx SECOND Bülow
Remained in position 31 Aug

Change of direction 31 Aug

xxxx FIRST Kluck
Oise
Compiègne
Soissons
Aisne

xxxx THIRD Hausen
xxxx FOURTH Albrecht
xxxx FIFTH Crown Prince
Meuse
Verdun

xxxx FIFTH Lanrezac
Rheims
Épernay
Marne
xxxx FOURTH Lanrezac

xxxx SIXTH Maunoury
Paris
Melun
Jouarre
xxxx BEF French

FRANCE
Troyes •
Sens •
Auxerre •

GHQ
Joffre

Nancy •
xxxx SIXTH Rupprecht
Meurthe
xxxx FIRST Dubail
Épinal •
xxxx SEVENTH Heeringen
Colmar •
Mulhouse •
Belfort •
Freiburg •

Key:
German troop movements
Allied troop movements
xxxx Army
1 Saint-Ouen-sur-Aisne
2 Vailly-sur-Aisne

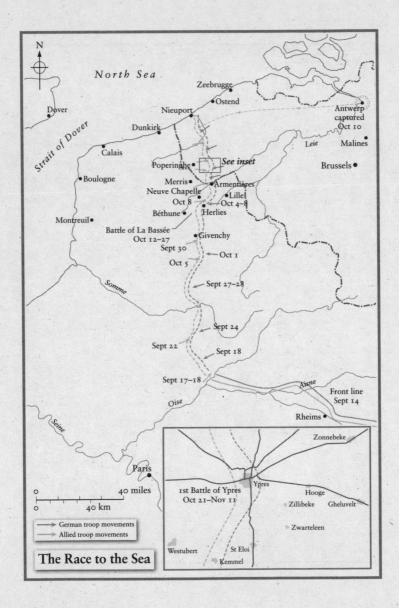

The Race to the Sea